Mister
WOLF

Chris Petit has written a trio of acclaimed 'beyond black' political thrillers covering a serial killer operating in sectarian Northern Ireland (*The Psalm Killer*); dirty money in World War II (*The Human Pool*); and terror, arms trading and the bombing of a civilian aircraft (*The Passenger*); as well as *The Butchers of Berlin* and *Pale Horse Riding*, which also feature the characters Schlegel and Morgen. He is an internationally renowned filmmaker.

Also by Chris Petit

Robinson
The Psalm Killer
Back from the Dead
The Hard Shoulder
The Human Pool
The Passenger
The Butchers of Berlin
Pale Horse Riding

Mister
WOLF

CHRIS PETIT

**SIMON &
SCHUSTER**

London · New York · Sydney · Toronto · New Delhi

A CBS COMPANY

First published in Great Britain by Simon & Schuster UK Ltd, 2019
A CBS COMPANY

Copyright © Chris Petit, 2019

1 3 5 7 9 10 8 6 4 2

Simon & Schuster UK Ltd
1st Floor
222 Gray's Inn Road
London WC1X 8HB

Simon & Schuster Australia, Sydney
Simon & Schuster India, New Delhi

www.simonandschuster.co.uk
www.simonandschuster.com.au
www.simonandschuster.co.in

A CIP catalogue record for this book
is available from the British Library

Hardback ISBN: 978-1-4711-7143-7
Trade Paperback ISBN: 978-1-4711-7144-4
eBook ISBN: 978-1-4711-7145-1

Typeset in Hoefler by M Rules
Printed and bound by CPI Group (UK) Ltd, Croydon, CR0 4YY

MIX
Paper from
responsible sources
FSC® C020471

*For Martin Müller, and in memory of
Peter Przygodda*

In the face of omnipotent terror, everything is fictional.

(Hans Bernd Gisevius,
To the Bitter End)

Hitler for his part no longer read fiction.

(Nerin E. Gun,
Eva Braun: Hitler's Mistress)

Wouldn't know the difference between a real blonde and a fake.

(Bob Dylan,
'My Heart's in the Highlands')

PROLOGUE

I

Munich, Harlaching, Saturday, 1 July 1934

The hunted animal thinks: blind instinct, like a repeat of a recurring dream, except played for real and not a dream, which does not detract from the nightmarish, unreal quality in that he half expects – prays – for it to end and he to wake, relieved and panting with fright, gradually aware of familiar surroundings, instead of running from and to his death. The inexorable. Charging on, lungs bursting, really not in shape, haring through woods, tinder dry, whipped by branches; the trees alive. He can't remember the last time he had been in woods. The pursuers behind; the unseen trap ahead, waiting. Stumbling, legs give way, taking a tumble, rolling and staggering up, weaving now, no energy left to run straight, lungs rasping, like they were full of iron filings, the shooting stitch in his side anticipation of the pain to come.

The hunters make a game of it, injecting a bit of fun for themselves, turning it into more than just another execution – face the wall and wait for the bullet to the back of the neck. With so much work on that weekend they have grown bored of straightforward killing. Spice it up a bit, throw in some suspense, stretch the fear.

Having driven him there, they'd all got out and stood around on the lonely roadside, not even so far from the city. They smoked, saying nothing, then gestured that he should start the race. Perhaps they were amused by the idea of such a habitué of night clubs and cafés forced to take physical action. They pointed towards the trees and shooed him away as if giving him a chance.

Three thugs; old-school. Holstered pistols and crow-bars. Their leader Emil Maurice, going all the way back: henchman, bodyguard, hoodlum, handy with his fists; and, curiously, a Jew – the exception that proves the rule. The sun shone on Maurice until that business with the Führer's niece. Ah, Geli. Were it not for her, none of this would be happening. Almost three years gone, and it was as if she had just tapped him on the shoulder to say, 'Your turn now.'

The legs stop running out of hopelessness as much as exhaustion. Why delay when it was as good as over; a few extra minutes or seconds make no difference. Now and at the hour of our death, he remembered. What a strange scene to anyone watching. Four gasping men, doubled over, hands on knees, struggling to catch their breath. None of them in great shape. The other two he didn't know: blond beasts, body builders, dumb, all brawn, zero brains. Maurice was different. Maurice was personal. They had history together. Maurice possessed a crooked soul. Maurice, though fallen from grace, was still indulged, a reward for all those faithful, obedient years of service, let out to do what he did best: dirty work.

For a moment, everyone seemed to find it funny, all this chasing around woods, out of condition. The cornered quarry: he had never seen himself dying out in the open, among trees. He feinted left and ducked right, going for the gap between Maurice and the man to Maurice's left. Maurice half shrugged, as if to say they were letting him off this time. He ran on, glancing back to see if they were in pursuit. They were, but ambling, like they were on a stroll.

A shot rang out from ahead and his legs went from under him. He lay there waiting for the end, trying to decide which was worse, the pain or the fear of what was to come, while dimly aware of Maurice and his thugs taking their time, the stickiness of blood on his smashed foot, seeing the men unholster their pistols, and tote their crowbars.

'Just us now, Anton,' said Emil Maurice.

2

Ten years later almost to the day, on 30 June 1944, two cars left the Führer's Berghof mountain retreat and drove west. The first vehicle departing that evening was an ordinary unmarked saloon rather than the usual armour-plated Mercedes. In it sat the Führer, Party Secretary Martin Bormann and the Führer's favourite German shepherd. Bormann drove fast and aggressively, as instructed. The following car, also unmarked, contained bodyguards.

The Führer's double-breasted civilian suit lacked even a Party badge. A surprisingly loud tie had what looked like a soup stain. A tuft of hair stuck up at the back of his head, untamed even by brilliantine. The hair looked darker and Bormann wondered if he was dyeing it. No sign of any loss, which was more than could be said for his own receding hairline. To compensate, he was growing a belly, not so big that he couldn't still see his dick, which was more than could be said of some.

There was no record in the Führer's diary of that night's appointment, only note of attendance the following day at a state funeral in Salzburg. They drove in silence and stopped once to let the dog do its duty. Bormann watched the Führer stretch his legs, thinking how stooped and vulnerable he looked outside the Berghof's lofty surroundings, standing alone on the remote wooded roadside, watching the dog take its crap.

Their destination was an exclusive lakeside resort where the guest house Hanselbauer had last been visited by the Führer on 30 June 1934 to arrest his oldest friend. Seeing the placid waters in the soft twilight of their arrival, Bormann was struck by such tranquil romantic surroundings marking the start of a bloodbath. As for the timber folksiness of the Hanselbauer, he was rather reminded of a giant cuckoo clock. The purge had been executed as Operation Hummingbird. Only later, when Dr Goebbels and his propaganda boys insisted that such a shining example of political and historical intrigue needed a title with a more classical and theatrical edge did it become known as the Night of the Long Knives.

The Führer paused outside the hotel, patting his pockets, seeming reluctant to enter. Bormann wondered if he had been the same on that morning a decade ago, dithering while winding himself up to launch himself as a force of nature. Bormann guided him towards a back entrance. The Führer had insisted their visit remain incognito. That night's party was booked under the name of Wolf. 'Nothing special,' Bormann had warned the management, but guests needed to be moved for security men to take over the corridor to allow the Führer the sentimental gesture of staying in the same room as the man he had gone there to arrest in 1934.

Bormann suspected that day had been a rare crisis of conscience for the Führer, despite evidence of betrayal by his great friend. Ernst Röhm was one of very few permitted to address him with the informal 'du'. The legend now went that fury at such treachery had driven the Führer to arrest

Röhm in person to witness his humiliation. A less gracious version had the Führer a reluctant participant in a publicity stunt organised for maximum effect by Dr Goebbels; reluctant because he suspected the case against Röhm was not as iron-cast as everyone made out.

The waters of the lake glistened in the last of the balmy evening as Bormann and his master sat down to dine in a private room. Though warm enough for balcony windows to be open, theirs were not. The table was set back. Two guards stationed outside came in and stood over the waitress. She was a plump, motherly woman whose hands shook as she served them.

They ate a simple meal of herb omelette, potatoes and peas. Bormann took the precaution of tasting the Führer's in case it was poisoned, and said it was good. The hotel offered Apollinaris mineral water, which the Führer didn't drink. He looked thunderous upon being told no Fachinger, until Bormann produced a bottle, having brought their own supply just in case. His briefcase also contained a flask of schnapps for himself, for later.

The Führer was unusually quiet and left half his meal. He showed a flash of his old charm as he sought to reassure the disappointed waitress as she cleared their plates that nothing was wrong with the food. In an unparalleled exception he told Bormann he could smoke. Bormann was about to protest when the Führer cut him short, knowing he did. Bormann fumbled for his cigarette case then decided not to after all.

'That morning wasn't the rowdy orgy Goebbels reported it being,' said the Führer. 'Ernst was here with, what, half a dozen others? Everyone was still in bed when we arrived. A beautiful morning, the lake like glass. Frau Hanselbauer made an excellent coffee, which I drank in this very room.

I had some sent up to Ernst who had been ordered to get dressed.'

It had been the Führer's idea to return for the anniversary of the putsch. Bormann had been surprised by this unlikely rendezvous with the past and presumed the Führer was nostalgic for his role as man of action that day, a rare exception to his usual sedentariness: the bolt of lightning that heralds the storm. That same afternoon Bormann had watched the Führer back in Munich foam at the mouth as he accused Röhm and his traitors of being guilty of the greatest act of disloyalty in the history of the world.

Bormann had always considered Röhm's demise as inevitable as the sun going down. To the other plotters, falling over themselves to prove loyalty to the Führer, Röhm was eminently back-stabbable. Now they had power, they were all becoming assimilated, no longer outsiders, with wives and mistresses and second homes and interior decorators. Bachelor Ernst and his dissolute rabble army of brownshirt boys were not.

Röhm had dug his own grave anyway, as the author of careless letters, written home while serving in Bolivia, bemoaning that backward country's lack of understanding of manly love. The correspondence had ended up in a newspaper scandal, not that the letters' recipient was around any more to explain how. Bormann exclaimed to himself: The number of indiscreet letters that fall into the wrong hands! The Führer had been no better in his day. Write the letter but don't leave it lying around for others to pick up!

The Führer asked, 'Do you ever think of Geli?'

Bormann was immediately alert to the unmentionable subject of the Führer's dead niece, unmentionable unless raised by him alone, then hardly ever. No mention of her in his table talk.

Bormann knew how he was supposed to answer. 'Such a sweet child. Such a tragic loss.'

He wondered about the real point of the evening. It wasn't as though anything was left to celebrate. Had they come there so the Führer could bring up the subject of Geli, which he would never do in front of Fräulein Braun? Or perhaps he was just nostalgic for the lost world of going out and eating like normal people. In the old Munich days his life had been public, with Geli on his arm. Twelve and more sat down to dinner of an evening in the Osteria or the Bratwurst Glöckl: hoots of merriment, tears of laughter, slapped thighs, with the Führer contributing one of his wicked impersonations of absent colleagues, and making up for lost time after years of poverty and social isolation.

Outside, the sky blackened against the silhouette of blacker mountains. July tomorrow, yet the terrace showed little sign of any holiday season. A solitary man stood smoking at the end of a jetty, his cigarette tip a glowing pinprick. Bormann, not usually given to reflection, wondered whether it was the man or his cigarette he envied.

Röhm had spent his last night of freedom downstairs in the bar getting smashed, or not, according to whose version you believed. At dawn the following morning, a long motorcade left Munich, with the Führer leading a gang of reliable thugs and brawlers from the old days, including his former driver, Emil Maurice. Goebbels, along for the ride, lied afterwards that Röhm was found in bed with a boy.

Accounts varied. That before arresting Röhm, the Führer beat a man senseless with the iron end of his whip.

That the Führer alone confronted and roundly abused a silent, chastened Röhm. That Röhm raged back and refused the pistol offered with which to shoot himself. Bormann had trouble picturing that. The Führer could get carried away but he was hardly going to hand Röhm a loaded gun.

What the Führer still didn't know, or preferred not to, was that the coup had been manipulated by using the old trick of feeding false information of impending insurrection to the man's many enemies when Röhm and his boys had had no more in mind than drunken carousing and climbing into bed with each other while on a month's furlough.

Goebbels reported evidence of epic degeneracy in that unlikely setting, exceeding even the last days of Tiberius, with experts in deviant intercourse known as analists performing elaborate, mind-boggling copulations. In the room next to Röhm's, two men were discovered together – Röhm's deputy and a mincing bum boy. The Führer had them dragged off to be shot by Emil Maurice in a car. First dead of the day.

The death hunt commenced, cheered on in Berlin and Munich. Envelopes opened, lists read out. Weekend of terror! Shot while resisting arrest. Hacked to death in a swamp near Dachau. Gunned down in the woods of Harlaching. Numerous brownshirt thugs, pansies and street-corner boys were rounded up. Many, not the brightest buttons in the box, believed they were being executed as loyalists after a coup against the Führer. Clean sweep. A scorcher of a Saturday as ordinary people went about their business. Röhm's Berlin chief off on honeymoon to Madeira was arrested on his way to the airport. He protested that the Führer had been at his wedding only the day before.

Made no difference. Up against the wall. Short marriage; long widowhood.

Röhm, seeing sense at last, declared, 'All revolutions devour their children.' You bet, thought Bormann, when he heard that. Bormann, being second generation and a desk man, was resented for not having been around for the old rough and tumble. He had them shafted now. See you later, boys!

By Sunday, the Führer was back at the Chancellery holding a garden party. He dithered over Röhm, who was finally offered the officer's way out and left a pistol in his cell with a single bullet to do the job. He refused and it was down to Commandant Eicke of camp Dachau, a graduate of the school of hard knocks, with a taste for theatrical punishment. The official version was that he and another SS man gunned down Röhm in his cell and Röhm died protesting his loyalty to the Führer.

The alternative, told to Bormann, had more of an air of flamboyant poetic justice. Such was Eicke's hatred of homos, and disgust at Röhm for not shooting himself as befitted an officer, that he had him held down and took the pistol Röhm was to have used on himself, fucked him up the arse with it and, with Ernst screaming for his Führer, pulled the trigger. Tell that to the history books, thought Bormann.

At the Chancellery garden party, everyone was champagne giddy over what they had pulled off. With internal power now secure, the Führer walked like a man reborn, resplendent in a cream jacket, smiling shyly and exchanging witticisms with the guests, most of whom remained oblivious of the slaughter. The others were crowing. Himmler's smirk was plastered all over his face. Goebbels was bouncing with excitement. Göring was extravagantly drunk, his eyes still cruel. Bormann lined them all up in his sights and thought: I will have you all one by one, just as you had Röhm.

Apropos of nothing, the Führer said, 'I am thinking of shaving off my moustache.'

They were still in the Hanselbauer dining room, from which the Führer showed no sign of budging.

'It's your trademark!' protested Bormann, in a rare uncensored moment. He was rewarded with the sight of the man laughing, lifting his hand to his mouth to hide rotten teeth. The Führer grew serious again and said, 'I shan't sleep tonight.'

One thing Bormann understood about the man he served was he was as much a mystery to himself as he was to others, or pretended to be. There remained an element of shape-shifting after all those years of touring and hogging the limelight. Bormann knew only too well how the gramophone record went: the actor who starts to believe the part he is playing; the author obliged to perform, who secretly yearns for a life of contemplation in his beloved mountains. The fact remained, the Jew was always the problem, so do away with him, and, while they were about it, the Roman Catholic Church too. Then you remove the schism that has bedevilled two thousand years of Christianity.

'Why should life be cursed by the notion of fallen man?'

Bormann couldn't agree more as he watched the Führer run out of steam when once he had been able to go on and on, in full voice, just as iron will drove him to maintain the stiff-armed salute for hours whereas Göring could manage his for all of ten minutes. The Führer kept a chest-expander under his bed, according to the housekeeper (and no spunk was reported on the sheets, suggesting that the relationship with Fräulein Braun was unphysical, or very fastidious).

Bormann was still puzzling over that when the Führer said, 'There are some private drawings I did once, of my niece, quite personal to me.'

Bormann must have clutched the table because the Führer asked what was wrong with him.

The drawings were in his safe in the Brown House in Munich, the Führer went on.

No, they weren't.

Bormann knew because he'd had them removed only the day before, thinking never in a million years would it cross the Führer's mind to ask for them.

Two days later, Bormann was forced to drive from the Berghof to Munich to pretend to look for them. He was in a rare state of nerves as he reviewed his options. Telling the truth was out of the question. Doing nothing was a possibility, in the hope that the Führer would not mention the drawings again, brought up in a sentimental moment on an emotional evening. Or, he could admit they were not there, but this was not wise as rule number one was never be the bearer of bad news.

Bormann brooded for the duration of the drive back. Fields approaching harvest under a baby blue sky against the spectacular Alpine backdrop made little impression. The cocooned interior of the vehicle, upholstered in the finest napped leather, was another matter. Bormann was a car nut; the Führer, too, though he had never learned to drive.

The immediate and vexing problem of the drawings being raised again by the Führer took up the rest of the journey, and just as well because after dinner the Führer drew him aside.

Bormann pulled a long face and said some idiot had taken the initiative of transferring the safe to the Führer's private office in Berlin, thinking it was needed there.

Bormann stared at the floor and thought of noodles, sauerkraut, knuckles of ham, sausages and onion tarts.

'Which idiot?' asked the Führer.

Bormann reeled off a name and added, 'He has been transferred as of today,' thinking, pâté de foie gras, Coq au Riesling.

Because the Führer knew nothing of how offices worked, Bormann was gambling that the transfer of an entire safe 600 kilometres north would not strike him as in any way odd. The implication was that the Führer's privacy had been respected. If Bormann reported that its contents had been transferred that would have led to spittle-flecked accusations of interference. But the Führer seemed quite pleased by the weight of the operation – a whole safe moved – even if it was an administrative balls-up.

With the Führer satisfied for the moment, Bormann sat back and contemplated his labyrinth. He was not a sophisticated man – quite the opposite, being culturally clueless and proud of it, other than acquiring stuff on the advice of so-called experts (it was the age of such people) – but at intrigue he excelled, through a combination of peasant cunning, bureaucratic blocking, grinding hard work, excellent memory, personal loans dished out left, right and centre from Party funds, and extensive files on everyone. Like it or not, nearly all were indebted.

Anywhere else he would have been chief of secret police but he had identified precisely the power base of the regime: the desk. Others had too but Bormann had identified the right desk, the secretarial one that sat right outside the Führer's kennel.

That evening, Bormann stayed late in the hope of running into the strapping kitchen maid who was usually up for a quickie. The Führer was in conference long into the night. Fräulein Braun was in her quarters, no doubt reading romantic trash, even more of a prisoner than the late Princess Geli. Bormann felt almost sorry for Braun.

The kitchen maid said she had the painters in. That didn't bother Bormann, but he had to make do with a hand job. Afterwards he took a beer onto the deserted terrace. The Führer's bedroom light was still on. Bormann thought it safe to risk a cigarette and lit up, only to be caught by the Führer creeping out of the shadows. Bormann whipped the cigarette behind his back and blew smoke out of the side of his mouth, hoping it didn't show. It was the first time he had seen the man in a dressing gown. Black with grey trimming. Noticing Bormann looking, the Führer said it was a birthday present from Fräulein Braun.

'Give,' he said. He meant the cigarette. Bormann handed it over like a caught-out schoolboy. In all his years, he had never been the subject of one of the Führer's towering rages and wondered if his moment had come. Heini Himmler he had seen reduced to a squeaking wreck.

To Bormann's astonishment, the Führer took a drag, handed it back and said, 'Filthy habit. Now put it out.'

For lack of an ashtray, Bormann stepped on the butt and stayed standing on it.

'We need to talk about what happens next,' said the Führer.

Bormann had never seen the man so fragile or human, even in the depths of his depressions.

That night they hatched the future.

Bormann said all the signs were that an attempt on the Führer's life was imminent and the Army was behind it. His agents were at work and names would be forthcoming.

The Führer, whose instinct for surviving such attempts was uncanny, said he had known in his bones.

But it was Bormann who voiced what the Führer dared not think when he said, 'Why not let the assassination go ahead?'

BERLIN

July 1944

I

August Schlegel flew into Berlin from Budapest via Vienna on the regular Lufthansa flight on the evening of Wednesday, 19 July, after what looked like another stinking hot day. Berlin was no longer the city it was. The extent to which it had been knocked about was more visible from the air, with flattened industrial outskirts as grey and pitted as a moon landscape. No air raids for most of the summer but destruction was a fact of life. Rubble, shortages and dust, the city more stuffed than ever with foreign workers in their wooden huts, sprung up like weeds on waste land.

The plane banked and Schlegel watched one train beetle-crawl past another on its elevated track. The city still functioned but not like Budapest where waiters continued to serve real coffee and cream. A cabin attendant handed out boiled sweets. Schlegel sucked hard on his, depressed at being back. BERLIN spelled out in huge letters on the runway struck him as faintly ominous.

The aeroplane wallowed in to land, engines whining in protest.

They all disembarked and walked across the wide concrete apron to the arrivals hall.

Passport control was a formality. Customs on the other hand singled him out, two badly shaven elderly goons keen to make the most of their authority. Open the bag. Close the bag. Papers. Purpose of trip. Open the bag again. Schlegel supposed it amused them. He was asked if he was carrying any gifts and to state the purpose of his visit.

'No gifts. Courier,' he said.

He had to show them the papers. 'Inventory of art works for sale,' he said and pointed to the signed documents, stamped by the SS and Hungarian customs.

Still they detained him with their pointless questions. For two minutes it was funny then Schlegel started to sweat. Did they know something he didn't?

The folder and papers were taken away for copying. Something seemed odd about them when they were returned. Schlegel flipped through the document. It seemed to be all there. The two goons looked at him. Authority confronted by another authority was always an uncomfortable experience. But they said he could go. Schlegel stuffed the folder back in his case, wondering if the men had been tipped off. As the waiter in Budapest's Gerbeaud café had said to him, not so many young men with white hair.

Much later he would try to decide the best point of entry into the events that were about to unfold. He could have cut the cake at any point really. What he didn't understand then was how deep correlations of historical coincidence could turn out to be so personal.

The one lesson Schlegel would learn was that you have to understand how the past telescopes into the present.

By that troubled summer of 1944 there was no past in the sense of lives being joined up by the usual connections of memory or nostalgia. If one did look back, it was only over one's shoulder, to check no one was following.

Anyone observing Schlegel on that evening of 19 July would have seen a tall, ordinary young man still in his twenties, wearing a hat and a suit too hot for the weather, carrying an overnight valise. His shoes were in a state of poor repair. He looked like he got not enough sleep and too little to eat, but by then sleeplessness, hunger and shoes with holes were the norm.

The city lay baked by the oppressive heat. Even the language was a welcome return after Hungarian, not a word of which Schlegel had recognised, not even the one for beer (sör). He took the S-bahn to Ostkreuz, changed and got off at Alexanderplatz. His apartment was a twenty-minute walk, through quiet dusty streets. He crossed a small square of trees with tired leaves and peeling bark. Cafés and restaurants were gone, their staff and owners long since mobilised, practically cheered off, given their reputation for universal rudeness. What was left was not worth patronising. The Hungarians were still serious about their cafés. The Gerbeaud was like a salon, with its formal layout of separate tables and heavy brocade.

Schlegel walked past mostly young women sitting on doorsteps, watching what was left of life go by. One saluted him with a beer bottle. He experienced a stab of desire at the sight of her skirt pulled up over her thighs to catch the last of the sun. Who might she think he worked for, he wondered; Ministry of Propaganda?

His tiny lodgings were up five flights, above a closed dance hall. The climb still left him breathless. He counted the ninety-six steps and paused as always on the third turn. The letdown of homecoming, he thought, as he entered his little box that stood alone at the top of the stairs.

He paused, alert. Something intangible in the dead air made him think it had been disturbed during his absence.

It was still light outside, the start of getting dark.

Everything was where he had left it: his service pistol, not taken to Budapest, under the floorboards; a heel of a stale loaf in the bread bin. The feeling of disturbance persisted.

Perhaps it was a result of now working for the Gestapo.

He knew as well as anyone that people had grown most afraid of themselves.

He resolved to go out and get drunk. His own form of deviancy amounted to seeking out illicit roving venues where forbidden music was played and teenagers – mainly boys with long hair – gathered to get high and enjoy the last of their freedom before conscription.

His purpose was to go in undercover to expose the scene he was patronising, though he had done nothing about that, having rather fallen for this forbidden world.

He'd hung around student venues, claiming to be a freelance photographer on a ministry grant, compiling an archive of endangered frescoes. Schlegel had once met such a fellow, who couldn't believe his luck: excused active service for undemanding work, with travel and accommodation thrown in. Schlegel told the students he was back from Köln where he had come across hot jazz parties. Thanks to Gestapo files, he knew what he was talking about. One gang called itself the Edelweiss Pirates, another the Raving Dudes.

Inside the venues, usually cellars of bombed-out buildings, maybe thirty to fifty kids crammed into a dark, sweaty space where they drank and smoked and necked and danced. A basic sound system amplified the gramophone and the tinny rhythms of crude, urgent music were transmitted like messages from another planet.

On the night of the nineteenth, Schlegel went looking for such a club. These visits had been going on for about six weeks. He knew he was playing a dangerous game. By then he was going for the pleasurable distractions of Gerda, who was a bit older than the general crowd. He didn't know what she did, other than postgraduate work connected to the university. Like many young women in Berlin, she was sexually generous.

They hadn't talked much or introduced themselves rather than bump into each other and start jigging to the music. Then it was first names and kissing in the dark and a few times after that easy gratification in shadows and doorways before going their separate ways. The blackout encouraged casual sex. Schlegel would have liked to get to know her better – she seemed lively and interesting – but it was an unwritten code that such encounters took place apart from the rest of life.

That night the local venues he tried weren't being used. It was dark with almost no moon and when he cracked his shin on a concrete pillar he gave up and went home.

He checked his mailbox. A couple of envelopes, one a bill, the other plain and unaddressed. Inside he found a folded sheet of foolscap and a list of names.

Upstairs, Schlegel looked at it properly – a column of typed names and initials, single spaced, with nothing to say what they meant; perhaps thirty in all. None of the names he recognised. He was irritated more than puzzled, until down near the end he saw his own.

'Schlegel'.

And his initial.

'Schlegel A'.

Above his name: 'Stempfle B.' Below: 'Zehnter K.' He had never heard of them but finding his own name on a list was bound to rack up a man's persecution complex. The regime specialised in secret lists. List after list. Was it a warning?

He slept badly and got up in the night, more worried about the Budapest documents. Papers in order; he decided the folder was wrong – it looked the same, but not quite: marbled paper, two ribbons for tying, a standard product. It felt newer. Sloppy fuckers, not bothering to return the original folder, he thought, and told himself it was just another irritating detail in an irritating day. As for the real point of the trip, Schlegel hadn't a clue, but more had been going on than he knew. He sighed. No use wasting time on imponderables. Some mysteries weren't there to be solved.

He went back to bed, slept badly and this time got up and inspected the foolscap list. The creases, folded for the envelope, looked new but the page itself felt old. He stared at his name and thought that was what had woken him. Whether he had been dreaming about his long-lost father – however hard that was when he knew nothing of the man or even what he looked like – somewhere in the depths of his unconscious he had made the connection.

Schlegel was August, his father Anton. Both Schlegel A. Was it his father's name on the list rather than his?

But his father had gone to Argentina in the early 1920s never to be heard from again, or to be mentioned by his mother, except once when Schlegel was fifteen to announce she had been told by the German embassy he had drowned in Argentina, swimming in a river. By then Schlegel remembered nothing of the man, so he didn't miss him. He was annoyed to be reminded of this vague, forgotten presence, like the first ripple of a breeze that brings bad weather, and he recalled a dim childhood memory of imagining him working for the Argentinian railway, building high spectacular bridges that spanned wild gorges over tumbling rivers. Why he should think his father had built bridges, he had no idea.

2

Schlegel went to work as usual on the morning of Thursday, 20 July after two days off sick – at least, according to what he had told the office. Another hot day was promised. It was still cool as he crossed the river. He preferred the forty-minute walk to the stink and squash of rush hour transport.

On Friedrichstrasse a section of S-Bahn track was down. The city was a smash-up. Everyone was so nerve-tested that Schlegel wondered if his hair hadn't gone white for a second time.

The list was in his pocket. He didn't know what to make of it but his organisation possessed a huge central index for all capitals, regions and zones of occupation, and if any names on the list had come to the attention of the Gestapo they would feature in its files. He decided to check, thinking if it really was his father, he must have not gone to South America or gone and come back without telling anyone.

'Feeling better?' Dunkelwert asked. There was nothing solicitous about the remark. Nor could Schlegel detect sarcasm, only flat disbelief.

'Food poisoning,' he said.

Dunkelwert was barely taller than he was sitting. He had watched her beady tracking of his arrival as he hung up his hat. Schlegel looked around the office. Such busy bees.

Dunkelwert had a slogan for everything – 'Efficiency and punctuality'; 'Time given to the state is dedicated time,' whatever that meant. The ineffectual Bletsch, nominally in charge, sat in his glass hutch, but Dunkelwert was taking over because the Party increasingly ran the show. She was its mouthpiece and usher of reforms, with performance assessment and forty- and fifty-year old men being treated like kids.

Control was easier since their offices had been damaged in an air raid. They were now lumped together in a former typing pool with cubby holes, fancily described as carrels, partitioned shoulder high, with no natural light because broken windows were boarded up and awaiting repair after months.

Dunkelwert with her nicotine moustache and tobacco stained fingers made Schlegel think of a malevolent animated doll wound up to tread a fine line between persecutor and victim. She wasn't his actual superior but being ambitious had positioned herself as *de facto* team leader, making her one of an emerging breed of a species thought to be extinct – the career woman. She had consolidated her base by setting up committees no one bothered about until it was too late. Technically she worked for the same department as Schlegel. Section 5a covered antisocial behaviour and shirking, which, as the cynics said, covered a multitude of sins, but through control of joint committees with sections 2 (sabotage) and 4a (Catholicism, Protestantism, Freemasonry), she was able constantly to interfere and exploited the condescension with which she was treated by retorting, 'You are only saying that because I am a woman.' As for any personal life, Schlegel couldn't imagine her sharing anything, let alone her body, yet from the way she sometimes looked at him he wondered if she was a sexual

predator, but of what? Boys? Girls? He suspecte
ical cruelty then at least a degree of mental tor.

The day started with the usual endless Thursday
Bletsch was an old timeserver, with a big quiff and   ...-
brush moustache, who made a point of giving Dunkelwert
a hard time because she was after his job.

Bletsch did his rah-rah act to gee them all up. Most
couldn't care less. Despite a heavy caseload, the job was
not complicated. It was the work of a network of informers
more than any active investigation on their part. After that
it was about what the apprehended could share about others.
Schlegel and Dunkelwert had two such cases on their books:
a farmer's wife shopped by her vindictive mother-in-law
and a juvenile delinquent looking to wriggle off the hook by
offering up a molesting priest. Schlegel was familiar enough
by then with the process. It was like watching a plug being
pulled as it dawned on the accused that everything had just
changed. Guilty or not, there were no mitigating circumstances. Actually that was not quite true. Situations were
often more negotiable than they appeared. Dogs could learn
new tricks. Thus did the informed on become the informers.

The meeting grew restless as Bletsch banged on. It was
stifling by then and had there been windows they would
have been open. Schlegel thought about Budapest, wondered about hidden purpose on the part of those that had
sent him, and wished he could have his trip over again, in a
better frame of mind.

The meeting at last adjourned and Schlegel intended to
sneak off to check the names on his list against the central
file. Instead he found himself summoned by Bletsch who
had left a note on his desk saying: see me. Schoolboy stuff.

Schlegel thought of ignoring it but Bletsch was in his glass cage, beckoning impatiently.

The cage had previously been used by the typing pool supervisor. There was hardly room inside for two. Schlegel wasn't invited to sit. He was aware of Dunkelwert watching them.

'You don't look so ill,' Bletsch said.

Schlegel said it had been a 48-hour thing; something he had eaten. Three days and he would have needed a doctor's certificate. Bunking off sick, once an accepted form of truancy, was being cracked down on like everything else.

Bletsch didn't like Schlegel. Schlegel hadn't worked his passage and had been dumped on them. He was seen to have a senior patron in his former boss, Arthur Nebe, head of CID, who had been responsible for his transfer, leaving Bletsch convinced that Schlegel had been put there to spy. Everyone had spies. The funny thing was Nebe had not asked Schlegel to spy when he had asked plenty of others. On the other hand, it was Nebe, along with his stepfather, who had sent him to Budapest and said not to tell his employer.

'Why *are* you here?' Bletsch insisted.

Schlegel said, 'I thought I could do more good here than in financial crime,' thinking that was true. He had been useless there.

'Why hasn't your file been forwarded by the criminal police?' Bletsch asked.

'I didn't know it hadn't been, sir.'

That was alarming. Schlegel hadn't known and supposed someone had sidelined it in order to do some digging.

Bletsch changed the subject to ask, 'How long have you been working on that underground club scene?'

Schlegel sighed to indicate the magnitude of the task. 'It's very tight-knit and secretive.'

He knew his card was being marked. Time to close the whole thing down. The kinder alternative would be to warn the kids off.

As Schlegel was about to go Bletsch asked, 'How do you get on with Dunkelwert?'

'I don't,' he replied, which was true but more to the point it was what Bletsch wanted to hear.

'Any reason?'

'Bossy woman.' Again what Bletsch wanted to hear. 'She meddles.' Ditto.

'Keep an eye on her.'

In other words, go through her desk.

The rest of the morning was given over to a Party meeting, chaired by Dunkelwert. These consciousness-raising affairs were dedicated to motivation, improvement and doctrine, and everyone had to be seen to subscribe, Party member or not. The problem was every state department had its shadow organisation within the Party so no one quite knew how anything worked, other than as a series of rivalries and duplications.

Dunkelwert disapproved of everything outside of Party dictates. She had reported an office clerk for defeatist talk after he complained about a disrupted bus service. Schlegel suspected she could make out a watertight case against an infant in a pram. He often thought she was there to expose him as one of those lukewarms with too many career compromises. He could see how she believed men had fucked it up and not wanting to be anyone's mother left the Party as the only way forward.

With the meeting over, Schlegel used a call box to telephone his stepfather. The housekeeper answered. His stepfather came on saying he couldn't talk. He sounded agitated. 'I am waiting for some rather important news.'

Schlegel said he had a quick question about his actual father. 'I was always told he had gone off to South America, where he died, but I came across something that suggests he might not have.'

'I am sure I don't know. Your mother never discussed him.'

'Can't you tell me anything about him? His name has come up.'

'Very little and not now. I too heard he'd gone abroad. Call me later. Sorry to rush.'

Schlegel hung up puzzled because his stepfather was not a man ever to be in a hurry about anything.

3

The Wolf's Lair, deep in the woods of East Prussia, was an enclave of tranquility, much transformed since being used to mastermind the 1941 invasion of Russia. Huge concrete bunkers. Deep camouflage. Grassed roofs. Brick-reinforced wooden buildings. Thousands of forced labourers continued to modernise the site. The Führer bunker awaited completion, leaving him to lodge in former guest quarters in the central security zone. Meetings were held a short stroll away in a reinforced wooden barracks whose partitions had been ripped out, leaving it light and airy with windows on three sides.

Bormann's appointments noted the arrival that afternoon of Il Duce, Benito Mussolini, a chastened figure since his arrest the year before and rescue by a team of crack SS commandos. Because of his visit the morning conference was being brought forward to 12.30. Göring would not attend, being keen to avoid Mussolini whom he detested. Himmler was on his private train nearby. Bormann reported the Führer being out of sorts, thanks to a raging toothache and a hefty dose of procaine. 'He's not at all himself,' he told everyone.

The bait had been laid with the relevant chief of staff summoned to report from Berlin for that morning's meeting. Several times Bormann questioned the wisdom of his own judgement, not something he was usually given to do.

He would not attend the conference. He would be working nearby, waiting. It was another hot morning with a forecast of rain in the afternoon.

At 12.42 local time, Bormann heard the explosion and ran from his office to be met with the sight of a shaken, reeling Führer, hair standing on end, white from fallen plaster, and trousers in shreds. The man's eyes shone with zeal as he declared providence had spared him to complete his work.

The conference room, with its windows blown out, looked like a butcher's abattoir or an idiots' carnival. The usually natty Hermann Fegelein was running around like a headless chicken. Groaning men lay on the floor, one spouting a geyser of blood, another clutching for a missing leg which had been blown across the room, and Bormann cursed to himself. The one thing he had not calculated for was the heroic nincompoop of a one-eyed, one-armed Colonel botching the fucking job.

4

Schlegel was waiting to check the names on his list with the central index when someone shouted, 'The Führer is dead!' The same voice shouted it again. Schlegel looked at the clerk he was dealing with and watched her mouth form a perfect O of surprise. He said, 'Surely it can't be true,' hoping it might be. The shocked silence was replaced by a hubbub of confusion.

His stepfather had been waiting for important news, he had told Schlegel. Could the Führer's death have been that news? He dismissed the idea. His stepfather was far too cautious to get involved in anything like that.

The building was in an uproar with people running around. Upstairs, it was being said terrorists disguised as labourers were responsible, or it was an air raid, or a bomb and the Army was taking over. Some of the secretaries were crying. Dunkelwert scrutinised Schlegel, trying to read his reaction. She said, 'Bletsch hasn't a clue, that's for sure.'

Schlegel watched everyone struggle to work out how to respond. He saw a terrible burden being lifted in one or two, followed by the equivalent of crashing gears as features were rearranged into expressions of appropriate shock and disbelief. He was sure his own initial reaction had contained that split-second giveaway. At the same time, he was indoctrinated by default to fear both authority and any change of it, enough to find the idea of rebellion faintly risible.

None of the news was certain. The Führer was dead. The Führer wasn't dead. Then he was dead again. No one knew where the attack was supposed to have taken place. Some said the Führer's military headquarters in East Prussia. Others that he was still in Berlin. Bletsch's white-knuckled grip on his telephone told Schlegel they were perhaps in the middle of a takeover which could see them all shot.

Switchboards were jammed. Schlegel rang his stepfather and got no answer. All lines to newspapers and broadcasters were busy. Foreign Office the same, the Ministry of Propaganda, and the Press Club. He tried Criminal Investigation, dialling the direct number for Homicide. It rang a long time. A gruff voice eventually said, 'Stoffel'.

Schlegel was almost more astonished by that than the news. Stoffel was supposed to have retired, and good riddance. 'Schlegel,' he said and enjoyed the evident surprise.

It was strange talking to Stoffel again. The man had always made his contempt for him clear. Stoffel was all blackjack and knuckleduster, knock heads together to make them see sense. By contrast, he now sounded almost cordial, given the urgency of events. He seemed to know that Schlegel worked for the Gestapo.

'You boys have been caught on the hop,' he said.

Schlegel asked him what he was doing back at work. Stoffel said he had been pulled out of retirement because of 'fucking staff shortages'. Of the business in hand, he said, 'I spoke to a man, who has spoken to a man who said a coup is underway but no one knows if it is the SS or the Army.'

Schlegel said they were in the dark at his end. 'But they're saying the radio is broadcasting as normal.'

Stoffel grunted. 'That's the first thing you knock out. Put your feet up, son. It sounds like they don't know what they are doing.'

Schlegel hung up and swapped notes with Dunkelwert. Reichsführer-SS Himmler was supposed to be flying back to Berlin. Dunkelwert looked strangely uncertain and Schlegel supposed her loyalties were being tested. She could not voice any opinion on the Reichsführer's role – whether he was returning to instigate the coup or quash it – because it was not clear where the Party stood. It was quite possible that the SS would surround the building and cart them all off.

'Here's what I think,' said Schlegel. Of all the leadership, Dr Goebbels was most likely to be in town and his ministry would probably be better informed than the Gestapo. He didn't add that in the event of a revolution the Ministry of Propaganda was probably the safer place.

They left Bletsch hanging on the telephone, looking like a man hastily revising his CV.

Outside, soldiers were on the street. Trams were running around empty, suggesting a curfew. The government quarter was being cordoned off. But none of the action appeared threatening, as if nobody was sure what was going on.

At a barricade they were told not to proceed. The sentry seemed almost apologetic, with none of the usual military snap. Schlegel asked to speak to the man in charge.

A junior officer came forward and explained they were on an emergency exercise to defend the government quarter in case of attack.

'Exercise?' repeated Schlegel, incredulous. 'They are saying the Führer is dead.'

The officer looked uncertain enough for Schlegel to show his badge and point to the propaganda building. 'We'll be inside the cordon and if it's not an exercise then you know where we are.'

Dunkelwert asked, 'Whose exercise?'

'The Reserve Army's.' He added that they had been on

standby on other occasions until they were stood down. So not the SS, thought Schlegel, but it seemed a very cack-handed way of conducting a coup, using troops that think they are on exercise.

Apart from soldiers and their vehicles, the area was deserted. Everything appeared more like a rehearsal than a real revolution.

They were allowed to pass. Schlegel and Dunkelwert's shadows – his elongated, hers squat – almost made him laugh. Inside the cordon they had the district to themselves: two figures dwarfed by the impersonal state and its vast, uncompromising buildings, reducing whatever was being played out beneath to insignificance.

The soldiers guarding the entrance of the Ministry of Propaganda seemed confused by the presence of a woman. Schlegel watched them reach the conclusion that if she was there at all she must be important. They were waved in.

The interior was pretentious in scale, an advertisement for its corridors of power, wide enough to drive a truck down. Although troops stood around, arms at the ready, the general atmosphere was more like a market, with staff gathered to trade the latest gossip. Least sure of their role seemed the soldiers, looking nervous about what they might be taking part in. Nothing appeared to be ordered with any great conviction. If a revolt was taking place it was a very lackadaisical one. A woman told them the ministry was supposed to be up in arms and the man next to her said, 'First I've heard,' and the woman added, 'We were sitting minding our own business until this lot stormed in.' No one knew whether the story of the Führer's death was true. Schlegel said they were there to find out.

'Shoot the messenger,' the woman said cheerfully.

5

The first that Minister of Propaganda Goebbels knew of the day's events was a communiqué from the Führer press office announcing that the Führer was uninjured following a bomb attack.

A further communication was sent for him to broadcast. This he sat on, as it sounded like the matter was in hand, which, in hindsight, was an error. By mid-afternoon it was being reported that the government area was being surrounded by troops. Goebbels telephoned the Führer headquarters to ask if the Army had gone mad.

Still he delayed the broadcast, which earned him a reprimand from Party Secretary Bormann who telephoned to ask what was going on. Goebbels said he was composing a fitting commentary to accompany it.

He could hear Bormann whispering with someone at the other the end of the line. Really, the situation was impossible! How this coarse and conniving little bureaucrat had elevated himself in the Führer's esteem was beyond comprehension. Or rather, how had the Führer fallen for such an arse-licking toad? The whispering went on then Bormann came back sounding like an angry speak-your-weight machine, saying, 'I didn't ask you for a commentary. I just want the news broadcast.'

Shortly after that, a highly decorated young Major was shown into Goebbels' office, where he was in conference, to announce he was occupying the Ministry of Propaganda on the grounds that Dr Goebbels, its minister, was in the process of trying to overthrow the Führer.

The situation was so preposterous that Goebbels started to enjoy himself and played to his audience who were all agog at the Major. They were then interrupted by two clowns from the Gestapo, a skinny beanpole with prematurely white hair and a dumpy little number with an ugly mug and what Goebbels suspected was a spectacular body, and who probably fucked like a stoat.

'Can the Gestapo tell us what is going on?' Goebbels asked with heavy irony.

Schlegel, still surprised by their easy passage through the building, saw Goebbels was playing to a full house. His lackeys, with a reputation for snappy dressing, looked dishevelled by events, compared to their immaculate master with not a strand of brilliantined hair out of place; a man who, perhaps because he was so short, appreciated scale. The office they were in was enormous and temple-like, which Schlegel supposed was the point, making the minister's utterances ones of religious command.

The other well-dressed man in the room was the highly decorated Major who was debating the course of the day with Goebbels, who was all sarcastic charm. The Major believed he was operating in a counter-revolutionary role. Goebbels scoffed. 'You have been tricked! We are all loyal here! The treason is yours!'

Goebbels really was tiny, thought Schlegel; no wonder he spent a fortune on tailors or he would be wearing children's sizes. Even in a crisis, Goebbels' eye for stage managing hadn't deserted him, with the doctor at its centre, surrounded by adoring acolytes, as he went about the business of converting the apostate Major.

Goebbels went for crude charm. 'I am shitting myself. Is there a revolution going on? First I've heard. Why don't we telephone and ask?'

There was only one way of countermanding the literal-minded Major's orders. Straight to the top.

The telephone rang. Goebbels picked up, paused and stiffened. The room was on tenterhooks. Goebbels relished the mounting tension as he refused to enlighten his audience, restricting himself to monosyllables, the only response to such a tumultuous event. Let them sweat. The Führer sounded away with the fairies. Goebbels supposed he had been given an anti-shock shot. For some reason the Führer was bellowing far louder than necessary; perforated eardrums, Goebbels learned later.

Eventually he held out the receiver. 'For you, Major. A word in your shell-like.'

Goebbels could hear the Führer asking if the Major recognised his voice. The Major clicked his heels and said he did. Goebbels leaned in, listening to the highly decorated young officer being given the full treatment while resembling a man being impaled as he realised that just by being there he was technically still acting for the conspirators.

'Only my commands are to be obeyed,' said the Führer. 'You are to restore order in Berlin for me.'

Suddenly the Major was the pin-up boy of the moment, chiselled, handsome, fanatical, just the man for the job.

The Führer fell silent. The Major wasn't sure if he was supposed to end the call. No, no, gestured Goebbels. Under no circumstances hang up on the Führer. Bormann was prompting in the background, shouting to the Führer, 'Tell him to use whatever force necessary and shoot anyone who disobeys.'

Schlegel wondered about the recriminations to follow.

He was willing to bet the Gestapo hadn't had a clue. In the space of a short call the young and highly decorated Major was rocketed into the stratosphere. He came off the telephone and informed them that he had been empowered to quash the *coup d'etat*.

Goebbels clapped his hands in delight. 'An extraordinary order for a battalion commander! For the moment you are superior to your superiors.'

The Major, utterly unimaginative and very relieved, played his part, leaving Goebbels to take command, pointing, sharing, shouting, restoring order.

'We are living through a momentous day. Again the Führer has been spared by destiny. He will address the nation tonight. It's the turn of those responsible for this miserable debacle to start crapping themselves. The Führer has promised no mercy.' He turned to the Major. 'Go and arrest some generals and let us get on with our job.'

The Major departed to perform his patriotic duty, leaving Goebbels to fume to his underlings at the very notion that he might be considered disloyal or even contemplate a coup.

Goebbels looked at Dunkelwert and asked, 'What is the Gestapo's line on this?'

'Awaiting orders, sir.'

'I suggest you go back and ask yourself why you weren't forewarned. Secrecy or incompetence?'

The answer was obvious to Schlegel: the Gestapo was inept at counterintelligence. The moment he said it he knew he should have kept his trap shut.

Goebbel's gaze swivelled in Schlegel's direction.

'How so?' he asked. 'Do go on.'

Schlegel had no choice but to answer. He couldn't think of anything other than to say that if the coup was Army business it fell outside the Gestapo's remit in terms of counterintelligence. This was strictly accurate but not what Goebbels wanted to hear.

'Name?' snapped Goebbels.

Schlegel told him.

'As in our illustrious translator of Shakespeare?'

Schlegel was afraid of this immaculate little man. Heads would roll for having his afternoon so inconvenienced.

They were told to go away and start compiling lists.

'A reign of terror,' said Goebbels with relish. 'To weed out the last of the naysayers, the recalcitrants and the traitors.'

6

Back at the Gestapo headquarters on Prinz-Albrecht-Strasse, the slumbering beast started to rouse itself. A one-eyed, one-handed military attaché who had left the conference early was being sought. A wag asked if he was one-eyed and missing the hand as a result of the bomb blast.

Tight little teams put on hats and departed to make the first arrests.

The room grew more committed to being seen to do its job as news spread of an imminent, almost unheard-of appearance from their chief, Gestapo Müller, whose invisibility was such that it was said he could be in a room for five minutes before anyone noticed. Schlegel supposed the man suddenly moving among them was Müller. Neither handsome nor unhandsome, he was strangely unmemorable, which perhaps had less to do with his looks – he wasn't *that* unmemorable – than a cultivated anonymity. His one disconcerting habit was a rapid eye movement, like flicking a switch. He departed as unobtrusively as he had come and moments later an underling announced an extraordinary general meeting, which Schlegel suspected would be the start of the dressing down. Failure of penetration would not be forgiven lightly and rival departments would be quick to advance themselves at the Gestapo's expense.

By the time Schlegel got to the theatre it was packed. The

room had filled up from the back, leaving seats only at the front. Schlegel found himself stuck in the second row, too close to the lectern.

Müller sidled in and addressed them in a monotone, giving thanks for the safe deliverance of the Führer. He didn't sound that enthusiastic about it. Insurrectionists were cowering in a barracks, he informed them, surrounded by troops loyal to the Führer. Whatever was intended had turned into a phantom revolt that would be matched by hard, unstinting punishment. He sounded more enthusiastic about that.

The eye flicker continued from side to side and every time seemed to settle on Schlegel, who was stuck in direct line with the outer range of this extraordinary movement. Müller took on an even greater greyness as he droned on. 'Questions must be asked about our own conduct. We knew of conspiratorial meetings, having penetrated a cell, made arrests, yet we failed to produce a correct evaluation.'

He fell silent. The room stirred. Was Müller suggesting an internal purge as a result of oversights?

He asked, 'Can anyone tell me why this should be?'

Even Dunkelwert, always eager to push herself forward, remained silent. Müller's eyes flickered again, coming to land on Schlegel, then away and back. Schlegel, realising he was about to be singled out, reckoned he had about ten seconds to prepare an answer.

'You, there,' said Müller. 'What do you think? Stand up so we can see you.'

Schlegel took his time, trying to think of something.

'A lack of comprehension,' he finally volunteered.

Müller looked interested. 'About what?'

Schlegel ploughed on. 'A true National Socialist would have difficulty understanding internal political difference, since the person of the Führer cannot be the subject of discussion.'

In other words, the cult of leadership precluded all opinion or analysis.

Schlegel sat down, sweating. The meeting broke up soon after but Müller's eyes continued to flick towards him, which resulted in his summons by one of Müller's entourage immediately after the man had walked out.

Trouble, Schlegel supposed.

Müller's office was on a floor Schlegel had never been to, and surprisingly modest, with a little anteroom and such a small space beyond that Schlegel wondered if the man had another office for formal business. Compared to Dr Goebbels's monumental statements, Müller's room was nothing.

Müller stayed standing. Closer to, he was even more insubstantial and inscrutable, but a glimmer of hard humour shone through, as though there was something funny about power.

Müller stared at Schlegel, the eyes temporarily still, boring into his. Schlegel supposed it was a trick, like a mesmerist's. The amusement was quite gone.

'What did you mean by your remarks to Dr Goebbels this afternoon?'

He'd known at the time he should have kept his trap shut. Müller's method was to offer nothing, letting Schlegel dangle. After bending over backwards to say that he was not being detrimental about the Gestapo's efforts, Schlegel realised he sounded pathetic and shut up. Twice that day and come to the attention of senior figures. It was unforgivable on his part: under no circumstances draw attention to yourself in the presence of any high ranking officer, and you couldn't get more senior than Goebbels and Müller.

Müller said, 'Your file makes for interesting reading.'

That morning Bletsch had complained it hadn't been forwarded by CID. Schlegel wasn't going to fall into the trap of opening his mouth again.

Müller repeated Bletsch's question. 'Why *are* you here?'

Should he lie, offer an approximation of the truth, or something more accurate that might leave him fatally exposed?

Müller stalled him, saying, 'If you are going to lie then do it properly. I want to see that golden thread of truth that knits together the really superior lie.'

It was getting dangerous, thought Schlegel, if Müller was getting metaphysical.

He countered by making the truth sound boring. 'Last year I was involved in a case of financial corruption in the SS,' he said. 'It backfired and I ended up being wrongly accused of the corruption I was investigating.'

'Hoist with your own petard. Someone was clever.'

'Yes, sir.' There was no point in naming names.

'Why aren't you dead then? There was a court hearing. The verdict was unequivocal. Yet here you are.'

'I was fortunate. A colleague knew of my innocence, arranged for my escape and kept it off my file.'

'Yes, an interesting gap. Yet according the court record you were executed. Am I talking to a dead man?'

Müller was so close to being a ghost that Schlegel thought that the idea of conversing with someone who was on record as being posthumous might appeal.

'It was arranged for me to be taken out after it had looked like I had been shot.'

'With one bound he was free,' Müller said sceptically. 'Is there a golden thread running through this story?'

'It's the truth, sir.'

More or less. The real cause of alarm was why Müller was taking such an interest in him and being appraised of facts omitted from his record.

'So what are you doing here, to repeat the question?'

Schlegel said he'd felt vulnerable returning to his old job so he had put in for a transfer.

Müller looked bored by the answer, and asked, 'This colleague of yours, who helped you escape, would that be Morgen?'

There was no point in denying it.

'Where is Morgen now?'

This was suddenly very difficult. The answer was Budapest, which Müller probably knew already. And if the next question was where Schlegel had last seen Morgen he would be in trouble because the answer was Budapest. He hadn't known Morgen would be there, but would Müller believe him?

'I don't know, sir.' Brazen it out, Schlegel thought.

'Budapest, I believe,' said Müller, mildly. 'Where he meets interesting people.' He treated Schlegel to a sphinx-like gaze. 'Have you been to Budapest?'

Every question a hurdle. A half-truth seemed best. Schlegel said he had been there once, not admitting it was only yesterday. He wondered if he had been watched all along, and Müller was letting him know as much in one of those destabilising acts the man no doubt specialised in.

Frankly, Schlegel was more puzzled by what Morgen – the last person he had expected to find in Budapest – *had* been doing there.

Müller said, 'You worked with Morgen from March until October last year, investigating corruption.'

The inference was clear: that Schlegel had been placed

in the Gestapo for the same reason and was reporting to
someone outside.

Schlegel suspected Müller was relentless in pursuit. Most
disconcerting was why he should bother with someone as
junior as himself, on a day of national emergency, unless it
was to persecute or cultivate him to some sinister end.

Müller looked as though he was about to dismiss him,
only to give him the flickering eye.

'Schlegel?' Müller asked.

'Yes, sir.'

'And Anton Schlegel?'

Schlegel thought of the list in his pocket and his hands
went clammy.

'My father, sir.'

'Could I have known him?'

Schlegel recognised a trick of Müller's: always be the one
asking the questions.

'He went to South America in the 1920s.'

'Not somewhere I have been.'

'Where did you know this other Anton Schlegel, sir?'

Müller looked put out at being asked.

'In Munich, in the twenties and thirties. He was around
quite a long time.'

Schlegel was sure he had not asked innocently. The obvious question was whether Müller was in fact responsible
for sending the list. Müller had Schlegel's file and knew
all about him. I am watching you, he seemed to be saying.
Within twenty-four hours of receiving the list Schlegel
had found himself being addressed by the Minister of
Propaganda and the head of the Gestapo; and his father,
whose name hadn't come up in years, had now been mentioned twice in two days. What were the chances? Schlegel
understood enough about subterfuge to know that if it was

played half in the open then point and motive became even more impenetrable.

Schlegel left convinced that if you stood Müller in sunlight he would cast no shadow. Most puzzling was the man's parting remark: 'Soup is never eaten as hot as it is cooked.'

7

For the rest of the day, Dr Goebbels kept an open line to the Führer headquarters. Like everyone, he had spies there. He was told the Führer was slumped in an armchair sucking pastilles and doped up on sedatives, waiting for a radio truck to be sent from Konigsberg so he could speak to the nation. The recording was finally made at 11.30 pm. The speech, all five minutes of it, was broadcast ninety minutes later. A lacklustre effort, thought Goebbels, and clearly written by Bormann: 'the warning finger of providence'. Never an easy cliché when a more leaden one would suffice. The sound quality was poor and the Führer had none of the old fizz. If only they had consulted him. Goebbels could have suggested ways of making the speech more rousing. The reading was variable and from the number of audible splicings sounded like it had been patched together from different takes. Goebbels supposed that for most just hearing the Führer would be enough but it fell short of his own professional standards.

He left his office and announced to his staff, 'The putsch is over.' He was buzzing now, his mood infectious. He ordered champagne and told them all in no uncertain terms that each and every one of them had been at the centre of history that day. No one else had been around to resist. Always on the lookout for the prettier secretaries, Goebbels swooped down on a group of them, brandishing his glass. 'Well, my dears, what a day!'

He decided on the pert, plumper one, with an attractive wave in her hair, what he suspected was a becoming blush and merry, dancing eyes.

He amused himself with the thought of what a long and wasted last day it had been for the traitor Stauffenberg. Up first thing. Fly out of Berlin. Five hour countdown to the Führer being dead. Blow up conference room. Fuck up the explosion. Fly back unawares. Botch putsch. Executed by midnight. Long live Germany!

8

At Prinz-Albrecht-Strasse they worked through the night, the gleaming beast now in full action. The coup ringleaders had already been shot elsewhere and the first detainees were being taken downstairs in chains. Dunkelwert said everything was being prepared to make life as unpleasant as possible.

Truck and car doors slammed as the first prisoners were taken down.

'More names will be forthcoming,' Dunkelwert said, 'and more cars dispatched to bring the next lot in, and so on.'

Schlegel supposed she would take up a position downstairs, showing herself to be as tough as any man. He feared she would ask him to accompany her and sidled off.

He used his ability for inconspicuousness – he'd had quite enough exposure for one day – to get assigned to Operation Second Wave, a compilation of also-rans, seen as an excuse to settle old scores.

The central file was like something out of science fiction – a tall, circular contraption so enormous it required an electric motor, with the operator able to produce any card at the push of a button. The latest punch-card technology logged each subject's details, including where individual files were held, which apparently wasn't that simple with everything grown so large that even local ones were held in several places.

To keep the system moving, no more than six names could be submitted by any agent at one time. Schlegel was reminded of a slow and cumbersome wheel of fortune.

He slipped in three names from the list in his pocket – Schlegel A. and the ones above and below – curious to see if any came up.

None did.

The names from the Second Wave operation had files in different parts of the building, involving more queues and forms to be filled. No files were allowed to be taken away.

By halfway through the night Schlegel had crossed eighteen names off his list, none of which seemed ever to have come to the attention of the Gestapo. He supposed there couldn't be a file on everyone but the mere existence of his list presupposed authority.

His notes on Second Wave files read like shaggy-dog stories: a man or woman who may or may not have done this or that, or belonged to something they shouldn't have. Schlegel had a railway official with former social democrat connections; a militant Christian female; a doctor suspected of performing illegal abortions; a dentist with unproved connections to a morphine racket; what was known as a 'factory shirker' with a history of illness as a cover for absenteeism; a woman in the Ministry of Propaganda with 'suspect relatives'. Schlegel asked himself if such relatives was what it came down to now.

In one of the filing rooms, the librarian, a middle-aged woman with a mournful face, struck Schlegel as not unfriendly. He asked her what happened when a case was closed.

She said it was removed from the system, not straight away, and taken who knows where. Schlegel thought perhaps a whole parallel clerical universe existed devoted to a death index. Would Gestapo Müller know what happened to these departed files, or would they be designated to some middle-ranker barely aware of their existence? Everyone was muddled enough as it was by all the strange overlaps and divisions of authority. Maybe even Müller was confused by the lack of rigid outline to the hierarchy. The observation seemed important – willed confusion would become chaos and many were already in the process of being swept aside.

Schlegel's shift left the office at 6 am due to be back at midday. A liverish sun hung in the sulphurous haze. The streets were full with those going to work, trudging, heads down. Newspaper posters of the first editions denounced the plot. No one Schlegel passed looked affected by the news. Careworn faces told their own stories.

Dog tired, he slept in his clothes and woke full of scrambled thoughts about his father. If Anton Schlegel's life hadn't involved going to South America it raised the question of why his mother had told him he had.

He couldn't ask her because she was in a concentration camp. How the mighty were fallen. In her pomp she had shared a box at the opera with the Führer himself. Now he received post cards from time to time saying, 'All well.'

Schlegel spent the first part of the afternoon assigned to arrests with a man he didn't know, who drove. Knock, knock. Five minutes to pack and come with us. Schlegel made a point of not looking at those taken away, most of them elderly couples and a few younger women. They all seemed to live several floors up. His colleague complained about his aching feet; otherwise he was the silent type.

Time passed. Schlegel took advantage of his role as passenger to try and think about nothing. Or, rather, he thought about a lot but nothing new, and it slid by as meaninglessly as the hot passing streets.

In the baking white heat the city took on an air of stunned surprise, indistinguishable from indifference. On one level, it had always looked like it couldn't care less. There were friendlier places. Schlegel supposed those they were carting off would end up in camps.

They dealt with only one case of histrionics. The rest came as meek as you like, as though what they dreaded most had come to pass.

They were polite taking them away.

Schlegel rang his stepfather a couple of times and got no reply, which was unusual because a housekeeper was there when he was out. After the last twenty-four hours, he grew worried that the man's habitual secrecy might be for a reason.

His list of potential arrests grew. Schlegel felt grubby and godlike peering down at ant-like lives.

He was ambushed by Dunkelwert while waiting in the canteen to be served, and had no choice but to sit with her.

Dunkelwert ate with gusto. Schlegel wondered if it excited her to watch men being tortured.

He stiffly recited, 'The Führer must be like a cat with nine lives, the luck he has. Imagine surviving a bomb in the room.'

Dunkelwert gave him a dead stare and asked, 'Why did you go to Budapest?'

He rocked back. Denial seemed pointless.

'Because I was asked.'

'On what business?'

'To get papers signed and returned. For the SS.'

'You didn't inform us.'

'I was asked not to.'

'By whom?'

'I am not at liberty to say, other than a senior officer.'

'Liberty is beside the point. You travelled under your own name.'

Schlegel said he had no reason not to and added with weak flippancy that he had only the one passport. While the work might have been confidential it hadn't been secret, as far as he knew.

'Why did you agree to go?'

He tried to make light of it. 'Wouldn't you? Forty-eight hours out of Berlin, expenses paid.'

The joke fell flat.

Dunkelwert said, 'Given the current emergency, a list of everyone flying in and out of Berlin over the past week was obtained from passport control. Your name was on it.'

Another bloody list, thought Schlegel.

He hoped she was guessing his meeting with Gestapo Müller was about that trip. At least he hadn't panicked when she raised the matter.

As he made to go, she said, 'One other thing.'

'What now?' He sounded as brusque as he could.

She produced a file card and showed it.

'Does the name mean anything?'

Schlegel hoped his reaction didn't betray him. How did Dunkelwert know about Christoph?

He admitted they were old childhood friends. 'But we lost touch.' True.

'When did you last see him?'

He sensed Dunkelwert knew already, again making denial pointless.

'On Wednesday, as a matter of fact, quite by chance and before that not for years.'

'Quite by chance?' Dunkelwert echoed.

Schlegel did his best to look casual. 'The papers I had to take to Budapest were a contract of sale for signing. I had no idea the address I was asked to collect them from belonged to Christoph – I told you, we weren't in touch, but it really isn't so much of a surprise. There aren't that many art dealers in Berlin. Even so, it never crossed my mind I would be fetching the papers from him.' Too long-winded, Schlegel thought; trying too hard. 'Why do you ask?'

Dunkelwert said Schlegel's name had come up on the flight list and a man of his description had also been noted entering and leaving Christoph's building.

'Noted how?'

'Your friend's apartment is being watched.'

'What for?' This was staring to sound bad.

'Are you aware your friend is homosexual?

Of course he was, instead of which, he said, 'I find that hard to believe,' thinking it sounded like the cold kiss of betrayal.

'Pansies aren't always easy to spot,' said Dunkelwert, with a treacly smile, then added, 'It's not pretty what happens downstairs.'

Schlegel got up and walked out on shaky legs, the crockery rattling on the tray as he stacked it with trembling hands.

He had been found out because of a passport check. Schlegel sensed Dunkelwert gave him the benefit of the doubt but her interest raised awkward questions. For authority the gap between the actual and the perceived turned everything into interpretation, the danger being what others could read into it.

Dunkelwert had implied Christoph was under sur-
veillance because of his homosexuality rather than any
business to do with Schlegel. But in the hall of mirrors
that constituted the secret state, one reason could contain its shadow, so a particular piece of business might
not be followed up until it came to the attention of secret
watchers concerned with something else, and then it in
turn fell under suspicion. Until Budapest, Schlegel had
been going about his business, keeping his head down,
and now he seemed to be associated with matters he knew
nothing about and therefore was bound to fear that he
had fallen into that Gestapo category known as guilty by
association.

Christoph's file was guarded by the sad-faced librarian.
It didn't take long to read. The bones of his career in the
art world were traced. Attached to the Art Historical
Institute and the Education Ministry, now working for
the Linz Project, had written government papers and
essays for art magazines, including an appreciation of a
Vermeer acquired by the state for the Führer in 1941. It
read like a clever fusion of the academic and bureaucratic,
with plenty of committees and consultancies. Christoph
was an acknowledged expert on ownerless Jewish art
properties in occupied Europe. He had obviously come to
terms with the regime: offering expertise in exchange for
suppressing his sexual inclinations, or practising them so
discreetly as to escape notice. No more jazz parties. The
extent to which he had successfully reinvented himself
was reflected in the report. One early note of homosexuality had an inked margin amendment stating: 'Not
proven; unreliable witness'. Nevertheless, Schlegel supposed Christoph's guardian angels could fly away at any

moment. It must be exhausting and dangerous operating at such a high level with a big secret when once he had been so frank and teasing.

Before the morning of the eighteenth, the last time Schlegel had seen Christoph was late in 1941. They had known each other since they were seven; what Christoph referred to as the 'age of knowledge'.

He had grown into a progressive young man of dark Italianate looks, attractive to all, who hated the gloomy north and its disgusting food. 'Give me light! Give me olive oil! Berlin is so Protestant!' 'So drab, so brown,' was Christoph's frequently heard lament. They were the last of a gilded youth, kicking out against cultural strictures in cellar clubs and the large, exclusive houses of the Berlin diplomatic.

Christoph had, according to him, a 'good but not exceptional' collection of Duke Ellington and American blues. However dedicated Schlegel tried to be, he came to find this worshipping at the shrine a little tedious. He wasn't *that* obsessive, however hard he tried to be a fan.

Christoph insisted on greeting him in English with, 'Hello, old swing boy!' and bidding farewell with, 'Swing heil!' Both jokes came to wear thin, as did Christoph's treating Schlegel's sexuality as an open question.

The occasion that marked the break of their friendship was one of Christoph's celebrated parties. Life remained expansive, the regime comparatively indulgent, with the fruits of victory being sent home from abroad. Christoph lived in a smaller apartment then and confided he had a sugar daddy – 'absolutely hands-off, totally platonic' – who kept him supplied with his favourite gin, which he drank neat. Christoph spent the evening needling Schlegel, his manner affectionate but increasingly irritating. 'You know you really like boys more.'

Schlegel protested it wasn't true.

Christoph would not give up. 'With boys you know what they are about. With women you just can't tell what they are thinking. Believe me, I've tried, and where's the fun?'

It was an all-male party, with a lot of young soldiers in attendance, mostly rough boys on leave from abroad, all of similar good looks, who appeared out of place among the understated artwork. 'Questionable decadence,' Christoph said of his collection. 'Rather than full degenerate.'

The evening was spent playing and trading records brought back from Holland and France. Amsterdam offered first-class jazz clubs and a lively black music scene from Surinam. The black guitarist Mike Hidalgo had a big German following.

They played records by Hidalgo and Kid Dynamite, clicking their fingers and getting in the groove. They trashed the reputation of what remained of German jazz and argued drunkenly over whether Surinam was in the Dutch East Indies or the Caribbean. Schlegel found it impossible to say whether the young men were there for the jazz or the jazz was a cover, until Christoph, the worse for wear, announced, 'The question we're all asking is shall Schlegel be saved for the girls or will he come and play with the boys?'

Where Schlegel once would have laughed it off, he left quietly and didn't go back.

Schlegel decided not to telephone his stepfather from the office again, in case of eavesdropping. Perhaps he was at home after all, and not answering.

He took the train round to Westend. It was still crowded

and he could not tell if he was being followed. The size of the political sweep was evidence of the extent of the Gestapo's suspicions, which excluded no one. He stood next to the exit of the carriage and twice stepped onto the platform as the doors were closing, feeling a little foolish as on both occasions no one got off after him.

The walk from the station took him through dead suburban streets, out towards the stadium. He was followed some of the way by a woman with a shopping basket and after that had the place to himself. The area was sedate, quietly prosperous and self-contained. It had been dull growing up there. He walked past the house, turned and walked back. No pedestrians, no suspiciously parked cars.

Schlegel walked up the drive through the soft dusk. The house was shut. No one answered the bell. The spare key for the back door was in its usual hiding place. As he let himself in and called out the house felt wrong. His stepfather stayed at home most of the time, and the housekeeper lived in. He supposed the most innocent explanation was she was on holiday and his stepfather was with friends.

Nothing was disturbed. When they came for his mother they had smashed stuff. Someone had scrawled 'Jew lover' on the garden wall. His stepfather had painted it over himself.

The clock in the hall had stopped. His stepfather was always meticulous about it being wound.

As Schlegel drew the blackout curtains he thought it extraordinary that his suspicion now extended to him wondering whether his stepfather was guilty of treason.

He searched cupboards, desks and drawers for some trace of his actual father, of whom he remembered nothing. He had been two at the time. Any later curiosity shown about his father had been blocked by his mother. There were no photographs or relatives or points of reference. The man may as well not have existed. Schlegel grew up supposing his father must somehow have hurt his mother terribly so he stopped asking.

All he knew was she was English, his father was German and they had lived in Shanghai where Schlegel was born in 1919. He wasn't even sure when they had come to Berlin, or why.

Apart from jewelry and an extensive wardrobe, carefully bagged and smelling of camphor, his mother had kept nothing in the way of mementos or the usual markers of time, apart from photographs of social occasions where the camera invariably favoured her.

At the back of a cupboard he found an album he had never seen before with milky images of what he supposed was Shanghai: a huge suburban house with stepped lawns. The photographs were always taken from too far away, giving everything the wrong perspective. What he presumed was a grand house was reduced to looking toylike. He supposed the blob in a pram on the lawn was him.

Significant gaps occurred where photographs had been carefully removed, leaving only the mounting corners and pale outline of the vanished picture, these spaces marking the removal of his father.

His own childhood was summed up in a dozen or so images, including a formal portrait with his mother radiant and he, aged six or so, chubby and unappealing. Her society photographs went on and on. She'd had her own parties photographed. In one Schlegel saw the back of himself, standing on the edge of frame. His hair was white, so it must have been in the last three years. Most men wore Party uniforms, their frumpy wives smartly turned out.

Through this endless parade his stepfather made a point of being unobtrusive, always peripheral, with the wariness of a man who disliked having his picture taken but as his wife's escort found it captured more than he would have wished.

His mother had entertained at the highest level, until her fall. Even their espousal of the new regime seemed normal, in that social climbers – of which there were plenty – came flocking. Schlegel hadn't been paying much attention, just as he hadn't thought about his real father in years.

There were no old diaries; not that Schlegel could imagine someone as purposefully superficial as his mother keeping a written record. She had never expressed an interest in anything inner, only the relentless projection of herself as a social creature. His stepfather by contrast was a distant man who spent time in his study on the telephone and travelled, often abroad. Schlegel supposed stocks and shares played their part.

He found his mother's desk so bare that he wondered if his stepfather had removed everything of significance. Its contents amounted to no more than expensive stationery, cheque books, bank statements, a jar of rubber bands and a stapling machine with no staples.

His stepfather's downstairs study was all browns and saturated with the smell of old tobacco. Trophies of stuffed animals hung on the walls. A glassed-in library, such as it was, consisted of social registers, books on hunting and fishing, horse racing and breeding, stock markets, business and economics.

Schlegel had no idea what he was looking for. He was sure his stepfather would have no reference to, or record of, his actual father, just as he doubted he would find an explanation for his stepfather's current absence.

The drawers contained pipe-smoking geegaws, envelopes and writing paper, which, unlike his mother's, was conspicuously not headed, unusual for a man of his class. Sheets of postage stamps suggested a volume of correspondence yet Schlegel found no letters received, bills or tax papers, not even a postcard.

There were ledgers of marching columns of numbers, with no explanation for where they were marching. His stepfather's hobby was accounted for by horse-racing news, betting forms and a lucky horseshoe.

The drawers beneath the book cabinets were used to stack board games, including chess and mahjong, not that he had ever seen his stepfather playing either. The last drawer was full of practical junk – twine, penknives, fuse wire, screwdrivers – and a photograph.

How different his stepfather looked, staring at the lens with none of his usual diffidence, dressed in bow tie and tails, with Schlegel's mother nowhere in sight. He looked about ten years younger, thinner, with darker hair in a widow's peak, since receded. He was flanked by two men: one a porcine youngish man in Party uniform, who contrived to look both servile and superior. His pose said that he deferred to Schlegel's stepfather. The third man was taller, with a moustache, silver hair, and spectacles. His manner seemed purposefully academic. He held a pipe and looked like he would be more at home in tweeds. He wasn't German, Schlegel thought, more English or American. Who either of them was he had no idea but his impression was the three knew each other.

Schlegel remembered the garage, that depository of the abandoned and forgotten which no one ever got around to sorting. Old fishing rods, tennis rackets with broken strings, what was left of his childhood toys, including an old wooden fortress. And his father?

Outside, he paused at the sight of the sky painted a dense, vivid orange, like after an air raid except there had been no warning sirens.

In the garage, the cars were covered in dust sheets. Growing up, Schlegel hadn't thought of the family as rich. His mother usually complained of not having enough.

At first, he found no more than what his mother called 'stuff', those odds and ends which one day might prove of further use. Old paintings and prints fallen out of fashion. Gumboots with perished rubber. Bald tennis balls. Cupboards revealed more of the same. He paused when he came across a guidebook for Munich, 1925. He doubted if it had belonged to his actual father, but Gestapo Müller had suggested Munich. Flicking through its pages, Schlegel found an old bus ticket in the restaurant section. Further on he sensed resistance between the pages and something fell out.

It lay on the floor face down. The crinkled edges told him it was a snapshot. Or more accurately, half of one because it had been torn. Schlegel picked it up and turned it over, half hoping he would be rewarded with an image of his father, not that he had a clue what the man looked like.

He saw a young woman instead. His father's lover?

More complicated than that, Schlegel realised, when he saw who else was in the picture.

The emulsion had gone silvery brown with age. An old photograph then, Schlegel thought, as he tried to make sense of it.

The centre of attention was a vivacious young woman, with bright eyes and flashing teeth, smartly dressed, and no older than her early twenties. The location was a restaurant. The quality of the photograph wasn't good, having been taken in insufficient light. The features of the young woman weren't sharp or clear, beyond an impression of liveliness.

It was a long time since Schlegel had seen anyone enjoying themselves like that. His mother had a version of the same look, saved for the camera – the one that said, 'Aren't we having fun, darling?' – but hers was rehearsed. This young woman came over as spontaneous, despite the coiffed hair and being dolled up.

The man to her left sat back, almost lost in the shadows. The forelock and smudge of moustache made him instantly recognisable. What Schlegel could make out of the face was expressionless, as if letting someone else take the spotlight for a change. One surprise was the informality of the pose, given the man's control of his published image. It caught him in the middle of blinking, eyes half-shut.

Schlegel wondered not so much why the Führer was in the photograph but how the photograph had ended up there.

The torn side of the frame was taken up with the back and shoulder of a man's dark jacket. Whether the picture had been deliberately torn, as though to cut someone out, Schlegel couldn't say.

Hitler and a young woman sharing a table in a restaurant. In Munich, Schlegel supposed, a long time ago.

He was bound to ask whether the partly missing figure was his father. Or had his father taken the photograph? And, again, if the guide was his father's copy how had it ended up in the garage? He stared at it, thinking how as a boy who had spent hours rooting around the garage he would have noticed the guide before.

Also in the same cupboard was a parcel wrapped in brown paper. Schlegel supposed a book. He was right about that – a two-volume edition, in fact, handsomely produced, bound in red leather, each in its own slipcase. As he unwrapped them, he was once again sure he would have looked inside out of curiosity had the parcel been there before. He read the title of the volumes with some surprise. The most widely published and unread book of the century was not what he was expecting. He supposed it must be his mother's copy, until he opened the cover and saw the bookplate and read the dedication: 'To Anton Schlegel, in eternal gratitude, Adolf Hitler. Munich, 24 December 1925'.

The book was not only inscribed, it was numbered 16 of a limited edition of 25 copies.

The Führer's *Mein Kampf*. Signed by the man.

'In eternal gratitude.'

Schlegel stepped out through the garage side door, feeling ambushed by the past. The sky's glow was even more vivid. Somewhere must be on fire, he realised, and quite a blaze, yet no alarm bells. Schlegel was undecided whether to stay the night or go home. He continued staring at the sky, thinking about the troubling contents in his briefcase and the eternal mysteries of family. He set off towards the blaze. There was no reason to see it as a portent but he did.

The fire was further away than it looked, up towards Spandauer Chaussee, which had marked the edge of safe childhood boundaries. Schlegel heard the first crack and snap of burning as the glow turned to sparks, followed by the spectacular sight of a substantial Wilhelmine villa being gutted by flames. Two plain, modern extensions were in the process of being engulfed. A wave of intense heat hit Schlegel as the upper windows of the main building blew out, showering glass, and the whole floor erupted.

The crowd of gawkers was small for the size of the blaze. Not a single authority in sight. It was as if the fire were being laid on as entertainment. Three teenage boys circled on bicycles, doing loopy figures of eight and looking cool about the whole thing.

The building appeared exclusive, standing in its own grounds. The extensions suggested more than a domestic residence. A drive ran underneath one, which stood on pillars. Schlegel supposed the building had a commercial purpose.

No reporters or photographers either; just the spellbound faces uplifted to the blaze.

He asked if a local Party representative was present. None was. The three boys lounged on their bicycles in youthful disdain, slouching as they made a point of looking unimpressed by Schlegel's badge.

Two fine blond boys, with crew cuts, and the third darker with acne and longer hair: future cannon fodder for circa 1949.

Schlegel asked, 'What's going on?'

The dark one, who looked like the leader, took his time. 'Empty building burning down.'

'What sort of building?'

The dark boy said, 'A clinic.'

'Then where are the staff and patients?'

There was no sign of evacuation, no gathering of white-coated staff or patients in dressing gowns.

The boy took so long answering that Schlegel couldn't decide whether he was stupid or insolent, or both. Eventually he volunteered that the place was closed for a fortnight's holiday. What they'd heard, he said.

Schlegel made them write down their names and addresses, saying they might be required to make a statement, thinking sourly to himself: Authority throws its weight around.

Obsessively neat handwriting had been dinned into all of them.

He wondered what kind of clinic closed for a vacation. Given its emptiness, it could be arson and an insurance job, which was a matter for the criminal police. He supposed he should file a report, if only to cover himself.

A dark pillar of smoke hung over the building. Black tendrils were starting to escape from under the roof tiles. The air was full of ash, debris and smoke haze, which made Schlegel's eyes water, causing the building to stutter and jump like film trapped in a projector.

He walked round the back and found the streets behind cordoned off with emergency tape and warning signs to stay away because of a gas leak. Schlegel passed under the tape. The house opposite the back of the clinic was empty. He supposed the area had been cleared and the clinic must have suffered a gas explosion. Such leaks were common. He considered chucking his briefcase into the flames and having done with it. What did he want to know anyway about his father? The man had been as good as dead; now the news of the Führer being dead, then not dead – two uncanny resurrections.

Flames cast dancing shadows over crisped leaves. The heat grew more intense. Schlegel sweated like he was in a sauna. His mouth was dry.

The back of the clinic had been converted into a space for vehicles. Another modern extension, part canopied, ran the width of the house. The flames consuming the upper floors hadn't reached down that far but it was only a matter of time. Through a tall window Schlegel saw a set of stairs being consumed by giant tongues that looked like they were being chucked from a flamethrower.

A single private ambulance was parked under the canopy, next to a motorcycle and sidecar, and beyond that an empty bicycle rack. A small, separate side building with a chimney suggested the clinic had its own incinerator. Distant bells at last announced the arrival of the fire brigade; a waste of time as there was nothing to save.

A huge explosion reverberated through the guts of the building and the whole lower area went up. The mansard roof was still intact, with a dirty black fog of smoke pouring out from under it. Schlegel's eyes stung until he could barely see. Up on the roof he thought he detected a movement in one of its windows, but his blurred vision made it impossible to tell. The start of the roof's collapse, he supposed. Then what looked like a shape appeared to struggle to climb out of the window, vanished in the smoke, then half emerged again, hunched and lurching like a drunk along the edge of the roof. Schlegel saw it only once more, plummeting through a gap in the smoke, any scream buried by another explosion which engulfed the parked ambulance in a fireball as the falling creature smashed through the awning, to be instantly consumed.

Schlegel blinked, not quite believing what he had seen. A derelict, maybe, or fugitive, or someone passed-out drunk, waking to everything in flames.

He went back to the front and found firemen setting up in a flurry of belated activity. The boys and the crowd were gone.

A single car slowly approached down the street and stopped. Schlegel saw the hatted shapes of two men inside.

Authority at last, and taking its time.

The men got out of the car and sauntered towards him, silhouetted by flames. They wore civilian dress. One was fat and short, a beefy farm boy who looked like a best man at a country wedding. His companion was cadaver thin, a human lollipop. Mid-fifties perhaps for the cadaver, the other about thirty-five, though his baby face made him appear younger. Their walk was unthreatening but against such an apocalyptic backdrop they appeared less like mortals than archetypes of a particular kind of violence.

Ministry of Works, Schlegel was told, when he asked.

They obviously weren't, and not Gestapo or they would have said when he showed his badge. They made no effort to take control though Schlegel guessed they were in charge.

Fatso looked at him and asked, 'What do you call a Pole with no arms?'

Schlegel, baffled, asked, 'What?'

'Trustworthy.'

The man cracked up while his companion looked for all the world as though rigor mortis had set in. The fat one carried on laughing while Schlegel thought they may as well be wearing clown suits.

He said, 'You may wish to question why the fire department took so long to answer the call.'

They looked like they couldn't care less.

Schlegel's impression remained of men best avoided. He made no mention of any falling body because he didn't want them coming back with questions. He still wasn't sure what he had seen. With the spectacle like a shadow play, he could easily have projected his own subconscious anxieties, with the falling man becoming a symbol for his father.

The S-Bahn, like everything else that evening, took its time arriving. Standing in the darkened, rattling carriage, Schlegel was aware of the reek of smoke on him. He was bound now to make a formal note of the fire, since he had shown the men his badge. Technically, it was none of his business. Oh, just write the bloody thing, he thought, rather than get caught out. He tried to make the image of the falling man disappear: whirling arms and thrashing legs, like someone trying to swim through space. But there had been no whirling arms. Just the opposite. It could have been the fat one's armless Pole falling to earth. The legs kicked as the top half plummeted head first. As to why a man should fall that way, Schlegel could come up with only one answer. Straitjacket.

9

Schlegel took several drafts until he had a report innocuous enough for no one to bother with. The fire had not been mentioned in the newspapers, either being censored or too late for morning editions. Any awkward aspects he ignored – such as the gas board having no record of leaks in the area of evacuation. A cursory search had revealed nothing on the clinic. Its telephone number was ex-directory – if anyone wanted to check, he could do so through the companies register or the health inspectorate.

Nor did he mention any falling body.

He cursed his luck. Were it not for a coincidence of geography and had he not gone to check on his stepfather, he would know nothing of the fire.

His final report offered a terse summary of location, circumstances, evacuated building, tardiness of the fire department, possible arson for insurance purposes (surmise; no proof), names and addresses of the three bicycle brats and the late arrival of uncooperative authorities who did not say what they were.

File and forget.

He remained preoccupied by the puzzle of his father's *Mein Kampf*. The night before, he had laid everything out on the table in his apartment: the book, the guide to Munich, the bus ticket, the photograph of the bright young girl, the smart photograph of his stepfather, and the list. On the bus ticket someone had written 'Room 202'. A hotel room? A room to report to? In the map part of the guide one of the streets, Nussbaumstrasse, had been underscored in ink. He couldn't get it out of his head that all these components were trying to tell him something. He looked at the two photographs: his stepfather, more central than usual, with the man in Party uniform; and the torn one, offering a glimpse perhaps of his missing father, appropriately removed. Complicated histories to both, Schlegel suspected, thinking he was bound to try and find out.

He sloped off early from work, telling himself he was just going back to his stepfather's, which he did, briefly, to find it the same. All the while he was wondering about the clinic. Don't pick the scab, he had been warned as a child, and he always had.

The gutted building, with its scorched brickwork, already looked neglected and forlorn, with the roof since collapsed. The municipal authorities, usually efficient at sealing off damaged property, had done nothing, leaving Schlegel free to walk down the drive, under what was left of the modern wing. He could still feel the heat from the ashes. The ambulance was a shell, its back doors blown off to reveal a deep bed of soft grey ash in which the remains of any dead body were not apparent. He didn't have to be there, Schlegel kept telling himself, checking automatically over his shoulder as he passed through the clinic's missing back door and stepped inside, conscious of his footprints in the virgin ash.

The building unnerved with its creaks and groans, as though making a last effort to transmit the trauma of its destruction.

The air was still acrid. The fire had swept everything before it. The ceiling had collapsed in several rooms and was still smouldering. He looked back at his wavering footprints that told him no one else had been in the building.

He didn't expect a cellar. The fire hadn't reached down there. There was less damage towards the front where corridors and rooms remained more intact.

Schlegel presumed the door was a cupboard until he found himself looking at descending steps. Turning to go, he saw the narrow shelf with a lantern and matches for power cuts.

He held the lit lamp tentatively in front of him as he made his way down. At the bottom was a bare space, with benches. The cellar served as a bomb shelter. The low ceiling forced him to stoop.

A second space revealed the same. On the threshold of a smaller annex he saw a solitary female shoe, turned sideways in the dirt. A practical shoe, for the sort of person who spent a lot of the day on her feet.

Some minutes later he left the building in a state of composed shock, scuffing his footprints in an effort to disguise his trail. At the doorway he paused and saw it looked like someone had tried to pretend he hadn't been there, with good reason.

Eight bodies in the cellar, two male, six female, shot in the back of the head, execution-stye. White coats. Clinic staff.

On the train back, Schlegel looked at the tired passengers, trying to guess which ones informed and decided he may as well go out, get drunk and look for Gerda. The rest could wait. What he had just discovered put him way out of his depth. The question was did he report what he had found? And to whom? There were no off-record conversations. No doubt a demolition crew would come and the bodies would be buried in the rubble, and that would be that, Schlegel thought, so leave it.

He found Gerda in one of the illicit clubs out near Wollankstrasse. The venue was a dive, full of smoke and sweat. She wasn't there at first, then she was, just as he was about to give up. They shouted meaningless pleasantries in the din and hopped to the music. The syncopated, scratchy rhythms compounded the tension in his body as he kept thinking of white coats and executed corpses.

When they left they groped around in a doorway, but in a perfunctory manner. It felt easier, walking in step, their sleeves occasionally brushing, than it had fumbling with her.

They walked on in silence until he asked how she knew about the cellar clubs.

'Wild fliers. Luftwaffe boys,' she said; a crowd on leave, most of them dead now. One with a rebellious kid brother introduced them to the scene.

He warned her it might not be safe to carry on going to the clubs.

'How do you know?'

'A friend in the Gestapo.'

'A reliable friend?' she asked, carefully.

'Most of the time.'

'Are you going to report me?' she asked, sounding worried.

'I would have already if I was going to.'

'Perhaps we could go out on a date instead.'

They both laughed to show it was meant as a joke.

A street or so later, she said, 'As in two people doing something together.'

'Haven't we rather got beyond that?'

He found her disconcerting.

'I am curious to see where you live,' she said.

Now that he was being offered, he wasn't sure. What would they talk about? He barely knew what she looked like. Their relationship had been confined to dark cellars and street blackouts. He was more familiar with her body in a blind way than he was with her.

'Don't worry,' she said. 'I'm not going to stay.'

She had read his mind, Schlegel thought.

'Ninety-six steps,' he said. 'It's right up in the roof.'

She was his first guest. He listened to her softly counting off the steps as he followed the soft moves of her legs.

She wandered around inspecting his meagre possessions. The *Mein Kampf* was open on the table. She read the dedication and the effect was electric. 'The Führer!' she gasped.

Schlegel suspected she was 120 per cent Nazi. He looked at her properly for the first time in the dawn light and couldn't decide if he would have been attracted had they met normally. She had a big-boned girl's forced cheerfulness. Quite sporty. Pleasingly fair hair, flawless skin and a tan. She shone with rude health. A tiny misalignment in one eye gave her an askance, seductive look.

10

On the Sunday after the bomb, Bormann returned briefly with the Führer to Berlin for a special party in the Chancellery gardens to celebrate his escape from death and to greet and walk among the Party faithful.

Bormann surveyed the gathering and thought: These are my days of greatness.

Most were so caught up in their own self-regard that they couldn't see what was under their noses. Bormann delighted in their contempt and dwindling influence.

The Führer was on his best behaviour, telling everyone it would take more than a bomb to get rid of him.

A kowtowing Goebbels declared the Führer a picture to melt the sternest heart. Silly ass, thought Bormann, watching Goebbels say how important it was the Führer did not become distracted from their deliverance.

Goebbels was resplendent in a white sharkskin jacket, his skull-like grin a lot more fixed than Bormann remembered it being ten years before. On that occasion – Sunday, 1 July 1934 – when Bormann and the Führer had landed at Berlin Tempelhof, the welcoming party had fumed at the sight of Bormann's unexpected presence by his master's side. Complaints were already flying about the underling's apparent indispensability. These the Führer ignored, telling Bormann that in the political equivalent of rock, paper and scissors, paper wins every time.

Himmler and Göring were waiting on the runway that blistering afternoon, as excited as two schoolboys. Himmler had a long and tattered list in his hand, which the Führer went through while Himmler and Göring poured honeyed poison in his ear.

When, ten years later, Bormann suggested a similar party in the Chancellery to celebrate the Führer's safe passage, the Führer jumped at the idea as it would allow him to reassert himself. The weather was just as kind on the second occasion; not a cloud in the sky.

Whereas the mood in 1934 had been euphoric, it was now marked by the eclipse of many of those present, allowing Bormann the satisfaction of assessing his decade's advance at the expense of faltering rivals.

Göring was conspicuous by his absence, 'retired sick', doped on morphine, the reputation of his airforce in tatters. Goebbels was sucking up to Bormann because there were only so many ways to paper over bad news, which reduced him to even more towering displays of sycophancy. Bormann watched him perform his usual seamless *volte face* after the Führer dismissed his suggestion of the soft pedal and insisted on a clean sweep. Goebbels was out of the traps in no time. Show trials! Everything to be recorded! Hang them with piano wire! Film that, too!

'Trouserless!' The crowing doctor was unstoppable. 'See how their pathetic cocks like that!'

How dearly Bormann would like to see the wire bite into the blubber of Göring's neck, watch scrawny Goebbels flap like a chicken, and hear Himmler squeak and squeal as he hung suspended.

Heini Himmler was swanning around, forever pleased with himself. Touch and go, but he had done well out of the failed coup. His pathetic military ambitions were being encouraged by Bormann because they were out of all proportion to his expertise, which was about up to running a scout troop. Bormann knew Heini was feeling out the future, which might yet see him drop through the same traitor's trapdoor as the rest.

Himmler was hard to like, despite making a point of appearing amenable and terrifyingly normal – good father, kind to animals, gentle, hesitant, soft-spoken, absorbed . . . a total crackpot. For all his modern bureaucratic know-how and worship at the altar of technology, the man was crippled by superstition. Bormann suspected he was a secret God lover. Himmler had modelled his elite on the Jesuits. In the first instance, given his preoccupation with racial purity, Bormann had watched him fill the SS with a remarkable collection of fair-haired morons who would have fared better as ships' cabin stewards. For Himmler the world was occulted and magical. He could bore for the nation on the subject of the hidden secrets of Nordic runes, which, if they could be deciphered, would reveal a close affinity with the characters of the Japanese alphabet, and that the Japanese, despite their alien appearance, were in fact Aryans. Thus did Heini make sense of the world. When relaying this, Bormann always got a laugh at Heini's expense, making slitty eyes with his fingers when it came to the bit about the Japanese.

Hermann Fegelein, Himmler's liaison officer to the Chancellery, was snaking around, being a charmer to the women. Fegelein fancied himself as a political player, which he wasn't; not really. He was putting it about that he and Himmler had been on to the conspiracy and their agents had penetrated a group of disaffected officers. Bormann was certain that this feint was a shoddy attempt to disguise the fact that Heini and Fegelein had been playing both sides.

Even as they celebrated in the garden and spoke in witty asides while their women trilled, people were being shot. Himmler reckoned it might be as high as six thousand in the end.

Bormann at the appropriate moment respectfully took the Führer aside and asked if he was tired. The effect of his booster shot would soon wear off, which could lead to sulks and petulance, but the Führer announced he was in tip-top form and said they should do it more often as it was good to get out. He gripped Bormann's sleeve and said, 'Do you really think none of them noticed?'

'Even if they did, no one dare say.'

To which the Führer added, 'To question the image of the Führer is treason.'

Plan B, Bormann thought, as he watched the Führer mingle again with his guests; always a plan B.

Even during a reign of terror there are days off. Go to the lakes on a hot sunny weekend and you still see women sunbathing, soft water lapping against the jetty, bottled fizzy drinks for sale from carts and something calling itself an ice cream cone that never was. Scorched grass, dog turd and litter, just like in summer peacetime. Warm tanned flesh. The white disc of the sun high in the lazy blue sky.

Gerda sunbathed in her underwear, with the strap of her brassiere undone. Schlegel wore an unprepossessing pair of woollen swimming trunks from before the war.

The day passed as ordinary for the first time in as long as Schlegel could remember. He recited to himself: *We got up late and spent our Sunday by the lake, lying in the sun and dozing.*

They rubbed suncream on each other and still got burned. Gerda could look stern in repose but a beguiling smile lit up her face, enough for Schlegel to wonder if what she had been raised to believe really mattered. He lay on his front, comfortably tumescent, resting his hand on the small of her hot back. All around lay loving couples made more poignant for the majority of men being home on brief leave. Gerda's gestures and movement suggested certainty about everything; yet, Schlegel sometimes thought he saw a shadow pass over her before deciding he was reading too much into her. He longed to be unimaginative and accepting, with a woman to come home to. He liked the idea of sex becoming more mysterious and elusive as they started to discover each other.

Impossible, he thought; lusting after this Nazi girl.

They did their share of laughing. They stuck to safe questions. Favourite colour. Film. Actors liked. Popular songs. Favourite leader after the Führer; her question. What could he say? She settled on Speer as he was good looking and seemed competent and sensible.

They were behaving like normal people, Schlegel told himself, and it was quite nice, realising he was qualifying a lot with the word 'quite'.

He pictured them sitting next to each other on the train home. He would put his arm around her waist and kiss her ear, making her shiver and squirm. They would look back at a moment of helpless laughter and wonder at themselves. It was a pleasant fantasy, going through the motions of falling in love. In a gallant gesture, down on one knee, Schlegel tied her shoelaces before they left, and on the way back, hanging around in the shadows of the railway station, they passed the blind and limbless, begging where they weren't supposed to.

On impulse they went to the cinema and arrived in the middle of some rubbish about love lost and found, full of overstated emotions. They held hands and laughed at the nonsense on the screen – it really was terrible – and kissed in the dark.

The film was followed by a newsreel reporting the Führer's miraculous escape. They were shown footage of the bomb-blasted room. From this devastation the Führer had walked out of alive, the commentator trumpeted, before reporting the resumption of business as usual with the steadfast Führer well enough to carry on with that afternoon's duties. Film was shown of him keeping an appointment with the Il Duce, meeting the Italian leader's train.

Schlegel found it strange seeing the Führer, who had become less and less of a recorded presence over the years. He looked much older. After the ordinariness of the day the newsreel appeared a bit unreal and Schlegel even found himself wondering if the bomb had ever in fact taken place. They were only being told on the newsreel's authority that Il Duce's visit came *after* the explosion when it could have been filmed on quite another occasion. The Führer was not shown inspecting the damage, either alone or with Il Duce, and those shots could have been dropped-in ones of any old blown-up room. By contrast, the torched clinic, the falling man and the dead staff appeared a far more comprehensive plot than what they were being shown, and nobody was broadcasting that. Schlegel thought: What if the newsreel was to distract from the awful state of everything else, and was as made up as the melodramatic nonsense they had just sat through?

Gerda was outraged that anyone could even think of killing the Führer.

II

The terror accelerated on the Monday morning with hundreds of arrests, but in Schlegel's office of more immediate concern was the disconcerting sight of Dunkelwert, blurred in the fog of her smoke, ensconced in Bletsch's glass hutch.

Bletsch was 'gone', as though he had never existed.

'Holy cow!' someone exclaimed, expressing what they all felt at a woman now in charge.

Dunkelwert spelled out their new terms: extra shifts and unpaid overtime; then, to stunned silence, she announced the arrest of von Helldorf, head of the Berlin police.

'A reckless man,' she declared. 'A compulsive gambler, with spiralling debts. Lack of moral fibre led him to throw in his hand with the conspirators.'

Von Helldorf had inveigled half the police department into his weekly poker sessions, which masqueraded as a social club, whose purpose Dunkelwert now questioned. Schlegel spotted at least six men looking nervous.

No doubt Gestapo Müller would make sure everyone knew von Helldorf had backed the wrong horse and anyone else at the races had better watch out.

The next plotter named was Nebe, head of Berlin CID. This was a huge shock in itself, but more worrying for Schlegel as it was Nebe, along with Schlegel's stepfather, who had sent him to Budapest. He feared it only was a matter of time before questions were asked about that.

Dunkelwert went on to declare the Führer's survival a blessing, marked by a resurgence of faith. Schlegel pictured blank, entranced faces parroting how they believed more than ever that after the hard upward slog, the sun-filled uplands and soft valleys of the high plateau would be revealed in their magnificence.

He suspected something psychologically complex and traumatic was going on underneath it all, rehearsals of guilt over being unworthy of the leader, making denunciation a matter of course, to divert from a process of mourning already underway because of a deep, secret feeling that the Führer had already abandoned them.

Terror and superstition go hand in hand.

Schlegel was summoned into Dunkelwert's smoky cage. His spirits sank when he saw his report on the clinic fire on her desk. It lay next to another folder, to which she pointed.

'The stuff crawling out of the woodwork. Mad correspondence about the Führer.'

She picked out a letter and read, '"The Führer hasn't been with us since 1943 and now works in the Vatican library and is unrecognisable." Signed, "A Friend."'

She read out another: '"The Führer has been abducted by aliens."' And another: '"This one says the Führer is a disciple of the English occultist, Aleister Crowley, which makes him a stooge of British intelligence."'

Schlegel said, 'Enemy propaganda,' implying that chasing any of it was a waste of time. The enemy was full of such tricks. It had even issued fake Himmler stamps to suggest a takeover was imminent. The joke was no one had noticed.

Silence filled the room until Schlegel eventually asked, 'What has this to do with my report?'

Dunkelwert produced a fourth letter and held it out.

'"In a Berlin clinic," it says.'

Everything about the letter was cheap, written in thick pencil, in ill-formed capitals on paper so coarse Schlegel could see the pulp in it. He wondered if the hand was pretending to be less educated than it appeared. The message itself was succinct enough.

'The Führer can't be in two places at once,' read the message, 'in a Berlin clinic, since burned down, *and* being blown up.'

'An anonymous letter,' he said. Sometimes it helped to point out the obvious. 'A crank.'

He felt far from sure of that.

'Get to the bottom of it,' Dunkelwert ordered.

He supposed there must be known suspects, one of whom could be 'persuaded' to own up. They lived in a cynical world where even the victims were becoming cynical in their resignation.

He said, 'I shall need men for door-to-door interviews.'

'None to spare,' said Dunkelwert briskly.

Schlegel wondered how seriously she was taking the case. She answered for him. 'The Führer's authority is being questioned.'

Schlegel couldn't see how. It wasn't as if the Führer had ever claimed he could be in two places at once.

Schlegel cursed his report, which had decided to bite back, unless the letter was a ploy to open up an unofficial investigation into the fire, and someone above Dunkelwert wished to know what lay behind it.

He felt almost sorry for her squatting behind her new desk. He suspected her zealousness did not stretch to intrigue, especially if political tectonic plates were shifting.

Schlegel asked, 'Was the letter addressed to anyone?'

'"To whom it may concern." That's you now. It's someone who works at the clinic, that's obvious! Round them up and find out who. No more hiding! Enough slacking! What's the matter?'

He couldn't say they were dead, having failed to mention that in his report. He drew scant consolation from seeing Dunkelwert, with no obvious Party directives to interpret, out of her depth.

She asked how with all clinic records destroyed in the fire he proposed to come up with a list of staff.

By picking up the telephone and getting on to the welfare, labour and tax offices, he said. 'As well as the doctors and nurses, there'll be cleaning and domestic staff, probably guest workers.'

Dunkelwert looked sulky. He was being patronising. Schlegel thought she must realise how unpopular she was. She told him he wasn't excused the rest of his workload.

Schlegel arranged with local police for the three boys whose addresses he had asked for to be held. He would enjoy watching them squirm, thinking they might be blamed for the letter.

With all the bureaucracy, inefficient switchboards and referrals it took Schlegel an age to obtain the names of the two male doctors and six female nurses. There was also an administrator, female, plus two drivers, elderly German males who performed other general duties. Six domestic staff covered cooking and cleaning, five Polish guest workers and a Lithuanian, allocated by the Labour Front, all transferred to other employment the week before.

He spoke to Missing Persons.

None of the staff had been reported absent.

Really? After several days? Didn't they have people who

cared about them? Then he realised. With mass arrests going on all over, the whereabouts of hundreds if not thousands were unknown.

Schlegel rang off and said to himself: I am not Homicide. Stick to facts.

He was hauled into Dunkelwert's smoked-filled cage again.

'Why report the fire in the first place?' she asked slyly.

He put on his most diligent face. 'It would have been irresponsible not to.'

'I have found out some things too.'

Schlegel sighed inwardly.

'The senior doctor was a famous cosmetic surgeon who ran a successful and fashionable practice dating back to the 1920s. A lot of rich Jewish nose jobs, for all the good that did them.'

Dunkelwert sniggered and said the employment office had given her the name of the hotel where one of the clinic's cleaners now worked.

Schlegel expected to be given it to call but Dunkelwert had done that already.

'Lithuanian, female, with some German,' she said. 'She and the rest were told the clinic was closing for vacation and they would transfer.'

'Was she given any reason?'

Dunkelwert shook her head emphatically. 'Sub-workers don't warrant explanations.'

That didn't mean they didn't have eyes, thought Schlegel.

He managed to speak to one of the clinic's drivers, who had been transferred overnight to a military hospital. The same with one of the cooks, a female Polish labourer, now working in a school. There was nothing unusual about people being reassigned at short notice, but not usually all at once.

Schlegel asked them to describe the clinic. Both said it was exclusive and discreet, specialising in surgery and burns, and wasn't for the regular sick. The driver obviously hadn't liked the owner and readily passed on that the man still did civilian cosmetic surgery for film stars and the rich.

Schlegel asked both the driver and the cook, 'Was the Führer ever a guest of the clinic?'

It was a difficult question for them as it was being asked by the Gestapo, but at the same time it was impossible that they question the Führer.

Schlegel was sure the driver's incomprehension was genuine. With the cook he wasn't so sure, so he asked if she had ever prepared meals for the Führer. She eventually answered, 'They never would have allowed me.'

If the Führer had been in the clinic on the Thursday then the woman would have already transferred. Did that mean there had been other visits?

She needed a lot of threatening before admitting that sometimes when important visitors came they brought their own people and the regular staff were farmed out.

'For how long?'

Usually a few days, she said, starting to sound frightened. She said there was never any mention of names.

As it was a only a short ride, Schlegel went to the hotel where the Lithuanian cleaner now worked. She was perhaps only eighteen or nineteen and easily bullied, with enough to lose, being relatively safe rather than in a camp. He offered her the choice of deportation if she didn't tell him what he wanted to know.

'The question is was the Führer ever a guest of the clinic?'

Schlegel could see as she stood there terrified that it was not for her to say.

'There obviously is something,' he said in a friendlier tone.

There was. It was said the Führer sometimes visited.

'And?' prompted Schlegel.

'Once, when I was changing sheets in a room and the door was open, he walked past.'

'Are you sure it was him?'

'He turned and stared for a long time. I thought I had broken the law even looking at him but in the end all he said was, "Good day," and he walked on. Very polite.'

She said he wore civilian clothes, was on his own and seemed preoccupied.

'What else can you tell me?'

Only that there was a steel door at the end of the corridor, which led up to an area at the top of the building where no one was permitted. Schlegel immediately thought of the falling man.

'High security, with a guard?'

'Just a locked door.'

'Did anyone know what was up there?'

'Everyone knew not to ask.'

He believed her and didn't know what to make of it.

Schlegel was still expected to fulfil his normal casework duties. The names on his Second Wave files required follow-up interviews, for further sorting. For this he could at least use the secretaries to make the necessary summons and he set aside time to deal with them: more sitting with frightened people in desperate rooms.

If Schlegel lacked a first impression of Anna Huber, it was an increasingly common phenomenon. On an everyday level, people had learned to give nothing away. Huber was the last of that day's Second Wave checks. Unlike those called before her, she retained her composure. She wore no wedding ring. Her demeanour was modest. No makeup, of course. Skin that could have been healthier with a better diet.

At second glance, Schlegel saw she was undeniably good looking – auburn hair, hazel eyes and two becoming worry lines over the bridge of an aquiline nose.

He gave his rehearsed speech, saying that in the light of recent events, everyone on file was being reconsidered. He looked at her card. Originally from Munich, early thirties. She would have been twelve when his father was gifted the *Mein Kampf*. Profession proofreader, Ministry of Propaganda.

Huber said reasonably, 'I didn't know I had a file.'

'By association. You are listed as having suspect relatives.'

She remained silent without looking particularly worried. Schlegel felt almost as though she were interviewing him.

'You know Munich.'

Huber confirmed she had been raised there, with an expression that said he must know because it was on her card.

'The cradle of National Socialism,' declared Schlegel crassly. What was the matter with him?

'Quite so.'

'What do you remember of those times?'

Huber blew out her cheeks. 'I was young.'

He waited for her to go on. When she didn't he filled in for her. 'Concerned with a young woman's things?' God, he sounded laboured.

'Whether to wear my hair up or down,' she admitted.

She wore it up at the moment.

'Which did you decide?' Schlegel asked, appalled by such leaden flirting.

'I never did,' she told him briskly.

Schlegel wanted very much to see what her hair looked like down.

'What did your family do in Munich?' he asked, in an effort to sound more professional.

He saw her hesitate at such a direct question.

'My brother joined the brownshirts,' she said.

The brownshirts had been neutralised after the big internal revolution of 1934, with many shot. Enough to make the brother suspect.

'What happened to him?'

'He moved to the Munich Chamber of Commerce where he still works.'

'Mother?'

'Housewife. Before that a kindergarten teacher.'

'Father?'

'He worked for the newspapers.'

'As a reporter?'

'Doesn't it say?' Huber asked.

Schlegel shook his head. 'It doesn't appear to be a very complete file. Worked for newspapers?'

'Yes. A typesetter.'

If he had been a union man, it would be enough to put him down as suspect.

'Where is he now?'

'He was supposed to have come here to Berlin after he and my mother separated.'

'When was that?'

'Ten years ago.'

'His name?'

'Frederick.'

'Did he and your mother stay in touch?'

'I don't know. She died in 1937.'

'Is he still alive?'

'I have no idea.'

She had a habit of touching her throat. Schlegel couldn't remember if this was a sign of lying.

'Did you and you father get on?'

She gave him a strange look as if to say, why ever do you ask?

It was his father he had been thinking about.

His father's departure had never been questioned at home. Schlegel grew up believing going away was something people did, not that other fathers had. He knew from eavesdropping on adults that they lived in an age of shame and concluded his father's absence was connected to that.

That evening he took the train to Charlottenburg in the hope of finding Christoph at home, nervous about seeing him. For all Christoph's having bought into the establishment, Schlegel suspected his old friend's compromises were fewer than his own.

Living as they did it was the impossible to question anything that fell outside proscribed areas. It was always better not to know. For that reason Schlegel had chosen not to address what else might have been happening in Budapest, much of it bizarre. Not that he expected Christoph to be frank but he was his only connection to anything else that might have gone on.

Christoph showed no surprise as he answered the door, and shrugged with a coolness bordering on indifference as he motioned him in.

A gramophone was playing. 'Bruckner,' said Christoph, knowing Schlegel wouldn't know.

Everything about Christoph was calculated: from the immaculate pressed white shirt, sharply creased flannels and tasselled loafers; to the rehearsed easy gestures and the positioning of furniture; to the size of the apartment in relation to Christoph's solitary presence. Schlegel was offered sherry, an unusual drink and a gift from the Portuguese embassy.

They sat in a formal reception room with parquet flooring, expensive rugs and a mixture of antique and modern furniture. The walls were covered with what Schlegel supposed was good art, landscapes mainly.

'Fairly dull,' said Christoph of the paintings. 'I have to entertain. Burghers, diplomats and matrons. There's an international aspect to the work.'

Christoph made a point of not enquiring after Schlegel.

'What paid for the sherry?' asked Schlegel.

'A Lisbon artist: Botelho – contemporary, quite collectible though not much outside Portugal. He once drew a weekly comic strip for children. A set was brought to my attention and I was able to arrange its sale.'

'When I was here the other day, did you know I was coming?'

Christoph picked imaginary fluff off his trousers. He was sitting on a high-backed French sofa with carved legs. Schlegel was in a disadvantageously low armchair with rattan side panels that he wanted to pick apart.

'Had no idea.'

'Who were you dealing with?'

'What do you mean?'

'I was asked to act on behalf of certain parties and I wondered if you were, too.'

'You first,' said Christoph.

'My stepfather was one,' he said.

'Not at my end. I remember your stepfather, of course,' Christoph added unnecessarily.

'Arthur Nebe?'

Christoph said he didn't know Nebe. He opened his hand, as if to say he had nothing to hide. All he knew of the matter was he was in the process of purchasing art works from Budapest and there was a contract for signing.

Artworks didn't sound like Nebe, thought Schlegel; nor his stepfather whose aesthetic appreciation didn't extend beyond racehorses.

'Is the buyer the SS?' he asked.

'Technically.' Christoph teased out the pause. 'But the SS could be procuring on behalf of someone else. The international art market is complicated. We are in something of a golden period.'

'And this particular purchase?'

'To be frank, the SS is being unusually aggressive. They are negotiating with a notable Hungarian family to lease its steelworks and buy its considerable art collection. While Himmler knows nothing of art he is always keen to purchase at the expense of rivals.'

'Such as Göring?'

'For example.'

'And the Führer?'

'Not in this case.'

'Has he already had his pick?'

'I vetted the collection. There is nothing of interest to him.'

In as much as he was able to pin Christoph down, Schlegel concluded that the deal was probably on behalf of Himmler. Christoph even knew the name of Himmler's man in Budapest, Becher, whom Schlegel had briefly met. Christoph threw in another name, Hermann Fegelein who was handling the Berlin end.

'Fegelein?' asked Schlegel sharply. 'Do you know him?'

'Only by repute. You sound as though you do. He races horses.'

Mention of Fegelein was not a welcome addition. Their paths had crossed before, not to Schlegel's advantage. 'That man can talk his way out of any corner,' he said and left it at that. It still didn't explain Nebe's involvement.

'Have you met the Führer?' he asked, changing the subject.

'Of course. He likes to discuss art. Within his field he is very knowledgeable.'

Even five years ago they would have considered the idea faintly risible. Schlegel would have dearly liked to know how much the remark cost Christoph, if anything.

'What's the Führer like?'

'Quiet and well-mannered,' said Christoph. 'He always asks after one. Very unassuming for such an important man.'

'He knew my father, apparently.'

'Your actual father? He went away.'

A silence fell. Christoph did not pursue the matter. Schlegel took it for his way of saying that he was no longer interested. He filled in the silence, saying, 'Your file makes no mention of homosexuality, or at least the one mention is discredited as unreliable.'

'Am I now in your debt?' Christoph asked irritably.

Schlegel was being mean. 'I thought you should know. These days the lists are starting to go on and on. It says you are an expert on ownerless Jewish art.'

Christoph sighed. 'It's more complicated than it looks.' With Christoph it always was. 'A blind eye is turned in exchange for foreign cash.'

'What about the embargo on currency transactions?'

'Don't be naive.'

'Do you know the Führer well enough to ask about my father?'

'It would be seen as presumptuous.'

Schlegel realised what a smooth operator Christoph had become, brushing him aside with the lightest deflection.

Schlegel looked at the art on the walls and thought of how the pictures Christoph bought separated themselves from their owners, to be followed up by correct documentation and legal paperwork to ensure their new purchase was in order.

Schlegel told him about his father's copy of *Mein Kampf*, thinking, I'll get you yet. Christoph was bound to be impressed because he was a snob. Ten years ago he would have mocked the vulgarity of the whole political show and now he didn't.

'It really is your father's copy?'

'I found it at home in the garage.'

'What is the story about him now?'

'It rather looks as though he went to Munich rather than South America.'

'Book dealing is not really my forté. Are you interested in selling?'

Schlegel said it depended.

'Given its provenance it's probably worth quite a lot,' Christoph went on. 'I can get it valued. You may find it would fetch most in the United States. I know of certain private collectors interested in memorabilia. They buy via Stockholm.'

Christoph stood and paused, staring at the carpet, before asking, 'Are you so interested in your father?'

Schlegel hadn't thought of it like that before. He wondered how much he really was. 'Yes, in that I was led to believe one thing and now I am being told another.'

Christoph said nothing. If being adult was about learning to live with one's compromises, Christoph struck Schlegel as very accommodating of himself.

Christoph glanced at his watch and said, 'I must be getting on.'

98

Schlegel wanted to say it was a pity how they had become strangers to each other when they had once had so much in common. They parted without saying goodbye and only as he walked downstairs did it strike Schlegel how much had changed between them and was he aware of how much hadn't been discussed – recent events, Christoph's life, Schlegel's work, old times, asking after family – and he saw how expert Christoph had been at steering the conversation. Schlegel supposed fair enough. He was the one who had put the distance between them.

Back at his apartment, whose meanness stood in stark contrast to Christoph's opulent surroundings, Schlegel was left feeling grubby and restless. He stared at the *Mein Kampf*, asking himself what he was letting himself in for. He put the book out of sight and picked up the Munich guide, wondering if his father's hands had flicked through it too.

He flipped through the guide's gallery section then its restaurant pages, noting their specialities. Italian. Hungarian. He salivated at the thought of full tables and regular service. Meatballs. Bolognese. Schnitzel. Strawberry cream cake. Entries listed telephone numbers for reservations and the names of proprietors.

The Bratwurst Glöckl advertised itself as specialising in local cuisine. It made him think of impossibly plump sausages, vats of potato salad, seasonal asparagus, foaming steins of beer, jolly dirndled waitresses, every cliché in the book, all the while staring at the name of the proprietor, Zehnter, asking himself why it seemed familiar.

He checked the original list. Zehnter's name was on it, next to his father's. Had Anton Schlegel eaten at the

Bratwurst Glöckl? Had he and Zehnter known each other? Schlegel's brief elation fell flat. If you weren't allowed to investigate the present no one would let you go digging up the past. Not only was the past past, the past was dead.

12

A brown sun beat down through the scratched dirty windows of the train. The rickety carriages should long ago have been assigned to scrap. Schlegel found the view from the elevated track endlessly depressing. For years the city had held together. Now even the grass looked like it had given up.

At the local police station, the three boys from the night of the fire were being held. The initial interviews took five or six minutes. Forms to be filled in, signed and witnessed in lieu of parental supervision. They didn't look so cocky now. A Hermann and two Martins; dark Martin and fair Martin.

Schlegel showed each the letter and asked what they knew, resulting in uniform shock and a quick shake of the head, then silence during which the detainee tried to stop his galloping imagination from running away with itself.

He brought the middle boy back first. Dark Martin looked like he possessed a shred more intelligence than his companions.

'Maybe you saw something, Martin, you can tell me about,' Schlegel said.

With younger offenders, first-naming was used as a form of belittling.

He saw Martin starting to cry on the inside. Spit it out, Schlegel thought. The boy had the makings of a young tough, with the war and his father away, and only a diet of violence to look forward to.

Dark Martin turned out to be a good little informer, once he had worked out his lifeline. After denying he had written the letter Schlegel asked him to suggest who might have.

The room was small, taller than wide, with a tiny window high up. Schlegel thought about all the words that had been spilled in it, questions and answers. If every word were represented by a nail paring, how high up the wall would it reach?

Martin delivered up three suspects without trying.

Schlegel was depressed by how casually the names were given. Before the afternoon was done, one of the boy's weasel friends would no doubt be naming one of his companions.

'What do you know about the women who worked at the clinic, Martin?' Schlegel asked.

Martin reacted as though he had been poked. From starting to look halfway confident, he grew furtive. It was obvious the boys spied on the women. Schlegel would have done the same at their age.

Martin licked his lips. A pustule on his chin needed squeezing. Schlegel looked away, faintly disgusted by the false intimacy of the process.

'Tell me about the nurses, Martin.'

'We know the smokers. They're not allowed to indoors so they come out the back.'

Martin went silent, looking like he couldn't think of any more.

Schlegel said, 'That's the problem with going first. You don't know what the others might say.'

Martin grew convoluted and mumbled. Schlegel told him to speak up.

What had happened was two of the domestic staff were

persuaded to take their clothes off in exchange for small presents. This striptease was performed in the window of the laundry room while Martin and his friends watched from the garden backing onto the clinic, from more or less where Schlegel had been standing on the night of the fire. The boy's face contained a trace of a smirk that made Schlegel want to hit him.

'These girls undressing for you were foreign.'

Martin spoke up, trying to sound reasoned and grown-up. 'We decided it wasn't racial defilement if no direct physical contact took place.'

'The law may not agree with you on that,' said Schlegel. 'And if these young guest workers had not complied with your wishes, what would you have done?'

Martin squirmed in his seat. 'They were easy about it.'

'And what did you and your friends do at the sight of these females?'

Martin stared hard at the floor. 'We wanked,' he finally whispered.

'Yourselves or each other?'

'Ourselves.'

Schlegel couldn't care less, other than finding himself pitched back to the boy's age, and he and Christoph fiddling with each other.

'In summary, you are telling me that in the week before the fire the clinic's patients and domestic staff moved out but its nursing staff and doctors stayed. Did anyone mention what was going on?'

'The nurses told us to mind our own business and say the clinic was shut for holidays.'

'Has anyone else where you live been asking about the clinic?'

Two men, he was told.

'Describe them.'

The boy did. The two thugs from the night of the fire.

'What did they want to know?'

'If anyone else had been asking.'

'What did you say?' asked Schlegel.

'We didn't know anything.'

'Have you told me everything?'

Martin looked uncertain.

'Think carefully,' Schlegel warned. 'If your companions were able to tell me more than you it would reflect badly. According to the law of juvenile punishment I can have you beaten in a way you would not forget for the rest of your life.'

They sat in silence while Martin considered.

Schlegel said, 'The nearer we come to the end, the harder it is, not in terms of what has been said but what has not. Do I make myself clear?'

'A car came,' the boy eventually said.

The vehicle had driven down the driveway ramp and drawn up outside the back.

'Then what?' asked Schlegel.

'A man with a completely bandaged head was taken into the building.'

'A single patient?'

'Yes.'

'Tell me exactly what you saw.'

'He was helped out of the car into the building.'

'Walking or on a stretcher?'

'Walking.'

'Assisted or on his own?'

'On his own.'

'You just said he was helped into the building.'

Martin corrected himself. 'I mean the car door was held

open for him, then the door to the clinic.' He added that two white-coated men were in attendance.

Medical orderlies. Schlegel dared not pause to think about the implications of what they were discussing. An invisible man, he thought. How would he report any of this? Would Dunkelwert be amenable to burying the story, or, and here came the hammer blow, *was this what he was supposed to discover?*

'What vehicle did they come in? An ambulance?'

'Not an ambulance. Grosser Offener Tourenwagen.'

The boy's answer cast everything in a new light.

'Armour-plated and bullet-proof,' he went on.

'How do you know?'

'By how they sit so low to the ground.'

'When was this?'

'About a week ago.'

'Be more exact.'

It was the previous Tuesday, two days before the bomb, and three days after the clinic officially closed.

Schlegel thought: Even the Führer can't be two places at once, so what the hell had been going on?

Dunkelwert's feet barely touched the ground sitting down. Schlegel looked at her and slowly said, 'I am told the clinic made preparations to receive a secret guest in the week the attempt was made on the Führer's life . . .'

He emphasised there was nothing to connect the two.

'Apart from the letter,' said Dunkelwert.

They looked at each other. Schlegel was betting she was keen not to venture any deeper.

'Why would anyone write a letter that is obviously a lie?' asked Dunkelwert, unwilling to let it go.

Because the whole thing is a lie, from top to bottom, Schlegel wanted to shout.

If he walked the case back to secret bodies in a cellar he had conspiracy to murder, unless the killing was state-authorised. Schlegel was sure all the elements could be made to join up but it wasn't in his interests – as a servant of said state – to do so.

He tried stashing the bodies in the back of his mind, along with the falling man, but the foolish, persistent part of his brain kept returning to the puzzle. In any immediate historical context, it would make more sense if the guest had been received *after* the bomb, as a result of his wounds being worse than had been stated. A completely bandaged head: was it to protect injuries or to prevent anyone from seeing who he was? Or was he a decoy?

The first news to come through on the Thursday stated the Führer was dead. Had someone decided the illusion of his being alive must be maintained to stop the country from being thrown into chaos? Schlegel supposed an actor could have reproduced the Führer's speech on the night of the 20th. Perhaps that explained why it had taken so long to put together. Almost twelve hours passed before its broadcast.

Schlegel chased all the arguments into dead ends. Had the bomb plot taken place *before* 20 July and the news been suppressed? Or had there been no bomb at all? Stuff was made up all the time. The point was, the upper echelon was now so detached it might as well exist on its own planet.

None of this he shared with Dunkelwert.

However hard Schlegel tried to shake off the idea, a sense of secret crisis persisted.

Curious about Herr K. Zehnter – on Schlegel's list, next to his father, and Munich restaurant proprietor – Schlegel went down to the public telephone kiosks in the lobby.

Dunkelwert had been bombarding them with memoranda. One stated no more private calls on office lines. He bought a pile of tokens from the cashier's office. Sitting in the cramped booth, with its awkwardly folding door, Schlegel thought of space rockets, coffins and vacuum chambers.

Long-distance connections took time. 'Lines are busy, caller,' the operator repeated in her dreary voice.

At last the number rang. A man picked up. He spoke bad German with an Italian accent. Schlegel repeated Zehnter's name and got nowhere. He said he was calling from Berlin, as in, 'Get a move on.' He supposed he was speaking to a waiter and the Bratwurst Glöckl was reducing to hiring anyone these days.

Schlegel asked for the manager, repeating the word several times, loudly and ever more slowly.

Someone came on the line after a wait long enough to be rude; Bavarian, thick accent, tetchy, and unwelcoming of any Berlin caller.

Not Herr Zehnter, Schlegel suspected. He asked if he was and was met with silence.

Schlegel persisted. 'Herr Zehnter?'

The name meant nothing said the man. The accent grew more curdled, as if to say fuck off, posh boy.

Schlegel asked if he was speaking to the proprietor.

Yes, but he was not Zehnter.

Strange, thought Schlegel. Restaurants were usually family businesses, with traditions and continuity. Schlegel asked if he knew when Zehnter had been the listed proprietor.

'Not for as long as I remember,' said the man just as Schlegel's tokens ran out and the call was cut off.

*

Outside, the weather had broken. It took a heavy shower for Schlegel to notice. It was like that these days. He barely looked up anymore, ignoring the dead sky full of vague dread, leaving him in a state of mounting unease.

With a growing sense of premonition he took to sitting in cafés and scouring newspapers in anticipation of finding just such a report, which he eventually did: a small, innocuous agency bulletin at the bottom of an inside page, reporting an air crash on the Austro-Hungarian border involving a specialist medical team on emergency relief work.

No survivors. No names, pending relatives being informed, other than the team leader whose name matched the owner of the clinic. That was it. End of article. The cover story for the bodies in the cellar. Now they were officially written off and there wasn't a thing anyone could do. Give them one death and now give them another, for the record.

13

Homicide cops reminded Schlegel of badly drawn cartoons, big men with little shading: thick necks, meaty hands, steel-hard paunches and years of hardbitten service. They played up to their image and answered to nobody, yet among themselves called each other 'girl'.

With no one he could turn to or trust, but desperate for someone to tell him what he should do, Schlegel thought of Stoffel. While he sneered at Dunkelwert for being out of her depth, his own feet were barely on the ground. Although bent, Stoffel was nobody's fool and had been around long enough before the current mob took over not to be impressed.

Schlegel had found Stoffel terrifying. If challenged, everything was dismissed as a joke. He once witnessed Stoffel rabbit punch a man and hold him almost tenderly after he doubled up. It was then Schlegel realised men like Stoffel had a superior appreciation of the art of terror and treated violence as almost balletic, compared to his own clumsy efforts to exert himself. However much of a bully, Stoffel stuck by his own and in that respect Schlegel knew he was bound to listen.

Like 99 per cent of homicide, Stoffel was a man of regular habits: same bar, same time.

Stoffel, comfortably drunk, his bowler hat tilted, glass halfway to his mouth, did a slow take and said, 'Your round.'

The waiter, a geriatric known as Puffing Billy, prided himself on remembering everyone, except Schlegel.

Stoffel said, 'Looking for me?'

Schlegel wondered how Stoffel managed to get drunk on such watery piss until he saw it was supplemented with mouth-gargle-sized swigs from a flask.

They were sitting in a large bar with deal tables, in a raised section that Stoffel had to himself. An ashtray contained several of Stoffel's cigar butts. Eighteen months ago the man wouldn't have been seen dead sitting with Schlegel. Now he seemed almost pleased. In the old days there was always a crowd in of Homicide braggarts needling all comers. Not any more.

'Funny how things change,' Stoffel said equably.

They started with Nebe.

'Who would have guessed?' said Stoffel. 'Von Helldorf too.'

Stoffel had been part of von Helldorf's poker school. They had all been grilled, he said. 'But can those asking the questions be trusted any more than anyone else? Have they had you in yet?'

'Not yet.'

'They will. Any dirt on your walking stick?'

'They have their suspicions.'

'I'm past caring. Drink up.'

Puffing Billy was summoned for another round.

Schlegel asked Stoffel, 'How's business?'

'Whatever is going on in the rest of the world, it doesn't stop people murdering each other. Thirty-four homicides last quarter. Thirty-five, if you count the dead theatrical agent.' Stoffel mimed a high fall with his hand. 'A jumper, officially.'

'Unofficially?'

'Who's going to listen?'

Chucking someone out of a window; the dead staff at

the clinic. Under normal circumstances Schlegel wouldn't connect them.

Stoffel leaned back, settling on the meat of his haunches. Schlegel thought the man must have run out of drinking companions, which was the only reason he was being tolerated.

Schlegel showed Stoffel the list he had been sent.

Stoffel needed reading glasses, carefully hooking the arms behind his ears with the belligerence of a man angry at having to wear them.

He scanned the list and handed it back. 'No names apart from the obvious. Is that you?'

'Or my father.'

Stoffel sat there, puddled, with the dazed look of a beaten-up boxer between rounds.

'How fucked are you?' he eventually asked.

Schlegel took a deep breath, exhaled and said, 'Pretty much.'

'Try me,' said Stoffel and sat back trancelike, as though he wasn't listening.

Schlegel walked the case backwards.

Stoffel raised his eyebrows when Schlegel got to the armour-plated Mercedes. 'Not many of those.'

And again when Schlegel told how the clinic had burned down.

'With or without guest?'

'A man fell off the roof, I think.'

'What do you mean, "I think"?'

'The smoke, the flames. It was night . . .'

Stoffel grunted. '"I think." Don't.'

'Then an anonymous letter turns up saying the Führer was at the clinic.'

Schlegel watched Stoffel process that.

'What are you saying?' asked Stoffel.

That it was he who fell off the roof? Schlegel said, 'I'd rather not for obvious reasons.'

'What's your business in this?'

'I was told to find whoever wrote the letter.'

'Say it's bollocks.'

'I did.'

'Not enough, if I know you.' Stoffel snorted. '"I think!"'

Schlegel said he feared a secret agenda.

'You don't know that. Stick to the facts.'

'There is a punchline.'

Schlegel leaned forward. Stoffel smelled like a brewery. He cupped his ear and Schlegel told him about the plane crash.

'Who knows about that?' Stoffel asked sharply.

'Me and whoever did it, as far as I know.'

'Keep it that way, and you haven't told me. And here's something I haven't told you. Is your stepfather's name Rohrer?'

Schlegel couldn't see how Stoffel knew that.

It concerned Nebe, Stoffel said, and a strange episode on the morning of the 20th when Stoffel passed him pacing in the corridor.

'He had a list in his hand. He grabbed hold of me and said a coup was imminent and showed me the list, which was for members of a provisional government.'

Stoffel had presumed Nebe was in the process of having the coup put down.

'It never occurred to me he was bragging. Anyway, he said, "Do you remember Schlegel? That's his stepfather."'

Schlegel had just said he didn't know what he was suspected of. Now it seemed he did: conspiracy at one remove. More suspect relatives.

'This is not a conversation we ever had,' Stoffel said.

After that they talked about nothing of consequence, then didn't talk much at all. Schlegel drank several more beers in a vain effort to feel in the slightest drunk. It turned out Stoffel's wife had died of a malignant tumour, which was part of the reason he had gone back to work.

They parted in the street. Stoffel gripped Schlegel's neck, uncharacteristically avuncular, as though he even cared.

'Let it go, son. No time to go sticking your hand in the fire.'

14

Schlegel continued to be visited by Gerda on some nights for what he supposed was a reasonable facsimile of a relationship. The sex on the whole made up for his anxious days. Despite the healthy noises she made in bed, he thought he probably failed to satisfy her. He found sex with her an approximate business, like fumbling with a combination lock, trying to guess its code.

He supposed she would start coming to his apartment every second or third evening, making her usual joke of being breathless at the top of the stairs. There was talk of a larger bed and finding anyone able enough to carry it up all those stairs. Gerda wore summer frocks that showed off her figure. A wholesome, yet troubling young woman, Schlegel thought, showing her insecurity by always asking whether they were having a good time.

If there was a bad omen or spell cast over them it came when they were walking in the street only a minute or so from the apartment when a passing young man in uniform turned, punched Gerda in the back of the head and ran off. The pointlessness of the act stayed with Schlegel and he thought about it endlessly, probably as a way of distracting himself from the mess of all the rest.

Schlegel remained curious about Anna Huber, given that she had lied about her father. The man whose file Schlegel

had just pulled was Frederick 'Fredi' Huber. Munich jour-
nalist, right age, relocated to Berlin in 1934. Although the
information was incomplete, with no mention of marital
status or dependents, or his death, it had to be Anna's father.
Trained as a typesetter, graduating to journalism via night
school, suggesting Anna Huber had been evasive rather
than entirely dishonest.

Schlegel found it impossible to imagine working for
newspapers in those days, with few reporting restrictions
beyond the legal ones of libel, writing whatever you wanted
without fear of censure, and not living in a world of made-
up air crashes.

He decided to call her back in. They sat in the same room
as before. Anna Huber looked less sure of herself when
Schlegel said, 'You should have told me your father was a
reporter.'

She asked, 'Are you investigating me?'

He sat back and said, 'There is something you might be
able to do for me.'

He didn't say in return for letting her off. She regarded
him warily as if he wanted a sexual favour, which was the
usual way.

'A very early edition of *Mein Kampf* has come to our attention, published in 1925 and limited to 25 dedicated copies.
There must be a list of recipients somewhere.'

He wondered why he was asking her, other than in the
foolish belief that she could somehow help him find out
more about his father just because she came from Munich
and seemed smart.

If Huber was surprised by his request she didn't show it,
but Schlegel sensed her unease turn to irritation. She looked
the sort that had to put up with her share of pestering.

*

Whatever else Huber was, she was efficient and called back within an hour, obviously hoping this would be the end of the matter.

She said, 'I have a list of the names you wanted.'

Good telephone manner, Schlegel thought.

'There is a ministry library and archive, part of which is dedicated to *Mein Kampf*, with a record and details of all editions, including the one you mentioned. I can get the list sent over.'

Schlegel, impatient, said, 'I'll take the names down now if you have the time.'

She remained polite, having little choice.

He asked her to spell the more difficult names. Most were obvious top Party ones. There were no women. He asked Huber if she recognised any of them.

She said she didn't and there was no legend to say who anyone was. In that respect it was just another list.

He said, 'Two names are of interest to me. Anton Schlegel and Karl Zehnter. Perhaps you could try and find out more about them.'

He sensed her hesitation and added, 'It's important.'

He remembered her gesture of touching her throat and thought she had probably made the connection between him and Anton Schlegel. He had only given her his extension number earlier, but when he picked up her call he had answered with his name.

Schlegel passed Müller in the corridor and wondered later whether events would have unfolded as they did had he not. He had spotted him approaching down an endless and unfortunately empty corridor, walking fast and alone. Metal tips on Müller's heels made his footsteps ring out on the stone floor in a commanding way.

Schlegel decided on a sideways glance and curt nod of acknowledgement, and seemed to have got away with that when the footsteps stopped and his name was called.

'Follow me,' said Müller.

Up wide shallow stairs, down more corridors, past offices with open doors, obviously used to Müller's footfall as they revealed pictures of intense concentration, no childish office behaviour, no paper darts being thrown.

Müller moved at a clip and Schlegel struggled to keep up.

Müller took them into his small office, sat, with no offer of a seat to Schlegel, and blinked at him in surprise, as if to remind himself why he might be there. The eyes flickered.

'Tell me about this business with the clinic. What exactly are you investigating?'

Schlegel experienced a rush of dizziness. What a relief in some ways to be able to topple and fall.

'Claims being made by a false anonymous letter.'

Müller stared at the ceiling then produced a copy from a drawer.

'You mean this?'

'Yes, sir.'

'Written by?'

'We have a list of suspects.'

Müller grunted. 'Who will turn out to be just that.'

Which was why Schlegel had done nothing about them.

'Motive for writing?' Müller went on.

'It can only be mischief, sir.'

Müller continued his eye flicker and banged the desk.

Schlegel hurried on. 'The clinic was cleared for an important visitor. The writer of the letter confused the visitor with the Führer, because we know—'

'Yes, I know. What else do you know?'

He had dreaded Müller taking an interest. Perhaps

something really had gone on that Müller wanted exposed. Schlegel had seen this sort of feuding before. It acted like a suction pump.

He offered an interpretation.

'The letter is considered the work of a subversive, to discredit the Führer, obviously. But there may be another motive, if it was written by someone connected to the clinic, which is to distract from it being deliberately set ablaze for insurance purposes.'

Müller tossed the letter aside. 'What do you really think?'

'We may be interfering with someone else's operation.'

'Pray, tell,' said Müller with as close to an arch look as he probably ever gave.

'Without meaning to,' Schlegel added.

He told how he had met two men in the vicinity on the night of the fire.

'They were plainclothes and were clearly taking charge but refused to say who they were, other than Ministry of Works, which they obviously weren't.'

Müller pondered. The eye movement came into play as he reached for his stationery, unscrewed a fountain pen and started writing. He used a violet ink.

Schlegel stared at the bent head, with its smarmed hair, and the aggressive pink line of the parting.

Müller blotted the page, folded it, put it in an expensive-looking envelope and showed brown tongue as he sealed it. 'Take this in person to Dr Goebbels. Deliver it in person. Wait in person for his immediate reply and return it in person to me.'

Schlegel stood stunned. Did Müller suspect, as Schlegel had, that the bomb plot had been a stunt?

'You do know who Dr Goebbels is?' asked Müller sarcastically.

As Schlegel left, Müller said, 'I am taking this business of the clinic seriously and suggest you do too.'

Schlegel walked out dazed, trying to work out if he was now reporting directly to Müller.

15

Dr Goebbels sat behind a giant desk at the end of a long room overlooking the square. He made a show of quiet, contemplative work as Schlegel was led forward by a male secretary who silently withdrew. Goebbels worked on, letting Schlegel sweat.

'You know what they say about young men with prematurely white hair?' asked Goebbels, still not looking up.

Schlegel, self-conscious, touched his without meaning to.

Goebbels went on. 'A sign of insincerity. I am sure that is not so in your case.'

The combination of slight and compliment seemed typical, Schlegel thought. Goebbels at last looked up with a smile that said: Of all people, the one standing in front of me is the one I most desire to see.

It was an outrageously insincere performance and Schlegel was flattered despite himself.

There was even time to chat. No mention was made of their previous encounter, though Goebbels made a show of remembering him. The talent for false rapport – discussing whatever was on his mind, seemingly sharing confidences and appearing fascinated by what the other person might think – was, Schlegel realised, just another form of showing off.

This time it was the foreign press.

'It publishes such lies, so do I tell the Führer, who likes

to kept informed? Do I show him, knowing it will only unnecessarily upset him, or not, because their pernicious lies are waste of time? Then of course I can be accused of withholding information. What would you do?'

'I think these foreign lies must always be exposed,' Schlegel said carefully.

Goebbels stood, arms akimbo, and smiled broadly.

'Of course, you are right.' He snapped his fingers. 'Schlegel? I remember now. Your mother, of course.'

Schlegel groaned inwardly. Not another of the woman's conquests. The little doctor was notorious for putting it about with starlets on the casting couch, and was known to extol the virtues of older women too.

The old joke, less heard these days, was that the man was so sexually demented he would fuck a corpse. Schlegel remembered general hilarity in a cinema showing one of the doctor's personally supervised features, when the heroine died in the hero's arms and he, heartbroken, asked what he should do, and a male voice from the darkened auditorium shouted in good-natured encouragement that he should fuck her while she was still warm. Waves of knowing laughter had been directed as much at Goebbels – because most of them knew the corpse joke – as at his silly film.

Goebbels folded his arms and stroked his chin. 'English, your mother. So sad what happened.'

Schlegel said yes to both, presuming Goebbels was aware that she had been carted off to a concentration camp.

Schlegel marvelled at the frightening ridiculousness of sharing confidences with a minister. Were they all like this and so eager for intimacy, once past the *cordon sanitaire*?

The moment passed. Goebbels looked at Schlegel haughtily and asked, 'What does Müller want?'

His tone made clear his distaste for the man. How they all loathed each other at the top.

Schlegel produced the envelope. Goebbels snatched it, no longer polite, took a paper knife to open it, read the letter and tutted.

The answer took all of ten seconds. Goebbels used green ink to write his reply on Müller's note, replaced it back in the envelope, which he returned to Schlegel with a terse smile.

The envelope was not sealed. Schlegel wondered if it was an unspoken invitation for him to read it later.

He stood waiting to be dismissed. Goebbels sat lost in thought. Schlegel coughed discreetly. Goebbels glanced up and went back to brooding.

'Tell me,' he eventually asked, 'did your mother teach you English?'

'Yes, we speak it together.'

'Then you are capable of more than a literal translation in terms of nuance.'

'I would hope so.'

'Do me a favour and look at something before you go trotting back to Müller. Let him wait!'

Goebbels grinned. Schlegel presumed such corralling was typical, as well as making a point about spontaneity, in marked contrast to Müller's desk-bound orthodoxy.

Schlegel had heard it said Goebbels sought power because he didn't want anyone else to have it, and worked hard to make it fun, whereas for Müller it seemed more like a private narcotic.

'Come, tell me what you think. Be honest.'

Schlegel found himself in a small viewing theatre with Goebbels in the row behind and a couple of hangers-on in attendance. At a sign from Goebbels, the lights dimmed and the curtains parted.

Urgent music swelled. 'Hitler Bomb Plot' read a caption in English. The film was an allied Pathé newsreel. A cartoon drawing of a joke bomb, like in a comic strip, already suggested it wasn't taking the story seriously.

The film footage was the same as he had seen with Gerda. How the British had got hold of it wasn't clear, but they used it to poke fun. The veracity of the whole episode was questioned, the Führer mocked, his survival laughed at.

'A staged publicity stunt or cover-up,' the commentary sneered, 'to dispel rumour in the Reich as to whether the Führer had escaped or succumbed later to his injuries. Rumour which if anything has grown.'

Schlegel sat rigid as he listened to his own deeply guarded, unvoiced thoughts being amplified around the room in such a rollicking way.

Goebbels clearly knew the material and had had it translated because he leaned forward to speak in Schlegel's ear. 'If the war were being fought with sarcasm the British might be in with a chance!'

He blew a raspberry when Himmler was described as the present virtual dictator of Germany.

The newsreel's tone grew even more incredulous, as it questioned if it was even the real Führer on show, or whether fanciful notions about the doubles the man was supposed to use were being put to the test.

Of a blank-looking Führer, the commentator, barely able to contain his mirth, asked: 'Is this Mr Schicklgruber or a stooge?'

The casual insolence was breathtaking, but for Schlegel not as disconcerting as being bombarded with the very speculation he had been wrestling with, for which he had no outlet.

Light was thrown into the room as someone entered and came down to hand something to Dr Goebbels. Schlegel half turned and thought he saw Anna Huber leaving, just as his attention was drawn to a man on screen, a short, stout figure, in profile, standing with hands clasped behind his back, on the edge of a small group listening attentively to the Führer. The plain uniform without insignia said he was not army.

Schlegel was prepared to bet it was an older, fatter version of the third man in the photograph of his stepfather and the professorial man with a pipe.

A brief closer shot of the same group showed the fingers of the man's clasped hands in a frenzy of agitation.

It was heretical. There was no getting away from it. No wonder Goebbels was concerned. The film questioned the very existence of the Führer.

Schlegel was bound to ask if the stiff celluloid figures were just acting for the camera. In terms of any comparison, it wasn't as though the Führer had been an accessible figure for years.

Goebbels halted the screening several times to question Schlegel on points of translation and to ask how serious the film was about the man on show not being the Führer.

Schlegel said, 'The film refers to the idea of doubles in a fanciful manner.'

'Meaning?'

'It is making a joke against the Führer, rather than accusing him of having an actual impersonator,' Schlegel said carefully.

'Is it that English upper-class rudeness, the way they look down on others? Your mother is very aristocratic in that respect.'

'No, it's just rude in a philistine way.'

Goebbels looked pleased. 'Philistine?'

'Being uncultured lets them be rude about most things.'

The point was proved as the newsreel moved on to disparage the highly decorated young Major whom Schlegel had watched being told over the telephone in Goebbels' office to quash the coup. Goebbels sniggered when the commentary talked of how the Major out-Hollywooded every screen Nazi.

'That's very good. "Out-Hollywoods!" So they are obtusely rude because they fear us.'

No, Schlegel thought: They are rude because they despise everything we stand for.

He was starting to feel as though he had been kidnapped by this persistent little man and transported into another dimension in which different strands of his life converged . . . Whatever he had been expecting from this stage-managed interlude, it wasn't the uncomfortable coalescing of so many elements, with the Minister of Propaganda looking over his shoulder.

The commentary roused itself for one last sally, declaring: 'This time there must be no comeback for Germany! Who was it who said if an ass goes travelling it will not come back a horse?'

The lights came up and Goebbels gripped Schlegel's shoulder.

'What is that business about an ass?'

Schlegel looked at Goebbels, his mind blank. The man indulged only to a point. The whole screening now seemed to take on the form of a test from which Schlegel would be allowed to return depending on the satisfactoriness of his performance.

'The bit about the ass, man! Don't the British call a fool an ass?'

Perhaps the man understood English after all. Schlegel ploughed on.

'The ass is also known as the beast of burden. What is being said here is like a leopard not changing its spots. It means we can't and won't be made to change, however hard anyone tries to.'

Goebbels looked around at his acolytes. 'This man is wasted in the Gestapo.'

The hangers-on stared at the floor. Schlegel suspected they understood perfectly what the business with the ass meant and perhaps even Goebbels did too, but it amused him to watch others squirm. Schlegel seemed to have passed his test.

'Most illuminating!' said Goebbels. With that, he and his acolytes swept out, leaving Schlegel thinking about whether he had in fact seen Anna Huber slipping in and out of the dark.

As Schlegel was in the building, it made sense to speak to Anna Huber. He had been impressed by how quickly she had come up with the list of dedicatees and he wanted to see her again, though he wasn't aware of any special attraction.

She did not sound pleased when he called to say he was downstairs and needed ten minutes. As she could not be seen to be uncooperative, she reluctantly agreed to meet in the square outside.

He watched her approach. She wore a red suede jacket that had seen better days and looked like it had been expensive. To judge from her preoccupied walk, Schlegel guessed she was used to keeping her thoughts to herself.

'I don't have long,' she said.

'Was that you I saw coming into the cinema earlier?'

She gave him a quizzical look and asked, 'What *is* it you want?'

She could see he wasn't going to satisfy her with an answer. It must sound like he was trying to spy on her. What he was about to say wouldn't sound any less clumsy.

The square was so enormous it isolated everyone on it. If Dr Goebbels looked out of his window he might even see them talking.

Huber, cautious, asked, 'Are you investigating me?'

He took a long time answering. 'No. I'm more investigating myself.'

She looked mystified as he explained badly about wanting to find out more about his father.

Huber said, 'Surely your office has the means to come up with the answer.'

True. He could call the Munich Gestapo. Such transactions were made every day. One advantage of a police state was being able to request information on almost anyone. Schlegel knew he was being tiresome. No one solicited the company of the Gestapo.

He said, 'Regardless of where I work, my mother is in a camp for harbouring a Jew. My stepfather is in hiding and now I am being told my real father, whom I wrote off as dead years ago, was close enough to the Führer to have been included among his most dedicated followers. Wouldn't you be curious?'

Huber shrugged and asked, 'Why are you telling me?'

'You have a journalistic background.'

'I am a proofreader.'

'You come from a family of reporters. Is you father still alive?'

'I told you, he disappeared years ago.'

'Was he ever arrested?'

'No record of it. Usually they are only too happy to tell the family. It keeps them in line.'

'Do you think he is still alive?'

Huber stared at the ground. 'I doubt it. They got everyone in the end. I must go back now.'

Schlegel stared at the pulsing blue vein in her long white throat.

'We have a missing father in common,' she eventually said. 'I suggest I find out what I can about yours from my brother and you can use all the discretionary powers of your organisation to find out what happened to mine.'

Schlegel held out his hand until she shook it, her grip firm.

'One last thing,' he said.

She looked around as if aware of being watched.

'Do you remember the Bratwurst Glöckl?' he asked.

'Yes, it was a common meeting place, favoured by the Führer's crowd in its day.'

Schlegel explained how its proprietor was among the names she had just given him.

'Zehnter,' he prompted.

'Was that his name?'

'He no longer runs it.'

'No, he wouldn't. They carted him off years ago.' Huber had no trouble remembering that. 'It was something of a scandal. I don't think I ever knew his name. He was just referred to as the owner.'

'What did he do?'

'At first it was said he had been taken ill. Then it was a nervous breakdown. Later it was said he had been interfering with a boy.'

'When was this?'

'Ten years ago.'

Was the Führer dedicating copies of his book to child molesters?

Huber said, 'Be careful what you wish for regarding your father. In those early days there were said to be very disreputable elements, until they all went in the big clear-out of 1934.'

Schlegel watched her walk back into the building and wondered what had really precipitated Zehnter's fall and presumably his father's, wiping their names from the record.

16

Schlegel was hoping it would be too late for Müller when he got back but Müller was keeping his evening watch in his little darkened office. Like Dr Goebbels, he kept a clear desk. Müller sat there, apparently staring into space, but giving off a discharge of energy like a machine for processing information.

He made a point of looking at the time when he finally noticed Schlegel and asked what he had been up to with Dr Goebbels.

Müller graced the answer with the ghost of a smile.

'That British newsreel?'

Schlegel nodded.

'He shows that to everyone.'

Müller held out his hand for the letter, noting it hadn't been resealed. He raised an eyebrow.

'Of course not, sir.' Tempted, but hadn't.

Müller read Goebbels' reply and grunted.

Schlegel suspected the note was of little relevance and the point was to expose Schlegel to Goebbels, either as part of a hostile opening move or as a sacrificial pawn.

Schlegel waited to be dismissed. Instead Müller produced a file from a drawer, placed it on the desk and said, 'You are familiar with Hermann Fegelein.'

It wasn't a question. Schlegel groaned inwardly.

'Yes, sir. He is the Reichsführer-SS's special envoy to Chancellery.'

Müller looked at him as though he were an idiot. 'Thank you for pointing that out. Fegelein has complained of false charges brought by you.'

'We had a witness to a hit-and-run accident that left a woman dead. Fegelein was driving.'

'The incident was a couple of years ago.' Müller's look said: ancient history. 'You tried pressing charges last year. What about your witness?'

'Unable to testify.'

Müller maintained his graveyard expression. 'Your word against Fegelein's and he is more important than you, by far. Your summary of Fegelein. Be candid.'

The question wasn't as hard as it looked. Fegelein was widely loathed. Schlegel thought it unlikely Müller was in favour.

'He has a bad reputation going back years but he enjoys a great deal of protection. Popular with the ladies.'

Schlegel had once believed men like Fegelein got their comeuppance, in the end.

Müller pondered before resuming in his dust-dry voice: 'Fegelein claims he had agents who penetrated a conspirators' cell. Which raises the question of why he did nothing about it.'

Schlegel cast around for something plausible and suggested events could have overtaken Fegelein, if his agents didn't know the actual date of the plot. Realising what he was about to add, Schlegel dried.

Müller looked at him. 'There are no microphones in this room.'

'I was going to say everyone was overtaken by events.'

Müller looked about as friendly as a cobra as he said, 'Fegelein maintains he kept quiet about his penetration for fear of compromise, because there are spies everywhere, in case you hadn't noticed.' He gave a thin smile. 'Then a clinic burns down the day after the bomb. The question I want you to ask yourself as you go about your business is, *which* conspiracy?'

'Are you saying there is more than one, sir?'

Müller merely said, 'There is much opaque behaviour surrounding the events of the last days, regarding the motives of several parties, some senior. Do you understand what I am saying?'

Unfortunately it couldn't be clearer: he was being dangled and had already been brought to the attention of Dr Goebbels.

Schlegel carefully asked Müller for an example of such behaviour.

Müller assumed an air of academic distraction. 'What was Dr Goebbels most exercised about when showing you his silly newsreel?'

'Its exact tone and whether—'

Müller interrupted. 'Not interpretation. Content.'

'How the film questioned the Führer's existence.'

'Then you have just answered your own question. Proceed, with caution. Take Fegelein's file, sit outside in my secretary's office, read it and leave it when you go.'

He picked up his pen in a way that suggested it was a far more valuable tool than Schlegel.

Schlegel took the file and crept out, hoping to reach the door without further ado.

Müller spoke as Schlegel grasped the handle.

'Think of yourself as an astronaut. I can launch you but you won't necessarily be able to come back if it is not in the interests of the opaque gentlemen.'

Not a dangle then; more an honorary sacrifice, on a plate.

'Oh, and your father,' said Müller. 'No good can come of

it. Heed the platitudes. Ignorance is bliss. Let sleeping dogs lie.' Müller nodded and Schlegel turned away and was again about to grasp the handle when Müller said, 'However, should you find yourself in Munich ask Emil Maurice. He might have a tale or two.'

Schlegel recognised the name: one of the twenty-five recipients of *Mein Kampf.*

'Emil Maurice?' he ventured, fearing he was exceeding his boundaries.

'The Führer's driver and bodyguard in the early days.'

Schlegel could see he wasn't going to get more and left quietly.

Schlegel thought: the higher you climb, the fewer the shadows. He had entered the world of high intrigue that left him dangerously exposed. What was he supposed to do? He had no access to Fegelein and any request would result in the usual runaround.

He had an uncomfortable memory of the man's superior smile, the moue of a pout, the moment of sloth before the insult. The flesh was not as taut as in his equestrian days. He was rumoured to be married to the sister of the Führer's secret mistress, which was typical of the man's self-advancement. Fegelein had spoiling good looks, a weak chin and a nasty manner when crossed. His most disconcerting aspect was how the smile *did* extend to the eyes. Nothing gave more pleasure and amusement than the discomfort of others.

He sat and went through Fegelein's file.

It started with a case involving a Munich man, referred to only as T.T., the receiver of stolen goods which were found located at the Fegelein family riding school after military transportation from Warsaw where Fegelein was stationed.

A copy of Fegelein's letter to the Reichsführer-SS claimed the goods were of legitimate origin, and that was the end of that, with a rubber stamp saying 'Case Dismissed'.

The goods were connected to a Warsaw case which Morgen had pursued in vain. Following the confiscation and Aryanisation of an international Jewish fur company, a liquidator was appointed. The shock for Schlegel was seeing the man's name, Becher – the same SS man to whom Schlegel had delivered Christoph's documents for signing in Budapest the week before. According to the report, Becher was a cavalry officer in Fegelein's regiment.

It meant the present tangle went back years, with all kinds of unsuspected backstitching. Small world, Morgen had said in Budapest; and about to get smaller, Schlegel suspected. Again, the higher you go, the fewer the faces, until it is just the same men in the room.

Fegelein and Becher had taken two of the firm's female employees as mistresses and proceeded to gut the company, passing on fur coats to society women at home, including the Führer's secret mistress. Morgen's investigation into 'gifts from the firm to powerful members of the SS' was blocked at the highest level. The name of Becher's mistress was blacked out, suggesting she too had protection, despite it being noted she was almost certainly a Polish agent. Schlegel experienced the sensation of being lowered in a swinging bucket into pitch black as he asked himself whether Fegelein had been aware of the double role of the woman with the deleted name. He doubted if Fegelein was a foreign agent but criminal and intelligence activity grew so overlapping that blackmail was always a possibility, and Fegelein was vulnerable in that respect. It also made Fegelein's claims of penetrating the recent conspiracy questionable in terms of his actual role.

Schlegel saw his own problem clearly: how to investigate a case he had no inclination to pursue against someone he had not the slightest chance of getting close to.

Müller had hinted at a second conspiracy, or a conspiracy within the conspiracy. Did that mean any questioning of the role of Fegelein must extend to his master and patron, Reichsführer-SS Himmler, who had a history of going out of his way to protect his protégé?

Müller had also implied Dr Goebbels was not above suspicion. In a world of infinite interpretations, there was always room for another reading, and in the palace of intrigue it was not out of the question that Müller himself was implicated and putting up a smokescreen. Schlegel suspected they all played the courtly game of pointing the finger, just to keep their hand in, and always at the expense of the little man.

Gerda was supposed to distract him, which she did but not how he wanted. They ate out. Soup of a sort. Bread of a sort. Thin beer. Schlegel was already a bit drunk and Gerda had gone moody on him. For a treat they had tinned tangerines for afters.

'From where?' asked Gerda, sulky.

Schlegel had no idea. Japan or Spain maybe.

'South America?' added Gerda, not interested.

The evening suddenly felt more like the start of a break-up, and out of nowhere.

They were in the large and dowdy Bollenmüller, which was more or less full, with pockets of liveliness. Not a haunt exactly, but Schlegel often went as it had a lot of people eating alone.

He couldn't decide whether he was a passing fancy and Gerda was the type to move on. That evening he had little small talk. What *did* two people talk about, he wondered. He sensed she didn't want to come back with him. He asked if she was all right.

'Fine,' she said. Always a bad sign.

'How's work?'

'Fine.'

Tangerines of the brightest orange. Schlegel thought the manufacturer must add artificial colouring. They tasted of a sickly sweetness. Gerda pushed hers around while Schlegel imagined her writhing on his bed, the night saved.

'There's someone else,' she said.

Schlegel affected nonchalance. 'Does that matter?'

'Maybe. He's coming home.'

'One of the fearless fliers?' He didn't mean to sound jealous.

'At least he fought.'

Touché, Schlegel thought. The mean part of him rather relished the prospect of a row. Perhaps it would give him an excuse to dump her first. He nearly laughed out loud. All of thirty seconds from fantasising about her naked to chucking her.

Gerda thought he was laughing at her.

The boyfriend predated him by some time. He was returning minus an arm. Again Schlegel found himself on the brink of inappropriate laughter as he stared at his hands resting on the table.

'When does he come back?' he asked, trying to sound conciliatory.

'In about a fortnight.'

It seemed tactless to ask if they could continue to see each other in the meantime, and even after that. But he sensed she was still available; it was just more complicated now.

'I am not such good company,' she conceded, and

admitted to hating the Bollenmüller. She had been there once before. Schlegel expected some sad boyfriend story but she told him she had been eating alone when plainclothes police came and snatched a man at the table next to her.

'He tried to run and when they jumped on him he made this high-pitched squealing over and over, which embarrassed even the policemen, and he messed his trousers and the waitresses didn't bother to clean up because it wasn't their job to tidy up after Jews. He left wet and the rest all over the floor.'

'You should have said. We could have gone elsewhere.'

Schlegel couldn't shake the feeling there was more she wanted to say. He guessed she was going to tell him she couldn't see him again, and was saving it for last.

Again he was wrong. She in fact wanted to be talked out of going home. She confessed that the thought of crippling frightened her and she was not sure how she would cope, and more or less pleaded to go back with him. So Schlegel obliged. He sensed decorum should prevail and he didn't kiss her on the walk back, or on the stairs, waiting until they were in the apartment, then suggesting they go straight to bed, but not how he wanted as it turned out: five minutes later, Gerda was in his bed and he was on the floor, after she had made a big show of apology, saying she was feeling off-colour.

'And a bit blue.'

She called him darling. Maybe she would feel more like it in the morning, she offered, giving him a chaste goodnight kiss and asking if there was an alarm clock so they made sure they had time.

There wasn't. Schlegel said he woke early.

'Honestly, darling, you don't mind, really?' Darling again.

Of course he minded. 'Not at all,' he said.

He had trouble sleeping. He was very aware of Gerda in the room. She was a noisy, restless sleeper, tossing and turning, groaning and muttering, which was both distracting and frustrating because Schlegel couldn't make out what she said.

He moved into the main room and must have slept because when he awoke Gerda was sitting at the table in the dark.

'You should go back to bed,' he said.

She wanted him to take her, so he did. For all the buck and tremor, he sensed her trying to blot something out, and he in turn was very aware of the armless boyfriend over his shoulder. She turned over straight after and he thought she was going to sleep.

Instead, after a long time, she said, 'I saw something today at work I shouldn't have done.'

So here we are, thought Schlegel. They had got there at last.

'Saw what?'

'A report.'

'What kind of report?'

'A recommendation.'

'Where did you see it?'

'It had been left lying in a laboratory at the University Medical School. In a folder. I didn't mean to look. I wondered whose it was, in order to return it.'

If Gerda worked in a sensitive area, Schlegel supposed she had found out something unwelcome about the job. Experiments were rumoured to go on in cancer research using human guinea pigs.

She said she had seen a series of memos involving the case of a severely hydrocephalic child.

'Hydrocephalic?'

'Water on the brain.'

The child had been examined by the university head of psychiatry, who also worked at the Charité hospital, whose case the child was.

What exercised Gerda was that she knew the man, had attended some of his lectures and he was much admired, charming and professional, which made the whole thing much more difficult.

'What thing?' asked Schlegel.

'He is saving children that shouldn't be saved.'

Schlegel protested that he must know what he was doing.

'Children beyond repair. There are channels. When the question arose whether this child should be transferred for full treatment this professor wrote: "He has to go some-where else."'

Full treatment? Schlegel said, 'Forget what you have seen. It was only chance you saw it in the first place.'

Or snooping.

But Gerda was of the mind that how she knew was irrelevant. She *knew* and was therefore bound to inform.

'He might be a secret Jew.'

'I doubt that,' said Schlegel.

'Psychiatry is a Jewish pursuit, after all.'

Schlegel thought: And still I want to see her, and talk her out of seeing her disabled boyfriend.

17

Schlegel didn't know what to tell Dunkelwert, to whom he still officially answered. She was insisting on a written report. Schlegel was a rotten typist, using two painfully slow fingers, hovering over the keyboard in search of the right letters.

He could say the 'mystery' of the clinic staff was solved. They had died in an aeroplane crash. He could say the 'mystery' of the anonymous letter was 'ongoing', not a word Schlegel cared for.

In fact, he had done some basic checking on the three 'suspects' given to him by Dark Martin. One of them, a carpenter, turned out to be the boy's maternal grandfather. The man's file showed arrests for drunkenness and suspicion of seditious comment. According to Martin, he was given to shouting, 'Heil Moscow!' when drunk. The boy had not revealed that the man was a relative.

Schlegel had found a harmless old sot sitting in his workshop surrounded by soft-lead pencils and coarse paper. The carpenter was a consumptive drunk, with a terminal cough, who didn't look like he was capable of holding a thought from one moment to the next. Schlegel made the man write down his name and address. The writing was a match yet he was inclined not to pursue the matter. He was sure the letter was a prank at the old boy's expense, dictated by Martin, with the help of his nasty little friends, when he was too drunk to know what he was doing. Let it go, Schlegel thought. The man looked on his last legs and would probably be dead in a few weeks.

Schlegel wasn't under any pressure to solve the case in any normal sense, so he decided to make no mention of the carpenter. Besides, the author of the actual letter was of little consequence now it was being treated by Müller as a gambit in some altogether deeper game. Desperate not to get any more ensnared, Schlegel produced a couple of paragraphs of impeccable jargon: 'central thrust', 'working through'.

No mention of the Müller–Goebbels merry-go-round. Or Fegelein. Or Morgen. Or old cases in Fegelein's file involving stolen furs and the Warsaw black market, whose clients included the Führer's mistress, about whom no one was supposed to know. Or the porky man in the bomb-plot newsreel who had once stood next to his stepfather for a photograph. Or his stepfather's name being down on a list for a new government. Or his own recent visits to illegal jazz clubs and not reporting them. Or the list with his father's name on. Or the dedicated copy of *Mein Kampf*. Or the young woman in a torn snapshot sitting next to the Führer. Or the mystery of his real father and what would no doubt turn out to be a catastrophic relationship with the Führer. Or his youthful indiscretions with Christoph or the fact of Christoph's homosexuality or his own feelings for Gerda, whom he suspected was both right and all wrong for him. Or having been followed by two Japanese gentlemen in Budapest, one of whom had later tried to rob his hotel room – what had *that* been about?

Anyone join that lot up and they would have him strung up before his feet could touch the ground.

What *had* the Japanese gentlemen been to do with

anything? Schlegel asked himself. He had edited them out of the Budapest episode, which he had surreptitiously been putting together in his head ever since in the likelihood of being questioned, desperately searching for Müller's golden thread that made the lie come alive.

Schlegel had returned from Budapest with random tourist memories, like postcards or snapshots – a shiny chrome-plated bicycle leaning against a movie bulletin board behind a monument; old shop signs in faded Yiddish; a grimy buffet with a few mouldy pieces of cake and a miserable fruit stack of three apples and five plums. He tried to convince himself that if he could string some story around these pathetic, innocuous images he might yet come up with a blameless version to satisfy anyone he told it to. But he feared that everything would be seen to connect in the end and when he was shown the full picture it would be him standing in the middle and what the Americans called the fall guy.

Schlegel was aware of Dunkelwert's entrance. She loitered, watching him. He looked at the mess he had typed and panicked, fearing that Müller was playing them off against each other, and Dunkelwert knew more than she was letting on in terms of what he was withholding from his report. She came over and asked in disbelief, 'Is that your typing?'

'No correction fluid left in the stationery cupboard,' he said, ripping the sheet from the machine and throwing it away before she could start reading it.

'Your report?' she asked.

He said he needed more time. She told him he had until Sunday to produce a full one, putting heavy emphasis on 'full'. 'No excuses,' she said.

Schlegel felt the room quieten as everyone watched. Just then his telephone rang. Dunkelwert snatched it before he could answer. She held out the receiver looking almost gleeful. 'Huber. For you.'

With Dunkelwert showing no sign of going away, Schlegel didn't know whether to take the call or tell Huber he would ring back. He accepted the receiver.

'Yes, hello,' said Huber and he was reminded how good her telephone voice was.

It occurred to him her real reason for calling was to check he was who he had said he was.

Dunkelwert watched, suspicious.

Huber said there existed a Munich Hotel and Restaurant Association. She had spoken to it about Herr Zehnter and the woman there remembered him because he had been on the association's committee.

'She told me he sadly passed soon after he was taken away.'

'What, just died?'

'Of heart failure.'

'And the official reason for his arrest?'

'Tax evasion, according to her, which was a shock because he had a reputation for being a scrupulous bookkeeper.'

Schlegel sensed there was more but he was too aware of Dunkelwert listening. He rang off and Dunkelwert asked, 'Who is Huber?'

'No one important,' Schlegel said and made up a story about it being an old case in CID financial crime which he was being asked about.

'Tax evasion.'

'And heart failure,' Dunkelwert added.

Schlegel sensed she had already heard too much.

He caught the glint of malice in her eye as he walked out, aware of her watching his departing back.

Outside, Schlegel stood on the pavement, momentarily overwhelmed. The only one he knew with access to the past was Christoph, who was in the occasionally shady business of appropriation. So he called Christoph, who sounded cautious, wanting to know what it was concerning.

'The family matter we discussed.' Schlegel was aware of how stilted he sounded but he knew enough not to volunteer more information over the telephone, with so many busy ears listening in. He suspected Christoph was wary too and wondered whether he was about to be given the brush-off when Christoph said he had twenty minutes if Schlegel came now.

'Fredi Huber?' asked Christoph. 'What on earth do you want to know about him?'

'His name came up.'

'The man was notorious.' Schlegel looked at Christoph, who continued, 'For hounding the Führer. The newspaper he worked for even put a mock-up on the cover showing the Führer in wedding clothes with a Negress bride.'

In the old days they would have laughed at that.

'Anything that says Fredi Huber knew your father?' Christoph asked.

Schlegel said Huber's name had come up by chance and he knew the man's daughter, slightly.

'I wouldn't trust her,' said Christoph.

'Do you know her?' asked Schlegel, surprised.

'By reputation,' said Christoph. 'She hangs around the art scene and some think she's reporting back, but they say that about everyone, so what do I know?' He paused thoughtfully then said, 'With regard to Fredi, I may be able to help you and you may be able to help me. The past is becoming quite collectible again. Old newspapers. Memorabilia. Rare items. Posters. Flyers. The more disposable it once was the more desirable now. Rare editions too, such as your father's copy of the Führer book.'

'Is Fredi Huber collectible?'

'As an alternative voice, shall we say. A lot of respectable buyers are mad for the past.'

'So Fredi Huber becomes collectable as an example of previous depravity?'

'Exactly.'

'What do you propose?'

'There's this man—'

'It sounds like the start of a joke.'

'You probably won't thank me.'

The man in question was a dealer operating out of a falling-down house in Kreuzberg, stuffed full of rubbish he claimed was priceless.

'Everyone knows him as Rösti, don't ask me why. Ninety percent of what he offers is worthless. He'll try and sell you a used piece of toilet paper, claiming Göring wiped his arse with it. Then once in a while he comes up with gold.'

Rarity had its own value, Christoph said. The fact of something being not available put a price on it. 'Who said, "Yes to decency and morality in family and state! I consign to the flames the writings of Heinrich Mann, Ernst Glaeser, Erich Kästner"?'

'Doctor Goebbels.'

'Quite. Kästner has since made his peace with the authorities but his books were burned, so if I were to offer an original edition of *Going to the Dogs,* several collectors would be interested; and if such an edition was in mint condition and signed by Kästner, or a dedicated copy inscribed to someone famous, it would be worth a considerable amount.'

'And Rösti?'

'Strangely enough, he has had several such copies available over the last months. Top of the range. Signed and dedicated. Coincidentally the recipients have all gone away, so, for instance, Eric Pommer isn't around to dispute the authenticity of his dedication.'

'Pommer?'

Christoph sighed at Schlegel's ignorance.

'Produced a lot of big early movies.'

'Are the dedications forgeries?'

'Either Rösti has come across a cache of books and is embellishing them, or the esteemed Kästner is selling off his own private copies suitably inscribed to make a bit on the side. The point is, several collectors have been assembling whole libraries from surviving copies of books that were burned. There's no end to it. Foreign editions. English editions.'

'You asked if I can help.'

'For some time now, Rösti has been trying to interest me in a package. It includes a typed copy of one of the Führer's earliest speeches. Probably authentic. Various Führer signatures and sketches, including napkin doodles. The actual pistol used to kill the traitor Ernst Röhm in 1934, with independent verification from the man whose gun it was. And all this a prelude to what Rösti calls the "hot stuff", which he will reveal only in person.'

'Why would anyone be interested?'

Christoph snorted. 'It's like the dance of the seven veils.' He crooked his finger and gestured with a beckoning motion. 'Come hither! That's how he works, only to reveal a fat nothing. I can contact him to say you are coming. See what's on offer. Don't buy anything. Say you have to report back. Appear enthusiastic. Quiz him about the Röhm item and suggest that's what interests me. He will play hard to

146

get about the secret stuff but insist on a couple of examples as *bona fides*. As for yourself, tell him I am interested in anything concerning Fredi Huber. He is bound to have something. What is it you are after, exactly?'

'I don't know.'

'You always knew what you didn't want.' Christoph half smiled. 'In that case offer Rösti something to get him on your side. If he doesn't know about Anton Schlegel he will make it his business to find out.'

'You mean show him the *Mein Kampf*.'

'Bring it up at the end. Act a bit coy.'

'He'll ask why I am not offering it to you.'

'Say you want a second opinion. Give me a time and I'll tell Rösti you will be there.'

Christoph further instructed Schlegel on how to handle Rösti then held out his hand to shake. It was slightly moist. Schlegel realised Christoph was nervous. He found it odd shaking hands, as it had never been a habit between them. The gesture seemed cool and rather dismissive, undoing Schlegel's impression of reconciliation, leaving him thrown again.

Christoph lived off Savignyplatz. Schlegel was in no hurry to return to work. He bought a newspaper from a kiosk and waited for a bus in Kantstrasse, gave up and sat on a bench in the small park and read the paper. The obituary section reminded him of the dead theatrical agent mentioned by Stoffel: the man was the subject of an insultingly terse entry, mentioning a life's service to the entertainment industry. Whether his death was assisted or unaided was beside the point now as the obituary blamed 'a short illness'. Contracted in the time it took him to fall, Schlegel thought grimly. He presumed it must be the same man Stoffel had told him about, as it seemed unlikely two such agents would die at once.

Schlegel walked to the Zoo Station telephone rank and looked up the agent in the book. He rang the number, curious to know if anyone would answer. A woman eventually did, her voice tremulous. He supposed her a secretary sitting in view of the window through which her employer had been defenestrated.

She sounded terrified when he said who he was, so much so that he wondered what she knew. He told her not to go anywhere, he would come straight over. He suspected he failed to reassure her by saying his enquiry was only a matter of routine. The trip would probably turn out to be a waste of time but it gave him an excuse to avoid the office.

The theatrical agency was on the fifth floor of a private block off Alte Jakob Strasse down towards Belle Alliance Platz. An elevator had an 'out of order' sign. The standard red sisal stair runner was the first mark of a typical, more well-to-do Berlin apartment, but the impression of shabbiness grew as Schlegel climbed. One of the back windows between floors had been blown out and boarded over. The push-button timer lights for the landing no longer worked after the third floor.

The woman took her time coming to the door.

For a moment everything was quiet. The noise of street traffic died. No birdsong. Only the quivering light coming through a high back window. Schlegel heard footsteps on parquet flooring.

He was confronted by a rail-thin woman of indeterminate age. The hair was dyed a garish chestnut, grown out to leave a grey run like a landing strip across the top of her head. Although it was still warm, she looked cold and as Schlegel stepped inside he felt the chill of something more than lack of sunlight. A corridor stretched ahead. Posters of films and theatrical productions lined the walls. The office was immediately to the left.

Her name was Frau Busl. Busl was the name of the agency too so Schlegel asked if she was the wife.

'Widow,' he corrected himself.

'Sister,' she said. 'My brother never married.'

A theatrical man, thought Schlegel.

Whether Frau Busl shook or shivered he couldn't tell, but she trembled slightly and held one hand clasped in front of the other to stop it shaking.

She appeared alarmed by Schlegel's white hair.

His eyes were drawn to the window. Big enough to chuck someone out of without any trouble. The atmosphere in the room felt spooked.

Two desks both placed sideways – one behind the door, the other down by the window. A couple of reading chairs. Reference books on shelves. Framed photographs on the wall. More posters. What looked like some awards. A chaise longue.

'The casting couch,' said Frau Busl. Schlegel hadn't been expecting a sense of humour from such a mouse.

His image of Busl was of someone corpulent and jolly, conforming to what he thought a convivial, social man should look like. Instead the many photographs on the walls showed an inconspicuous, dapper little fellow, wearing large spectacles, who looked more like an accountant; if Gestapo Müller were ever looking for a stand-in then Busl was his man. As an agent, his social reach appeared considerable. Many photographs showed him with Dr Goebbels – perhaps Busl was a humorist because the doctor was invariably shown laughing his head off. Busl with Hermann Göring. Schlegel needed help with some of the famous faces he didn't recognise. Frau Goebbels was a regular. Actors. Actresses. Child stars. Other agents. The whole show business panoply caught in the light of a flash gun.

Schlegel was saddened by the pointlessness of the parade, and all these photographs of Busl being silent witnesses to his demise.

On the evening of his death, Busl was supposed to have gone out to the theatre but at the last moment he announced he had a late appointment.

'They say he jumped.' Frau Busl snorted.

'The newspaper said after an illness.'

'That's true. You don't smoke sixty cigarettes a day and not get ill.'

So maybe Busl had a terminal diagnosis and decided to take the quick way out after all. Schlegel pictured Busl on the ledge alone, having a final cigarette, waiting for the moment, whereas a minute or two earlier he'd had him being dragged across the floor to be pitched headfirst out of the open window.

In such a murky world any interpretation could be shown to the right one.

Schlegel asked Frau Busl about their job.

Business was still good. Films were being made, plenty of radio and stage work, recitals, travelling repertory and entertainments for the troops. Frau Busl told him they handled everything from classical actors to radio announcers and variety acts.

'The one with dancing dogs is very popular,' she said.

Schlegel asked himself: Why chuck an agent out of the window? Because he knew too much, but how did that relate to the clinic, if at all?

Schlegel asked Frau Busl how long she and her brother had been working together.

More or less back to the beginning of the motion picture industry, she said. They had worked with all the directors who had since left – the work which hadn't deserved a mention in Busl's obituary, Schlegel supposed. A lot had changed: the clamorous variety of the previous era against the strident flatness of everything now. Even Hollywood films had been available until the end of 1941, albeit horrendously dubbed, at least offering some alternative: cowboys, slapstick, gangsters.

It was more than just forgetting, Schlegel thought. Everything had grown corrosive and toxic.

Frau Busl didn't have to say she was frightened it might be her turn next in such an abrupt world. The window seemed to have grown bigger, like a mechanical backdrop on a stage set. She looked at him and said, 'I though at first you were the angel of death with your hair, come to throw me out of the window too. I don't understand how for one past caring it is possible to be so frightened.'

Schlegel said, 'In the chaos of the last days many things have gone on that we are trying to understand.'

He sounded suspiciously sincere, he thought.

'He was homosexual,' she said. 'I sense you guessed that. You seem a sensitive man. In the theatrical profession there is always leeway. If they had packed them all off there would be no chorus line or male dancers at all.'

Schlegel wondered why he was being told, then understood. Information was like passing on a sickness or virus, in the hope that the infection would transmit. It was important too that he was authority, so she could say to anyone else that she had already talked to the Gestapo. She more or less admitted as much, asking how to contact him, in case.

In exchange for his number, Frau Busl, as though honouring her side of the bargain, reached up to a shelf and got down several directories. For casting, she said. She handed Schlegel one. It was in alphabetical order, with formal portraits of actors, sometimes with a note of whether they specialised in drama, comedy or variety. The comic ones tended to pull funny faces.

She showed him where several pages had been turned down.

'He must have been working on a casting call,' she said. Schlegel looked at the folded pages – dark-haired actors of middle age and somehow familiar. Their resemblance was obvious in a general way but seemed not to have been spotted by Frau Busl, or perhaps she was too afraid to point it out. Her brother had died immediately after the bomb plot. Again, coincidence?

Frau Busl said, 'My brother's telephone pad was blank but what he wrote on the top page was traced on the one below.'

She had shaded it with a soft pencil, like a brass rubbing. Schlegel read: 'Thursday, 20, 8am Babelsberg. Room 175'.

'Babelsberg film studios,' said Frau Busl, the shake of her head becoming more pronounced. 'Room 175 is one of the meeting rooms used for casting.'

18

Film studios are factories like anywhere. Several productions were being shot during Schlegel's visit to Babelsberg the following morning, a Saturday. His badge got him past a guard on the main gate who noted his name. Inside, men and women in wigs and period costume strolled and smoked as they paraded down neatly verged lanes.

An air of privileged boredom hung over the waiting sound stages, with their huge arc lamps and much banging of last-minute carpentry as sets were readied. Schlegel felt a little starstruck at the thought of seeing someone famous.

Through the windows of a building marked 'Canteen' he saw more people sitting around in costume and wigs, and spilling outside onto the lawn to sun themselves.

The boring parts were further back, in single-storey, pebbledash barracks – accountancy, administration, editing suites and all the rest.

The place struck Schlegel as a benign version of the slaughterhouse at Zentral-Viehoff and the concentration camp in the Occupied Eastern Zone, which shared some of the same architectural detailing and presentation of an ordered existence. A factory was a factory after all, whether killing animals and people on an industrial scale or manufacturing dreams: same process, different outcomes.

He was seduced by the unreality of the place. People were friendly when he asked what films were being made.

Working there must be one of the nicest jobs of the war and the canteen was good when he tried it. He walked down a street of facades, supported at the back by a complicated network of scaffolding. The contrast between this perfect illusion and the bombed streets in the city made him rather question the point of everything.

He finally addressed himself to a building slightly grander than the rest, which housed a central reception, with a directions board pointing out where everything was. Screening theatres. Writers' offices. Production rooms. Guest suites and dressing rooms. Casting. Room 175 was on the first floor.

Its door was open and people were sitting waiting for a meeting. Schlegel glanced in. The room looked identical to the empty ones along the corridor: table and upright chairs, a couple of armchairs for comfort with chintz fabric.

Downstairs reception held the appointments book for the meeting rooms. It was casually handed over without question, as if it were the most natural thing in the world. The woman who gave it to him even said, 'There you go,' with a cheerful smile.

The three desk women were all young and beautiful, bright and chatty. Schlegel wondered if they were out-of-work actresses, hired to present the right image, making it all as much of an illusion as the fake street outside.

When Schlegel pointed out the page for 20 July was missing, the young woman – she really was startlingly beautiful – said, 'Yes, ink got poured over it by mistake. The page was totally ruined.' She gave him a dazzling smile.

It must have been a remarkably neat spill with none of the other pages showing any sign of splatter. He asked if anyone remembered the agent Busl being in on the morning of the twentieth. 'Early appointment. First thing.'

The three women did perfect impressions of not

remembering and Schlegel wondered if they were as empty-headed as they looked.

He returned to the canteen and fell into conversation with an old electrician who was already drunk. He had been on a night shoot, he said, and raised his glass. The man's advanced network of broken veins told of a long career of studio drinking. For the price of several beers he entertained Schlegel with stories from the old days. The silents then the first sound pictures. He remembered Busl. They had worked together for the director Lang on *Spione*.

'I knew Busl quite well, actually,' he said, slurring his words.

'He was here last Thursday,' Schlegel said.

'Was he?' asked the sparks. 'Maybe.'

The old boy clearly knew nothing of Busl's death, which went unmentioned.

'Lang was a cunt,' the electrician volunteered in the middle of a roundabout conversation involving Schlegel trying to explain about the missing page in the appointments book, and whether he could find out what Busl had been doing and who he had been seeing.

The old sparks duly performed his sole useful task of the session by reminding Schlegel of what he already knew: the studio front gate kept its own record of all admissions and departures.

Schlegel bought the man a last beer and left him to it. He was drunk and at the gate he tried not to breathe over the guard, whom he suspected was as drunk as he was.

The record of visitors' ins and outs was kept in what looked like a child's exercise book. The pages were filled in by a variety of hands, most barely legible. At the end of each day, a line was drawn across the page. Schlegel flipped back to the twentieth.

First in for the day at 7.45: Dr Goebbels; second in at 8.00, the agent Busl; 9.10 Dr Goebbels out, followed immediately by Busl.

Process of elimination, Schlegel thought; who didn't want anyone to know? With Busl dead, it could only be Dr Goebbels.

Back in the main building he asked if there was any kind of section for casting and was directed up to the second floor where an older woman of the same sort of indeterminate age as Frau Busl, with hair of equally suspect colour, presided over the studio's photographic and reference library.

Like the drunk electrician, here was another who was a walking history. She too remembered Busl and concurred with the electrician that Lang was 'not a nice man'. All of this was done with an easy familiarity, with the woman calling him 'dear' from the start. Schlegel knew she knew he was drunk. Like everyone else, she showed no curiosity about why he might be there, as if to say everything comes and goes. She did, however, display a glimmer of interest when Schlegel produced the names of the actors singled out in Busl's casting directory. They went through her copy of the directory together.

'Can you tell me anything about them?' he asked.

'Jobbers, dear. Nothing special.'

She appeared amused.

'A certain resemblance between them, wouldn't you say?' ventured Schlegel.

'If you are looking for a type,' she agreed.

Her books were often used in actual casting sessions, she said, seemingly apropos of nothing. The covers had a stamp of ownership and said 'Please return'.

'Look how this one came back,' the woman said. 'Honestly! No respect for others' property.'

She found the page showing an actor like the others in

age and looks. But over his picture someone using green ink had doodled a forelock and toothbrush moustache. Next to the altered face were several exclamation marks, also in green.

Schlegel said, 'Dr Goebbels uses green ink.'

The woman snorted. 'He should know better. Not a classy colour.' She studied the photograph and said with a mixture of amusement and irritation, 'You have to admit, there is a resemblance.'

'But what was it for?' asked Schlegel.

She said the gossip was Busl and Goebbels were secretly auditioning actors to play the Führer in a forthcoming feature film. 'Not that anyone has heard a squeak about it since that bomb went off.'

'I hear Busl has since passed on.'

'No surprise there, dear. He'd been on his last legs for years. I hear he took his own life but they're trying to say it was illness.'

'Why?'

'So his wife can squeeze some money out of his insurance policy.'

'Wife?'

The woman laughed. 'Not so you'd notice.'

After several misunderstandings Schlegel gathered that the Frau Busl he'd met claiming to be the man's sister was in fact his wife.

The woman gave a bark of laughter at this turn of events. 'Fed up with all that chasing after boys, I don't suppose. Well, mind how you go, dear.'

Schlegel left Babelsberg thinking: what on earth was Dr Goebbels doing casting Hitler actors on the morning of the bomb plot?

*

The dealer Rösti lived in a tall, narrow house near a canal and a long way from transport. It took Schlegel ages to find. Even before he stepped inside, the place smelt of cat. The *Mein Kampf* was in his brief case.

Rösti was an unshaven greasy man, elderly and almost as tall as Schlegel. His collarless shirt appeared never to have been washed. Despite the heat of the day he had on a long woollen overgarment that struggled to make up its mind whether it was a coat or a dressing gown. A habit of licking his lips before he spoke gave a suggestive moistness to any utterance. Most extraordinary was the wig, which could have been one of the cats sitting on his head.

While Rösti's appearance was questionable and his surroundings a tip, the voice and manners were impeccable. He ushered Schlegel to an upstairs living area with two facing armchairs, surrounded by junk that reached almost to the ceiling. Tea was offered and served in dainty cups and saucers. Perhaps sensing Schlegel's inebriation, Rösti pressed an Obstler on him. Schlegel sat down gingerly. His armchair was covered with a fine blanket of shed cat fur. At least the window shutters were more closed than open, making it harder to discern the full foulness of the room. He saw mouse droppings and smelt cat shit.

Rösti said, 'I spoke with your friend, Christoph. I am sorry he is unable to come in person. I fear he considers me rather beneath him, but there you are. Still, you are here recommended.'

A suggestive look implied that Schlegel was some sort of boyfriend.

'I've just come back from Budapest, as a matter of fact,' Schlegel observed inconsequentially, with what he hoped was cheery insouciance.

'A fabulous city, I have heard.' More Obstler was poured. 'Let's get companionably drunk now you are here.'

Schlegel couldn't decide whether the man was harmless as they continued to make small talk. Rösti had disconcerting a habit of throwing Jewish words and phrases into his speech.

'You're worried I am Jewish,' he said at one point.

The remark was clearly offered as a test.

Schlegel ignored him and asked if the name Anton Schlegel meant anything. Even if it did, he suspected Rösti wouldn't say because it went against his instinct as a hoarder of information.

'Is he a relative?'

'A distant one,' said Schlegel not wanting to commit himself. 'Something of a black sheep, I believe.'

Rösti winked at Schlegel. The tower of books behind him looked like it was about to topple and bury them both.

'Christoph is interested in the gun,' Schlegel said.

Rösti nodded. 'The one used to shoot Röhm. They shot him up the arse. Do you suppose your friend Christoph would still be interested?'

Schlegel stared at the glass in his hand and felt mildly entranced as Rösti turned the cuff on his sleeve and went on. 'Röhm was a homo, which was why he went, along with the rest of the old Party rebels and queers – 1934, the Night of the Long Knives; not strictly accurate as no knives were used as far as I know.'

He laughed loudly as he stood and searched through his junk.

After taking a long time to find what he was looking for, Rösti crouched next to Schegel's chair and lovingly turned the album's cellophane pages, which displayed photographs of items for sale, until there was one of the pistol used for Röhm's execution.

'Why is Christoph interested in this item?' Rösti asked.

'Because Dr Goebbels wants it.'

'Of course the doctor would. He was a witness to Röhm's arrest.'

'Christoph is also interested in Fredi Huber.'

Rösti chuckled knowingly. 'What kind of game is our friend playing?'

'I don't understand.'

'Huber meant nothing last week – a forgotten man – and means nothing now unless our friend is aware of a particular item being talked about as perhaps available for sale, in which case Christoph might suddenly be very interested.'

'What sort of item?'

'Ah-ha! I nearly gave it away. Let's say some sort of record.'

'A phonograph?' Schlegel asked, trying to sound stupid.

'Ah-ha again! Let's just say a written record.'

'Do you have anything by Huber?'

'Whether I show you or not depends.'

'On what?'

'How can I vouch for you, other than on your friend's say so? These are difficult times. Showing you seditious material, written against the Führer, is not something to be contemplated unless both parties are straight with each other. I think there needs to be a price.'

Schegel supposed that was how it worked. He was getting sucked in.

'As a matter of fact,' he said, 'I have something that may be of interest to you.'

He produced Anton Schlegel's copy of *Mein Kampf* and watched Rösti's eyes grow round.

'Can I touch it?' Rösti asked.

Schlegel made to hand the volumes over.

'Wait,' said Rösti, who made a show of putting on white

cotton gloves before inspecting both books with reverence. He produced a magnifying glass from a pocket and peered at the dedication. 'It's genuine. You can't be too careful these days. Anton Schlegel must have been a very special person to have earned one of these. Are you thinking of selling?'

'It depends. I am not sure. How much is it worth?'

'Do you have a figure in mind?'

Schlegel named an outrageous sum, as Christoph had told him to.

Rösti gave him a sharp look. 'Rather out of my league, but I am nonetheless tempted. It is unique. I have never heard of another copy of this edition being offered for sale. What does your friend Christoph say?'

'Books aren't really his thing.'

Rösti gave him another look as if to say that the price just offered by Schlegel was more likely to be Christoph's estimate. 'But it is a collector's holy grail. And still in its slipcase.'

'The whole thing looks like it has barely been touched.' Schlegel stopped short of saying 'unread'.

Rösti gurgled with unrestrained delight. 'Perhaps you would let me ask around on your behalf. My commission is twenty percent.'

'Maybe in the meantime you can show me some samples of Huber,' Schlegel suggested.

Rösti pondered and said, 'Follow me.'

He led the way into a back room where everything was even more topsy-turvy, with more leaning book towers, held up by stacked paintings and bric-à-brac. There was barely a path to the table under the window, which contained bound editions of old newspapers. 'Not filed in any particular order,' said Rösti.

For lack of space, Schlegel had to stand much closer to the

man than he wanted. Rösti continued flicking through the pages, paused and asked meaningfully, 'What do you know of the Führer's niece?'

Schlegel said he didn't recall any family.

'I expect you are too young to remember. It was in 1931. On the morning of Saturday, 19 September, the man's niece, Geli Raubal, was found dead after shooting herself, according to reports, on the floor of her room in the apartment she shared with her uncle. She even used his pistol, a Walther 6.35 – and what a choice item, if that were ever to come to sale. He was away on the road at the time.'

'Why did she do it?'

'In the end, the mystery remains. Perhaps she was a hysterical girl who could not reciprocate the love of a man almost twice her age.'

It sounded like bad opera, Schlegel thought. Hitler in love! The man's image insisted he was above all that. He asked what it had to do with Huber.

'Huber cried foul play. A big scandal, however you looked at it, but Huber really went for it, claiming the Führer was in the apartment at the time and not away as was being said. Huber reported that the girl's nose was broken and the body had extensive bruising.'

Schlegel knew the Party had a habit of getting rid of those it didn't like, but the man's niece? Or was Huber saying Hitler had done it himself? Warmonger or not, a domestic murder sounded altogether too far-fetched, and in the current climate of control both unimaginable and irretrievable.

Schlegel thought of the torn photograph of the Führer and his young female companion and asked Rösti, 'Do you have a picture of her?'

Rösti eventually unearthed a pile of society magazines,

some of which had articles on her 'fairy-tale rise', reporting how she had been plucked from obscurity as a sixteen-year-old by the Führer taking her 'under his wing'. More or less the same material was repeated each time, like it had been written up from a press release. At the time of her death the girl was about to embark on a distinguished musical career thanks to voice training undertaken at the Führer's expense so she could reward him by performing on the public stage.

Several magazines featured photographs of the girl, formal portraits all attributed to Heinrich Hoffman. There was no question. It was the same girl as in his photo. A bit bovine but bright and cheerful looking.

Rösti pondered. 'Look at this,' he said.

He turned back to the newspaper collection.

'Ah, yes. Here we are. The Führer, who was reported to be devastated by the death of the girl, was forced to issue a public denial, refuting the claims, in the very newspaper in which Huber was accusing him. Here's what it says: Not true that he was forever fighting with his niece Raubal or that they had a big fight on the Friday or anytime before. Not true that he was against her going to Vienna or her planned trip there. Not true that she was going to get engaged in Vienna or that he was against any engagement. However, it is true that she was tormented with worry over a forthcoming public appearance and wanted to go to Vienna to have her voice checked by a voice teacher. Not true that he left his apartment on 18 September after a fierce row, and he concludes by stating, "There was no row, no excitement, when I left my apartment on that day."'

Rösti closed the folder. 'A lot of muckraking went on over the Führer's love life. It was widely put about that he was a secret homo. His obvious devotion to his niece was taken as a way of disproving that. Perhaps I shouldn't be telling you this. Are you shocked?'

'Surprised. I hadn't realised the depths to which his enemies could stoop.'

'A dirty bunch. You can see why the press had to be tamed.'

'Does anyone know where Huber is now?'

'Scattered to the four winds is the thinking, but rumours persist that somewhere in a safe exists his completed account of the niece's death, with sworn affidavits.'

'Is this the document you were referring to in terms of Huber being relevant again?'

Rösti wouldn't confirm that but added smoothly, 'There is more.'

Schlegel suspected with Rösti there always was.

'What do I tell Christoph?'

'Tell him there is a signed confession.'

'Whose?'

Rösti smirked, refusing to say.

'Regarding the niece? A broken nose, you said.'

'My lips are sealed.'

'Are you saying the man confessed to killing the niece?'

'It would be a sensational document, even as mischief and a fake.'

'Why would anyone be interested in a forgery?'

Rösti spoke very slowly as though he were addressing a dim pupil. 'Because someone would have to have been *au fait* enough to create a plausible version. We are all familiar with *The Protocols of the Elders of Zion*.'

Schlegel dutifully parroted that it was taught in schools as an example of the Jewish plan for global domination.

'Quite so,' said Rösti. Except the original text was a series of fabrications by Tsarist Russia's secret police, so it was a deliberate act of misinformation which is still taken for fact.'

It was like being in a hall of mirrors, thought Schlegel, were it not for one obvious link between Rösti's story and recent events: on both occasions, the Führer was supposed to have been in two places at once. On 20 July in his field headquarters or in a Berlin clinic. And on the night of Friday, 18 September 1931 – away, as claimed, or at home with his soon-to-be-dead niece. Schlegel knew enough of the world to know if a lie works once it's worth repeating. He watched Rösti moisten his lips with his tongue and wondered if he was being dragged into something that was perhaps a splinter of the current conspiracy, and the two plot lines, past and present, would meet and join.

He asked, 'Was there any motive to get rid of the niece, if Huber is right?'

Rösti sighed. 'Who can say? Perhaps the most poignant detail: a pet canary, called Hansi, was found dead with her. Two birds, as it were, stopped from singing.'

He slopped drink down his front, sniggered and raised his glass. 'Cheers! It is interesting that you are here.'

'How so?'

'In terms of timing. You are an innocent from what I can see but I am bound to note the name.'

'With regard to Anton Schlegel?'

'Fredi Huber, Anton Schlegel – neither one meant anything a week ago and now you pop up here just as so many rumours are surfacing.'

'Is there more?'

'Oh, yes. Stories of private pornographic drawings made by him of the niece, and a highly indiscreet letter to her, oh-la-la.'

'Why now?' Schlegel asked.

'The drawings are said to be in play after all these years, but no one knows why or where they are. Now there's even talk of the girl's lost diary which, if she could string two sentences together, could be quite a bombshell. Some say it was the current mistress, Miss Quiet as a Mouse, that stole the diary.'

Schlegel decided the whole thing had the air of a confidence trick. But again why now and why was he being told? He decided to volunteer something of his own and said, 'I have a photograph of the niece taken in a restaurant with the Führer. Would that be of value?'

Rösti waggled his hand. 'That would have been Hoffmann, the Führer's official photographer. Two-a-penny, I am afraid.'

'It's not a formal photograph, it's a snapshot and badly taken. The Führer is caught in the middle of blinking.'

Rösti sat back seemingly overawed. 'There are no unofficial pictures of the man. I would need to see it. It might be worth a small fortune.'

'How do you account for this renewed interest in the niece?'

'Let's look at what there is. Huber's so-called exposé; the niece's so-called diary; various attributed artefacts ...'

'The drawings and the letter.'

'Yes, and the confession so-called.'

'All "so-called"?'

'It's a grey area. The fact of its existence makes the right object collectible, even if inauthentic, and was perhaps even forged deliberately, with a view to enticing such interest.'

'Is it coincidence, all of these items coming up now?'

'I would say it is almost certainly a controlled exercise.'

Schlegel was slow to gather the point. Rösti patiently had to explain that it was important to identify which was the key article in question. 'Let us say it is the girl's diary and, for the sake of argument, it is a fake, but the hope is to pass it off as real. The other material is put around it to build interest in that particular item. Of course, it is not out of the question that any such diary has been fabricated for subversive reasons, with the purpose perhaps of it surfacing abroad, don't you think?'

'Are you saying one person is behind all this?'

'Or a small group. It's called controlling the market. You have to admit you became more interested the more you were told.'

'Are you behind it?'

'Dear heart! Of course not. This is coming out of Munich and we're sitting here in Berlin.'

Schlegel questioned Christoph's motives in introducing him to Rösti, who was enticing him with a lot of alluring nonsense about secret diaries, improbable confessions, indiscreet letters and salacious drawings ... At the same time, he suspected the higher in the Party, the greater the stakes and the dirtier the gossip. Any of the material being floated by Rösti would be of value to the Führer's political rivals and take on an almost talismanic quality, if possessed. As for a 'confession' in which the man purportedly admitted killing the girl ...

Schlegel asked, 'The Führer last saw his niece after lunch on Friday the eighteenth but Huber disputed this?'

'Not very successfully. The Führer's car was issued with a speeding ticket the next morning.'

'Then he had a cast-iron alibi. What's to question?'

'Huber insisted there were inconsistencies to the man's schedule. In the official version, the Führer returned to Munich only on the Friday morning but Huber maintained the Führer was in town all along and on the Thursday he dined out with her until very late with her in a private room in a favourite restaurant. They were reported arguing and the Führer, unusually for him, was drinking alcohol.' Rösti raised his glass. 'Cheers!'

Schlegel said, 'The Führer's published statement denied a big fight on the Friday "or anytime before", so, if that was a reference to the Thursday row, who was the source?'

'The restaurant owner.'

Fuck, thought Schlegel. He knew the answer. Rösti confirmed that it was the Bratwurst Glöckl and Herr Zehnter. Schlegel asked himself if that was the real reason for Zehnter's name being on the same list as his father's.

They sat in silence until Rösti pulled a mournful face and announced that he had been perhaps a tad disingenuous.

Schlegel protested. 'On the contrary, you have told me everything I have asked.' Quite why, he couldn't tell.

'I wasn't sure how to bring it up.'

'What?'

'Anton Schlegel.' Rösti stared at the ceiling before going on. 'The death of the niece was a dirty business. Political opponents exploited it. The lies surrounding everything only grew. It wouldn't surprise me if the girl's diary turned out not to exist.'

'Then what's the point?'

'Most items surrounding the case are old hat. Stories about Huber's document go back years, the letter and the drawings too. The other stuff is new, suspiciously so.'

'I still don't see.'

'Probably hot air, but that's the point. Whatever is passed on by word of mouth can contain nuggets of planted information yet to be revealed.'

'And the confession?'

'Too good to be true, wouldn't you say? The story has been peddled for years that he did her in but nothing stuck.

That lot in Munich at the time couldn't keep a secret if their lives depended on it, so stories of any confession would have circulated from the beginning.'

'And Anton Schlegel?'

'Another new rumour. In among all this you sometimes hear that the supposed confession is wrongly ascribed. It is not the Führer confessing, but Anton Schlegel.'

'Saying he killed the girl?'

Rösti shrugged. 'Stories carry on the wind.'

Schlegel's first thought about what he had just been told was: Well, that makes sense. It was doubtless just another addition to the farrago of surmise being peddled by Rösti, but even if it weren't true it did at least make sense to Schlegel. Perhaps he wanted it to be true. Perhaps he wanted his father to have crossed a line that made any hope of reclaiming him irretrievable.

'What do you think?' Schlegel asked.

'If either confession ever existed someone, against the run of play, was very good at keeping secrets.'

'But something is going on.'

'Something is definitely going on.' Rösti looked at him with amusement. 'You must come again. I must say a package for sale involving Anton Schlegel's *Mein Kampf*, your photograph of the niece and a copy of Anton's confession would make for a mouthwatering collection.'

Schlegel felt suddenly quite giddy. He couldn't decide if it was the drink or overall bamboozlement at what he had learned that day: first, casting calls for the Führer and now being pitched back into a phantasmagorical past, with his father being paraded as the possible murderer of the Führer's niece. In contrast to all the usual censorship and oppression, it was quite exhilarating.

The answer to his next question left him sober and

surprised. He asked what more Rösti could tell him about Anton Schlegel.

Rösti took his time answering. 'When his name first came up not long ago, I did some checking. Dark horse. No trace, apart from an archivist in Munich who was surprised I was asking as no one had enquired after the man in years. He said in those days Anton Schlegel was the only one that did not come to the Führer. The Führer went to him.'

'His role?'

'Unspecified. But according to my man, Anton Schlegel was the man who made the Führer what he is.'

As Schlegel left, Rösti asked if he could 'borrow' the *Mein Kampf* as there were a couple of wealthy customers he had in mind. Schlegel said he wasn't sure. In the end he was too drunk to care. Cajoling resulted in Rösti promising he would guard the book with his life. On the train back Schlegel sat wondering if he was being conned and decided instead that he was pleased to be rid of the thing. It wasn't just his briefcase that felt lighter.

The following morning, none of what Rösti had told Schlegel counted in the cold light of day as he sat down to begin his report on that dull Sunday. He stared at the blank page, nursing a crashing hangover. The previous afternoon felt like an unpleasant interlude presided over by a comic but malignant presence. Anton Schlegel, Huber and all the rest were of no help to the task in hand. It even crossed Schlegel's mind that the episode was a prank set up by Christoph; that's what his hangover told him as he glumly contemplated what he should write in his report. Besides, even if Anton Schlegel had been involved with the Führer's niece, it was not a stone Schlegel was about to overturn, through choice or opportunity. He sighed and addressed himself to the blank sheet of paper.

They were now expected to work every other Sunday, according to a roster. A week ago, Schlegel had been at the lakes with Gerda. He had a message to call Frau Busl. He got no answer. Did it matter? Dunkelwert wasn't in, he was pleased to see. It was being said she was spending more time in important Party meetings. She seemed to have the office whipped into shape. Schlegel had heard the first remarks of grudging respect: tougher than any man. Everyone was giddy from the number of arrests. Cells were so full that a temporary holding centre had to be set up. Colleagues smacked palms together in shows of celebration as if their team had won.

As for his predicament, Schlegel identified two different motions at work: they suck you in then they hang you out to dry. He suspected he had been marked all along. The same arguments flew around his head: malign intent versus incompetence, currents of subterfuge so deep they would buckle the plates on a bathysphere; all interpretations equally valid.

He continued to stare at the empty page, incapable of writing. How many Führers were there? Several had been auditioned. Given that the agent Busl knew too much, what had become of them since? If there was a pattern of secret duplicates or stand-ins or doubles or decoys, were they sent to the clinic to emerge more Führer-like? Schlegel supposed the point was to fool the enemy into believing the Führer was in several places at once.

The more he stared at the blank sheet the more he was left wondering whether there was even an actual Führer, and if he hadn't become a phantom, leaving only an image to be manipulated by others. Perhaps the man was long gone, either dispatched or in secret retreat as stated in the letter which claimed he had been gone since 1943 and could now be found working in the Vatican library. An absurd notion suddenly no longer seemed so far-fetched. The man hadn't been openly seen in years and had barely uttered a word in public for eighteen months.

In terms of the various Führers, Schlegel noted the one that had narrowly avoided being blown up and whether he was a stooge as suggested by the Allied newsreel. Second, there was the one briefly glimpsed standing in the clinic corridor by the cleaning woman. Schlegel had an impression of many Führer secrets being kept behind the clinic's steel door in some kind of scientific laboratory. Third, there was the invisible man who had checked into the clinic on the Tuesday.

Schlegel found himself unable to dismiss the falling man and whether that had been some terrible image of the abandoned Führer. Who else would warrant such a cover up?

Schlegel stared at the still empty page. He could hardly write that the fate of the clinic was indistinguishable from the identity of the Führer.

19

The next morning, Schlegel was in Müller's office within minutes of arriving, picked off by Dunkelwert.

'Upstairs,' she said, giving nothing away.

Müller was perched on the secretary's desk in his outer office and the two were giggling, a sight so astonishing that Schlegel gawped. The woman was such a hatchet face she looked like she had never cracked a smile in her life.

Müller stood and motioned for him to follow. He seemed in a good mood, which lasted all of ten seconds.

Standing behind his desk, Müller asked, 'Do you have anything to say?'

Quite a lot actually, Schlegel thought, and said, 'No, sir.'

He felt the air being sucked out of him while Müller looked at him like he was a bug that deserved squishing.

'What am I supposed to do with you?'

Schlegel stared hard at the floor.

Müller flicked through Schlegel's report. 'Writer of anonymous letter, unidentified. A suggestion that a man seen checking into the clinic on the Tuesday *may* have been the Führer.' Müller gave Schlegel a sarcastic look. 'Not an appointment confirmed by the Führer's diary. I checked with Party Secretary Bormann. The day passed in transit. Security prevents me from saying more.' He returned to Schlegel's document. 'And your extraordinary assertion that Dr Goebbels spent the morning of 20 July interviewing actors who could pass for the Führer. What are we to make of that? You don't say.' Müller tossed the paper aside. 'A report that is remarkably short of conclusions. Are you aware of any talk of Dr Goebbels staging an assassination attempt as a publicity stunt?'

'To rally support for the Führer? Not in so many words.'

'Then what?' asked Müller irritably. 'Don't try and do clever fencing with me.'

Schlegel had cold sweats.

'The British newsreel said as much.'

'Then you did hear it in so many words.'

'I put that down to enemy propaganda.'

'Then why does the good doctor indulge in a casting call on the morning the Führer is due to be assassinated?'

Schlegel had no answer to that. He was in danger of visibly shaking.

Müller snorted, 'I trust what you've got isn't catching.'

'I sometimes get dizzy spells.' He didn't add: Since shooting a lot of people in a ditch.

Müller said, 'Let's hear what Dr Goebbels has to say.'

Goebbels made Schlegel wait an hour in the outer office. Sometimes he emerged, waving papers, was charming to secretaries, ignored Schlegel and went back in. Schlegel, having spent the walk over gazing in a state of disbelief at ordinary life going on, thought he should usefully spend the time reviewing his options and gave up as he didn't seem to have any.

'Explain,' Goebbels ordered when at last Schlegel was shown in, his mind dead from churning anxiety.

Goebbels was sitting behind his huge desk, the size of a small atoll.

Schlegel deliberately explained himself badly, in the hope

that he would be taken for a bumbling idiot; he stopped well short of any mention of Dr Goebbels defacing the casting directory.

Goebbels screwed the top back on his fountain pen, sat back and sighed. 'What do you know about the Führer?'

'What you tell us, Minister,' said Schlegel in a desperate attempt to show some spine.

Goebbels threw back his head and gave an unfunny laugh, showing gold teeth.

'And these stories about doubles used for the Führer? What the British call stooges.'

'For strategic reasons, I presume.'

'More complicated than that, theological even. What do you remember of your divinity and the Holy Trinity?'

Schlegel said it was the union of three persons in one godhead.

'Exactly. Similarly, the Führer is a man, a leader and a figurehead. The Führer is unique, so the man cannot be replaced. His leadership cannot be duplicated, but he can under special circumstances be represented as a figurehead.'

A tutorial from Dr Goebbels.

'What you have to understand, Schlegel, is that the Führer's image was always the point. From the very start, he presented himself as an enigma, to build curiosity about the movement. No photographs! The charismatic leader who refuses to stoop to cheap reproduction. The only way people can find out what he looks like is by attending the meetings.'

The transformation in Goebbels was extraordinary. Talking of the Führer, he became transfixed by religious adoration. He spoke on, apparently oblivious of Schlegel.

'No photos! Cameras smashed! The buzz grows tremendous. What does the man look like? As early as 1922, an

American photographic agency puts a price on the Führer's head. One hundred dollars for a picture when the going rate is five! And no one collects the bounty, thanks to the vigilance of the Führer's praetorian guard.' Goebbels growled, 'They kick the shit out of anyone who tries.'

The inference was obvious. They still do.

Goebbels stood and paced in an arc behind Schlegel, who was thrown for being unable to see him.

The lecture resumed. 'The first time a double was used other than as a decoy, was in 1924 when the Führer was a political prisoner.'

Goebbels circled in front of Schlegel, gesturing to say that the thought of an incarcerated Führer was impossible to imagine.

'Anyway, what we might call the more artistic among his followers decide to stage a Christmas *tableau vivant* in the Café Blüte in honour of him.'

Goebbels moved behind Schlegel as he continued. 'Picture a prison cell on a half-lit stage, showing a man sitting with his back to the audience, face buried in his hands, while an invisible male choir sings "Stille Nacht, Heilige Nacht".' Through a barred window, snowflakes are seen falling. As the music ends a tiny angel enters and places an illuminated Christmas tree on the table beside the lonely man.'

Goebbels found it impossible not to laugh. 'In film production the biggest battles are always hair and makeup. In this job the greatest struggle is against kitsch, and in those early days there was an awful lot of it. But when the prisoner turns to the audience many think it is indeed the Führer – miraculously transported from his cell – and a half-sob goes up. You may think the whole thing sounds like tosh but the *effect* is what counts.'

Schlegel noticed how Goebbels seemed able to switch effortlessly between the ecstatic and sarcastic.

'Achenbach, the stooge cast by Hoffmann: uncanny resemblance, everyone said.' Goebbels gave a bark. 'The man has been duly rewarded, with the Bureau of Investigation for Aryan Racial Purity to run.'

Goebbels looked at his watch, an expensive Heuer. It was typical of the man to share his appreciation. 'Nice, isn't it? Three more minutes in which we decide what to do with you.'

Goebbels had the same shiny currant-bun eyes as children's teddy bears, which Schlegel had once found so sinister. See nothing and record everything.

Goebbels snapped his fingers. 'You were here that afternoon the Army made its pathetic attempt to take over. Imagine how I felt booking a call to the Führer and thinking, oh the irony because only that morning, as you say, I was at Babelsberg, seeking actors who can pass for him.'

Schlegel thought the appearance of Goebbels sharing the confidence was probably a way of lulling him into a sense of false security.

'With the Führer otherwise so engaged' – Goebbels broke off with his winning smile – 'a think tank concluded it would enormously help public relations to have a substitute, to boost morale, visiting war-damaged areas, like the British Royal Family and the warmonger Churchill. Given what happened next, perhaps better if no record of that morning's session is available. Imagine. Casting for a stand-in on the very day someone decides to try and kill the Führer. Then you go and find me out!'

It was all so light and teasing and skittish, with every hurdle effortlessly jumped.

Schlegel asked about Busl, since he was dead. Goebbels

stopped, apparently stricken, and reached for Schlegel's arm with a clawlike hand. Schlegel resisted flinching.

'My God! What a tragedy! We discussed his illness. Busl didn't have long. He asked me my thoughts on suicide. I said as long as there is hope he should banish them. He said there was none. Well, there's nothing you can say to that. The man went back years – he discovered Peter Lorre and worked with Lang. A pity so much talent had to leave to churn out third-rate rubbish in Hollywood. The maker of the fabulous *Metropolis* reduced what they call oaters. Cowboy stuff, bang-bang shoot-'em-ups, compared to the visions we would have entrusted him with. I begged him to stay! But poor Busl. There was hope, though too late. The hospital had muddled his diagnosis with another. Such a sad story.'

Told with such brio, it seemed churlish not to believe him, however obvious it was that Goebbels was making it up on the spot. It was like watching a supreme piece of improvisation by a musician.

Schlegel pictured Goebbels's memorandum to himself the moment Schlegel had left the room, writing him off: Be rid of him.

Green ink.

Schlegel's impression as he walked out and marched jerkily down the long corridors was of everything starting to move at double speed. People seemed to come at him very fast, slowed for a second, and were gone, swallowed up in the wake of the corridor, as if chucked overboard.

Outside he panicked. He had questioned Goebbels' authority, and also offended his vanity by daring to question him. The reflex action of such men was disposal. The price of the shared secret would be his removal, one way or another. Schlegel had never been so aware of his insignificance and expendability. A relief almost.

The streets seemed to be full of men following him. He walked on aimlessly, half expecting to be picked up and bundled into a car, no doubt by the same two thugs as before. All the while he was thinking how they had worked out that you could remove people from the system and those still in it would be too scared or grateful or obedient to object to all the bodies in cellars, high falls, deported cleaners and the countless others he didn't know about. Schlegel knew the world wouldn't stop for a second when his turn came. It was only a matter of time now. Presumably death had a backlog too, with so many still to dispose of before it got around to him.

It wasn't even an imposed, totalitarian vision, these state-sanctioned deaths; more like housekeeping and the will to tidy, with a lot of 'follow my leader' and attention paid to what they were sold. No more crooked lines – a bright new future, pale wood, clean technology, private washing machines, family automobiles, the radio network. All that was understandable: away with the dark past, no shadows, don't look back, self-reliance, helping each other out, a daily brightness, a healthy future. Then the small print about what doesn't belong. 'Oh, excuse me, you're in the way, stand over there . . .' 'Oh, you don't want to? Why not?' Thump.

Everyone else is looking the other way.

Schlegel went home and waited for Gerda and was about to give up and go to bed when he heard her light footstep on the stairs and her voice counting them off.

She asked what he thought about children. He said he didn't on the whole, sensing what was coming, thinking it far too soon to be having such a conversation.

Gerda announced that she wanted their child. Schlegel was unable to tell if she was being flirtatious or in earnest, until she said, 'Perhaps I am having it already.'

'Are you serious?'

'Only teasing.'

Schlegel wasn't so sure. They had been careless about contraception.

'Not straight away,' she went on. 'But let's soon.'

He still couldn't tell if she meant it. She seemed in a strange unreadable mood. He wanted only to talk about something else.

'It's not the right time of month yet,' she said, adding suggestively, 'But practice makes perfect.'

He wondered if she suspected she was already pregnant and telling him she wanted a child was so it would not look like an accident.

As she surrendered herself, Schlegel decided her wish was a fantasy to distract from the impending return of the maimed boyfriend, and as he thrust at her he wondered at this strange female world, even more impenetrable than all the others he was dealing with.

20

The following morning, Schlegel found himself deep in the heart of the Chancellery as if in the middle of a dream of malign intent, summoned there with no idea of what to expect.

Dunkelwert had confronted him in the office, telling him, 'You are instructed to present yourself to Party Secretary Bormann at the Chancellery at eleven o'clock.'

Schlegel knew nothing of Bormann, except that he was known as the Brown Eminence. He looked at Dunkelwert for an explanation.

She repeated, 'Eleven o'clock. Report back here afterwards. We have questions for you. And get a haircut. You can't turn up looking like that.'

Schlegel was so fidgety during the barber's shave that he got cut and had to be left in the chair, waiting for the bleeding to stop while avoiding himself in the mirror. He was still unsettled by Gerda's announcement the night before. The matter had not been referred to again and when Gerda left she was back to her brisk, usual self. Schlegel wondered if she was more unstable or emotionally excitable than she let on.

The barber, annoyed at having his hand disturbed, proceeded to give Schlegel a brutal haircut when he had asked for a trim, leaving his ears sticking out.

He went home and ironed his least unpresentable suit

using a damp cloth. He pressed the cuffs, collar and front of a once-white shirt, trying hard not to think.

Shoes were more of a problem as Schlegel had run out of polish and there was a shortage. He stopped off at the Adlon which still had a shoe-shine man. He had lost the best part of a leg and knelt on the stump. Schlegel watched as cardboard was stuck down the side of his shoes to protect the socks and the tired leather was coaxed into something resembling respectability. He was surprised in the end at how presentable he looked. His haircut gave him an altogether graver appearance, like a professional mourner or undertaker ... about to attend his own funeral.

The scale of the government buildings performed their usual task of reminding all approaching outsiders of their puny existence. More marbled corridors of power. More unholy acolytes. Nothing frivolous. The Chancellery trumped even Dr Goebbels' preposterous ministry in proclaiming itself the temple of orthodoxy.

Schlegel's name was ticked off as he passed through several security locks that took him into the nerve centre of the building until he reached the Party Secretary's office, where he was told by a frighteningly efficient secretary to wait in an outer sanctum the size of a tennis court and full of horrible practical furniture.

Schlegel sweated into his suit as he sat there in the forlorn hope that someone would come out and send him back after telling him it was a mistake.

The short man with a belly and a receding hairline who hurried in, cupping a cigarette on which he took a last drag before putting it out, Schlegel recognised immediately as the official standing attentively with agitated hands in the bomb-plot newsreel, and, before that, next to his stepfather in the photograph.

He introduced himself as Party Secretary Bormann. He seemed in a jolly mood, capable and friendly.

Schlegel gave his name in return. The other man took a step back, in surprise, and said, 'You are different from what I was expecting.'

Expecting?

Bormann led the way to a tall window looking out onto the extensive Chancellery gardens. He lit another cigarette and motioned for Schlegel to join him. Schlegel doubted if he had been brought there to admire the view.

Bormann asked, 'Why were you in Budapest last week?'

It was the last question Schlegel was expecting.

He could hear how doubtful he sounded as he said he had been delivering papers for signature and return.

Bormann looked crafty and amused. 'And the Japanese gentleman who broke into your room?'

Schlegel's knees sagged. How on earth did the man know about that? He considered and decided it wasn't so surprising. The Budapest Astoria was a hotbed of international intrigue and no doubt Bormann was kept fully informed and probably knew more about why Schlegel had been there than he did.

'He must have mistaken me for someone else. I had nothing worth stealing.'

Again, Bormann appeared amused as he said, 'I will leave that to Dunkelwert.'

Christ! thought Schlegel. Was Dunkelwert working directly for Bormann as one of his apparatchiks? That put a completely different complexion on everything.

'Fine view,' said Bormann conversationally.

A couple of gardeners busied themselves with weeding. Fuel restrictions seemed not to have reached the Chancellery because Schlegel could hear a two-stroke mower.

He decided to offer a small gambit of his own, having nothing to lose. 'I have a photograph of you with my stepfather.'

Bormann knew immediately what he was talking about. 'Taken ages ago. Seven, maybe eight years.'

'There's a third man in the photograph.'

'An American,' said Bormann. 'They were around then. Think carefully what you say to Dunkelwert about Budapest, given that two men wanted for conspiracy sent you. Of course, if you hear from your stepfather I would be obliged if you inform me directly.'

Schlegel had the sensation of being about to put his foot in a mantrap and watch it snap shut.

Bormann took Schlegel by the crook of the elbow and said, 'As for your mother and that unfortunate business of harbouring a Jew, there are facilities elsewhere, better than her present ones, where confinement more resembles a sanitarium with medical attention and the guests are of a better class. I can arrange for her to be sent there.'

Depending on what? Was Schlegel being bought off in some obscure way?

There was no time to find out. The gardeners outside were making themselves scarce and the lawnmower stopped. Schlegel stood watching the empty view, then a man and a German Shepherd came into view. The man threw a stick for the dog to fetch. The dog broke off from its chasing to deposit a huge turd on the lawn.

Schlegel stared at the trademark forelock and moustache. It was obvious who it was. It was equally obvious Schlegel had been brought there to see it was.

His first impression was how stooped and aged the man was compared to the propaganda images. He even wondered for a moment if it really was the Führer, then realised it had to be because they wouldn't show him such a decrepit-looking double.

The Führer was capless. Schlegel had heard the man's eyes were light-sensitive but suspected it was probably just a story to enhance the impression of their glorious leader seeing the world more acutely than the rest of them; a benign version of the Nosferatu legend.

The doughy features reminded Schlegel of childhood gingerbread men before they got fired in the oven. Not the most appropriate image, and Schlegel thought he might yet break into peals of deadly, hysterical laughter, and Bormann would produce a pistol and put him down like a mad dog.

'Well?' asked Bormann. 'Do you know why you are here?'

'You want me to confirm I have seen the Führer.'

'According to Müller, your mind has been in some doubt; turmoil, even.'

Schlegel understood. Bormann was showing him the Führer to put an end to any speculation. His role was a variation of a line-up witness identifying a party.

'And your best theory?' Bormann asked mildly.

Schlegel suspected Bormann was insatiable in his quest for knowledge in pursuit of power, which was why he wanted to hear Schlegel's version. There seemed no point in not saying as he was probably as good as done for anyway.

'I mistakenly came to believe the Führer was in a clinic at the time of the failed assassination.'

Schlegel decided his only plea was temporary insanity.

'Which clinic is that?'

'One in Westend. It burned down.'

The Führer and his dog were back to their stick games. After each retrieval the dog sat waiting to be rewarded with a treat and a pat on the head.

The Führer had a rather girly throw, Schlegel noticed as he said, 'I saw a man falling from the roof of the clinic.'

'Excuse me?' asked Bormann, sounding properly surprised.

'I foolishly thought the man falling from the roof was the Führer.' He still did in a way, for all the evidence in front of his eyes.

'Why on earth?' asked Bormann.

'I came to believe he had been abandoned. It was a time of great confusion.'

'Yet the Führer walks before us.'

'I see that now. I was wrong to have doubted.'

Schlegel suspected he was fighting for his life, and that Bormann knew what Schlegel was talking about and wasn't telling.

'You were deluded,' said Bormann as he thought: Closer than you know, my friend.

'The clinic had been evacuated. I thought at first it must be someone who had got drunk and passed out and woken up too late, then I didn't know what to think because the falling figure appeared to be wearing a straightjacket.'

'But you couldn't have seen the body, otherwise you would have known.'

'It was engulfed in the flames.'

Bormann laughed with what sounded like relief and asked, 'What on earth led you to believe the Führer was alone in a blazing building?'

Schlegel said he didn't know. He saw that wasn't enough and hurried on. 'There was a steel door and a secret section and the Führer was once seen in the corridor. Because of that . . .'

He trailed off. He supposed now – watching the man play with his dog – that the falling man had been more like some monstrous sacrifice to appease the gods. He was sure that the fact of talking to Bormann about it meant the two were connected.

Instead he said, 'I questioned the Führer's existence when I should not have done.'

Bormann gave him a lecture on doubt and misunderstanding while Schlegel retained the almost certainly misguided opinion that he was seen as more of a curiosity than a threat.

'Is disloyalty hereditary?' Bormann asked. 'Your mother and stepfather have betrayed the regime. It is time you proved yourself.'

Schlegel ventured, 'And my father before that?'

Bormann made a whistling noise. 'An upsetting subject does not need further upset. Tread with great care as you climb down from the high and dangerous ledge you are on.'

Said in a way more friendly than not, it nevertheless left Schlegel in no doubt of the man's brute force.

Outside, the Führer was passing under their window, glancing up at Schlegel with a look that said he might as well not exist. With that he was gone, like a vampire leaving no trace, his presence more like a visitation, representing not belonging, the messiah who sacrifices himself for his people. Schlegel found it impossible to connect the subdued, intense man playing with his dog to Rösti's salacious tales of sexual scandal and the death of the Führer's niece, and if she were somehow the man's Achilles heel, where did that leave Anton Schlegel?

Schlegel didn't expect to find himself reminded of the bodies in the clinic, yet the connection between what he had just been shown and their deaths made complete sense in that moment. The man's eyes, in which Schlegel had expected to see the depths of something, had revealed nothing but pointlessness. Schlegel now understood how this superior indifference, and the machine's response to that, ended in meaningless death.

The identity of the Führer was resolved. Whatever had gone on in the clinic could be written off and in exchange for Schlegel's silence his mother would benefit. But it wasn't that straightforward. If Bormann knew all the answers, Schlegel's future was now in the man's hands.

'We understand each other?' Bormann asked.

Did they? Whatever had gone on, equilibrium now looked to be restored and Schlegel could be counted on to sing the authorised version.

Unless of course it wasn't over; or, rather, was over for him, being next in line, if his role was considered done. There was still the hurdle of Dunkelwert. They wouldn't do anything before that.

Schlegel's dismissal was like shutters coming down, within the space of time it took Bormann to tell him he could go. He could see he was forgotten before he had left the room.

There was one last unwelcome surprise in the anteroom: the odious Hermann Fegelein flirting with the secretaries. He looked up as Schlegel walked out as stiffly as an automaton. Schlegel stared, disconcerted by the sight of the man. He registered Fegelein's flicker of recognition and the start of a sneer before he was blanked as the man brushed past him. Fegelein opened the door to the office and Schlegel heard Bormann on the telephone saying, 'He's all yours.'

He departed with the uncomfortable impression it was said deliberately loud enough for him to hear and that Bormann had meant for Fegelein to be in the room when he left.

21

Bormann put down the receiver, thinking it was not often he was caught on the hop. The falling man was not part of the script. On reflection, it was almost funny: the fake Führer proving so hard to finish off, having survived the blast when he should not have. One botched job and so nearly a second, leaving the bloody understudy crashing about on a burning roof. Some idiot must have got the dose wrong. Still, a spectacular curtain call for an audience of one, soon to be none. Better than almost funny.

'Drinkies?' suggested Fegelein as he swanned in, wanting to know what Schlegel had been doing there.

'I am curious to know whether he has the foggiest idea why he was in Budapest,' Bormann said, thinking what a cock-up that had proved, thanks partly to the man standing before him.

Fegelein said, 'He's too stupid to work anything out.'

Bormann was still thinking about the falling man. Too close a call, but providence was on his side. Time to get loaded.

The Führer's timetable was scheduled to allow Bormann and Fegelein, a serious toper, to get drunk at lunchtime. The Führer siesta often meant he didn't surface before evening. Work got done at night, as a substitute for insomnia. Bormann preferred attending to his duties with a hangover.

Bormann poured drinks. They sat, loosened their collars and got down to the serious business of Fegelein's moist tales of his latest conquests, his recent marriage notwithstanding. The talk was of sex and women: ones had, ones wanted, those fancied, all seen with a practiced eye. Contrast and compare, quality of flesh, line of beauty; two lovers of women testing dangerous curves and the limits of desire, with toasts to the proud knights of the flaming bush. Grubby fucking, in other words. Bormann did not delude himself, whereas Fegelein did. They were not selective. Bormann took refuge where he could, which translated as 'pick them plain, they are ever so grateful.' Ploughed conquest being the point.

Fegelein's rosebud mouth went slack after a couple of drinks. Bormann knew he could be indiscreet because Fegelein liked to drink himself to a standstill even in the middle of the day. When Bormann saw he was pie-eyed he announced, 'We swapped the Führer.'

Bormann wanted to know how it sounded aloud. Good, actually.

Fegelein made saucer eyes.

'Reeeally?'

Like many cavalry men, Fegelein was mannered and drawled. He gave a big blink, an exaggerated double take, and said, 'You what?' as smoke poured from his nose.

Bormann saw Fegelein already wasn't capable of taking in much. The voice was starting to slide and the memory puddle. Bormann could say more or less anything because Fegelein when drunk was the mental equivalent of a lost luggage office: whole trunks went missing, never to be retrieved.

'You did what?' Fegelein asked again, not sure he had heard.

Bormann ignored him and wondered aloud at what point everything had got fucked. He could have men shot for asking less, but with Fegelein any talk stayed in the room.

'There's fucked and fucked,' said Fegelein sagely.

Stalingrad was a big fuck, they agreed. Tiny Goebbels' finest hour; gigantic speech at the Sportpalast. Standing ovation, unending stormy applause. Total war.

'Now there's a slogan to get your teeth into,' slurred Fegelein.

'What wouldn't the little fellow do for such rapture now?' asked Bormann.

Fegelein reminisced instead about the noisy thrusting of a big-breasted actress – an extra more like, who maintained she was a supporting player; blink and you would miss her. This one, passed on by Fegelein for what they called road testing, was between a blonde and a redhead, a collector's item that made Bormann think of strawberries. He had gone at her with the pump and vigour of a barnyard animal, pummelling her soft fruit until she was squeaking, lathered, hair stuck to forehead, arm thrown back in surrender, the sight of a wet tinge of underarm hair driving him on as she panted for him not to stop.

He made her take him in her mouth, promising not to come.

'Too frightened not to swallow,' Fegelein sniggered, nodding off.

Fucked, Bormann remembered thinking in the moment of release. She said she preferred the girth of Bormann's prick to Fegelein's pencil shaft. One subject he and Fegelein never discussed was the Führer's dick.

'Did you think it would work?' Fegelein asked vaguely. He meant the swap. Bormann saw the man hadn't a clue.

While Bormann was getting Fegelein drunk enough not to remember, an increasingly uncomfortable Schlegel was being stared at by a portrait of the Führer, looking more focused and alert than he had in the flesh.

Chris Petit

It was a standard interview room, with basic table and chairs, unadorned apart from the portrait on the wall facing the interrogation chair.

The window looked inwards onto the yard.

Schlegel supposed Dunkelwert as inquisitor was Bormann's immediate Party representative.

She was with an older officer Schlegel had never seen before, probably some form of obscure, higher SS security, with the hard look that was all the rage these days. Dunkelwert smoked. The sidekick smoked. There were no ashtrays and they flicked ash on the floor. The room would soon become a haze. Schlegel asked if he could open the window, forgetting the window didn't open.

When Dunkelwert asked when he had last seen his stepfather, her eyes glittered behind smudged glasses and she showed her teeth in anticipation. He answered by saying he had seen very little of his mother and stepfather in recent years.

'For what reason?' asked Dunkelwert.

'They struck me as frivolous. They were entertainers.'

He knew he was on dangerous ground and it took him a long time to say, 'I came to suspect my stepfather of denouncing my mother.'

Did he believe that? Why not? It so often turned out to be the case. The point was to divert Dunkelwert from any possible connection between himself and his stepfather and the events of 20 July. It was obvious she had her traps set.

Schlegel ploughed on. 'He was right to do so but I found it hard to come to terms. I even considered psychiatric help.'

Dunkelwert chased him on that.

Schlegel said he felt blighted by the association of his mother harbouring a Jew.

'Were you angry with your stepfather for not bringing the matter to your attention?'

192

'At least I could have tried to dissuade her from such foolishness.'

'And not report it?'

'She is my mother, after all. I am sure she would have seen reason.'

Schlegel wondered what Dunkelwert's mother was like.

He hoped he was getting across that he was generally rather useless and not worth their bother. This seemed to be confirmed by Dunkelwert's companion regarding him like he was shit on his shoe.

Dunkelwert asked, 'Where is your stepfather now?'

'I have no idea. We are not in the business of keeping each other informed,' Schlegel said primly.

'He is currently a wanted man.'

'Yes, so I heard.'

'How come?'

'I was told his name was on a provisional government list.'

'How come?'

Schlegel passed on the story about Nebe being seen waving such a list on the morning of the 20th.

'And your reaction?'

'I consider my stepfather far too timid for anything like that. He never gave any evidence of having a single conviction in his life.'

Schlegel hoped Dunklewert took that to mean Schlegel was talking about himself as much as his stepfather. He needed to be careful of growing blasé. Keep it as tight and as personal as possible, he thought, while privately ashamed of such bartering.

They moved on to Nebe. Schlegel was able to say he was an old friend of the family who had been asked to take care of his career.

'I was ineligible for military service.'

'Asthma,' said Dunkelwert, consulting her notes, looking doubtful.

Schlegel waved his hand to show their smoke was upsetting him.

Schlegel wondered when the sidekick would take over but the man just stared at his crushed butts on the floor.

Dunkelwert tried to build a case against Christoph by getting Schlegel to admit Christoph had seduced him when they were younger.

'We were friends! Categorically, *no*.'

'When did you become aware of his persuasion?'

When he said he loved me was the correct answer.

'Christoph never struck me as flamboyant. He was just a friend.'

Five more minutes of wrangling got Dunkelwert nowhere.

'Let's move on to why you went to Budapest.'

'I think everyone knows now I took papers to be signed and returned concerning acquisition of an art collection. By the SS.'

'Budapest is a city of notorious international intrigue,' Dunkelwert recited stiffly. 'Nothing else? Given the date.'

'No.'

'Did you wonder why you had been selected?'

'Gruppenführer Nebe asked me to go.'

'But as you no longer work for him he must have asked you privately.'

'That's right.'

'You agreed, obviously. Why, if it wasn't an order?'

'I felt obligated. Gruppenführer Nebe had taken an interest in my career.'

Dunkelwert snorted. 'What career?'

'Gruppenführer Nebe is also a friend of my stepfather.'

'Why did you report sick to the office and not say what you were doing?'

'Gruppenführer Nebe asked me not to.' Schlegel leaned forward, as if confiding. 'He thought there was a risk of the operation being compromised because of spies. He was mistrustful of the Gestapo being too open to what he called "all bidders".'

Dunkelwert pounced. 'What operation? You said it was about signing documents.'

Schlegel brushed the question aside. 'It was. But it was a sensitive sale, with other interested parties. It was important to get in first.'

He sat back, doing his best to appear relaxed.

Dunkelwert looked sulky. She had thought she'd had him.

'Gruppenführer Nebe and your stepfather have since been exposed as part of the conspiracy. Have you thought if your mission had any connection with that?'

Obviously, he had. He was scared witless at the thought that he was part of several overlapping intrigues. He was just about bright enough to understand it was a time of variable and conflicting offences.

He also saw it was necessary to persuade Dunkelwert he had known exactly what he was about.

He said, 'I wish to speak off the record.'

The sidekick looked at Schlegel as though he were talking Double Dutch. He turned to Dunkelwert, who said she supposed it was all right.

Schlegel took a deep breath and decided to improvise by dumping on Fegelein, reciting the choicest details from the man's file.

'Fegelein has a history of corruption going back years. There was a case of looted fur coats from Warsaw being sold on the domestic market '

Next, he told them who Morgen was. 'An investigative prosecutor. We worked together when I was in financial crime at CID.'

'When?' asked Dunkelwert.

'March last year until November. Morgen is now in Budapest, still chasing Fegelein, who has an associate there from his Warsaw days, Becher. Morgen believes the same corrupt operation is being repeated in Budapest, under Fegelein's hand.'

Schlegel had no idea if that were the case. He was beyond any point of truth and determined only to convince Dunkelwert with the aid of a well-placed lie that he had a plausible hidden motive.

'And your real reason for being there,' Dunkelwert said.

'Money,' Schlegel said.

'Money?'

'I went to Budapest to give Morgen money. He was running low on funds.'

The truth was, he still hadn't the faintest idea about had really been going on.

'Explain about these funds,' said Dunkelwert.

'Morgen was freelancing for Nebe, who was running the operation off the books and underwriting it because he believed Fegelein has a case to answer.'

Schlegel decided his version was messy enough to pass for the truth. He almost believed it himself: Müller's golden thread. But that didn't explain Morgen's blunt hostility towards him in Budapest or why when Schlegel walked in the room Morgen had looked like a man caught out.

22

Morgen was standing at a tall window, overlooking a large semi-tropical garden, his hands clasped behind his back. He turned as they entered. Because he was silhouetted Schlegel wasn't sure for a moment if it was actually Morgen.

They were in a grand stucco house on a spectacular boulevard in the centre of the modern part of Budapest. A manservant had answered the door to Schlegel. The occupants were in the process of moving out. Pictures had been taken down, leaving lighter patches on silk wallpaper. A smooth, good-looking man in shirtsleeves strolled into the hall, smiled amiably, introduced himself as Becher and took Schlegel through a billiard room, where an unfinished game lay on the table, into a large library.

Schlegel supposed he must have have stared. Morgen was the last person he expected to see.

Becher asked, 'You know each other?' He appeared piqued. Schlegel supposed it was his show.

Morgen shrugged and lit up. 'Berlin, then near Kattowitz, last year.'

Schlegel thought Kattowitz a very coy way of describing Auschwitz and the largest concentration camp in Europe. He wondered in passing if Morgen was in Budapest on some undercover assignment, hence his brusqueness, but he looked so at ease in such opulent surroundings that Schlegel concluded he was probably part of the shakedown now.

'You look awful,' was all Morgen said.

He did. Schlegel still felt wretched after air turbulence on the short flight following a change of planes in Vienna. It had reduced him to vomiting in a sick bag while the rest of the passengers flew on unconcerned, flicking through their magazines, accompanied by the noise of his retching.

Still staring at Morgen, he thought to himself: Unforewarned, unprepared and shaky.

Becher told Schlegel to put the papers on the table, ready for signing, then went off, leaving Schlegel and Morgen, who smoked with exaggerated show, as if to say the pleasure of the nicotine was all he cared about. Schlegel finally broke the silence by asking, 'What's going on?'

'Not much,' said Morgen, refusing to be drawn.

'Did you know I was coming?'

Morgen said he was as surprised as Schlegel evidently was. Before they could continue Becher returned with an elderly aristocratic gentleman, immaculate in an English-style cravat and hunting jacket, to sign Schlegel's documents. This was done with a certain *froideur*, using a Mont Blanc fountain pen presented ready for use by Becher, who watched with good-humoured detachment.

The elderly gentleman turned away with a look of contempt towards Becher, who missed it because he was blotting the ink.

'Job done,' Becher said cheerfully, as he returned the papers to Schlegel. As he replaced them in their folder he realised the family were Jews, of course, and in the process of buying a safe passage, probably in exchange for a pittance, hence the contract, otherwise they would have been shipped off like everyone else.

Morgen continued to give nothing away.

Schlegel asked him, 'Do you want to catch up now or later?'

Morgen said, 'That's unlikely as I am busy.'

It was a rebuff. For a moment, Schlegel had thought Morgen might have been Nebe's reason for sending him there.

Becher remained friendlier, asking as Schlegel left, 'How long are you here?'

'Just for the night.'

Schlegel wondered if Becher would extend some kind of invitation. It wasn't as though he had anything specific to do for the rest of his stay, but Becher only said, 'It's still a good posting. The locals haven't woken up to what's happening. You can get a good lunch at the golf club, though it's a bit late for that.'

It was already after two. Schlegel was tired after his early start and still thrown by that morning's unexpected encounter with Christoph, and now on top of that, the shock of seeing Morgen.

Becher went on. 'Well, enjoy your stay. Pleasant female companions, if you are interested in that sort of thing. But be careful with the women, however beguiling. One put industrial-strength itching powder in the rubber johnny of a general making use of her services.'

Becher clapped Schlegel lightly on the shoulder in an easy gesture of dismissal, leaving him standing on the steps.

Later, Schlegel decided his time there only made sense as a series of inconsequential 'and thens'. Incidents made sense on their own but none appeared to join up. Moments of apparent significance soon blurred, leaving only a pile of random, pointless details, of the kind usually forgotten, stuck in his memory like dead flies on flypaper.

After leaving the big house he wandered through a smart part of town with wide streets and big detached houses. He brought a German street map from a news kiosk. His hotel looked about a twenty-minute walk. Only then did he realise that Nebe had set his itinerary without appearing to, by saying, 'Stay at the Astoria. It's where everyone is.'

Nebe had also given him the name of a café he 'had to visit'.

After buying the map, Schlegel first spotted the Japanese. It was impossible not to when everyone else was Caucasian, despite their comic efforts to appear inconspicuous. Schlegel supposed there must be a Japanese embassy or legation in the neighbourhood. At first he treated them as a novelty and assumed they were going in the same direction, but when he crossed the road they did too, and when he changed his mind they crossed back. They weren't threatening. They kept their distance. Nevertheless, he walked fast for a couple of blocks, doubled back, cut down side streets, jumped on a bus and quickly got off when he didn't know how to pay, but at least he was rid of any Japanese watchers.

He found himself on a busy thoroughfare in a trading area with fruit and vegetable displays, and shops with awnings, which chopped up the street up into shafts of hard light and charcoal shade. Probably because he was inspecting his map and looking like a gormless tourist he attracted the attention of a young tough. Only because he happened to look up, Schlegel spotted him walking fast towards him, not deviating, with the intention of forcing him to step aside. His briefcase was obviously the target. Schlegel was more annoyed than afraid as he had no wish to waste time at the local police station, followed by the embarrassment of telephoning Berlin to say he had managed to lose important signed documents. He feinted left and moved right, keeping the case out of reach, and kept walking, cutting through the crowd. When he looked back the yob was gone. Two Japanese gentlemen and the putative thief; were they linked?

With all the nonsense that had gone on, it was well after three before he reached his hotel. Schlegel dismissed the attempted theft as one of those things, drove Morgen from his disgruntled mind and resolved to entertain himself for the rest of the trip. Compared to Berlin, Budapest still looked pleasantly normal.

The Astoria had been requisitioned for German use and it was easy to see why, being large, extravagantly marbled and a perfect hangover from the *belle époque*. Anyone parading through its well-proportioned spaces was bound to feel enhanced.

The reception desk spoke German. Lufthansa had a travel office in the lobby. Schlegel was given a very ordinary room on a high floor with no view and a dead atmosphere. Too much transit, he thought, as he sat on the bed, mildly depressed.

He went back downstairs. The uniformed lift operator wearing white gloves called out the floors, working the large brass lever as though he was a precision engineer.

On the ground floor, ushers, as extravagantly turned out as hussars, directed guests towards the next lift. The lobby extended into a smart café area with imperious waiters in long white aprons giving lessons in advanced superciliousness. Plenty of German uniforms and suits hung around, combining business with pleasure. The mood was relaxed. Good-looking women with an inviting air sat alone on banquettes. Schlegel, reminded of the street market, presumed the fruit was for sale.

He ordered a coffee and exclaimed aloud when he tasted it; not only real but excellent. A handsome woman, older, in her thirties, came over and asked if he was new in town.

Schlegel asked how she knew.

'The coffee. Everyone does that with the first cup, looking like they are in an advertisement.'

She smiled easily, showing white teeth, attractively smudged with a smear of lipstick. The women all wore makeup, unlike at home. Mascara, eye shadow and face powder made them blurred and alluring. Again Schlegel was reminded of the market, with its inviting pools of shade.

His companion said she was an actress. She leaned forward revealing a hint of cleavage and smiled invitingly. Her German was fair. Her English turned out to be better. Schlegel explained that his mother was English, which was why he spoke it.

She told him she had done a spell in London in cabaret.

'I was in a show called *Going, Going – Gong!* Have you heard of it?'

Schlegel said he had never been to England.

'London is so big I sometimes felt quite overwhelmed,' she said.

They prattled on in a stiff, relaxed way. It was strange to speak English. The woman assumed a pose of exaggerated interest.

'It's quite funny to land somewhere and find yourself being followed by two Japanese gentlemen,' Schlegel observed, with the air of a man of the world.

The woman obliged by lightly brushing his sleeve.

'Is there much street crime in Budapest?' he asked, matter-of-factly.

'Oh, no. The police are very strict. Well, there is some.' She looked around and added, 'They come here sometimes.'

'Who?'

'The Japanese. But they never mix. They do look so funny.'

Schlegel supposed he should invite her upstairs then

thought he must be mad. Her approach was the third time he had been singled out that day. She continued to gaze at him, seemingly with nothing but desire. He sat entranced, about to make a fool of himself.

The woman's eyes flicked up and it was like watching a light being switched off as a voice asked angrily why they were speaking English.

Schlegel turned and was confronted not by the bullet-headed Nazi he was expecting but a suave man, not in uniform, with almost unfashionably long hair.

For all his smooth manner, the other man appeared genuinely affronted, especially as Schlegel was obviously German.

Schlegel explained about his mother. The man snapped back that it was his responsibility to be teaching his companion better German.

Schlegel looked at the woman and wondered if she knew the other man and some complication was going on between them.

That rather put the kibosh on the afternoon; probably just as well. The woman made her excuses, saying vaguely she might see him later.

After that other women were reluctant to approach him. Schlegel looked around ostentatiously, as if waiting for someone. He supposed he should check out Nebe's recommended café so he could report that he had.

The Hungarians were extravagant about their cafés. The Gerbeaud was like a salon, with its formal layout of separate tables and heavy brocade. Schlegel drank another coffee better than the last. His waiter approached and said in passable German he was wanted on the telephone. Schlegel asked how he knew it was for him.

The waiter said, 'There are no other young men here with white hair.'

The whole episode felt unreal as Schlegel crossed the floor, wondering if he was being watched.

A woman on the telephone told him to go to the Café Central and hung up before he could ask. Schlegel paid for his coffee and suspected he had over-tipped when he was given fulsome directions to the Central, a ten-minute walk.

The Central was a lavish art nouveau establishment and like the Gerbeaud did a good trade. Schlegel thought: It could be before the war.

Eventually, he was approached by a short, shabby man with carroty hair who looked all wrong in such elegant surroundings. He bowed, revealing a big gap between his front upper teeth when he asked in German, 'Are you the one with the violin for repair?'

Schlegel couldn't place the accent. It didn't sound Hungarian. In keeping with the otherworldly feeling to everything since his arrival, Schlegel ignored the question and asked where the man was from.

'Bucharest.' The man smiled, showing an expanse of gum.

Schlegel didn't know what to say, other than the man must be mistaken as he had nothing for repair.

The man doffed his hat, apologised and withdrew. Schlegel sat there perplexed. Nebe had said nothing about being approached. He looked around, fearing a trap. He knew nothing about Hungarian secret police but if it were the Gestapo, that was when they would make their move. Schlegel had been careful to note whether anyone was watching, but could not be sure.

Later on, with Nebe and his stepfather both wanted men, Schlegel supposed that his hidden role had been passive, as some sort of harbinger. He decided he had been sent to

Budapest simply to be seen – the young man noticeable for his white hair – as a sign of momentous events to come.

Free of obligation until his return to Berlin, Schlegel supposed he would take advantage of the hotel, see if the actress was around, treat himself or both of them to a decent dinner and sleep in late. The luxury of such idleness was unheard of for as long as he could remember.

He spent a lazy evening in the hotel lobby, watching the parade. Unlike in Berlin, the party went on. Women were fragrant. Men of confident gesture ordered from superior waiters. What looked like real cream cakes were being guzzled. No wake-up call yet.

The actress was now sitting with the suave complainer from earlier. She ignored Schlegel. The marbled lobby was crowded and buzzing with gossip. The galleried balcony overlooking the reception area was full too. The Japanese were up there, their heads together, showing no sign of having spotted him.

Schlegel looked around. The location and its cosmopolitan air reminded him of his stepfather, a man of international connections and he wondered if they had anything to do with him being sent there. His mood deteriorated. He felt like he had somehow been used. His spirits lifted momentarily when he saw Morgen come through the revolving entrance. From the way he glanced about he appeared to be looking for someone. Schlegel, supposing it might be him, half-rose and waved, only to be stared through. He watched Morgen march across the lobby, head deliberately down, and disappear into a lift. Schlegel sat back, deflated.

Some minutes later Becher strolled in looking relaxed and smart in a tailored double-breasted suit. Unlike

Morgen, he gave Schlegel an easy wave before he too disappeared into a lift.

Schlegel thought it was like one of those mystery stories his mother used to read where the cast assembled for the denouement. All that was missing were the Hungarian gentleman being fleeced by Becher and the street thug. Schlegel looked to check if the latter was disguised as a bellboy.

Drifting through the hubbub came the sound of a cocktail piano playing bittersweet tunes easy on the ear. Schlegel experienced a sudden spasm of disgust, realising he was as much a part of the problem as the rest of them. He thought about Berlin and realised he was homesick for a shit hole.

Staring at the hotel's garish opulence, he decided the day's events were more like watching cards being flicked down in a game. The cabaret artist a Queen of Hearts, playing herself onto the table; Becher a Jack of Spades, or was he a Joker? Morgen, it was hard to say what he was, but he was clearly playing a hand.

And all this was before Schlegel went upstairs to find one of the Japanese gentlemen searching his room; not that it had amounted to anything because the man ran off like a scalded cat; then there was the subsequent bad-tempered exchange with Becher the following morning, leaving Schlegel wondering at the real point of the trip, and all of it for what? A set of so-called binding legal documents that probably amounted to daylight robbery. It made no sense. Even the episode with the intruder, which should have been frightening or dramatic, was more like mistimed farce. Schlegel remembered switching on the light, thinking as the man ran off that it was he, Schlegel, who had been mistakenly given the wrong key and was in the wrong room. Whatever the man had been doing, he hadn't got very far because nothing was undisturbed. Schlegel went to bed thinking the Japanese must have mistaken him for someone else as there was no earthly reason he could think of for attracting their attention.

On the flight home, his recollections of Budapest were of a mischievous, wilful confusion, a back-to-front world too encrypted for him to decipher, surrounded by high drama. Budapest was a play – intensely self-regarding – and he an extra; or Budapest was one of those dreams where you find yourself onstage in the wrong scene.

23

What a wild goose chase Budapest had turned out to be, thought Bormann, and all for some dirty drawings of the Führer's dead niece, done years ago.

'Excuse me?' asked Bormann when Fegelein first raised the matter at the end of June. Bormann equipped himself to deal with every eventuality, but never could he have come up with this.

Word had been passed through reliable back channels that General Secretary Stalin in Moscow was keen to acquire certain drawings executed by the Führer.

Fegelein recited all this as though it were a perfectly normal request while doing his best not to look confounded.

'How and what the fuck does he know about them?' Bormann asked.

He suspected Fegelein knew quite a lot about them too, being married to the sister of the Führer's mistress, who had led the charge to trample what was left of the dead niece's reputation. The Braun sisters believed the obscene drawings were proof of the diabolical hold the girl had once had over her uncle.

Munich in the old days before power was full of gossip the size of a huge floating dirigible, most of it gaseous, all of it leaky. The kept secret was unheard of. The well-placed lie became worth more than real currency, with inflation through the roof. If the drawings hadn't existed the Führer's enemies would have invented them.

The spies Bormann had been sending out for years into the café-bars and fairy haunts reported back the various scandalous stories about the Führer that were circulating. The latest – by then it was the summer of 1931 – was that dirty drawings of the niece executed by the Führer, 'an artist in his own right', had been 'stolen' and were doing the rounds. Real or fake didn't matter; they existed.

Bormann, in an exercise in damage limitation, put out that they were fakes by a scurrilous Jew. The Führer then queered that pitch by privately claiming them as his. Why so eager? Appropriation, Bormann decided. The man wished he had done them and was willing to play along so he could acquire them for his private collection and pretend they were his when, frankly, he couldn't draw a cunt to save his life.

Bormann put the squeeze on the usual suspects. Money exchanged hands, not for the first time, and silence was bought. The drawings were returned. Bormann was more trusting then. He told himself he was not a prurient man. He had no need to see the actual drawings and back in the Führer's safe they were of no negotiable value. And that was the end of the story, until now.

That the drawings acquired a new life in that turbulent summer of 1944 was the unanticipated consequence of a Führer initiative. For some time now the Führer had been privately aware that he did not stand to gain from continuing war in the East, and he told Bormann it was time for their Nippon friends to play an active role in mediating talks with the Ivans. Bormann, who had the facts at his fingertips, was able to confirm that the omens were good.

The Soviets were exhausted from war fatigue. The Japanese approach was then condoned by the Führer pretending to turn a deaf ear. Deaf ears and blind eyes were increasing ailments that summer.

Fegelein boasted of a back channel to neutral Istanbul via his old chum Becher in Budapest. Bormann opted for that rather than Military Intelligence, which had so many leaks it may as well have published a newspaper advertising its activities. Fegelein also had contacts in the Japanese embassy in Berlin, thanks to the strategic dishing out of honorary SS memberships.

Word came back that Stalin was amenable, with a proviso.

'Only if the Führer is removed before anyone sits down at the table,' Fegelein announced then added, 'As a sign of our *bona fides*, General Secretary Stalin wants a sweetener.'

That was when Fegelein first mentioned the drawings.

'What do you know about them?' Bormann thought it as well to ask.

'The Braun sisters say the minx had the Führer under her spell. She was depraved and obsessed with her own shit and made the Führer draw her doing caca.'

Bormann wondered how far Fegelein's sexual kinks went.

On 29 June – the day before the Führer raised the subject over dinner – Bormann had the drawings removed from the Führer's private safe. The transfer was managed by Fegelein, who was flitting between Berlin and his bride in Munich.

When Bormann finally got to see the drawings, his first thought was: Fuck me.

'What do you think?' he asked.

'They're not very good,' volunteered Fegelein.

They were so amateurish Stalin would think they were having him on and throw a fit. They were not even schoolboy art – they looked like they could have been done by that degenerate Picasso on a bad day. One showed spread female genitalia and a healthy bush and the other a well-formed turd about to drop from a plump squatting female arse.

Something more credible had to be produced fast – requiring an artist and a plump-arsed model whose auditions Bormann took upon himself – allowing for the originals to be returned to the Führer, leaving that part of the problem solved.

The new drawings were to be passed on to Stalin's agents in Istanbul via the Japanese in Budapest. Bormann was aware of Fegelein's contempt for, and mistrust of, the slitty-eyed honorary Aryans. The real reason Fegelein was leery was irate Nippon husbands, subsequent to his pursuit of horizontal relations with the wives of Japanese embassy staff. Sometimes Bormann wondered why Fegelein didn't just wear his dick outside his pants for all the world to see.

With Fegelein revealed as a liability and showboater, Bormann preferred to deal directly with the man's old partner in crime, the more thorough Kurt Becher, who was in Budapest negotiating a twelve-year lease for a Jewish family's steel factories and acquiring their art collection in exchange for safe passage to Lisbon, all according to legal contracts not worth the paper, etcetera. Bormann was impressed by how the crafty and urbane Becher was laying down personal survival strategies, by being seen to be nego-tiating with local Zionists about saving those that could be extracted from death's maw. Becher's infamous ransom train allowed some Jews to buy their way out, in exchange for safe passage to neutral territory.

Fleecing ploys were there to be repeated; Bormann appreciated that. The ransom train was a bucket-class version of Becher's brokered deal with the industrialist family. In both cases, a fortune got paid and Becher took what became known as the Becher deposit.

Morgen's reports told Bormann that Becher was operating at a level far above anything Fegelein was capable of, probably on his way to becoming a millionaire and getting away scot-free.

What Becher didn't know was that Morgen at the time was answering to Bormann. It was a Machiavellian arrangement, which involved the unscrupulous passing on of details of Bormann's personal enemies for Morgen to sort for corruption. By then practically the entire upper echelon was corrupt anyway, having been bought off, so it was a matter of Bormann taking his pick. He and Morgen had squabbled over Fegelein. Epic corruption, Morgen said. Non-negotiable, countered Bormann. Bormann admired Morgen's persistence but found his stubbornness verged on stupidity. Becher was agreed upon as a possible compromise target, hence Morgen in Budapest, playing an elaborate and probably useless game, in keeping with the strange dream-like atmosphere of that summer.

For the commission and delivery of the drawings, Bormann turned to the compromised art dealer; queer and pretending not to be. Bormann could always sniff a homo. This one had the waspish humour of one, which he didn't mind.

It was one of those situations where it was impossible to tell exactly the extent of everyone's involvement. Bormann, the spider at the centre, knew as much as anyone but even he was not at first aware that the courier was the same man that would cause him so much discomfort by filing a report on the mysterious burning down of a Berlin clinic.

The drawings were secreted by sealing them within the

actual cover of the document folder and the switch was supposed to have involved a straightforward swap of one folder for another, with the original passed on to the Japanese. In a less suspicious world, that would have been done during the signing of the contract, but Becher ducked it, telephoning Bormann to say he feared he was being watched by Morgen and too many others. The Hungarians were mad at him because they had been promised there would be no confiscations. Göring was livid because he had been cut out of the art deal. The Hungarian secret police were taking careful note. Becher got on his high horse and said such cheap tricks were beneath a man of his rank and class. The man's sublime cynicism was rendered more exquisite by impeccable manners. Bormann – tiring of kid-gloved dilettantes – told him to make it work. Only later did he learn that this consisted of Becher informing the Budapest Japanese Trade Delegation, which was fronting their end, that it was up to them to make the switch.

From then on the situation deteriorated.

When the courier's name eventually surfaced it was a shock to Bormann. Suddenly, Schlegel was everywhere. Schlegel the Budapest courier. Schlegel and the clinic. Schlegel hobnobbing with Dr Goebbels. Müller kept Bormann informed. They talked every day as it was, and had done so for years, climbing the greasy pole together since their lowly beginnings in Munich.

Bormann assembled a full account of Schlegel's moves in Budapest. From Becher. From Morgen. From several sources in the Astoria, which was riddled with informers, including women who hang around lobbies. The only thing he hadn't known was the wretched man's name, abbreviated to WHM ('white-haired man').

Bormann's report noted that WHM had complained to the hotel management about finding a Japanese gentleman going through his room on the evening of the eighteenth. WHM reported nothing stolen. The house detective said he would keep an eye out for any further errant Japanese behaviour and WHM agreed it was not necessary to involve the police.

Why the search of the hotel room had proved fruitless was because the desired object had been deposited by WHM in the hotel safe.

When the Japanese informed Becher they had failed, it fell to a reluctant Becher to go to the hotel the next morning and inform WHM he needed to make an amendment to the contract.

But then only the contract was removed by WHM from the safe. According to desk staff, a 'childish' standoff followed. A testy Becher announced a change of plan and he was now to take the contract *and* the folder. WHM refused, insisting his orders were to return the contract.

What should have been a straightforward swap never took place, leaving the courier to return home with the original folder, which was why he was stopped by Berlin customs, the folder swapped then flown back to Budapest on the night mail plane for collection by Becher for forwarding to the Japanese. As it happened, the whole operation turned out to be a complete waste of time, given what happened the next day with the failure of the bomb plot, after which the Japanese initiative collapsed.

As for the dopey courier, if he noticed when he returned the papers it wasn't the same folder, so what?

What delighted Bormann more than anything was discovering how secret puzzles joined up, especially those of his own making, and the whereabouts of missing pieces: the roles of those running and being run; the nobodies who think they are somebody and the plain nobodies; the accidental damage and the women who get fucked along the way (plump-arsed model there for the taking, as well as others he had auditioned). Then there were the overlaps and coincidences: for instance, how the Führer had raised the matter of the drawings on the very evening after Bormann had arranged to have them removed. And all this wild goose chase going on while the world was being rocked on its heels, at the whim of two of its foremost leaders, who perhaps should have been concentrating more on steering the ship of state than thinking about mucky drawings. But in this Bormann understood exactly how the world worked, which was why he was rather good at running it.

24

Schlegel reached Gerda at his first attempt. She sounded cheerful and happy and he thought perhaps the day was salvageable after all. He was sitting at his desk. Everyone gave him a wide berth. Dunkelwert was back in her hutch, giving someone a hard time on the telephone.

Dunkelwert had told him his case was 'under review'. They had sweated him for the rest of the afternoon, going over his time in Budapest. He stuck to his edited highlights. No Hungarian actress. No attempted snatch in the street. No mention of violin repairs. No mention of being followed by two Japanese gentlemen, though he did mention the one found in his room, only because he had reported it to the hotel. He tried to look as baffled as they were.

Dunkelwert had nothing she could make stick but was reluctant to let him go. She looked exhausted, with black smudges under her eyes. Schlegel felt almost sorry for her. She had wanted to break him and not succeeded. In the end, she was forced to admit defeat.

There was the awkwardness of leaving the room together. He supposed he should feel relief rather than nothing. If they let him live he would continue to burrow his way through the days with no sense of future, his inner life as empty as a winter greenhouse.

He told Gerda, 'I saw the Führer today,' to see how it sounded. He didn't quite believe it even as he said it.

Her enthusiasm was touching and he laughed. Sounding bashful she said, 'A child conceived on the day you saw the Führer!'

Schlegel cringed. He still could not tell whether she was serious and wondered if he shouldn't go out and get plastered instead. She told him she would be as quick as she could. It would take her an hour or so to finish up.

Schlegel was doodling on the old message telling him to call Frau Busl. He decided he couldn't be bothered, then called to avoid a bad conscience, hoping she wouldn't answer.

Someone picked up as he was about to give up, listened to him ask for Frau Busl and replaced the receiver. He called back and the line rang unanswered.

He still had time, he supposed. He should check. The bit players, extending to himself, were the most expendable – those in the wrong place at the wrong time.

He called again from the station. No answer.

Schlegel was amazed that the structure of the day still resembled something that passed for normal: see the mother wipe the nose of the snotty child; see the two secretaries meet after work. There were fewer men and those that were left looked a mite furtive about it, and a lot more widows, younger and younger these days, with their black armbands.

The train sat for a long time between stations. Apart from the dimmest lights in the tunnel, which served only to give definition to the darkness, Schlegel could see nothing. Were it not for the sound of collective breathing and a child's occasional snivels he could have been buried alive.

Schlegel was across the street from Frau Busl's block, catching his breath because he had jogged the last part, being late – Gerda would let herself in anyway – when he saw two men leave the building, and ducked back into a doorway.

It was the two thugs from the night of the fire, moving with easy assurance, scoping the street as they hit the pavement. They went the other way from Schlegel, who was in no doubt they were the ones doing the tidying. Bormann's henchmen, he supposed, or Gestapo Müller's, or maybe even Dr Goebbels had been told that all traces of his potentially embarrassing extracurricular activity must be removed.

The downstairs main door was open.

More worrying, Schlegel found the door to the Busl apartment open too. He called out, fearing the worst. No answer.

The office showed no sign of disturbance. Dr Goebbels grinned out at him from the wall.

He checked the rest. With every reveal, he expected Frau Busl's body.

The wooden floor squeaked when walked on. Schlegel tried cupboards in case she was hiding. He checked the building's inner well, to see if they had chucked her down that.

Gradually he formed an impression she was alive and had managed to avoid her hunters. If she wasn't in the building, she would have locked her front door. Schlegel searched the back stairs. He looked in the cellar. There was no concierge or warden to ask. He was reluctant to leave. He felt responsible. Outside, he continued to hang around. He looked at the time. He really was late now. He had done what he could.

Public transport as usual was infrequent and full, with crowds waiting at stops. Schlegel half-ran up Friedrichstrasse, pausing to wait at the next stop, then hurried on, to be overtaken by buses and trams sailing past.

He gave up on them and decided to walk the rest of the way. Half an hour late was nothing these days.

It was staring to get dark as Schlegel came to his street. He didn't make much of the crowd, staring up, necks craned, a gathering of maybe thirty or forty, spilling into the road. Cops were on the scene. An ambulance was parked. It looked like an accident.

Two men moved through the crowd. Schlegel knew already who they were. The fat one gave a nod and what could be taken for a rueful look. They took up a position on the edge of the crowd, keeping him in sight. Schlegel understood. He looked up, barely daring to. The window of his apartment was open. He knew the rest.

Someone said, 'Girl fell from a high window.'

The window would have been open anyway. In summer it was always stifling.

Schlegel knew the two men were waiting for him from the way they lingered. If he left, they would follow. If he stayed, they would stay. Either way, they would finish their intended business, even if it meant sticking a knife in him in the confusion of the crowd. Perhaps he should provoke a fight and be done with it. He had nothing left. Gerda should have been exempt. She had nothing to do with it. They must have found the door open upstairs, barged in and thrown her out, for no reason other than to show Schlegel what was in store for him or just because they were irritated to have missed Frau Busl.

Schlegel pushed his way through the crowd. The cops at least had had the decency to put a tent around the body. Even so, a leg stuck out, without its shoe.

When he thought there were no more surprises left, there was one in the shape of the big, ugly man walking out of the entrance. Stoffel.

He was with two uniformed cops.

Stoffel asked Schlegel what he was doing. Schlegel suspected Stoffel was drunk. It was like the old days, with Stoffel in no mood to be friendly, seeming to regard Schlegel turning up a huge inconvenience, just as everyone was packing up. Stoffel took his time working out that it was Schlegel who lived upstairs.

'She fell from *your* apartment?'

Schlegel nodded.

Stoffel said, 'In that case, identify the body for me. Instant death. Very little mess. I've seen worse.'

He produced a hip flask and didn't offer.

Schlegel was shown the body. He looked away. Smashed teeth.

Stoffel repeated that he'd had her down as a jumper. He didn't need to add, 'Until you showed up.'

He lit up one of his cheroots that always ended up looking like a dog's dick.

Schlegel pointed out the two men who were responsible, still hanging around. Stoffel looked at the two thugs and told Schlegel he didn't want to know. Schlegel's control snapped.

'You there!' he shouted at them, but before he could go on Stoffel had his arm in a vice-like grip.

'Don't go causing me trouble. Let's go inside.'

Stoffel followed Schlegel upstairs. Schlegel couldn't tell what Stoffel had in mind. Stoffel kept having to stop to catch his breath.

The room showed no sign of struggle. Schlegel crossed to the window and looked down. The tent and Gerda's body were in the process of being taken away. The crowd was dispersing. The two thugs loitered, looking up, waiting.

Schlegel turned away and said to Stoffel, 'Cigarette butt on the floor. She didn't and I don't smoke.'

Stoffel shrugged. 'Probably one of ours. A lot of sloppy work these days.'

The man was impossible. Schlegel realised what it was: even by pointing out the two thugs he was telling Stoffel it was a case of no trespass. There was nothing Stoffel could do.

Schlegel pleaded in desperation, 'Say it was me who pushed her.'

'Get on,' said Stoffel. The man was wheezing like a pair of old bellows from the climb.

'I *need* to be arrested.'

Stoffel focused for a moment and said, 'Never made a false arrest in my life.'

'Otherwise those men will do for me.'

Stoffel looked at Schlegel expectantly. Schlegel couldn't work out why, then realised and stepped forward and socked Stoffel as hard as he could across the jaw with his right fist. It was like hitting cast iron. Stoffel barely staggered. He came back and thumped Schlegel in the gut and the air left him in a rush, like it was taking his insides with it.

Stoffel put Schlegel's arm in a half nelson and held him almost gently by the neck, telling him to breathe deep however much it hurt.

'There you are, son. Nearly there.'

When Schlegel finally managed to pull himself upright Stoffel punched him in the stomach again, not so hard.

'Just to remind you how we do things,' he said. 'Turn round and put your hands behind your back.'

Schlegel felt the handcuffs snap shut, so tight they bit into his flesh, which was when it hit him that Gerda really was dead.

Stoffel manhandled a staggering Schlegel out of the building, none too kindly. The two thugs sauntered over like they owned Schlegel.

The cadaverous one said, 'We'll take over now.'

The fat man opened his wallet showing documentation. Stoffel looked unimpressed. The cadaverous one took a step forward. Schlegel flinched, thinking he was about to be gut-shot. Stoffel showed his gun first. The two thugs checked and looked undecided.

Stoffel said, 'Now step aside.'

The men shrugged and stared at Schlegel. The fat one smiled amiably and said, 'Catch you later.'

When the desk sergeant wrote down the charges, Stoffel said, 'Throw him in the drunk tank. Can't be seen to be doing favours.'

Typical Stoffel. He may have helped out but he would always find a way of telling Schlegel he didn't hold him in any more regard than before.

'You get one phone call.'

Schlegel said he wanted to speak to Morgen.

Stoffel knew Morgen and asked where he was.

'Budapest,' said Schlegel.

'Fuck off, son. I'm not paying for an international call. Local only.'

Schlegel couldn't think of anyone. Not Christoph. They had grown too distant. By a simple process of elimination he arrived at Anna Huber.

The next morning he used his one local call to ring her at the ministry. She answered sounding cool and efficient. He said he had a favour to ask and wasn't sure how best to explain it.

'Tell me,' she said, sounding ironic.

'I am unable to make calls abroad at the moment and urgently need to contact a friend and thought perhaps I could ask you to ring on my behalf.'

'An unusual request,' she said drily. 'As long as you are not asking me to do anything illegal.'

'Not at all,' he said quickly, thinking it must all sound very questionable.

The telephone was attached to the wall in a grey corridor and was without any booth. Schlegel felt exposed and ridiculous standing there; they had taken away his belt, tie and shoe laces, for the obvious reason. Stoffel was waiting nearby, whistling as he smoked, and looking amused by Schlegel's predicament.

'Spot of trouble?' echoed Anna Huber.

She could mean only one thing: that he had got swept up in the reprisals.

'Nothing to do with recent events,' Schlegel offered; well, not really. 'If you contact Morgen, he will know what to do.'

'Where are you at the moment?' she asked.

'Quite safe for the time being, staying with old friends.' She probably thought he meant he was on the run and quickly added, 'You can call Inspector Stoffel in Berlin Homicide. He will vouch for me.'

Stoffel laughed out loud at that and told him his two minutes was up.

Schlegel said he had to go. Hoping he didn't sound too desperate, he asked Huber to call the Budapest Astoria as Morgen's likeliest point of contact. He wondered what she was thinking.

'Will you pay me back for the call?' she asked, making it sound ambiguous, as though he were putting himself in her debt for more than just the cost of telephoning Budapest.

25

Stoffel came to Schlegel's cell and said, 'Upstairs!' Schlegel suspected Stoffel had tired of the charade and it was the two thugs come for him.

'Visitor,' Stoffel said, seeing his alarm.

Schlegel had been transferred to his own cell. Already he was losing any sense of time. They had taken his watch. He had slept a lot and woken disorientated. He had no idea if Huber had managed to contact Morgen. He supposed thirty-six or even forty-eight hours had passed. As they walked upstairs Stoffel told him that the thugs had put in the paperwork for his transfer.

'Under whose authority?' Schlegel asked.

'Fire Protection Police, according to the docket.' Stoffel snorted. 'It says you are wanted for questioning about burning down a clinic.'

Schlegel supposed the fat man and the cadaver could hide behind whatever bureaucracy they wanted – Ministry of Works one day, Fire Protection Police the next. Schlegel was forced to admit a grudging admiration for the cleverness of the charge. It was a perfect frame.

Stoffel said, 'Apparently you have previous form.'

It was true. The year before he had been accused of starting a fire in Auschwitz to destroy evidence.

'It was a fit-up, like this,' he protested. 'Morgen got me off and there's no record of it on my file.'

'Tell that to the judge!' said Stoffel.

As to whom the two thugs really answered, Schlegel

supposed it was Bormann. The Party Secretary was the great manipulator when it came to scene shifting, and a lot of that had been going on since 20 July. No doubt the clean sweep was an excuse for settling many old scores. They were all bound to have their lists: Bormann, Goebbels, Himmler . . .

Schlegel asked Stoffel, 'How long do you think before my transfer?'

'They appear in no hurry. I doubt if you're top of anyone's list. They know where you are and will be happy to let you sweat.'

Stoffel showed Schlegel into a private visiting room rather than the common area. He found Anna Huber when he was expecting Morgen and stood tongue-tied. Huber looked even more beautiful in such grubby surroundings. She surprised him by stepping forward and putting her hand on his shoulder.

'I am so sorry to hear about your friend,' she said.

What had she been told?

'Morgen said there was a terrible accident,' she went on, stepping back.

'How much do you know?' he asked. 'About everything.'

The worry lines above her nose deepened.

'Only that you have a habit of getting into trouble and it falls to Morgen to bale you out. But that's not why I am here. I want to tell you about your father. You had better sit down.'

She was smartly turned out and Schlegel wondered if she was on her way to meet a man.

Huber sat. She said nothing for a moment, and then: 'After everything that has happened, I hope this doesn't come as too much of a shock.'

*

If there was one thing Schlegel was convinced of it was that his father's existence had long since ceased, and if he had not drowned in an Argentinian river in 1934 then he had met his end around that time in Munich.

'Alive?' he repeated after Anna Huber.

'Might be. I didn't know whether to tell you. Nothing is certain.' She trailed off. 'He's not the most reliable, my brother, but I tell it for what it is.'

Having given so little thought to his father in all those years, Schlegel could not absorb the fact that the man might not be dead. The idea of him still living and breathing was almost too much.

Anna Huber said, 'Anton Schlegel was not a Party member so I made some discreet enquiries.'

Schlegel couldn't imagine what form they took.

Huber brightened. 'Next year is the twentieth anniversary of the publishing of *Mein Kampf.* I said we were thinking of doing a 'where are they now' for the twenty-five dedicated recipients of the signed limited edition. Quite clever, I thought.'

Schlegel agreed. Suitably innocuous and the kind of idea the ministry would come up with.

'And your brother? The one you said was a brownshirt.'

'Do you know who I mean by Emil Maurice?'

Gestapo Müller had first made the connection, suggesting Maurice might have a tale to tell about Anton Schlegel.

'My brother told me Emil Maurice was supposed to have shot your father, but, for whatever reason, let him off.'

'When was this?'

'In 1934, after the brownshirt putsch failed.'

It was a long way from drowning in Argentina. Schlegel wondered if his mother had known and made up the other story in denial of the dishonour.

'How does your brother know?'

'He was friendly with one of the two men who did the job with Emil Maurice.'

Schlegel found it hard to imagine his father caught up in a revolution, then had to ask himself what did he know of anyone? He never would have guessed that his stepfather was plotting against the government. Gerda he had known only two or three things about. Morgen remained an enigma and Schlegel was a stranger to himself most of the time. And the woman opposite, although she no doubt led a real life, appeared more like a screen for a phantom projection of his own flimsy imaginings.

'Why was Anton Schlegel down for execution, does anyone know?' It seemed presumptuous to say his father.

'For the same reason as everyone else. He probably knew too much.'

Schlegel watched her watching him as they realised they were in dangerous waters.

'Does Morgen know?'

'I thought I should tell you first.'

26

Schlegel continued to exasperate Morgen, looking at everything as if it didn't quite belong, or he to it, with the dazed wonder of a man stumbling through a party to which he hasn't been invited and doesn't know how to leave.

Or perhaps Morgen's own sense of order and propriety had taken such a kicking that he rather envied Schlegel's lackadaisical approach. The law Morgen was there to uphold was repeatedly shown to be meaningless.

For two years his casework had amounted to exposing rot for others to cover up. In Warsaw 1942, Fegelein, Becher and others, steeped in corruption, became mysteriously protected. Ditto Auschwitz 1943, a racket from top to bottom. Deportation trains brought hundreds of thousands, turning up with their baggage allowance of fifty kilos, confiscated on arrival. What happened next was state-sanctioned, Morgen was told in no uncertain terms. Piles of money, piles of bodies, death factory politics – there was an actual *reformist* movement, Morgen was staggered to learn – and shopping in Auschwitz. The commandant and his wife were in it up to their necks, with her jewellery 'enterprise' servicing her husband's boss in Berlin. Threatened with exposure, the commandant got kicked upstairs, a makeweight replacement was sent to appease the reformists, and, in an act of apparently spontaneous combustion, for which they tried to blame Schlegel, all Morgen's collected evidence went up in flames.

That was eight months ago. The bitter footnote was that the commandant had since been restored to his post, with extended powers not unconnected to that summer's influx of trains from Hungary.

Morgen found it increasingly hard to ignore the voice shouting in his ear that there was nothing he could do because nothing mattered.

They would all be running soon. As to what he believed or did: who would care in six or nine months? Even his self-estimation he saw as the vanity of wanting to think well of himself in the mirror, but who was to judge? In five hundred years the whole debacle would be no more than a speck on the historical horizon.

Schlegel's summons came more as an irritation than a distraction. Morgen had paused hard, wondering whether to bale him out again. If he had snubbed Schlegel in Budapest it was because the man never seemed quite to trust him, and seeing him with the smooth and dubious Becher had no doubt only confirmed that. The trouble was it was true. Morgen had found himself unable to decide whether he was exploiting situations to expose them or was just following suit. Budapest was a case in point. He could pretend he was on the job rather than in retreat from his own failures and living well into the bargain.

When Anna Huber contacted him because, as she put it, present circumstances prevented Schlegel from making calls abroad, Morgen decided he was wasting his time in Budapest. With no real dirt on Becher, and intrigued by the sound of Anna Huber, he packed his bags and flew back to Berlin, ready to give Schlegel short shrift, only to find a broken and bewildered man.

*

It took Schlegel the best part of a day to explain how he had ended up in a prison cell. Morgen often had to get him to go over things he didn't understand. Schlegel was like that. Ambiguous in his interpretation of events. Afterwards, Morgen was not sure what to make of it all. Schlegel appeared to be trying to rewrite history while having his own family history rewritten into the bargain.

Morgen supposed Schlegel's young woman had been there when it should have been Schlegel. The two thugs weren't done for the night either. Morgen checked: the drama agent's wife or sister or whatever she was had also taken the high dive. Stoffel told him they were being instructed to treat the case as self-inflicted. Suicides by then were commonplace.

The other half of Schlegel's account Morgen didn't know what to make of either: the long-lost father, spectacularly re-emerged as an old Führer darling, about whom everyone was unwilling to utter a word, though that wasn't so unusual these days. The problem was getting anyone to remember. But if Schlegel had a gift, it was to stumble across some wild connection that he, Morgen, being more methodical, would have missed. Schlegel had come up with a dubious bomb plot, unresolved, and the scandal of the dead niece, also unresolved. What strange bookends, Morgen thought.

When Schlegel first brought up the business of the niece, Morgen wondered if the spectre of Schlegel's father was inviting them to expose the present by digging up the past.

Morgen remembered at the time of the niece's death being a podgy, gauche young man, completing his studies at the Institute for World Economy and Ocean Traffic in Kiel. Even then the story struck him as blown out of proportion: a sensational, distant provincial scandal, involving a man known for public hysteria and barely able to contain himself on stage. The death's occurrence during the hot-house of Munich's Oktoberfest was noted, suggesting dark undercurrents of collective frenzy.

Munich was a long way from Kiel, a tough, blowhard navy town, where it was regularly pointed out that Hitler had barely seen the sea. It was fashionable anyway to ignore the noisy squabbles of a thuggish provincial minority. Morgen could not picture a man as sexless as Hitler obsessing over anything as inconsequential as a female. Back then he saw only a comic figure – his mistake – a bogus faith healer who should be peddling miracle cures and religious crack-potism, and a weird super-narcissist who, however noisy and effective on a soapbox, would turn out to be a political damp squib.

As for pursuing the no doubt sordid business of the niece, there were plenty of unanswered questions, but if he couldn't nail someone as openly corrupt as Fegelein, what chance of bagging the biggest tiger of all? But then, if none of it mattered, what did he have to lose?

It would be enough even to have the man in his sights.

Morgen had it in mind to go to Munich and not take Schlegel. The two thugs seemed in no hurry to remove Schlegel, and Morgen had discussed with Stoffel whether to transfer him to somewhere remote and lose him in the system. Morgen couldn't decide who, *precisely*, wanted Schlegel dead, and Schlegel was doing himself no favours trying to resurrect Anton Schlegel, who belonged in a locked drawer marked: Things We Keep Quiet About.

The question was whether Morgen gravitated towards Bormann or Müller, to neither of whom could he say: I want to expose a big skeleton in the Führer's closet.

Morgen made a simple bet with himself: that Bormann

knew more than Gestapo Müller, but Müller was always keen to learn more and he would see him on the same day when others had to wait weeks.

The problem with dredging up former lives was the regime's talent for unwriting the past. In terms of who was who in Munich in the old days, the Führer's driver, Emil Maurice, was the most curious because he hadn't moved to Berlin with the rest. Emil Maurice was listed in the Party register as chairman of the Munich Chamber of Commerce. His record showed years of loyal service. He was among the first hundred Party members in 1919. By 1923, he was head of Hitler's elite new bodyguard, which two years later became the SS. Maurice seemed to be something of a local hero yet it was an odd career. Although in effect the SS's actual founder, immediately after Hitler, he now ran a local Chamber of Commerce, which could be taken for a sideways shunt, a fall from grace, or a sinecure.

Then Morgen stumbled across the undreamed-of connection. Thinking how paperwork always held its own secrets and being curious, he went back to company records for the clinic. If life had taught him anything it was that there was no such thing as coincidence. The clinic had four major shareholders. The deceased surgeon, two others and Emil Maurice.

Müller received Morgen in his more formal office. Morgen disagreed with Schlegel's description of Müller as the ultimate grey man. Müller always struck him as full of fizz, like a cheap brown drink.

Morgen got straight to the point, wanting to know if the case of the burned clinic was closed.

'I can't see why not,' Müller said, taking care not to look surprised by Morgen's angle.

Morgen explained about Emil Maurice being one of the shareholders. A lesser dissembler would have recoiled in surprise. Müller blinked and his eyes travelled across the ceiling.

Müller said, 'Emil Maurice is a Jew, you might like to know.'

That didn't make sense. Morgen was careful to say nothing.

'Protected by the Führer's benevolence. Up to a point. You will find the clinic shares are a reward for past loyal service. The Führer is not as intolerant as is sometimes made out if he befriends a Jew like Emil. But this is not really about the clinic.'

Müller was not a man to bluff, so Morgen remained silent.

'It's about the niece,' Müller went on.

'The niece?'

'Let me explain. I sometimes think we never got to the bottom of it. Girls of twenty-three don't usually shoot themselves with pistols as far as I know, not held at such an angle.'

Müller demonstrated with his fingers, pointing down towards his heart. He appeared amused. 'I know Fräulein Braun subsequently managed to shoot herself unsuccessfully, but that was the act of a copycat, in imitation of her rival. Anyway, she is more the cry-for-help type.'

'Fräulein Braun?'

'A friend of the Führer. You can ask her. She's around, with nothing to do.'

Müller stared at his desktop in mild disbelief at the ways of women before going on. 'It might not be a bad time to review the Raubal case to show a Jew was responsible. Of course that Jew could be Emil Maurice.'

Morgen felt outmanoeuvred. It now looked like he was expected to provide some cooked-up story so Dr Goebbels' press could go to town with another load of lies.

'Isn't the business of the girl best forgotten?' Morgen ventured, curious to know the answer.

'I agree. The case has been dead for years, except now it is being dug up again.' Müller paused. 'Given recent events, we have to presume a plot to destabilise, perhaps connected to the previous one.'

So that was what it was about, thought Morgen.

Müller counted off on his fingers. 'One: a long-lost tell-all diary, supposedly written by the niece – political dynamite even if fake, which it probably is – apparently not so lost after all. Why now? Two: an old hack's secret exposé of the case of the niece, pointing fingers, same rumour of it surfacing. Again why now? And third and most preposterous: a so-called confession – if we can credit that – signed by the Führer saying he killed his niece.' Müller rolled his eyes.

Morgen thought the confession had to be a hoax. Why would the man admit to what he hadn't done – and even if he had, why confess after getting away with it?

Müller concurred without being asked, saying, 'It can only be the work of fifth columnists in the pay of foreign agents.'

Morgen wondered if Müller wanted the confession for himself. Authentic or not, such a document would be of inestimable value as leverage.

'How might it be connected to the other plot?' Morgen enquired innocently.

'Say the Führer had been killed by that bomb. Phase two would have been strategic mud-slinging. Perhaps some of the conspirators are persisting in the vain hope some will stick.'

'Why would anyone believe it?'

'Indeed, but there is a long history of outrageous muckraking against the Führer.'

'A political initiative then?'

'Making it a time bomb that could be even more damaging than the recent one. Look how that caught everyone out. See it doesn't happen again.'

'Do I need to know anything about the circumstances of the girl's death?' Morgen asked.

'One version you can discount was that it came about after talking to Reichsführer-SS Himmler.' A glint of amusement let Morgen see this was probably Müller's way of letting him know he could implicate Heini if he chose to. 'He was meant to have browbeaten her into doing the decent thing after so compromising the Führer by her outrageous behaviour.'

Morgen could picture Heini's creepy smiling manner, telling her it was the honourable way out, with lots of nonsense about the traditions of the Bushido.

'Outrageous behaviour?' asked Morgen going back to the niece.

Müller rolled his wrist. 'A Jewish lover, or some such, perhaps even pregnant by him. Do you see what I am saying?'

Morgen could – whatever had gone on had had to be hushed up because the Führer's niece had been consorting with a Jew.

'And the confession and so forth?' Morgen ventured.

'He's so tiny you might miss him, but try the Party archivist, a fellow by the name of Rehse, been around for years, deals on the side with a lot of dubious material. Fakes can do untold damage in the wrong hands. The text of this ridiculous confession in, say, a Swiss newspaper – there are an awful lot of gullible people out there who believe what they see printed in black and white. The foreign press would have a field day. Find it and bring it to me. As for the diary and and the hack's exposé, bring them too if you find them. And what role is the Huber woman playing in this?'

Morgen was surprised and he tried not to show it. 'She was Schlegel's contact for getting in touch with me.'

'Did he mention that she is the hack's daughter?'

No, he hadn't. Clearly Schlegel wasn't telling him everything.

'And are you aware that her brother works with Emil Maurice?' Müller went on.

No, he wasn't. More and more curious, Morgen thought.

'I have arranged with her employer for her to take leave forthwith. Take her. She might be useful. Are you taking Schlegel?' asked Müller.

'I was thinking he is better off where he is.'

'I keep hearing his stepfather is hiding in Munich. The boy has been questioned and I still think he is more connected than he makes out. Take him and see if he makes any moves. All clear?'

Müller looked at Morgen, again amused, knowing it was anything but. Morgen sighed inwardly at being lumbered with two extra lots of baggage. Still, if Huber had connections she might prove useful.

'What is my authority?' asked Morgen.

'Checking Führer security in connection with various residences as a consequence of the recent breach of security. And tell him to dye his hair.'

'Schlegel?'

'Who else? I can't vouch for his safety. He seems to have upset a lot of people. Dr Goebbels is incandescent.' Müller looked at Morgen blandly. 'Shall we say five days? If you're not back by then, I will presume someone has set the dogs on you.'

As for the business of the bomb, Morgen was inclined to go along with Schlegel's version that some sort of a Führer trick had been performed and the plot made most sense as a stage-managed event. In a location of such high security they could have lions and elephants living there and no one would be the wiser. If there had been any Führer swap, the man seemed to have been restored to himself by the time Schlegel was invited to see him with his own eyes as proof, thus closing the case from any other interpretation. Bormann now acted with impunity, having built the Party into a black Vatican and reduced the power of all rivals through controlled channels of information and access. But the trick would not be revealed because the last thing Bormann would say is, 'Sit down and let me tell you how I did it.'

27

Agatha Christie, the English Queen of Crime, had a big following in the Chancellery. Her latest, *Ten Little Niggers*, had been published that year. Even the Führer, who claimed not to read fiction, was a secret fan. The mystery had given Bormann the solution to the puzzle he had been struggling to solve regarding the Stalin initiative and the removal of the Führer prior to any negotiation. Of course! The murderer fakes his own death. Bormann understood that to mean if the Führer could be shown to be dead the future became negotiable.

Sometimes, Bormann and the Führer referred to the others as FF, fake Führers. Bormann was always careful not to remind him of that stupid Charlie Chaplin film, which had revolved around a Führer swap. How the Führer had sat as stony-faced as Buster Keaton through that.

Realising such a big switch was possible came to Bormann while studying the esteemed Minister of Armaments and all-round toady Speer, so consumed by his own reflected glory that the man's eyes could have been rotated towards the back of his skull for all he saw. After that the idea of such an intimate switch did not seem so impossible.

Bormann wondered if the Führer even knew how many doubles he had. They weren't entertained. They didn't put on Führer shows. They were kept apart and were as jealous as cats in terms of being the most authentic. Long-distance fake. Medium-range fake. Close-up double. You had to laugh.

Once, in the heady days of early power, Bormann brought an especially convincing one to the Berghof and the Führer fled in terror, declaring it bad luck to meet one's double. It was the nearest Bormann had come to getting one of the Führer's legendary rockets.

At the height of the Führer's exposure, no political leader had ever been in such demand in terms of mass consumption. Führer substitutions came to be known as 'working round' the Führer, providing cover for the man's helter-skelter schedule, the need to be several places at once, insatiable audience demand, crazed female fans worked to a pitch of sexual frenzy, and the man's exhaustion and nervous collapse. Within the inner circle, the use of doubles was often prefaced by the man himself saying in a mock gruff voice, 'A Führer for the boring stuff.'

It was an old joke between them, the amount of over-acting required to get his message across to the people. 'Double ham with mustard tonight,' the Führer would say to Bormann in easier, more cheerful days.

Sharing the role the Führer thought legitimate and *modern*. It appealed to his divided nature. Distancing himself from tough decisions, he had grown able to feel it was not really him making them but a doppelgänger.

In a recent late night confession he had confided to Bormann that he feared his willed destiny of victory followed by a withdrawal into a life of contemplation would elude him. Bormann sought to assure him that if victory was no longer realisable the dream of personal release still was.

*

Until the one-eyed hero of the hour made a total bollocks of the job.

In the week of 20 July, the Wolf's Lair was on full military alert with the 'Führer' at last present after a long sojourn in the mountains.

For the dwindling few, the rigmarole of admission with its endless security checks amounted to a magician's sleight of hand; as in, after all this and that, it's not going to *not* be the Führer. The Führer was anyway controlled by Bormann's appointments diary and who else could the man be sitting at his desk, wearing his clothes? The image was so firmly stamped on servile minds that no one was going to blurt out, 'But this is not the Führer!' Bormann thought that with all the surrounding protocol it would probably take a shaven-headed dwarf masquerading as the Führer before anyone noticed: you see what you expect to see. For those ushered in, warning of a possible Führer rocket was enough to reduce them to standing with eyes glued to the floor. 'No, my Führer.' 'Yes, my Führer.'

Bormann the perfect acolyte was there to maintain his own faultless performance of deference. The head bowed. 'My Führer,' said with such utter conviction.

A good coaching job had been done, Bormann said it himself, with plastic surgery to enhance the resemblance. This top fake knew the leader's record of greatest hits off by heart. The real reason Bormann had insisted on tape-recording the Führer's table talk wasn't posterity. It was a vital tool for imitators: the mesmerising voice was most of the trick.

When resting, the lives of these surrogates were very like that of the Führer's mistress: sidelined, cosseted, cloistered, endless waiting, ignored, semi-captive; insecure actors filling in days with study and rote, trying to make sense of their existence. Bormann suspected they lolled around slack and bored to tears, in the expectation of not being called, and anxious too, with redundancy being an unwritten part of the contract.

In Bormann's down-on-his-luck version of life after the war he pictured himself as master of ceremonies for a travelling show of these Führer freaks.

During that critical week, the understudy was required for a vital period of a few days before getting blown up. His main duty was to attend the daily war conference where he could fall back on the Führer's entitlement to silence and make a point of intense study of maps with a huge magnifying glass. Bormann told the man that he carried the country on his shoulders while the Führer recuperated from an essential operation at a time when he could not afford to be seen to be vulnerable through absence.

Bormann manipulated the Führer timetable even more ruthlessly than usual. The actor's props included a large handkerchief held to the face to soothe a raging toothache. The detail Bormann was proudest of was the same voluptuously bad breath, to remind you that you are in the presence, lest you forget. He permitted himself a private joke, telling those about to be shown in that the Führer was not himself, so tread gently.

As for the secretaries, the man had the Führer's courtesy to staff down to a tee, with Bormann cracking the whip so hard they were too scared silly to look up. To make sure, he made an example of a questioning adjutant with an immediate transfer to the Front.

As for the Führer's valet, the man was there to serve, however sloppily. If he guessed, it was not for him to question.

Bormann had him down anyway to be among the first to be shot, along with the blabbermouth quack Morell, who knew the Führer's pin-cushion arm better than his own. Bormann got his message across by standing too close and ordering Morell to carry on as normal.

After the bomb failed to do its job, Bormann saw how the explosion had performed a miraculous act of transubstantiation, as though the shockwave had soldered the essence of the Führer onto the understudy, at the cost of only lacerations and perforated eardrums. The man didn't break performance for a second and such was the chaos that no one would have noticed anyway. Bormann could only marvel – to the point of being tempted to applaud – at how the understudy swanned through the newsreel footage with a glazed stare, courtesy of Morell, in a more than passable imitation of a dazed and grateful Führer, spared by the hand of fate. Huge chutzpah – no other word for it – on Bormann's part, but no one was going to question whether the survivor of an enormous explosion was not the real thing until foreign newsreels got snide about it. And Heini and Göring weren't going to blow the whistle, being too compromised by their own positions.

It was the old lesson: foghorn the lie and they all still fall for it.

HERR WOLF

1931

28

Martin Bormann, 1931

Whether any story is true or not doesn't matter beyond the fact of its existence. The Führer is a master of the lie, which when it comes to his personal life is his blind spot. Call yourself Herr Wolf and promote yourself as a man of alias and intrigue then others bound to speculate. The stories about Herr Wolf had been going on for years. The ones about him picking up boys. People swore they had seen the police reports. It was said that Emil Maurice, ex-bodyguard and ex-chauffeur, who had marched alongside him during the failed putsch of 1923 and gone to prison with him, was his bum boy and the two were involved in a complicated ménage à trois with the Führer's niece. The murk and stew of the milieu made anything technically possible and, yes, something had been going on; the gossip – smut and giggles, most of it rank – said so. Drunken idleness and poor pay mean more or less anyone can be bought off.

Herr Wolf,'s trench coat, the whip and the holster and pistol were part of his Wild West image (well, not the Lederhosen); 'risqué' was part of the man's bohemian act, though Bormann was willing to bet the sex trophy cupboard wasn't nearly as full as Herr Wolf made out. As for Emil being his bum boy (and pimp, it was said, too), that was offered as the reason for Herr Wolf's tolerance of Emil's Jew grandmother. Bormann had no wish or desire to blackmail the Führer; he was there to serve and protect the man from his naivety. Emil he couldn't care less about. Come the time, any story could be made to stick – Jew-schmew, take it up the arse like a man. The pederasts would have to go, and in the case of the fairer sex Herr Wolf needed to settle for something a little duller.

From Bormann's side, Geli was a disaster. Gold-digger on the make, a classic good-time girl, 'fun loving' (and how!), leaving a soppy Führer making goo-goo eyes. Bormann personally found nothing complicated about sticking his dick between a woman's legs. Not the Führer. All infatuation, playing hard to get, and never real women, more girls, then making them miserable because they couldn't compete with a man wedded to his political destiny. Look at that shopgirl who tried to hang herself from a doorknob!

With Geli, the distraction was colossal. People sniggered as he escorted her around town; possessive uncle, idiot paramour – and the gossip! His niece! Regardless of what she was up to with her 'Onk', she was putting it about. Oversexed, a hormone fountain. The gossip wasn't good. Jews. A Jew musician. Another Jew lover. The latest rumour: she had stopped menstruating ... If the child were a little Wolf? Out of the question. Bormann had been told categorically: not on the cards. No reason was given but digging had been done: family in-breeding had produced a load of cretins. The relationship with his niece was incestuous: what would happen if another idiot were spawned? And if the Geli baby belonged to one of her Jew lovers? Even more out of the question.

Bormann couldn't see it, how everyone said she lit up the room. He tended to agree with Putzi (great name,

Bormann thought, but you're not going to hear from him again), who thought her a slut. Geli had been slutty enough with Bormann in making clear her availability. Tempted as he was, he had declined, apart from putting his hand up her skirt between her hot little legs and working her until she was gasping. Both knew that didn't count, technically, and left her in the role of guilty party. After that, they seemed to understand each other and Bormann made it clear that he saw himself as her protector if she ever wanted help or needed someone to confide in. He could see she didn't trust him but after an arrest for public drunkenness Bormann made sure no record was kept. Tearful gratitude told him what he needed to know in terms of her debt.

What she didn't tell him, he knew anyway, being on bidding terms with her father confessor (in some respects she remained the dutiful young woman). Father Peter was amenable to trading secrets of the confessional in exchange for charitable donations. She told him she had stopped menstruating and asked what she should do. Bormann supposed he could arrange a doctor if asked. He knew of three scrapers.

With Bormann, Geli was quite open on one subject: her frustration. She suspected the marriage she wanted more than anything was never going to happen. Was it possible to love too much? she asked. She was living in a gilded cage. She was trapped. Bormann thought that a little excessive. The girl put herself about as much as she liked, although he could see that her uncle was demanding and obsessive for little romance in return; and it must be creepy, if that wasn't too strong a word, to be kept semi-prisoner by a man nearly twice her age. And of course he paid. The latest was singing lessons. No great talent; so another waste, to go with all the rest Bormann shelled out for from Party funds.

He suspected Adolf was privately tiring of the farce, leaving him sulky and insecure, hence the plan to steer him in the direction of the photographer Hoffmann's undemanding little assistant. No tits, Fritz, but you can't have everything. Young Eva was eager to please and aware of her place; as was Bormann, who was as invisible as a top waiter, leaving him to operate the levers behind the scenes.

He was the factotum, the one who did the boring desk work when the rest couldn't be bothered, being too busy swanking. He kept the books, ensuring everything was organised, restaurant tables arranged, theatre tickets sorted. When the Führer bought his apartment it was Bormann who arranged for a top lawyer to negotiate the contract. It was Bormann who recommended he put a second home in the mountains in the name of his half-sister to avoid tax complications. It was Bormann who handled the Führer's financial affairs, at which the Führer was deliberately hopeless as it they interfered with his artistic image of himself; Bormann who dealt with the disputatious Munich tax office; Bormann who did everything for the man short of wipe his arse. The Führer was disorganised. A dreamer. A seer. He needed a desk jockey. 'Table for twelve, nine o'clock.' And Bormann was good. He didn't forget. He distilled information into what the Führer wanted to hear and gave it in spoon-sized bites. He made a point of being deferential, standing one step back, attentive, head inclined in a show of thoughtful enquiry. It was an act but one that suited, and Bormann made sure there was never cause for dissatisfaction or disagreement. The Führer approved of Bormann's aggressive womanising: no mistaking their master-servant relationship. The Führer could be effeminate, so it wouldn't do to have a secretary who was in any way swishy. Bormann wasn't even technically the Führer's secretary. He was secretary to deputy Hess, who probably was a fairy, despite having a little wife tucked away. Hess was no more interested in his desk than the Führer, always being off somewhere or consulting with astrological quacks. Bormann and the Führer could joke about such things, and when the Führer was in a good mood he addressed Bormann as Bubi, a pet name between Munich homos; a joke, of course.

Workload didn't matter to him. He left his wife at home, banged up with another child. The only sacrifice was not being able to smoke around the man. Bormann not only managed the Führer's money, his control of Party funds meant that many were forced to come to him for discretionary loans, being in hock and desperate for cash. Bormann had told the Führer that the cost of his new apartment was paid for out of his publishing royalties. The Führer was vain in liking to think his own efforts were responsible for what was a huge hike in lifestyle – nine rooms in the smartest part of town. Royalties were fair but nothing like enough for the current outlay.

With better quality investors financing the movement came the tricks of the trade, locating funds beyond the prying eyes of the tax office. Thanks to Anton Schlegel, tidy piles were building up in Swiss accounts, money that only Bormann and Anton knew the exact whereabouts of. Yet anyone looking at him would have thought him nothing more than his master's dogsbody. He made a point of good-dog behaviour when seen with the Führer and appeared friendly in his dealings with others. He knew what they said about him. Unctuous. Arse-licker. A pig when the rest were so aspirational now the Führer was climbing the social ladder.

*

Bormann the desk man knew he counted for nothing in the eyes of Ernst Röhm and his brownshirt shit. Nevertheless, Röhm condescended to drink with Bormann. He drank with anyone, and the favoured bars weren't that many. He preferred cheap standing ones, with beer shoved through a hatch. The Führer opted for seated dining areas, along with the rest of the head honchos.

The small room was noisy and heaving. Others had spilled out to drink in the street. Children came in with flagons to be filled to take home. Bormann spotted Anton Schlegel outside with a brownshirt lad. They didn't acknowledge each other. Bormann thought it wouldn't hurt if Schlegel thought he was Röhm's informer. Keep everyone on their toes. In fact Bormann was spying on Röhm for the Party.

He came to look back on that encounter with Röhm as defining the internal struggle. Straight versus homo. Political infiltration versus revolutionary violence. One in the ascendant, the other too blind to read the writing on the wall, leading three years later to the big clear out.

They pissed together, spraying copious amounts into the urinal trench. Röhm, shameless, leaned over with exaggerated amusement to inspect Bormann's cock.

Back outside, more drinks. Bormann watched the pansies strut. How he despised them. They thugged it up but none put in a shift. If Bormann had his way he would cut off the lot of their dicks.

Röhm tried to convince Bormann of his persuasion. 'It's not about handholding or any of that nonsense. It's based less on mutual attraction than the power of cock.' He gripped Bormann's knee. 'A beast like yours is wasted on women.'

Bormann held Röhm's eye. 'Cunt over arse any day.'

Röhm laughed loud and said, 'I hear your wife is a baby-making machine.'

'That's what they are there for.'

'Play away for a while.'

Bormann switched to the one subject that would see the hand removed – Röhm's beloved Führer – knowing that Röhm believed he was the only one tough enough to extract his master from the mire into which he had let himself fall.

'Female dalliance, social blandishments. He needs me back to reinstall some of the old revolutionary zeal. Everything has grown too bourgeois.'

Bormann tended to agree but Röhm had failed to grasp that social infiltration was integral to political advance.

'Hitler in love!' protested Röhm. 'And not just any old "in love". His fucking niece!'

Bormann had first become aware of this unlikely pair at his wedding, two years earlier. Marriage marked a big hike up the ladder after years of snubs. Fisticuffs counted; Bormann, who was running the Party pension and insurance fund at the time, did not. Plan B – target a daughter of good political standing. A big cold shoulder from the potential in-laws. Persistence. Peasant cunning and dick the girl couldn't get enough of. Nineteen. Pliable. In love and banged up before the wedding. Sour-faced in-laws make the best of a bad job, calling in the Führer to witness, with a view to him godfathering the firstborn. On the Führer's recommendation, Geli was a bridesmaid and the mother made the wedding cake.

The girl was a daredevil, Bormann could tell from her saucy air upon setting eyes on her at the party after the ceremony, where she did everything other than stick her tongue down his throat to steal the limelight from his bride.

On an occasion of visiting his godson, two years later,

dandling the baby awkwardly, the Führer said to Bormann unsolicited, 'It is an idyllic interlude I know must end – and she will go off and marry and have children and become like everyone else. How can we save her from that?'

Bormann's involvement with the shadier side of the Führer's private affairs had begun in the spring of 1929, two years before the business of the dirty drawings: what happens repeats. Looking back, he wondered if his success in dealing with the case of the potentially compromising letter had been his audition for admission into the inner circle, marked by the occasion of his marriage six months later. The bride's parents were what was known as 'Party people'.

The story of the letter had been passed on to Bormann by Party Treasurer Schwarz – an old fart with a leaky gut – for the simple reason that Schwarz didn't want to get embroiled in such a dubious business, so he delegated it to his ambitious junior, hoping that Bormann would make a mess of the job and damage his rising star.

At the time the Führer still lodged in his old bedsit, presenting himself to the world as the poor, have-not revolutionary. He had apparently written an indiscreet letter to his niece, containing 'some pretty dark stuff' according to Schwarz. The letter wasn't sent and had been taken from the Führer's desk. Bormann knew such thefts were not untypical, with a lot of souvenir hunters around by then. While the Führer was fiercely protected in public, he was negligent about domestic security, claiming he had nothing to steal.

That was less true than it had been. The Führer's tax return for 1925 claimed his only property was a desk and two bookcases, along with the books. The difference now was the man was a public commodity. The most dedicated collectors let it be known that even the contents of the Führer's wastepaper basket were of potential value. Draft speeches, musings, doodles – everything counted.

No one took such scavenging seriously – apart from the collectors – until the letter in question. Bormann's first move was to contact a couple of creeps who called themselves Party archivists and traded in such material: Father Bernhard Stempfle, Roman Catholic priest and antisemitic scribbler of dubious repute, lurking behind the manner of a plausible academic, and his teeny sidekick Rehse.

Stempfle's claim to fame was that he had rewritten and edited large chunks of the Führer's *Mein Kampf*, whereas the Führer considered it all his own work, so was not well disposed, leaving Stempfle with a grudge about not getting a cut of the royalties. The gnomelike Rehse was a mad collector and self-appointed curator of Party memorabilia, which amounted to the sum of his personal collection of posters, bulletins, scraps and tat going back years, which now took up so much space in his apartment that the floor was buckling. Rehse had kept every possible souvenir, anticipating that his investment would one day pay off, but if he had no money the Party didn't either, or said it hadn't, and the so-called archive received no financial support, despite his repeated requests. The Führer was not inclined, dismissing Rehse as little more than a tramp. Bormann witnessed an embarrassing confrontation in the Park Café beer garden, with Rehse twisting a greasy cap in his hands as he stood before the Führer begging for money while the rest of the table, including Bormann, laughed. Bormann knew Rehse as one of those toadies who made himself indispensable by volunteering for everything; he was uncomfortably aware of their similarities.

Bormann arranged to meet Stemple and Rehse in the same beer garden that had witnessed Rehse's humiliation.

It was the first of the good spring weather. They sat under dusty trees coming into leaf.

Stempfle assumed a knowing air, claiming to have seen the letter and saying it was being offered for sale.

Bormann argued that with the Führer's reputation at risk discretion was essential. Stempfle must buy back the letter to stop it falling into the wrong hands.

'Of course,' said Stempfle. 'Exactly what I had in mind.' He looked at Rehse, who said, 'But we're strapped for cash.'

'We have no budget,' Stempfle added meaningfully. 'The point is we are discreet. Others might not be.' He pursed fleshy lips.

'How compromising is this wretched letter?' Bormann asked.

'Depraved.'

Bormann asked, 'What's the worst of it?'

Stempfle leaned forward and whispered, 'The writer expresses a desire to be defecated on.' He recoiled in horror.

Bormann shrugged that off. 'I spend my whole time being shat on.'

He noted Rehse's canniness, making out he hadn't actually seen the letter, and letting Stempfle make the running.

'Gentlemen,' Bormann told them in conclusion, 'if it is a matter of buying it back then that is what you must do. I leave it to you to sort out. The money will be found.'

Seeing their exchange of looks, Bormann wondered if Stempfle and Rehse were not quite the innocent go-betweens and the letter was veiled blackmail to raise some cash for themselves.

Bormann considered the matter settled and told Schwarz so. It wasn't. Stempfle came straight back to report what he called a 'complication'. The letter wasn't the problem. Party assets were at risk. The very future of the archive was in jeopardy.

'What has that to do with the letter?' Bormann demanded. 'I said the money would be forthcoming.'

He had expected Stempfle to haggle over his fee but had not expected any further wrangling. He was even more inclined to believe Stempfle and Rehse had cooked up the whole thing.

'I thought you should be aware of the wider picture,' said Stempfle. 'Others are expressing interest in buying the archive, including Moscow.'

'Moscow!'

'Clearly, they appreciate its value. There is more than one offer on the table.'

'How long has this been going on?'

'I have only just heard. I merely pass on what I know.'

'Is it Rehse?'

'Apparently he is just as much in the dark as I am. But serious sums are being talked about, offering a degree of financial security. We have dedicated ourselves to the Party for years, for nothing in return, even after others started being looked after.'

'Just buy back the bloody letter,' said Bormann, losing patience.

Stempfle pointed out that if the Party had the money to retrieve the letter it should also take financial responsibility for the archive.

Bormann suspected that these higher stakes were what Stempfle had had in mind all along and the letter itself was little more than a gambit.

Bormann told Stempfle not to do anything. He would make enquiries and get straight back to him. He cursed to himself. He had underestimated Stempfle's reputation for haggling and intrigue.

His first reaction was to have Emil Maurice and his gang drop Stempfle from a high building.

But Anton Schlegel had other ideas.

By then he and Bormann conferred regularly. Although Anton was not a Party member, they had a shared interest in hiding money. Anton had taught Bormann how to build up secret funds, away from the prying eyes of the tax office and the Party.

That evening Bormann and Anton Schlegel happened to run across each other, not so unusual in Munich where regular haunts were no more than a handful, and Bormann complained how Stempfle was making a fool of him.

Anton Schlegel listened and said he should see it more as an opportunity than a hindrance.

'Whether these potential buyers exist, Stempfle is right,' he went on. 'Any thought of the Party losing its historical record is out of the question. In exchange for their fixing for the letter to be taken off the table, tell Stempfle that the Party accepts that the archive needs to be preserved and run properly.'

'But everyone knows the archive is a joke.'

'Not in the long run. I am sure Herr Wolf can be persuaded of its potential value. Funds could be made available and these would be tax-deductible.'

Bormann came to accept the sense of the idea, especially the tax break.

'Are you saying leave them to sort out the business of the letter in exchange for the larger reward?'

Anton nodded. 'Give them a budget for cataloguing, storage and fees for themselves as curators. Tell Rehse and Stempfle they are visionaries who have shown how order and organisation of assets will become the backbone of the Party. That way they will be beholden to you and the archive will come under your virtual control.'

Bormann saw that Anton was right.

'Besides,' Anton continued, 'documentation is power and an archive is memory and a useful deposit for all kinds of information. What, for instance, shall you do with the letter in question?'

'Have it, destroyed, I suppose, so it can do no damage.'

'It's of importance as a historical document.'

Bormann snorted. 'It's probably a cheap fake written by Stempfle, if it exists. We only have his word.'

'The point is, all such documentation has a value and should be protected.'

Considered by others a dark, labyrinthine force, Anton saw himself as quite easy, in that he sat above. Later, Bormann heard stories that it was Anton who was behind the whole business of the letter, having identified the archive as somewhere into which he could insert himself. Others even attributed the letter's authorship to Anton. Some form of *quid pro quo* seemed to have occurred because soon after Anton became responsible for acquiring books for the Herr Wolf's library. A lot of shelves to fill in the man's dreary new apartment.

His accommodation was discussed on the occasion of that evening's meeting, saved for last when Anton Schlegel gave Bormann a meaningful look and said, 'You need a plan B for Herr Wolf.'

'In what way?'

'He should start to be seen making his way in the world. Decent accommodation is now essential; no more bedsits. He needs proper security and a household staff that can be relied on to report to you. We both know Herr Wolf needs looking after.'

As for Stempfle, Bormann thought: I will have you yet. He did too, a patient three years later, in the purge of the Night of the Long Knives. Emil Maurice broke the man's spine before finishing him off, after Bormann had told him not to make it quick.

MUNICH

1944

29

Schlegel and Morgen arrived at Munich station on the night train, mysteriously without Anna Huber, who had failed to show up, leaving them guessing. Schlegel worried she had been detained.

The shabby tourist office in the station told them everywhere was booked and with almost no rooms to be had. All the woman on the desk could offer was sharing a double in a cheap hotel behind the station. Schlegel supposed some kind of refugee crisis. Were the bombed-out being put up in four star hotels?

The hotel – more of a dive really – came in shades of dirty brown. A girl who looked about twelve sat behind a tiny reception counter under a turn of the stairs, and being an efficient little Nazi was bossy about them filling out their registration forms.

The room, more shades of brown, consisted of two single beds with lumpy mattresses and faded covers, a table in between, grimy linoleum, and curtains so threadbare they were transparent. The window overlooked a cul-de-sac off a main street. Schlegel could hear distant traffic. Whatever his love–hate relationship with Berlin, it was at least a known quantity.

Munich was in the process of being even more rearranged than Berlin. Being smaller, the air raids were more intense, leaving skeleton buildings and rubble everywhere.

Its southern remoteness was emphasised by Schlegel's feeling of looking at everything the wrong way round since Gerda's death. There was no obvious way into the past. Even attempting to access it seemed futile in the context of such a blasted present. Everything took longer. Munich was more provincial, less commercial and metropolitan, lazier, Catholic and God-fearing, nearly Austrian, with a bewitched quality that a hard-headed Berlin could never aspire to. Ill winds and deeper waters, despite the forceful air of cosy cheer; a greater clarity to the sky, with the mountains not far off. Not Berlin's grey city.

It was a landscape traversed, more than Berlin, as they were reduced to bicycles, after the promised car from the local police department failed to materialise. Morgen announced they were from Berlin, using the temporary title granted him by Müller that went on forever. It included the phrase 'special investigative powers', which made the local police sit up but not enough to find them a car. The bicycles rather belittled the fanciness of Morgen's title.

As for the Raubal case, it remained ring-fenced. They were given copies of four sheets. Morgen asked, 'Is this it?' They were informed it was the sum of available paperwork. They were told the two officers that had handled the case were no longer around and the police doctor was dead. Gestapo Müller had said he could offer no official help, but, even so, Morgen expected more in the way of liaison. The Munich cops made it clear they weren't interested in Berlin butting in. Morgen suspected it was because their original investigation wouldn't bear re-examination.

Schlegel soon hated Munich. Old Party haunts hung around like second-rate museum exhibits. From the perspective of his wobbly bicycle, everything struck him as old-fashioned, boring and traditional, down to the ponderous neo-classical works of the last dozen years.

No one was sightseeing by then. Barely a dozen years and a whole world replaced. The former Party headquarters in the Brown House had boarded windows, pitted brickwork and walls missing. Inside they found a skeleton staff of elderly and infirm deadbeats. Among the organisations listed as being in the building was the Chamber of Commerce. They were told it had moved. Where nobody could say as they were waiting for the directory to be updated.

In bars and cafés once patronised by the Party, the old waiters were gone and the few left made a show of not remembering. The Bratwurst Glöckl smelled of harsh cleaning fluid. Schlegel noted uncomfortable looking chairs, knick-knacks on high shelves and leaded, stained glass windows that gave the place the feel of a dry aquarium. The manager he had spoken to on the telephone was politer when physically confronted. He claimed he wasn't really the manager, and was standing in for a cousin in hospital. He pointed out the Party's old table and looked depressed at the thought of having missed out on such fine times. Zehnter's name was barely remembered.

In the once risqué and artistic Schwabing quarter, the cabaret artists and homos and rowdy press boys had long been chased out, leaving the rest keeping their heads down. Mention of Anton Schlegel sometimes produced a vague frown of recognition before the obligatory shake of the head. No one remembered being in the room with him. But cities were big places. Why should anyone in Munich have heard of his father, Schlegel thought, any more than people in Berlin knew about him?

Hoffmann's photography shop had a sign in the window saying it was closed for the afternoon. The reason to talk to its proprietor was that the Führer's official photographer was apparently among the last to see the niece alive.

The Party Archive informed them that Rehse was out of town for the day.

Munich at first seemed simple enough in terms of navigation but Schlegel could not get the hang of the place and, as in a maze, he felt he was constantly losing his bearings. Yet the feeling persisted that he was standing on the edge of a world where everyone had known everyone else. At the same time, he suspected denial would set the tone, and they would be met with the equivalent to signs everywhere saying 'no access'.

They ate despondently in the station café where cucumber and tomato was the only plate available from a menu boasting far more. The place, empty at first, was suddenly full of soldiers, most of them the latest conscription of boys.

They went over what little paperwork they had: a doctor's report, two morticians' statements and a speeding ticket.

Police doctor Müller's summary stated that death had occurred on the evening of Friday, 18 September 1931, and rigor mortis had set in several hours before the body's discovery the following morning.

'Not exactly forensic, is it?' said Morgen.

The rest of the statement was even sketchier: the fatal shot had penetrated through the dress to pass directly above the heart and lodge in the left side of the back, above the hip, where it could be felt beneath the skin.

'Is that all?' said Schlegel.

Morgen said, 'You would expect an autopsy, to confirm cause of death.'

They turned to the morticians' statements, both of which parroted each other, declaring no bruising to the body and in particular no breakage to the nose.

'Why say so if there wasn't?' asked Morgen.

'Unless they were coerced into stating otherwise.'

Morgen read, '"I noticed no injuries and in particular saw nothing suspicious about the nose." Sounds like it was dictated. What does that say to you?'

'That the Party was all over the case before anyone called the cops.'

'The speeding ticket's genuine, you can't argue with that. Issued to the Führer's Mercedes in Ebenhausen, soon after half past one on the afternoon of 19 September. Convenient, though, in proving that the man was away. It looks to me like more strings than in an orchestra were being pulled.'

'She was a Roman Catholic, I presume,' said Schlegel.

'Most Austrians are.'

'Do we know how she was buried?'

'Normally, I suppose.'

'Except suicides cannot be received for burial by the Catholic church.'

The hotel bathroom stood at the end of the landing. The toilet, displaying evidence of the last user's deposit, wouldn't flush. Schlegel pissed sideways into the bowl in an effort not to disturb its contents. He caught sight of himself in the mirror and thought how odd he appeared. Morgen had bought the hair dye and told him to use it, otherwise he was too conspicuous, should anyone come after him. He'd had to plaster gunk over his scalp and rinse it out. The water had come out of the tap brown and was as black as squid's ink by the time he was done.

Morgen made no comment but seemed privately amused. Schlegel hadn't liked his white hair but had grown used to it. Now he looked like everyone else, apart from the ferocious black of the dye.

They went to bed early, depressed at the prospect of sharing, and lay in the dark listening to each other not sleeping. Schlegel wondered what Morgen hoped to prove.

Morgen turned over restlessly and attempted to thump some shape into his tired pillow.

'Of course, on a point of law, we're wasting our time,' he said, more to himself than to Schlegel. 'It has been impossible to start legal proceedings against the Führer since 1933.'

Schlegel was surprised to find himself pessimistically cheered by that, and replied with an attempt at a brightness he did not feel: 'Perhaps the reason for that lies with what really happened to the niece.'

Morgen grunted.

Schlegel drifted off with sad images of Gerda in his head and wondered why Anna Huber hadn't showed up. When at last he slid into unconsciousness he had a feeling they hadn't heard the last of her.

30

The Führer's apartment in Prinzregentenplatz, a pregnant-looking building with bulging bays, stood across the river in a smart part of town, offset from the tight core of its central locations. The front door had an electrical release. No one answered number 16. Morgen tried the tradesman's bell and they were buzzed in, but when they rang the apartment door they heard someone coming. Schlegel wondered how long since the Führer was last there.

Schlegel's first impression of Frau Winter, the custodian of the apartment, was a woman conditioned by service, duty and obedience – and, to outsiders, an expert in proprietorial silence.

She was younger than Schlegel was expecting and presented herself as neither attractive nor unattractive. She dressed formally and carried herself with the self-contained air of one elevated above regular domestic service to a position of responsibility and trust, in exchange for total discretion. Frau Winter did not greet, she admitted. Schlegel wondered what she thought of her boss.

Morgen said they were there for a security inspection, a precaution after recent events. However reluctant she looked about letting them in, Frau Winter had no choice but to defer to Morgen's rank.

The apartment had been given a full makeover, with uncontroversial but no doubt extremely expensive interior design calculated to show evidence of a thoughtful, contemplative man of taste and judgement, surrounded by massive, dark furniture, so solid that most of it looked immovable. The first impression was of a space under-lived in for all the money chucked at it.

The grandest rooms overlooked the square, with huge doors out of all proportion to human scale. Schlegel decided it wasn't that the taste was bad, just wonky, with no personality beyond flat statements about acquisition and power. On a low table in a formal reception room stood a bronze bust of a young woman, clearly Raubal. Schlegel asked and Winter said it had been commissioned after the girl's death, making it plain that her job was to protect her master's privacy and not to act as a tour guide.

Morgen asked how many people had been there at the time of the niece's death.

Winter asked what did that have to do with present security.

Morgen snapped, 'Your job is to answer my questions, not question them.'

'None,' she replied coldly. 'We were dismissed as she meant to go out that evening, to the cinema with a friend.'

'Was she upset about anything?' asked Schlegel.

'Well, her pet canary had just died,' Winter eventually offered, with barely veiled insolence.

Morgen said, 'We have been asked to summarise the case of Fräulein Raubal, to refute certain false documentation recently come to light.'

Schlegel thought that sounded convincing enough; he had no idea if it were true. Morgen, as usual, continued to play his hand very close to his chest.

'When was this business of the canary?' Morgen went on.

'After the Führer left, I saw her wandering around the

apartment, crooning to the dead bird, which lay on cotton wool in a little box.'

Schlegel asked what staff had been present that day.

'Myself, as house manager. Frau Reichert, the live-in housekeeper; she had been the landlady at the Führer's former lodgings.' Winter made that sound rather infra dig. 'The daily housemaid and the cook. There was was Frau Drachs too.'

Drachs turned out to be Reichert's mother and profoundly deaf. She had no duties but the Führer had taken pity on her and let her live there.

Schlegel thought: And the lot of them conveniently out when it happened.

They were shown the library with the Führer's extensive collection of books. Morgen spotted several self-help manuals on how to improve your public speaking and pointed them out to Schlegel, who kept a straight face. He wondered if the Führer's relationship with Anton Schlegel had extended to being in this room, and under what circumstances.

The Führer's sleeping quarters were surprisingly modest. At first Frau Winter claimed the bedroom was out of bounds, being private. Morgen whipped out Müller's lengthy description of his responsibilities and held it up for inspection. 'Be quick, then,' she said and stopped Schlegel, establishing her authority by saying, 'Only one of you.'

She made it plain without saying so that in the absence of her master this dead space was hers to command. Schlegel supposed, given that it had been empty for so long, she had nothing to do other than treat their intrusion with resentment.

He contented himself with inspecting the bathroom, which had an air of impersonal luxury, like something in the Adlon Hotel. He found it impossible to imagine the man naked in his bath; and had the niece ever sat in it, having her back soaped by her uncle?

They were shown the kitchen and staff quarters: separate enough to ensure the apartment's privacy.

'And Fräulein Raubal's room?' Morgen asked.

Frau Winter took them there with the greatest reluctance. It was at the front, next to the main reception.

'The room is a shrine,' she said. 'To which no one is admitted but the Führer and myself, to change the flowers.'

Morgen insisted. 'We have authorisation.'

Frau Winter said she hadn't got around to replacing the flowers yet.

'Chrysanthemums. Her favourite.'

The door was locked. The key was produced unwillingly and Morgen asked, 'Did Fräulein Raubal lock the door before shooting herself?'

'Yes,' said Winter.

'When did anyone grow alarmed?'

'I came in on the Saturday morning and saw her breakfast and newspaper were still on the tray outside the door.'

'What time was this?' asked Morgen.

'About half past nine. I decided she must have had a late night.' Frau Winter said it in such a way that implied such nights were not infrequent. 'It was the Oktoberfest.'

'Did you knock?'

She sighed as if to say she couldn't see the point of their questioning. 'About an hour later I did to ask if she was all right. That was when I found the door locked.'

'Did she usually lock it?'

'I am not here at night.' Frau Winter said.

They were still standing outside the room. Schlegel

thought: If it turned out that the niece hadn't killed herself then it was like one of those old locked-room mysteries.

Frau Winter opened the door and they stepped over the threshold into the gloom of what resembled a theatrical set. The shuttered room made the presence of any flowers pointless. Those in the vase hadn't been changed in a long time. Schlegel suspected the room's neglected state reflected Frau Winter's depression at being abandoned by her master.

Frau Winter looked as though she wanted to stop Morgen as he turned on the main light. The room stood in stark contrast to the renovation of the rest of the apartment with nothing changed in the past thirteen years, frozen as in a fairy story. Schlegel noted the single bed, a desk under the window, a settee, and a gramophone. The furniture was painted with stencilled motifs. The walls were pastel green. An illusion of continuity was maintained by the made-up bed with its embroidered sheets. In contrast to the cavernous space next door the room was poky and ill-proportioned, with the ceiling too high for its width. Schlegel wondered how often the Führer thought of this morbid space as he put the world to rights.

'I need your version of what happened for the record,' said Morgen.

Frau Winter looked at him with great hauteur, as though he was questioning her loyalty.

Morgen went on. 'We can take it here or you will need to accompany us to a police station.'

Slowly she began to speak. Her automatic recital of how the girl died came out pat, as if it had been kept in mothballs all those years.

The bare facts were that the Führer and his niece had lunched together on that last Friday. Spaghetti, Frau Winter remembered; after which the Führer was fetched by his photographer Hoffmann to drive to Nuremberg. Soon after their departure the girl locked the door of her room and at some point later must have shot herself with the Führer's pistol. As Fräulein Raubal had the only key to the room, Frau Winter, upon growing alarmed the following morning, telephoned her husband to discuss whether to break down the door. In the end, not wanting to incur a bill for damages, a locksmith was summoned. The long and short of it was that it was midday before the police were contacted. By the time the Führer arrived back that afternoon they were done and gone.

'It doesn't sound as though the police were particularly thorough,' said Morgen.

Frau Winter said, 'If they acted in haste it was out of consideration. They were very efficient and sympathetic. Such a tragic death and they could see how upset we all were.'

Hoffmann's version blamed the weather. The autumn Föhn had been blowing, an ill wind causing everyone to be out of sorts.

'Enough to shoot yourself?' enquired Morgen mildly.

'It can be the very devil. The Führer remarked on it at the time, saying he had the most uneasy feeling of premonition.'

They had found Hoffmann in his shop. He was short, fat, with a vastly protruding belly and a head with an otter's sleekness. The first thing he asked was whether they had been sent by Bormann, to which Morgen replied, 'Why ever should we be?' and Hoffmann responded, 'I tell you, that man wants me dead.'

When he learned they were there to ask about the Führer's niece he assumed the air of a forgetful man.

'Whatever for? Yes, of course. Come through.'

He made a show of ushering them in and drew the blind on the door after him, taking them through the shop and down a corridor to a comfortable room with a tiled stove. Schlegel realised Hoffmann was drunk as he walked past him.

'Real coffee, gentlemen? Which I happen to have.' Hoffmann rubbed his hands in a show of bonhomie and said it was all such a long time ago that he doubted what he could remember.

He called, 'Fräulein Braun!'

A thin very well-dressed woman in her early thirties came through, in a haze of perfume, and regarded them haughtily.

'Would you mind serving these gentlemen coffee?'

Fräulein Braun looked at Hoffmann as if to say it was beyond her brief, whatever that was.

The woman was a perfect clothes horse. The tinted, permed blonde hair looked like it had just been set. The immaculate make-up was understated, with carefully applied lipstick in a cupid's bow. The presentation was in calculated contrast to the natural look advocated for women, but Braun got away with it by being obviously trim and sporty, and generally alert. The impression was of brimming good health. Only the startled brightness of the eyes suggested it might be enhanced.

Hoffmann said, 'Fräulein Braun was my assistant at the time of Fräulein Raubal's death. She still comes in when her other duties allow.'

Morgen supposed this was *the* Fräulein Braun, described by Gestapo Müller as Hitler's friend. The mutual dislike between her and Hoffmann was evident. Morgen noted straight seams on silk stockings as she turned away after agreeing to make coffee.

The point of that was to show how it was properly done.

They were called through to a set table, with silverware and a coffee aroma strong enough to turn their knees weak.

Why the woman should be in the shop at all, Morgen could not decide. It was clearly beneath her. He suspected the silver service was to put Hoffmann in his place. The man gave every appearance of letting standards slip. Fräulein Braun served them as though she were conducting an etiquette lesson, with a saccharine overlay (cake and fake cream). She withdrew, closing the door behind her, after pointedly asking, 'Is that all?'

'What does Fräulein Braun do?' enquired Morgen as they listened to her departing footsteps.

'She supervises the Führer's mountain retreat,' said Hoffmann with sufficient innuendo to make his meaning clear. 'She first met the Führer here in the shop when Herr Wolf came to visit.' Hoffmann chuckled obsequiously. 'He liked to present himself as a man of mystery and often went by that name. Fräulein Braun was up a ladder at the time and he admired her legs.'

A brittle creature, thought Morgen, certainly with airs and graces, given the way she had just put them all in their place.

'When did this historic meeting occur?' he asked.

'She was seventeen at the time, so fifteen years ago. In October, I do remember that. October was always a significant month for the Führer.'

'I say, this coffee is really good,' Morgen remarked conversationally. 'Yet Fräulein Braun still works for you.'

'When she's in town she handles my photographic press. She likes to use the darkroom here as she is a photographer in her own right.'

Hoffmann looked doubtful about that.

So the woman lived in the mountains, kept a place in town and used her employer's facilities; it didn't strike

Morgen as a particularly extravagant relationship between her and the Führer. Much younger. Nothing too grand. He wondered if the Führer had been running the two young women in tandem.

'Did Fräulein Raubal and Fräulein Braun know each other?' he asked.

Hoffmann gave another chuckle. 'Only as rivals.'

Hoffmann served himself a large belt of schnapps from a sideboard, after half-heartedly offering it in the expectation of their refusing. Hoffmann took a mouthful, smacked his lips and set the glass down with the steadiness of a seasoned drunk. A sentimental one, too, Schlegel saw from the way the man's eyes moistened at mention of the niece.

Fräulein Braun, in a hat and putting on gloves, came through to tell Hoffman she was going out and might be back later. She barely glanced at Morgen and Schlegel as she swept past, saying only, 'Gentlemen.'

She was opening the door when Morgen called her name and she turned with a look that told him he was exceeding himself.

'Well?' she asked as she continued to fiddle with her gloves.

'Were you at all familiar with Fräulein Raubal?'

'I don't see what business that is of yours.'

'We are looking for her diary.'

Even Hoffmann sat up at that.

'I am sure I wouldn't know. We never met. There was a mother and a brother, I believe,' she said with affected vagueness. She remained by the door, dismissive and expectant. Morgen said nothing and finally she turned to Hoffmann. 'Perhaps they are confusing me with Henny. She knew Fräulein Raubal well. Picnics and all that.'

Henny was his daughter, Hoffmann chipped in, and she

was now wife of the governor of Vienna. He sat back, the proud father.

'Yes,' concluded Fräulein Braun, 'she would be the one to ask.'

She left without further ado. Hoffmann muttered under his breath what sounded like, 'Stuck-up bitch,' but he would not be drawn further on the subject of Fräulein Braun. Instead he stood and said, 'Come.'

Hoffmann was an unstoppable show-off. He boasted that he was the only one who could talk the hind legs off the Führer. Although a man of immense self-regard, he was careful to make out he was just 'a humble snapper'.

They were shown photograph after photograph of the Führer. Boxes and boxes, albums and albums. Early self-conscious poses. Rallies. Speeches. Resting. Themed. And the books churned out! Hoffman reprised the story told to Schlegel by Goebbels, how in the earliest days an American agency had put a price on the Führer's head.

'A fabulous bounty for any photograph of the elusive, unsnapped Führer, and I got him too, only to have the film confiscated by his bodyguard.' Hoffmann looked at them with buzzing delight. 'What they don't know is I nailed him again, without anyone noticing. Let me show you.'

The photograph was proudly displayed: the young Führer leaving a building, accompanied by henchmen. Schlegel was struck by the strutting, naked thuggishness, with the entourage assuming the pose of gangsters.

Schlegel asked Hoffmann if he knew the others in the picture. Hoffmann named them. On the right, next to the Führer: Emil Maurice. He wore a uniform and cap, which distracted from any proper impression. Young. They were all young men. Maurice looked wiry.

Schlegel stared at the man who was supposed to have killed his father, yet apparently hadn't. The dark eyes, if not murderous, suggested huge indifference towards the general welfare of his fellow man. Schlegel found he couldn't look for long.

He turned to the rest of the photograph, noted the dressing up, as though they were trying on an image. Everyone appeared strangely unformed, even the glaring Führer and Emil Maurice, who had the air of an aspiring matinee idol with his narrow little moustache. Unpressed uniforms but shiny boots. A huge sense of playacting. Those that grew moustaches and those that didn't.

Hoffmann said he had always remained popular with the Führer, who was amused and entertained by him, but not so Bormann. 'You see, I shattered the wall of isolation that Bormann has been building around the Führer, so he plotted against me.'

Bormann had recently insisted anyone exposed to the Führer be subjected to a medical checkup and in Hoffmann's case rigged the results to show he was carrying a highly infectious strain of typhus, which disqualified him from any further contact.

'What rot! I am as fit as a fiddle. Even Fräulein Braun supports me on this because she knows Bormann is capable of any dirty trick that suits his book.'

Hoffmann turned back to the photographs with a bitter laugh, and said, 'Now, here's something. What's unusual about this photograph?'

'Two Führers,' said Morgen.

The occasion was the opening of an autobahn in 1936, when the man and one of his understudies had turned up for the same ceremony. One stood to the left, wearing a peaked cap, hands folded, as if protecting his crotch. He looked entertained, as did the senior Party officials around him, at the sight of an identical looking man cutting the tape, who wore the same cap and uniform, making it appear as though an act of teleportation had occurred.

'Why two?' asked Morgen.

'Admin cock-up, which was good for me. I sold this for big bucks to *Time* magazine, which reported the story and the good-natured response of the Führer to the amusement of the crowd.'

Living proof, thought Schlegel, of the existence of doubles.

'You must have photographed the niece too,' Morgen said.

'Never to my satisfaction. Something essential always seemed missing.'

'We heard Fräulein Raubal was a great beauty,' Morgen said.

'In the room, undoubtedly. Such *joie de vivre*.'

The photographs were disappointing. The subject over-projected. Hoffmann failed to hide a heavy jaw, or make much of her round face or capture any animation. The impression was of a pleasant-looking pudding of a young woman.

Hoffmann sighed. 'It's like being a sharpshooter. You may miss a lot but you bag them in the end. I never did that with her. The closest I came was one afternoon on a picnic. There's this one.'

The photograph showed her in profile leaning back on the grass, wearing a summer dress with a bold print, and gazing in adoration at her uncle, who was zonked out in a deck chair, making the picture unintentionally comic.

'And this one. A saucy moment,' said Hoffmann.

It showed her paddling on a lakeshore. She wore a pale sleeveless shift, and was standing up to her knees in water, turning to laugh at the lens.

'I was trying to catch her unawares. She was staring at the water lost in thought, a quite wonderful expression, but then she caught me watching and lifted her skirt and flashed her thigh, giving me that daring look.'

It was the only photograph in which she looked natural, Schlegel thought.

Hoffmann said mournfully that you had to be with her to appreciate her. 'Such spirit.'

'Such a tragic end,' said Morgen, with the air of a weary prompter. 'You must have been one of the last people to have seen her alive when you collected the Führer on the Friday afternoon.'

'Who could have known it would turn out like that when we said goodbye to her? I remember her leaning over the bannister as if it were yesterday. There had been a spat but nothing to suggest that she felt impelled to kill herself. The Führer admitted to me in the car that Fräulein Raubal had been in a mood because she thought he was neglecting her. He was embarrassed that staff had heard them arguing over lunch – he had asked the cook for spaghetti, one of his favourites, and a good meal was ruined by her running from the table and smashing things in her room, which could be heard all over the apartment. But nothing to suggest ...'

Schlegel pointed out that this was very different from the official statement which insisted there had been no disagreement between the Führer and his niece.

Hoffmann said, 'He only wished to protect her reputation. Well, she had confessed to me that she felt constrained and neglected ...'

Morgen asked what sort of constraints.

'She liked parties and dancing.' Hoffmann did a shimmy and gave them a glimpse of his act as life and soul of the party. 'But Herr Wolf don't boogie-woogie.'

'You're pretty light on your feet, Hoffmann,' said Morgen.

Hoffmann stopped, breathless, and smoothed down already smooth hair, passing both hands over his scalp, as he told them that the outcome of her social restrictions was a series of much older chaperones, himself included.

'The innocent fun of such outings was quite spoiled.' He assumed a serious expression to make up for the frivolity of a moment before. 'Frau Winter confided to me that Geli was not happy about living in the apartment, and on that last afternoon, after we had gone, she remained disconsolate and angry, and complained, "I have nothing in common with my uncle."'

'She told you that?' Morgen exclaimed. 'Frau Winter doesn't strike me as the type to volunteer anything.'

'To outsiders. When it came to the Führer's welfare, she was fiercely protective.'

Hoffmann and Winter's combined versions made complete sense to Schlegel. That said, he couldn't see Winter confiding anything to Hoffmann under normal circumstances: one a blabbermouth and the other a basilisk of discretion. Neither would speak ill of the niece – loyalty to the Führer would preclude that – but the impression was of a spoiled brat who was hard to handle. Although Schlegel didn't actively question anything that either had said, he thought it might be because they had both learned their lines like actors for a play.

'In the end, do you have any idea why she did it?' Morgen asked.

'The only thing I can think of is the letter,' said Hoffmann.

'What letter?'

'I don't wish to speak ill of the dead, but Fräulein Raubal must have gone through her uncle's pockets after he had left, found it, read it and tore it up. Frau Winter discovered it later in the wastepaper basket and taped it back together.'

Hoffmann shrugged and said, 'Geli could be a compulsive girl. The letter . . . and the Führer's pistol to hand . . .'

'A note from whom?' asked Morgen.

'Why, Fräulein Braun. Did I not say?'

The Führer's flame, the same woman who had just served them a fine cup of real coffee.

The torn-up taped-back letter and the business of the dead canary – Schlegel thought them like clues in a third-rate mystery. It occurred to him that for a woman who volunteered so little, Frau Winter had observed a lot.

GELI

31

Anton Schlegel, August 1931

In the summer of 1931, Anton Schlegel acquired a dog, and a central Munich apartment, which he house-sat, after being talked into taking care of the dog for a wealthy widow who had taken herself off on a long sea cruise. The dog was a wire-haired fox terrier and required her daily walk.

Anton had spent much of the previous year travelling, mainly in South America, before returning to Munich to find that the Führer had become like a movie star, with fans and autograph hunters, and a huge publicity machine. Then there was the big complication of his 'princess' niece, with all the gossip about her, everything from angel to slut, from meadow in full bloom to a field everyone had ploughed.

The niece declared herself in love with Anton's dog when they ran into each other in the English Garden. By then they knew each other enough to say hello.

'What an adorable dog!' she exclaimed and declared how much cuter it was than her uncle's German shepherds.

The next day she was there again.

Anton Schlegel found her uninhibited and uncensored. She said more or less straight away, 'I have decided to trust you.'

'What makes you think I am trustworthy?'

'I didn't say you were, just that I have decided to.' She gave a delightful peal of laughter. 'I may be lazy and not much up for work but I am not as stupid as I make out.'

He supposed her somewhat theatrical as a result of being thrust into the limelight.

They walked and talked most days.

She asked if Anton knew her uncle.

'I know him as Herr Wolf. We met first in 1925.'

'Let's call him Herr Wolf, then!' she said, playing along. 'Are you friends?'

'We talk a lot.'

'What about?'

'Books and films mainly. The importance of a library. Cinema as a projection for mass entertainment, which modern leadership must learn to emulate.'

She asked what he did.

He said he didn't have to do anything. 'I'm a man of leisure. Well, some stocks and shares, that sort of thing.'

'Money's so boring. What films do you like?'

He said he liked *M*, which had come out earlier than summer.

She said, 'Why would anyone want to see a film about a child murderer? What else do you like?'

He said he had liked *Dr Mabuse* but it was an old film.

'What was that about?'

'A criminal mastermind.'

She laughed and said, 'Child killers and criminal masterminds! Tell me something properly interesting about yourself.'

Anton Schlegel thought about that and said, 'I suspect I am what Herr Wolf most wishes he were.'

'What's that?'

'An orphan and a foundling. I have no idea who my real parents were and was raised by a wealthy, childless couple whom I detested. I find myself drawn to men who formed intense attachments to their mothers. I suspect it gives me – the motherless son – some kind of attraction to them.'

'Life would be a lot easier without families!' she said ruefully. She gave him a look as if to say he had passed some kind of test.

On the third or fourth meeting she showed him the gun she had been given.

'To protect myself in case I am attacked.'

'Do you know how to use it?'

It was a Walther. Hitler and his crew were security mad.

'I do target practice on the range.'

'Are you a good shot?'

'A deadeye, so don't mess with me.' She laughed again – she was a great laugher – and said she would show him how to strip the gun. She made it sound sexually suggestive.

The whole security malarkey Anton Schlegel suspected was just a way of keeping tabs on the girl.

Her moods could be changeable and fleeting. One minute up, the next down, admitting she could not really say what she thought in case it was reported back.

Anton Schlegel replied, 'I don't talk out of turn.'

She seemed to take him at his word and over time he came to see how desperate she was to share without fear of censure.

While expressing herself only in terms of gratitude towards her uncle, they both knew it was more complicated than that. She turned out to be more astute than Anton Schlegel was expecting.

'He manipulates me terrifically,' she admitted, 'but I

know how to work him back, and if sometimes he makes me do things I don't want to do, that's men, and it seems a small price to pay for everything he has given me.'

'Do you believe that?'

'Of course not. More often than not, the situation is close to intolerable.'

He found he could tell when she was being honest and when she was rehearsing, to test how it sounded, as when she said during their one of their first meetings: 'I would of course marry him as the drop of a hat if he asked, and there is nothing more I want than to be the mother of his child.'

When she learned how frank she could be with him, this sunny picture was revised. He took what she said to mean that Herr Wolf was controlling, blissed out on the girl but emotionally immature and insecure, with much talk of the loneliness of his vocation.

Geli laughed and said, 'It's Herr Wolf's way of saying he is afraid of women. Now do you see what my problem is?'

'I expect if he can't have you he doesn't want anyone else to either.'

'But I like boys. Can a good little Catholic girl say that? I like fucking boys.'

'So do I,' said Anton Schlegel.

A look of complicity passed between them.

'I knew we had lots in common. Only boys? No girls?'

'Most of the time boys. Not always.'

Anton Schlegel saw that Geli, for all her dissatisfaction, remained in thrall to her uncle's generosity and fame. She had understood early on how much it pleased him to please her. Given his laziness, she could easily talk him out of work and going on an outing instead.

Geli had a bright way with words, describing hot sunny

days spent by the lakes in summers gone. The Führer had just acquired a new car, his first big tourer, open-topped, too, a treat in itself, into which Geli and her many girlfriends were 'squashed like sardines', while her uncle sat in the front, dishing out mints, and Emil drove.

'Emil?' asked Anton.

'Emil Maurice. The chauffeur at the time.'

Anton detected a wistful look. 'One of your boys?'

Geli punched him playfully on the arm. 'There's no hiding from you.'

Her descriptions of those early picnics consisted of uninhibited frolics under the indulgent eye of an inhibited presence. Geli and her girlfriends skinny-dipped and sunbathed naked, working on all-over tans; nothing remarkable about that. They were easy and unselfconscious. Maurice bathed wearing trunks.

'Sometimes we could see his thingy was hard. Maurice always had his pick of the girls.'

'Where is he now?'

'Moved on. Somewhere around. He played the guitar and he brought it along to the picnics and we sat around making up silly songs.'

Her uncle relaxed, up to a point, being cheerful and appreciative of the sight of so much tanned, firm flesh, but he never bathed or undressed, removing only socks and shoes and rolling his trouser bottoms so he could paddle and skim flat stones along the surface of the lake, pointing out how good he was. No singalong for him, only the fixed smile of a man too shy to open his mouth.

Emil and Geli decided to get engaged after one thing led to another in terms of practice with Emil's thingy.

'How naive can a girl be!'

The engagement was Emil's idea, she said. He was one

of Herr Wolf's oldest friends. Once officially engaged, they could spend more time together.

The trouble was, Herr Wolf caught them nearly at it.

'I was playing lollipop with Emil's thingy. I tucked it away before Onk saw but he went crazy and thrashed Emil until I had to throw myself between them.'

His excuse afterwards was he thought Maurice had been threatening her.

Geli did a perfect imitation of the man smoothing his hair and recomposing himself.

'I have never seen anything like it, even when he beat his dogs.'

'When was this?'

'Christmas, nearly four years ago. Onk said I was underage and fired Emil.'

Yet, extraordinarily, Herr Wolf continued to entertain the idea of the engagement, as long as it was postponed for two years until Geli reached her majority.

Geli anyway decided to end it with Emil, telling Anton she had been foolish to let herself get talked into an engagement when Emil had completely misread the situation. She sensed how complicated her life was about to become. Her uncle saw part of his role towards her as matchmaker, finding what he called a suitable mate.

She saw how much the process tormented him. He would vet young men in public, asking, 'Is that one good looking?' or 'What do you think of him?' He told her he needed to know her taste.

Anton suspected the gossip was right and the man had made his own sexual demands.

A year or so before, Herr Wolf had acquired his first proper apartment. The ostensible reason for the move was to reflect his growing power, but Geli suspected a secret motive.

'He said we should live together and for a moment I thought he was proposing! He meant as a lodger. He said, "It makes no sense me rattling around on my own in a place this size."'

He claimed he had been forced into taking the apartment by the Party and he would have been much more at home in his usual modest surroundings.

He told her, 'But if it means we can be together more then I am happy.'

This she took to mean greater supervision and less freedom.

She became used to his brooding presence, waiting for her return after a night out and saying, with the eyes of a jealous lover, 'Tell me about your evening.'

She entered a world of chaperones and chauffeur-driven cars. When she protested she was perfectly capable of taking public transport she was told it was for her safety. There were rumours of a plot to kidnap her.

'What nonsense!' she told Anton Schlegel and looked sad. 'I went from being his little princess, for whom nothing was good enough, to being a prisoner whose every move was watched over.'

Even during their walks in the park a couple of body-guards followed at a distance.

'What do you do about boys?' Anton asked.

'Tricky but not impossible if I know Onk is away. The ski instructor was skiing lessons!'

She rewarded Anton Schlegel with her most delightful laugh before turning thoughtful. 'If only he could say he loves me when it is obvious that he does, and let me be with him. What does the job matter if he's with someone or not? Now they just look at him like he's odd or a fairy.'

Anton asked what she wanted.

'Not being wrapped in cotton wool. Lots of normal healthy fucking and not being asked to do weird stuff.'

He looked at her and she turned away saying, 'Another time; I don't want to say anything about it now. Anyway, it's the talk of the town. Ask anyone.'

32

Geli Raubal, August 1931

Geli Raubal considered herself an adventurous, somewhat headstrong young woman, aware of how much she could manipulate and be manipulated in return. To her it was a game, until she saw how her uncle was buying her piece by piece. Everyone gossiped, sometimes with her, with lots of swearing to secrecy, stories about his dark desires and the stupid shopgirl who tried to kill herself over him, and the besotted photographer's assistant, and the gigantic widow Wagner who wanted to marry him. When she asked about the prospect of a Wagner engagement, he had lost all the devoted chivalry with which he usually treated her and cursed like a sailor and locked her in the house.

In the long, empty hours when time hung heaviest, she studied herself in the mirror, his blackness infecting her as she dared to imagine tempting him into revealing himself. Perhaps through submission she could free him, by showing him the impossibility of his desires within the greater reckoning.

The reflection in the mirror told her the risk she ran: if he refused to release her, she would be destroyed, or destroy herself, fulfilling a tragic destiny that would allow him to progress.

Too late did she understand the deadly game of brinks-manship that had been embarked on. She made the mistake of sharing her secret with others, in the mistaken belief that the situation was somehow negotiable. Her uncle in turn confessed that she drove him to despair. He implied that she had defiled herself by succumbing to his wishes and was unworthy of his love. The psychological mechanisms became a series of hair-triggers.

Until she talked to Anton Schlegel, in the dog days of high summer, unaware that she had only a few weeks to live.

33

Martin Bormann, 19 September 1931

'We need to be seen to be on the same page,' said Bormann to Müller, who then was still just a Munich cop, years away from acquiring the soubriquet 'Gestapo'.

'Your version?' asked Bormann.

'Girl shoots herself while mentally unbalanced using the Führer's pistol.'

Bormann nodded. 'She was a complicated creature. She must have known that the relationship was coming to an end. She ran out of time, as simple as that.'

Müller was known for short cuts and messing with the system. Bormann had the man on a retainer to keep him informed about hostile reporters, who treated the station as a second home, bribing cops to feed them leads.

The two men were in a private room in an out-of-the-way bar, drinking convivially, a late afternoon break in a hectic Saturday that was far from over.

It had been Müller's idea to have the Führer's returning Mercedes issued with a speeding ticket, which was when Bormann realised he had met a man after his own heart. Both knew their careers would depend on how they handled the affair.

*

Soon after eleven o'clock that morning, before any police were called, three senior Party officials had gathered for a secret meeting in the Führer's apartment to decide how best to handle the news of Raubal's death in terms of damage limitation. When Bormann informed them that the girl was dead by her own hand and as a mark of respect she should be left undisturbed, Treasurer Schwarz was quick to agree that any inspection would be an intrusion on the Führer's privacy. He looked glum and tactically out of his depth. No one was keen about being there. Bormann saw they expected him to fix it, considering such work beneath them. Deputy Hess was wailing like a chorus in a Greek tragedy. He took Bormann aside to say there was the dreadful symbol of a dead canary.

At the risk of insubordination, Bormann asked, 'What are you talking about, man?'

Hess appeared on the verge of hysteria.

Frau Winter later told Bormann that the bird was called Hansi and Geli had treated its death as an omen.

The third man later shown as 'not present' that morning was Hoffmann's future son-in-law, von Schirach. What a quorum!

On two facts Bormann got them to agree. The door was *locked from the inside* and Raubal was the only one in the room.

How they resented Bormann, however desperate they were for him to do the tidying: an unparalleled opportunity in terms of a young man's ambition. If Bormann succeeded, the years of derision would be thrown back in their faces.

Bormann let them get on with it. Any public aspect of the case was not his business. After that it was a clowns' convention, going round in decreasing circles until they were in danger of vanishing up themselves. Von Shirach demanded a press-office release saying the Führer had gone into deep mourning after the suicide of his niece.

Bormann spoke up, only to be shouted down, saying shouldn't the police, let alone the Führer, be informed before the issue of any release. Von Shirach was already on the blower when Bormann left the room.

Straight sorting, he thought as he walked down the corridor to the kitchen. Plug any gaps with the local police, where Müller was the man. An open-and-shut case of suicide. Death certificate. Get body out and away. No autopsy – nothing good would come from revealing a possible bun in the oven. There would be enough crazy speculation as it was. Hacks would have a field day regardless.

The domestic staff sat around the kitchen table, looking blown about, like an audience that had just emerged from an extraordinary event.

Get your stories straight, Bormann thought.

There was the live-in housekeeper, Frau Reichert and Frau Winter, who lived off the premises, and a daily maid. Reichert's and Winter's husbands were both there, a couple of makeweight odd-jobbers. Capping it all was the disquieting presence of Reichert's mother, Frau Drachs, who lived in the apartment with her daughter and was stone deaf; disquieting because Geli had claimed to have woken one night to find Frau Drachs standing at the end of her bed brandishing a knife. After that she had made a point of locking her door.

Bormann saw how petrified Frau Reichert was, as was Frau Winter. Disaster had struck on their watch. Bormann sensed a private resentment towards the niece, for her selfishness in involving them, as well as the enormous repercussions on their master, with possibly unpleasant consequences for everyone.

With their complacency and security threatened, they

agreed wholeheartedly when Bormann said, 'We must do everything possible to protect the Führer.' He didn't add, 'Otherwise it's out of the door with the lot of you.'

Frau Reichert said, 'I can't explain why Fräulein Raubal killed herself.'

'Then that's what you tell the police,' said Bormann.

Frau Reichert recoiled at mention of the police. The thought seemed not to have crossed her mind.

Bormann said, 'Better no mention is made of the several gentlemen already here or my presence. We don't wish to complicate.'

Bormann made them learn and recite their rehearsed statements. Like backward schoolchildren, they struggled to remember, as if distraction had undone their minds.

Frau Reichert, at last: 'Around three o'clock yesterday afternoon, I heard the door of Fräulein Raubal's room being locked and shortly after I heard a faint noise coming from inside, as if something had been knocked over. I attached no particular significance to this.'

Frau Winter: 'I did see, around the same time, Fräulein Raubal, very flustered, go into the Führer's room and hurry back into her own.'

'Carrying the pistol with which she would shoot herself,' prompted Bormann.

'Carrying the pistol,' Frau Winter repeated obediently. 'She had informed me none of us was needed as she intended to go out later.'

'With a friend to the cinema,' Bormann suggested.

Frau Reichert: 'That night, at about ten, I went to Fräulein Raubal's room to turn the bed down, but finding the door locked and getting no answer I assumed she had gone out.'

*

Meanwhile, the idiots in the Party press office had issued a *second* statement saying Fräulein Raubal had killed herself as a result of exam nerves over a singing test. Rowdy reporters besieged the police station. In such chaos it wasn't so difficult for Bormann to organise the essentials and sow the seeds of contradiction.

The Führer had returned mid-afternoon and given a short statement to the police, telling them that his niece had always struck him as ill-fated. Bormann took the precaution of informing Hess and Schwarz, who were hanging around uselessly back at the apartment, that the Führer must be taken somewhere safe, away from reporters, and a watch kept at all times, in case he tried to harm himself.

'He will be distraught beyond belief,' Bormann told them.

Schwartz and Hess looked incapable of comprehending any of the six words just uttered.

'It will be touch and go,' Bormann said. 'The Führer is far too important to lose.'

When much later the Führer asked whether Bormann had in fact said that, and Bormann saw the Führer's moist-eyed gratitude, he knew the kingdom would be his.

Geli liked to do crosswords, the Führer said. Bormann knew. He had helped her. Nothing too demanding. Four-legged animal, three letters. Cow or dog? Or pig?

MUNICH

1944

34

Morgen supposed contemporary newspaper reports of the affair must still exist. Schlegel suggested the Party Archive. They telephoned and were told Rehse remained unavailable but when Morgen asked about newspapers the helpful man he spoke to told them that a collection of the Party's Völkischer Beobachter was held at the Brown House.

It was still there, despite the partial evacuation of the building, looking neglected in a dusty back room. Their impression after ten minutes of reading badly written, sensational copy was of a highly controlled version of events: the niece suffering from exam nerves over a forthcoming music test; an immediate verdict of suicide, precluding the need for a post-mortem; the body returned to its homeland for burial in accordance with the mother's wishes, taking place in Vienna on the Wednesday after the death.

'That was quick!' exclaimed Morgen.

The technical question of cases of suicide being ineligible for Roman Catholic burial was not covered by the newspaper. The tone throughout was tragic, sentimental and not without a tinge of cynicism. It made for depressing reading because it left nothing to question. Every angle had been covered.

Schlegel glumly concluded, 'Maybe the man just had a fancy for suicidal women. That Braun woman tried and failed.'

Morgen asked, 'How would you shoot yourself, if you had to?'

'Temple or mouth, I suppose.'

'Then not through the heart holding the gun at a downwards angle, which was how it was described.'

'Unless she was thinking it was her heart that was broken.'

Morgen said, 'Ah, the sentimental interpretation.'

'Or it was a cry for help.'

'She knew the apartment was empty. Frau Winter told us. No one would come.'

They left it at that and went and sat outside, depressed. Morgen smoked and eventually asked, 'Is there a way of looking at the whole thing from another angle?'

'You mean, how did the canary die?'

'Let's be serious.'

They sat in silence. Finally, Schlegel spoke. 'The Bratwurst Glöckl.'

'The Thursday night row? There's no evidence. No one left to remember.'

'Say it happened. Reports of an argument . . .'

'Then what?'

'He had been drinking – a famous teetotaller – and couldn't handle it.'

Morgen pondered. 'Are we saying it turned into a domestic row that got out of hand?'

'I have no idea, but what if everything happened earlier than anyone is admitting?'

Morgen said, 'Which means our windbag friend Hoffmann must be lying.'

For twenty minutes, Hoffmann, in the same back room of his studio as before, bluffed and blustered. It was like watching a man tiptoe backwards, downplaying his part when

previously the roles of the tragedienne and her uncle were
seen as incidental to his own blowy passage through life.
He dismissed any report of the couple being seen arguing
in town on the Thursday night, telling them, 'My friends,
there was so much gossip, all of it unfounded. Of course the
Führer's enemies wanted to make hay of it.'

He stuck stubbornly to his version then sighed deeply
and said, 'There is something else.' He stopped as if
unable to continue until prompted then added, 'It's an
intimate detail.'

He took his time, visibly embarrassed, and finally offered
that his daughter Henny had confided how Geli suffered
terribly during her time of the month and dreaded its
approach. Hoffman lowered his voice to a confidential whisper. 'Feelings of deep sadness and despair, irritability and
anger, frequent outbursts at loved ones. Feelings of anxiety,
panic attacks, mood swings. Irrational behaviour.'

'Including suicidal thoughts?'

'Those, too.' Hoffmann looked at them, morose
and puzzled. 'Women in the end are unfathomable,
wouldn't you say?'

Before either could answer they were interrupted by
approaching footsteps and Fräulein Braun made a reappear-
ance as if on cue, upstaging them all. She stopped in surprise
at seeing them. More of a shock was the uniformed man
standing behind her. Schlegel watched Morgen pale.

'My brother-in-law,' Fräulein Braun announced.

Fegelein smirked and said nothing. Morgen ignored
Fegelein in return. Schlegel was aware of pungent eau de
cologne competing with the woman's scent.

'We're not stopping,' said Fräulein Braun.

If Fegelein was thrown by seeing them he gave no sign.

'Chasing shadows, gentlemen?'

Morgen asked, 'What brings you?'

Fegelein, nonchalant as he inserted his cigarette into a holder, replied, 'International Racing Week, don't you know?'

Morgen wondered at such things still happening.

'For sure. Big social event out at Riem.'

That was why all the hotels were booked, Schlegel realised.

Hoffmann seemed disconcerted by Fräulein Braun's presence, as if it confirmed his fallen state, with Fegelein a further reminder of his exclusion.

Morgen said, 'Fräulein Braun, a question if you please.'

'Another time. We're late.'

'It will only take a moment. Did you write a letter to Fräulein Raubal's uncle shortly before she died?'

She kept her composure, Schlegel had to say that for her.

'A thank you note, plain and simple. It is only polite to write such letters after being taken out.' She did her best to sound imperious but lacked the authority.

'Fräulein Raubal found it and tore it up.'

Fegelein's hooded eyes flared with delight at the spectacle.

Fräulein Braun sighed. 'Whatever she may have read into it, there was nothing other than cordial politeness. I was well brought-up.'

'I can vouch for that,' Fegelein said. 'Well, there we are. Shall we go?'

Fräulein Braun hadn't finished. 'She was like a child, everyone said, a spoiled brat, and like all such creatures became resentful when she was not the centre of attention. Her uncle had more important things on his mind.'

Morgen said, 'I believe you tried to kill yourself, too.'

Fräulein Braun took a step back at that.

Fegelein continued to look entertained, composing himself only when Fräulein Braun exclaimed, 'How dare you!'

'Steady on,' he said to Morgen.

Hoffmann rallied too. 'What has this to do with anything?'

Fräulein Braun was determined to have the last word. 'I was told the girl wrapped the gun in a flannel to muffle the report and shot herself in the mouth.'

'Told by?' asked Morgen.

'The Führer, which is quite sufficient authority for you. Enough of this. Let's go, Hermann.'

Fegelein turned to leave, paused and, sounding forgetful, asked, 'Morgen, isn't it?

Morgen didn't grace him with a reply.

'The thing is, you should come over for lunch later at the old riding academy. I can show you around.'

'Why should I?'

'Kurt Becher said you spoke fondly of me in Budapest.'

Seeing Fegelein and Fräulein Braun turned out like a starry society couple, Schlegel was reminded that Fegelein was supposed to have provided her with fur coats from Warsaw.

Fräulein Braun tapped her foot. Hoffmann started knocking back schnapps.

Schlegel suspected Fegelein's invitation was gloating, disguised behind casual, impeccable manners.

'Very well,' Morgen said, with an attempt at equal manners.

Fegelein's nastiness reasserted itself as they were leaving. 'Just you. Not him,' he said, pointing to Schlegel. '*A bientôt*.'

'Nice chap, Hermann,' said Hoffmann. It was impossible to tell if he was serious.

Morgen looked as disconcerted as Schlegel had ever seen him as Hoffmann reverted to blaming Bormann for his exclusion from the court of the Führer.

'I was never hypocritical, unlike some. They all smoke behind the Führer's back.' He mimed smoke being blown away. 'Bormann surrounds the Führer with creeps and toadies. Fräulein Braun is a cow to servants.'

Not much of a surprise there, thought Schlegel.

'I have never seen anyone so desperate as Fräulein Braun to get her man,' Hoffmann went on. 'Of course, the fascination he held for women was quite astonishing. Old hags used to rave around him like young flappers. Married women wrote begging him to father their child. Others wrote in ways that revealed them to be quite deranged.' Hoffmann tittered at the recollection. 'I can tell you, there was a voluminous set of files in his office under the general title "Crackers!".'

He snorted, started to laugh and couldn't stop. The laugh became a hiccough that seemed about to turn to tears until a large slug of drink put him right.

'That reminds me,' he said. He fetched a box file standing alone on a shelf, on which someone had stuck a collage of pretty pictures. 'Geli wrote to my daughter once about her uncle – here it is.' He held up the letter. 'I quote – "whose slightest action, whether it concerned a lawsuit about some mysterious funds from Italy or the administration of a dose of poison to an old Alsatian dog, assumed the vast proportions of an event in a Wagner opera," unquote. It was all laughter or tears. Even the Führer could get quite weepy.'

Schlegel thought: *or the administration of a dose of poison to an old Alsatian dog.* Was this something uncles shared with their nieces? Let alone her knowledge of mysterious funds. Both suggested a woman who had her eyes about her.

Hoffmann ploughed on drunkenly, talking for the sake of it now. 'Much of Geli's charm was her Viennese accent. When she was together with her uncle, his own softened to become more like hers. He had worked hard on his voice, making himself sound proper. She said she despised stupid, blonde Bavarian girls.' He rolled his eyes in the direction of the departed Fräulein Braun. 'Geli was a terrific dresser. When I arrived to chaperone her to the Shrovetide Ball she appeared for her uncle's inspection absolutely ravishing in a design by Ingo Schröder and was told in no uncertain terms it was far too revealing and to change into something more ordinary. And be back by eleven. It was Bormann who killed her, of course.'

Hoffmann stopped and looked surprised at himself.

Schlegel had seen it before, how people could break quite suddenly. Chase them fifteen times round the houses to no avail, then all of a sudden they dump it in your lap.

'You had better tell us then,' said Morgen, as though they were indulging in teatime conversation.

'That calls for a drink,' said Hoffman with false cheer and insisted they join him. Glasses were produced and clinked.

'To victory!' said Hoffmann. 'Rockets will do their work yet.'

Killed her himself or had Bormann had her killed? wondered Schlegel. On the whole, the regime used others to do the job.

Bormann left little to chance, Hoffmann said. Even when quite low on the ladder he was able to throw his weight around because of his reputation as Mr Fix-it.

'Bormann sees everything in terms of opportunity.' Hoffmann leaned forward. 'Remember the 1939 anniversary meeting of the old guard when that bomb went off here in Munich in the Bürgerbräukeller?'

Hard not to. A huge story, talked up in terms of the man's uncanny instinct for survival.

'I was there,' Hoffmann went on. 'There was a panic over a security warning which had led to talk of cancelling. The Führer was crestfallen – it was one of the biggest dates in his calendar – until Bormann suggested it go ahead after all, but begin and end early to accommodate the Führer's hectic schedule, which required him to catch the night train to Berlin. That was what was agreed. I was standing next to the Führer on the podium. He was bursting with pride and could barely make himself heard above the cheers. He spoke to a standing ovation and soon after we left the bomb was timed to go off.'

'An inside job, then?' prompted Morgen.

Hoffmann shrugged. 'Circumstance. Timing. I have thought a lot about it since because if I hadn't been travelling with the Führer that night I could have been among the dead. I am sure he never knew. Old Party faithfuls among those blown to shreds – he never would have condoned that. But to Bormann and the propaganda boys, what were eight or nine lives of deadbeat old fighters against such a shining example of the Führer's infallibility?'

Controlled acts of apparent fate or chance made sense in terms of what Schlegel knew of Bormann. The recent bomb could be seen as a variation of the Bürgerbräukeller one, to prove the man's indestructibility when everything else was going so badly. At the time of the Bürgerbräukeller the war was only a couple of months old and what better way to demonstrate the Führer's invincibility and rally public support?

In his desperation to implicate Bormann, Hoffmann had to unpick his previous version, which he did without apology and in an astonishing *volte face*. His account now began in the middle of the night, with a telephone summons from Bormann to come to the Führer's apartment.

'In the early hours of the Friday?' asked Morgen.

Hoffmann nodded, passed his hand over his sweating brow, inspected it and told them how earlier that night the Führer – not now out of town as previously claimed – had dined out with his niece before returning home late.

'The Führer doesn't bother with keys,' said Hoffmann, 'so the girl must have forgotten to lock the door because after he had gone to bed she was attacked by an intruder.'

Hoffmann didn't look as if he believed that any more than they did.

'What did you find?' asked Morgen.

'Bormann was there with Doctor Müller, the same one that later pronounced her dead.'

'Did you see the girl?' Morgen asked.

'I was told she was sedated and resting.'

'And the Führer?'

'Sitting in the hall in a state of shock. He had been given a shot too.'

'Did any of this strike you as strange?' asked Morgen.

'Except for the fact that I have rarely seen him touch a drop, I could see the man was plastered. Bormann put it down to the effect of the sedative, but no, he was definitely drunk, which is one thing I do know about.'

Hoffmann also believed someone else was in the apartment.

'I had a sense of him being in the living room, listening, but no one came out.'

'And what did Bormann expect of you?'

'To take the Führer off and keep him safe at my place, then leave for Hamburg the next day as scheduled. Of course, we only got as far as Nuremberg.'

'How was the Führer when you took him off?'

'He was berating himself for dismissing the downstairs guard or the intruder would never have got in. He was still drunk.'

'And you had never seen him in such a state before?'

'Or since. The odd glass but no more. He loathes drunkenness. Funny that he puts up with me.'

Hoffmann looked like he was about to start crying.

'Did Bormann kill her that night?' asked Morgen. 'According to your theory.'

'He was forcing her to fuck him because he had dirt on her.'

'What dirt?' asked Morgen wearily. It was starting to sound like another turn of the merry-go-round. Hoffman's drunken confidence slipped a notch.

'She had a reputation for flightiness. Bormann likes beating women and must have gone too far and had to hush it up.'

'So Bormann beat the girl, not this intruder or anyone else?' asked Morgen, more sarcastic.

Hoffmann protested. 'The Führer would never lay a hand on her.'

'Are you saying Bormann shot her after you left?' asked Schlegel.

'I don't know the details.'

'Why are we sitting here pointing fingers when you saw nothing?' asked Morgen.

'Geli. Fräulein Raubal,' said Hoffmann. 'She said Bormann fucked people behind their backs.'

'Not the same as killing.'

'You'll see I am right,' said Hoffmann.

Schlegel suspected a pathetic attempt on Hoffmann's part to implicate Bormann in revenge for being removed from the Führer's inner circle.

Schlegel took over. 'So lunch on the Friday and all the rest never happened. No spaghetti, no throwing things around in her room?'

'We were told to say it to protect the Führer.'

'By whom?'

'Bormann, who else?'

Schlegel thought Hoffman was desperate to blame Bormann when it seemed more likely a case of an ambitious junior doing everything to protect his master.

Hoffmann threw up his hands. 'Women! I ask you. Fräulein Braun was no better. One day, the summer after Geli's death, Fräulein Braun didn't come to work. I didn't worry about it but, towards midday, my brother-in-law, a surgeon, came in looking very serious. "This is a bad business," he said. "During the night, Fräulein Braun rang me. Speaking with great difficulty, she told me she had shot herself through the heart with a 6.35 pistol. She said she had felt so lonely and neglected that she wanted to end it."'

'More and more bizarre,' said Morgen. 'She shoots herself through the heart, which, whatever she says to the contrary, is how the niece is supposed to have done it, using the same type of pistol.'

'They say imitation is the sincerest form of flattery. My daughter said the difference between them was Geli was opera and Fräulein Braun light operetta.'

Schlegel thought: one gets her tragic end and the other a pale, botched job.

35

They bicycled over the river back to the apartment in Prinzregentplatz, where Frau Winter admitted them as far as the hall and stood in the half-light with her hands clasped in front of her and one ankle crossed behind the other. Schlegel thought her like the caretaker of an abandoned museum.

She regarded them in slow amazement when they asked about the intruder's nocturnal attack on Fräulein Raubal.

'Whoever told you that needs his head examining.'

Morgen said, 'According to Hoffmann, the Führer left the apartment that night and didn't return.'

Frau Winter scoffed, 'Oh, Hoffmann!' She dismissed it as another of his stale warmed-over stories.

'Any revisions to your version?' asked Morgen.

'The Führer was many men to many people. Here was the one place he could put his feet up and be himself. I tell you he came on the Friday morning and left after the midday meal. The girl was being difficult. He took me aside to say he was worried about her agitated state.'

Schlegel didn't know who to believe. He decided Frau Winter was probably better at dissembling than Hoffmann was at telling the truth.

She insisted she knew nothing of the Führer and his niece dining out the night before because she wasn't live-in staff.

'So on the whole, you didn't know the Führer's whereabouts?' asked Morgen.

'I knew when he was away and when he was here,' she recited primly.

'Yet Hoffmann says the Führer never returned here on the Friday.'

'Believe who you like. Hoffmann makes things up and gets confused.'

'Drunk, you mean,' said Morgen.

Frau Winter's facade cracked a fraction. 'Well, he can certainly pack it away.'

Morgen brought up the Führer's drunkenness.

Frau Winter vehemently denied it.

'Not even once?'

'Hoffmann can talk! Most of the time he is so far gone it's a wonder he can take a photograph.'

Schlegel thought: the tomblike discretion of the loyal servant whose silence spoke volumes. The Führer was above question.

Frau Winter changed tack, volunteering for once. 'Fräulein Raubal's moods were like clouds passing the sun, sometimes very dark—'

Morgen interrupted to ask, 'From the state of the sheets would you say the relationship was a consummated one?'

The question was outrageous, as Morgen intended it to be. Winter held her ground. 'Ask the laundress. Dirty linen is not my business.'

'Did you like Fräulein Raubal, Frau Winter?' Morgen asked.

'Liking had nothing to do with it.'

'Even so, you must have had an opinion.'

Frau Winter wrung her hands, her face contorting as she decided what to tell. Perhaps because she was unused to being asked, she gabbled, using the niece's first name, which she hadn't done before.

'Geli was a flighty girl. She tried to seduce everybody, including her uncle when he merely wanted to protect her. She loved him in the way romantic films had taught her. She was always running after him. Naturally she wanted to become Frau Hitler. He was highly eligible but she flirted with everybody. She was not a serious girl.'

'Stupid, would you say?'

'More unthinking.'

'And not eligible, in the end.'

Frau Winter was quick to agree. 'However much she wished to better her station, she was out of her depth.'

Schlegel almost believed her.

Morgen went on. 'The doctor's report says Fräuein Raubal shot herself in the heart yet Fräulein Braun says she wrapped the gun in a flannel and put it in her mouth. You see why we are bound to question everything.'

Frau Winter grew discreet again and said she was sure Fräulein Braun had her reasons. 'I wouldn't know. I didn't see the body.'

'But by your own account you discovered it,' said Morgen reasonably.

'The room was dark. There was a shape on the floor and you could see something terrible had happened.'

'Who did you call?'

'The Brown House.' Party Headquarters.

'Who did you speak to?' asked Morgen.

'Party Secretary Bormann, except he wasn't Party Secretary then.'

Schlegel thought: So Bormann answered. By arrangement? The strange thing in all of it was Schlegel had no clear impression of the niece. Sometimes he could almost hear her laughter filling the apartment but he couldn't say how hollow it was.

36

The Bratwurst Glöckl was a six or seven minute ride back towards the centre. Schlegel thought they should see if there was an old reservations book showing that the niece and her uncle had dined there on the Thursday night. Morgen, bad tempered about Fegelein, grumbled, 'It was thirteen years ago, man! You're clutching at straws.'

The place was opening for business. They were told by a waiter with bad German that the manager wasn't in. Morgen marched through to the kitchen, telling the waiter when he tried to stop them to fuck off back to Italy or wherever.

Morgen asked the kitchen staff if anyone was from the old days. They all looked either sixteen or sixty and incapable of cooking. A boy chopping onions sliced his finger and carried on, too nervous to stop. Schlegel watched blood mix with the onions.

The waiter hung around by the door, all obsequiousness now. Morgen asked for his papers, just to be nasty. He really was in a foul mood. The man produced them with shaking hands, bowing and scraping.

'I was going to say,' he volunteered. A woman who had been been there a long time came in twice a week to do the books and she was in the manager's office now.

The waiter showed them to a windowless room whose main feature was a dull grey skylight, with a bucket on the floor where it leaked. Unlike the restaurant's decorative antique panels, the walls were bare, suggesting there was no point in wasting money on what was not seen.

The elderly woman sitting at the desk looked up. Large spectacles with magnifying lenses gave her a startled look. She wore bright pink and had hands more like a man's, but her voice was motherly and they immediately became her 'boys'.

Co-operation at last. Schlegel could have kissed her.

The room was small and tidy, apart from a mess on the desk, which the woman had shoved aside to clear a space for her own neat ledgers.

She was from Zehnter's time, it turned out, and she told them, 'He was a stickler but a convivial man and proud of the place's tradition. "Reservations are our history," he was always saying.'

She opened a narrow filing cupboard and proudly showed them the order books, lined up by year, alongside bound copies of accounts.

There it was, among the reservations for 17 September, 1931, in the same Gothic script as the rest: Wolf plus one. Private. Ten o'clock.

The woman didn't ask what they were doing. People knew when to keep their traps shut. Her magnified eyes were so pale they reminded Schlegel of oysters. You could still get them in Berlin, at a price. Funny what was still available, he thought.

Morgen asked, 'Is there anyone you know who would have been working here then?'

The woman made a show of thinking and offered them a wine waiter from the old days. 'An old boy. Not so well now.' She tapped her head. 'Some things he remembers. You can do worse than ask.'

318

He was in a rest home on Nussbaumstrasse where the woman visited him from time to time. Some days he was all right, she said, and on others he didn't know her. His name was Dreck, which she said he had always complained about for some reason.

They looked at the private dining room on the way out: not a large room, single round table with seating for six, and depressing for having its curtains drawn. Trying the curtains, Schlegel found they were only for effect, with no windows behind them. Candelabra on the walls. He supposed with the right lighting it could appear romantic. If rooms could talk.

Just as merchants and guilds grouped together in a particular part of town, the medical profession had taken over Nussbaumstrasse. Clinics. Research centres. University blocks. Schlegel tried to imagine his father's footsteps before him and what business might have caused him to underline the street name in the guide map, and what had brought him there, and what he looked like and what sort of contract he had made with life. Whenever Schlegel tried to picture the man, he saw only a blank. Perhaps he was resisting in case he found some strutting, swivelling, booted monster or snivelling courtier. He had no control over the reality, so why bother to imagine?

The rest home was more modest than most of the buildings in the street. A criss-cross little garden fence, a stretch of grass with a central path and a building as plain as a child's drawing.

Nurses more like prison wardens, for all their surface politeness; tough middle-aged women who could apply a headlock. A home for old people waiting for death, some no doubt troublesome, but on the evidence most passed the time by losing their minds, a not completely unpleasant experience, from what Schlegel could see. Two women sat with the same look of vacant contentment, never mind the puddle on the floor beneath one. Dreck was pointed out, sitting in a neglected garden, with his back to the house, wearing a check dressing gown, and with wispy sticking-up white hair. A few more like him sat dotted around, in solitary outcrops.

'You will need chairs if you are staying,' said the no-nonsense nurse, pointing to a stack in a conservatory whose corners still had last autumn's blown-in leaves. Schlegel felt like crying. All these husks once would have drunk, flirted, fought, fallen in love, and lived according to somebody else's plan. 'And then one day you die,' Schlegel wanted to shout. 'Was that a contract you were willing to sign and seal?'

'Hello, my young friends. Good to see you again,' said Dreck as they joined him with their chairs. He wore little round sunglasses with scratched lenses.

Morgen played along. 'How have you been keeping in the meantime?'

The old boy waggled his hand. He would have been tall once, now quite concertinaed in on himself. Dark hair grew along the ridge of his ears, like columns of tiny insects, in contrast to the snowy crown. Dreck was without teeth and had trouble with his consonants. Bulbous grey veins ran down the back of resting hands. In as much as Schlegel thought about waiters, he pictured them shorter rather than tall.

Morgen offered a cigarette, gratefully received. Dreck cupped his hands around the flame, lifted his head and inhaled deeply, looked at them and asked who on earth they were.

Morgen asked how he was doing.

Dreck gave a harsh laugh and said, 'Waiting.'

He wanted to know why Schlegel dyed his hair.

Schlegel was aware of blushing and muttered he was too young for it to be white. The waiter waiting, he thought, or the waiting waiter. An elderly female raised herself out of a chair to totter round the garden. Dreck offered long silences and gaps and detours, his grasp of the present variable to the point of non-existent. Pitched back, however, he stumbled across shards of intact memory, repeated verbatim.

Dreck would not be hurried. He resisted questions about his working days. Sometimes when Dreck remembered a detail with no context, Schlegel was reminded of those accidental photographs of nothing: a blur, a foot, sky. Dreck remembered the past, or bits of it, but was lost in the present. For the rest of them it was the other way round: washed away past, stuck in the present. The future didn't bear thinking about. Any random memory of himself from ten or fifteen years before, Schlegel always thought: That was someone else. Perhaps everyone felt the same. He had never talked to anyone about it. Dreck asked him, 'Why so glum?'

Schlegel said, 'I want you to tell us about—' He explained how once a long time ago the Führer had been reported drunk in the company of his niece at the Bratwurst Glöckl. Dreck's eyes screwed up behind the dark lenses, in a show of furious anger at forgetting. His body seemed to expand as though being pulled up by invisible wires, then collapsed.

Schlegel thought of something, nothing to do with Dreck, and wanted to get out.

Dreck appeared to have dozed off. His head still slumped, he suddenly asked what they wanted to drink.

Schlegel, in a moment of rare inspiration, snapped his fingers, and called, 'Herr Ober!'

Dreck looked at him and recited the wine list, with personal recommendations.

Morgen said he would have whatever Fräulein Raubal was having.

'That would be a Spätlese, a sweetish white wine if you like that sort of thing.'

'And her uncle?'

'Mineral water and never Apollinaris, always Fachinger. Except that time when he was on the Hacker Pschorr, enough to float a battleship. "Keep them coming!" he said. A first in my history. She was pissed too, and could put it away. She had her hand under the table – private room – and gave me a look that said she knew I knew what was going on.'

They both had liver dumplings and she fed him, taking the food off his plate with her fork. So much for the Führer's publicised vegetarianism, Schlegel thought. Turtle soup to start, not on the menu, specially made. A selection of sweet pastries and cream to end with.

Schlegel and Morgen exchanged glances: the man had to be talking about that last night, but when pressed Dreck faded on them.

'Herr Ober! Same again,' Morgen ordered, pointing at glasses, and they were back in the room. 'How would you describe the mood between them?'

'Like they both had a fever. Intense.'

'How?'

'As though they were plotting something.'

That didn't make sense, Schlegel thought. They were supposed to have been arguing.

'What sort of plotting?'

'Like two kids with a secret.'

Schlegel suspected Dreck was muddled and recalling another occasion. People pay no attention to the waiter, he thought, not realising the waiter is permanent and the guest there under sufferance.

Dreck looked at them both as though he had no idea why any of them were there, then barked, 'And that was the last we saw of her!'

'What do you mean?' asked Schlegel.

Dreck looked at him as though he were stupid. 'She didn't come back after that.'

So Dreck had been talking about that final night.

'Private room,' Morgen reminded Dreck. 'We heard they were arguing.'

'Later on they argued.'

Over what?' insisted Morgen.

Dreck snapped back into the moment and gave Morgen a look of professional hauteur. 'I may observe but I make a point of not listening.'

'Yes, of course,' said Morgen. 'Overall mood?'

'Lovebirds, then not lovebirds.'

Impossible to picture, Schlegel found. That was as much as they were going to get. Dreck had lost interest.

'Did Herr Schlegel dine there?' Schlegel ventured.

'Downstairs. On the pansies' table. With Herr Röhm, usually.'

'Was Herr Schlegel a pansy?'

'None of my business. Herr Röhm was and didn't care who knew. He went. Maybe Herr Schlegel did too. Night of the Long Knives. Night of settling any old score, if you ask me.'

A pansy? Was that possible? Schlegel asked himself.

'My boss, gone too,' said Dreck.

'Herr Zehnter?'

'Homo. Curtains. Head wine waiter. Homo. Curtains. Me. No homo. Are you homos?' He gave them a gummy smile. 'No dentures. They took them away. I bit a nurse last week. Herr Wolf didn't tip. Paid on account by Mr Pig. No extras. Not classy people. Herr Schlegel classy.'

A classy father who consorted with pansies and was pally with the subsequently deposed and executed leader of the brownshirts. Anna Huber's brother had been a brownshirt. He couldn't see his father as one.

Morgen was late for Fegelein. He'd had enough of bicycles, he said. He would wait for a taxi, which were more plentiful than in Berlin where finding one was like winning the lottery, never mind not being able to afford it unless you had lottery winnings.

His decision turned out to be irrelevant. The bikes were gone anyway. They had not been given locks. Schlegel didn't mind much. Munich was walkable, unlike Berlin.

Morgen lit up, smoked half the cigarette and.eventually said, 'One thing that gets you killed is knowing too much.'

'Are you speaking about us?'

'Probably. The business with the niece is like a deadly parlour game. This version of what happened. That version of what happened. Oh, no, it didn't happen like that at all. We were fortunate with Dreck. Come back tomorrow and we could get nothing. Everything wiped.'

Schlegel supposed Anton would have been among those to have clicked his fingers to summon Dreck. He thought 'classy' was probably more of a category than a compliment and Dreck in his heyday was a model of deferential contempt.

'Gossip before the girl's death,' Morgen said. 'Just because she's dead doesn't mean the gossip stops. It reaches fever pitch. But what if that were somehow the point?'

Schlegel couldn't see what Morgen was getting at. The

Raubal case was by definition insoluble. So many layers had been created that even if they did stumble across the answer it would be indistinguishable from the rest. In Gestapo Müller's terminology, it was shot through with enough golden threads for a tapestry, leaving them with the official version that no one quite bought but everyone generally believed, and that was what had stuck: a young woman firing a bullet into her heart in a fit of something or other and bleeding to death.

Schlegel watched Morgen wait by the side of the road for a taxi: light traffic, another fine day, the sky sharper than in Berlin, but dark clouds were building. Out of the corner of his mind's eye he saw Gerda fall through the night and his knees sagged.

Sitting with Dreck in the dreary garden, Schlegel had been struck by what he had already noticed: that the street was given over to clinics and suchlike. Was that why it had been underscored in the guide map, and did room 202 on the bus ticket refer to one of these buildings? It didn't amount to much of a clue but as he was there . . .

His persistence was eventually rewarded when he was told of a convent hospital whose nursing staff were nuns. The woman telling him had a nephew who was a porter there and said the Party paid to keep it exclusive.

The convent hospital stood hidden behind a high wall capped with green Roman-style tiles, the same as the roof. Paint-washed walls gave it a Mediterranean air. Schlegel used his badge to gain admission and inside found himself in a deliciously cool, translucent arched corridor along which cowled nuns glided, their habits muffling their footsteps. Schlegel trod softly, feeling large and self-conscious.

He addressed himself to the registrar, an old nun with a

pink face. He stumbled to come up with a reason for wanting to look through her admission records. He said it was complicated by having only a room number.

She made his job seem easier when she explained that room 202 was one of several private ones, logged separately from general ward admissions. She asked how far he wished to go back. To 1925, he said.

She led the way down to stack rooms even more silent than upstairs, into a maze of narrow walkways between tall shelves. She pointed to one too high for her to reach where private room admissions were kept. The spine of each book was marked by year and they went back to the turn of the century.

Schlegel watched her walk away and turned his attention to the books.

Room admissions and discharges were listed in columns, starting with the names and initials of patients on the left, with no reference to gender; perhaps the celibate sisters held it to be irrelevant, us all being God's children. Next came the name of the referring doctor and date of admission, with the room number in a final column on the right. A space must have been left under each entry because the date of discharge was recorded directly beneath. The first examples showed name after forgotten name admitted in 1925 and released a week or so and sometimes months later.

Schlegel supposed the hospital had a reputation for discretion, being cloistered. By the time he got to the 1930s he started to recognise some of the more famous Party members. Göring H. several times, booking in for ten days.

As for Room 202: three admissions in 1930 where the name in the patient's column was Wolf, no initial. Schlegel presumed recuperative bouts for the highly-strung Führer.

Moving on to 1931 and Room 202, Schlegel found no more Wolf.

The room had one long stay of a couple of months early in the year but no one he had ever heard of. July, August. Of no interest.

An admission into Room 202 on Monday, 21 September.

A tumultuous week, with the niece dead the Friday before. A busy time for Dr Müller, too, if it was the same police doctor who had made the referral. Schlegel felt like he was swimming in sand because of the name in the admissions column. Schlegel A.

37

Hermann Fegelein was immensely pleased with himself, living as he did in a world of justified smugness. Career and fun and plenty of both. Nothing else mattered. He could talk himself out of any corner, using his winning smile and silver tongue to convince his masters to overlook his bad boy pranks. His boss, Reichsführer-SS Himmler, a model of bourgeois probity – apart from a secretary mistress tucked away, but everyone had one of those – was jealous of how Fegelein flouted the rules. Letting him get away with it was Heini's surrogate thrill.

Heini, not a physical specimen, envied Fegelein's spring-heeled athleticism. Show jumping. Gymkhana. Dressage. Flat racing. The finest horseman in South Germany many said.

'I won the German Spring Derby in 1938,' Fegelein announced to Morgen over lunch. Gracious about Morgen's late arrival, he decided to bore him into the ground with tales of his riding exploits. Also in 1938, first past the winning post for the German Brown Ribbon.

'It's being run tomorrow, as a matter of fact. Not competing, sadly. Too much on.'

Fegelein quoted Xenophon at the dowdy and unprepossessing Morgen: how the horse in its essence has something very gracious and appealing and attracts all eyes under the command of a skilled rider. '"Honour to him who knows how to master one." Do you ride?'

Of course he didn't.

Morgen suspected his resistance to Fegelein's winning ways when others fell for it was what offended the man. It wasn't the usual charm offensive. There was deprecation and the diplomatic skills of a first-class liaison officer, no easy job when it came to communication between the Führer, Reichsführer-SS Himmler and Party Secretary Bormann. As for Gestapo Müller, Morgen suspected his antipathy was based on a local boy's resentment and the slow business of climbing the ranks compared to the short cuts offered to Fegelein, so famously good at games.

The depressing thing was Morgen suspected he might yet like Fegelein: the despicable man who knows he is despicable and makes no effort to hide it. The lunch was excellent, local river trout, the service impeccable, the wine exceptional. But what was the point?

It wasn't confession. It wasn't about coming clean. It was more than showing off. Morgen decided it was because Fegelein wanted to be taken seriously and for all his glory he was still considered a lightweight whose job in the end was to grease the wheels. The point was Morgen knew Fegelein's record better than most, and with the man's greatest triumphs being recidivist he could not boast too openly about them. It probably explained why Fegelein made a point of expressing his admiration for the gentleman thief Raffles, played by the English actor David Niven in the film from before the war.

'Niven could play me rather well. He rides because he was in *The Charge of the Light Brigade*.'

Morgen said he didn't go to the cinema much.

'That's your choice,' said Fegelein magnanimously. 'I have to admit to being spoiled as I can take my pick of private viewings. The Führer is a big movie fan. He screens most evenings.'

Fegelein had read his own file. 'It pays to know what people are saying about you. Was that you who wrote up the Warsaw affair in '42?'

Morgen said neither yes nor no.

'I thought so. It was an intelligence operation all along, a point which you—sorry, the report was very reluctant to concede or acknowledge.'

'And the furs?'

'Used to fund the operation of course.' Fegelein smirked. 'Didn't Heini pack you off to the Russian front just after that?'

'For six months.'

'Reason?'

Morgen thought Fegelein was bound to know, having read his file and probably everyone else's.

'Refusing to prosecute a case.'

'Well, there's a change from the usual. You probably deserved it. Jankers before that?'

'Six months' detention. Prussian exercises, so-called.'

'Well, there you are. You're the one who has been the jail-bird and I haven't. What does that tell us about the world?'

Morgen was beguiled watching Fegelein at close quarters. The man lied most of the time but had the rare quality of believing whatever he was saying.

They swapped military experiences. 'You first,' said Fegelein.

Morgen cared not to remember. 'Wiking Division.'

'Enough said.'

Morgen added that he had watched his company being wiped out several times over and he had been more than lucky to have survived.

Fegelein's uniform displayed his raft of medals, including Iron Crosses first and second class.

'Death's Head Cavalry,' he said nonchalantly.

The man was shown to be brave, which made him harder to dislike. Morgen wasn't greatly up on his medals so asked, knowing Fegelein would be entertained. Fegelein showed off well, in the same way he probably did as the gracious winner. Morgen suspected plenty of tantrums when he lost.

Morgen remembered from Fegelein's record that the man had failed to qualify for the 1936 Olympic riding team and to see what the answer was he asked, 'Didn't you ride in the Olympics?'

'Did, as a matter of fact.'

The lie was so throwaway that Morgen ended up questioning his memory.

A rueful smile and pout of the cherry lips. 'Well, not quite. I injured myself before I could compete. Didn't look where I was going, tripped and twisted an ankle.' A moue of regret. Fegelein's massaged version of getting knocked out in the selection qualifying rounds. 'Are you sporting?'

'Not at all.'

Fegelein all but said: Didn't think so.

Morgen decided there was probably some deep correlation between Fegelein's bent for fraudulent practice and private feelings of inadequacy – hence the lie about Olympic disqualification – before he glumly concluded Fegelein was just another highly evolved psychopath. Morgen went back to the medals.

'What's that one for?'

'Infantry Assault Badge. To be fair, they were handing out gongs like nobody's business.'

Morgen laughed at the thought of Schlegel and his strange sighting of the Führer. Fegelein thought Morgen was laughing at him. Morgen explained that Schlegel had got it into his head that the Führer had been using a stand-in.

'Know anything about that?'

'Not supposed to,' Fegelein said, making clear that he did, before offering the throwaway line, 'Polyps of the rectum, is what I heard.'

'Why not say the Führer is indisposed?'

'Goebbels is my guess. These days the Führer can't be seen to be anything but infallible. I was in that room when the bomb went off.'

Morgen thought: A pity the bomb didn't do a better job.

'And was it the actual Führer?' he asked lightly. 'In the room?'

Fegelein, sharing the joke, smoothly said, 'Never thought for a moment it wasn't.' Morgen couldn't tell if the man was lying. 'Mind you, he was being kept on a very short leash.'

'You must be able to spot the difference.'

Fegelein shrugged. 'The Führer is a rather withdrawn figure these days.'

Morgen wondered at the real reason for an assassination attempt, if a double was being used. Was he supposed to have gone in the explosion, as part of the bigger political picture?

'Have you met any of these doubles?' Morgen asked.

'Seen them around. They're quite good actually but bored to sobs most of the time. There's one at the Berghof at the moment, flying the flag.'

'Flying the flag?'

'Raised flag when the Führer is in residence. Decoy for enemy intelligence.'

'So he rattles around on his own all day?'

'Inspects the guard, I expect, not that the Führer bothers.'

Fegelein surprised Morgen with his next question. 'Is it right to kill civilians, do you think?'

'Depends on the circumstances.'

'Anti-partisan duties. Whole villages put to the sword. Pripet Marshes. Summer of '41.'

Morgen suspected the man's only objection was aesthetic, using an elite force to dispatch peasants.

'How did your men take it?' he asked.

'Lot of grumbling. Not proper action. Dirty work but someone has to do it. Ever kill anyone?'

'Only Ivans.'

'Close enough to see the whites of their eyes?'

'Bayonet in the stomach.'

'Well done you. Did they give you a medal?'

'No.'

'Any wounds?'

'Only frostbite.'

'Three times, me. Twice in two days. Snipers on the River Don, 21 and 22 December '42. Again in September last year. Shipped home and cushy jobs ever since. I want to put you straight about one thing.'

Morgen wondered if they were approaching the point of the meeting. Did the man have something to sell? No, he merely wanted to complain about his file.

'Remember my court martial a couple of years ago? That had quite a lot to do with you.'

'Stealing money and luxury goods from Warsaw, and found right here in your stables if I recall.'

'You bet you do,' Fegelein snarled, showing teeth. '"Murder motivated by greed." "Unlawful sex." Others – not you – said I made her have an abortion. Incorrect. She miscarried, but with the number of men she was carrying on with it could have been anyone's. And the so-called murder was a man shooting himself. All charges dismissed, as you know.'

He poured the last of the wine and ordered another bottle.

333

'May as well. What you need to appreciate is it's not about unmotivated greed or lining my pockets. There is always a point but the police here have it in for me.'

Morgen didn't follow.

'I always wanted to be a policeman, did officer's training until I got caught stealing exam paper answers and was kicked out. Hands up, I admit that, but they've gone for me ever since, no idea why. The place was full of cheats and men on the take; and tell your pal Gestapo Müller, I was never any kind of toff just because my father ran a riding school. I spent most of my youth shovelling shit, barely able to read.'

Poor Hermann – keen that Morgen understood it was all his own effort, no short cuts.

'When the war came I arranged for the state police stable to transfer to the riding academy, to stop the Army mobilising it, and got accused of theft!'

Morgen added 'misunderstood' Hermann to 'poor' Hermann.

'Do you know how much it costs to run a riding school?'

Morgen supposed a lot.

'And a whole lot more. After the '36 Olympics, Heini thought the SS should have its own academy and asked me to set it up but funding was never enough to match his ambitions and by 1940 we were struggling. I tried to bring the matter to his attention but he had other things on his plate. The academy – a state institution – had debts it couldn't cover, leaving Hermann with three choices.'

Morgen for a moment couldn't think who Fegelein was talking about when he started referring to himself in the third person.

'Apply for a fucking grant,' Fegelein went on, 'which takes months. Get Heini's approval on a nod and a wink for a bit of under-the-table, or exercise initiative and get on with it. And as you well know, what didn't one find lying around in Warsaw?'

The bottle arrived. Fegelein told the waiter tasting wasn't necessary.

'Do you know, in the marshes we had orders to drive the women and children into the swamps so they drowned. They don't give you a medal for that. So we charged them into the middle and they ended standing in water that didn't even cover their fucking knees.'

Fegelein struggled not to laugh.

'What did you do?'

'Had to hack them down, like something out of Cowboys and Indians. No budget for bullets. Bloodbath. What would you have done?'

'I was never asked.'

'Smart sidestep.' Fegelein gave Morgen a level stare. 'Not something you would wish on anyone.'

'Least of all the dead.'

Fegelein ignored the jibe. 'My men were a fighting unit who found it demeaning to be mopping up.'

He looked at his glass, making a show of regret. Morgen suspected Fegelein's men had had the time of their lives, at last able to use their sabres, which had long ceased to have any function in modern warfare.

'Actually, I am a complete fraud,' Fegelein announced with a disarming smile, leaving Morgen unable to detect the lie. Fegelein flicked dismissively at the medals on his chest. 'All of them flukes. I am an absolute coward and all of these were for a knack of looking heroic. In fact, I was terrified, so there you are.'

Morgen thought it a confession of sorts. Perhaps the man was sympathetic after all.

'Anyway, I was saying about costs,' Fegelein went on. 'I wasn't best pleased when as a result of your investigation a search of the premises here revealed what were described as goods looted in Warsaw. From what I remember, a lorry, and a six-cylinder Mercedes—'

'Two. One trimmed in black and another trimmed in brown.'

'Good memory or are you still harbouring a grudge?'

'I'll have you yet,' Morgen said equably.

'Bet on it?'

'Not for money.'

'Didn't have you down as a gambling man. I once broke the bank in Deauville.'

It was clearly offered as an example of 'This is me telling a lie'. He went on: 'Two-seater Skoda cabriolet, twenty-five kilos of coffee, fourteen packets of cocoa – all right, they were an exception; my mother has a sweet tooth. Chest of tea, two chests of chocolate, clothes, fur coats and what were listed as sundry items. All to finance the ailing riding academy, on my initiative. Things were dire for a while. I even sold on the bloody police horses when I probably shouldn't have. For a few months it was touch and go.'

'Am I supposed to care?'

'Just telling you. When I explained all this to Heini he understood, which is why the charge was quashed.'

Fegelein asked Morgen what he was doing in Munich.

'Security checks.'

'Not what I heard.'

The teasing silence was typical of the man, thought Morgen: the unsettling moment of destabilisation.

'And your lanky friend?' Fegelein looked contemptuous. There was nothing for Morgen to say other than signal he was ready to leave. He was feeling disgusted with himself for being half won over.

'Apropos of,' said Fegelein, 'you may remember my dossier starts with a reference to an unnamed man receiving stolen goods traced back to here. The obvious reason for not naming a man is that he is a police informer, no? I thought you might be interested, all things considered. Your lanky lad's dad.'

'Anton Schlegel?' asked Morgen in surprise. 'Do you know him?'

Fegelein wouldn't say.

What was more, thought Morgen, Fegelein was indicating that Anton was alive as recently as 1942, working in a criminal capacity.

'Isn't Anton Schlegel why you are really here?' Fegelein asked. 'I am told you are looking for certain documents connected to him.'

'I wouldn't know about that.'

'The difference between us, my dear Morgen, is that you couldn't tell a lie to save your life.' He paused, considering. 'I rather fancy getting my hands on one of these documents myself.'

'Which one would that be?' asked Morgen, supposing they were getting to the real point of the meeting.

'The confession everyone is talking about, of course.'

'I didn't know they were.'

'Well, not at your level. The thing is, it must be found to stop it falling into the wrong hands.'

'Are you the one to do that?' Morgen asked in disbelief.

'Would you trust Gestapo Müller with it? Isn't that who you are answering to? Or Bormann? Whereas I am almost part of the Führer's family now!'

Basing his credentials on being Fräulein Braun's

brother-in-law was a bit of a stretch, thought Morgen, but typical. He presumed Fegelein was referring to the Hitler confession.

'Now here's the deal,' Fegelein went on. 'Find it and bring it to me and we'll destroy it, and that'll be the end of that. If I find it first I'll do the same and bring it to you. In fact, race you for it!'

The man was making a game of it, thought Morgen, to distract from his real purpose. If he had to bet, it would be on Fegelein secretly acting for Heini Himmler. Heini was rumoured to have his eye on the leadership and, according to Schlegel, Heini and Fegelein had known about the bomb plot and done nothing about it, which could be taken for Heini biding his time, waiting in the wings to take over.

With Heini being a stickler for doing things 'by the book', Morgen could just as easily picture him in discussion with top SS lawyers about finding legal loopholes to bring about a possible overthrow of the Führer. What better way to demystify the man than reveal him as the self-confessed murderer of his own niece? Would anyone even come forward to defend the Führer? The man's pig-headedness and military incompetence were obvious, whatever the newspapers were not telling. Everyone was sick of the war. All but the diehards were starting to fear the end, which would see them all dragged into the abyss by a madman who listened to too much Wagner. Morgen thought he would almost prefer Heini.

The school's corridors served as galleries for photographs of former events. Many inevitably featured Fegelein, smartly turned out and mounted, horse and rider lazily photogenic, or caught in mid-air, equally composed, scaling an enormous jump, or racing flat out.

Other photographs showed children, top-hatted women and men. There were cups and prizes and ribbons galore. A grinning Fegelein holding a silver trophy. Oil paintings celebrated his biggest wins. Morgen wondered whether in the man's mind's eye this parade of triumph was interrupted by flashes of the Pripet Marshes and the exhilaration of hacking down screaming villagers. A photograph of a woman alone on a horse made Morgen look twice: a young woman, perhaps still adolescent, in hat and gleaming boots looking down with the air of one who knows the photographer and is easy around cameras and horses. Morgen looked again, thinking, where do I know you from?

'Who is that?' he asked Fegelein, who had screwed a monocle to his eye to inspect the photographs.

Fegelein made a point of remembering: dressage, 1934 or '35; very good; career cut tragically short after a fall.

'Huber,' said Fegelein. 'That's Anna Huber.' He looked at Morgen. 'D'you know her?'

If he lied, Fegelein wouldn't believe him so Morgen said, 'She works in propaganda now.' He asked if they were still in touch.

'Munich is like a village. The hard thing is avoiding people. The Chancellery and ministries aren't so different. Berlin is just Munich on Spree.'

Fegelein laughed easily, leaving Morgen quite clear now on the point of the lunch. It was Fegelein's way of announcing he was now at the table in whatever game was being played.

After leaving Fegelein, Morgen went and sat in a drab little park with yellow grass, dusty pathways and crisped horse chestnut leaves, watching an improbable future in the form of ferociously bad-tempered children being pushed around in perambulators. His main thought while lunching with

Fegelein had been: We're all in the same boat, however much I pretend otherwise. There wasn't much difference between them in the end. Morgen served the same state. He abided by its laws, even if his luncheon companion didn't. As for going after bad apples, what was the point when the whole barrel was rotten?

Still watching the squalling brats, Morgen thought the timing of the Raubal case had to be about buying exactly that: time. Hoffman's revised version had suggested as much, except he fingered Bormann because it suited him. With the death not announced until late on the Saturday morning, it could be shown that the Führer's elaborately detailed Friday afternoon departure had taken place before the stated time of death. Delaying any announcement also gave them the rest of Saturday and all Sunday to get their story straight and tidy away whatever was necessary before the first newspapers hit the stands on the Monday.

QED. Not that Morgen could prove it, unless Hitler was amenable to confessing.

38

The Nussbaumstrasse clinic kept its secrets. A date of discharge for Schlegel A., Room 202, was entered two months later, on 15 November 1931. Had his father really stayed that long? What had been wrong with him? It couldn't have been cheap. Schlegel was sure the sisters' discretion came at a price. There was no medical record for any Schlegel A. on file. Records for the deceased were destroyed after ten years or forwarded in any case of referral.

Another blank.

When he got back to the hotel the gloomy, shadowed street did nothing for Schlegel's mood and Morgen wasn't back. He hung around the station, drinking beer and watching trains until he decided to call the archive and try and speak to Rehse.

The bank of telephones was busy. Schlegel found himself waiting longer than everyone else for a gossipy young woman, who at last hung up and gave him a careless smile to say she was perfectly aware of having wasted his time.

Schlegel spoke to the archive switchboard and asked for Rehse's office. The line rang unanswered and Schlegel was about to hang up when a man picked up.

Schlegel said he must have been given the wrong extension. He wanted Herr Rehse's secretary.

The man said it was her desk; she just wasn't there. Could he assist, he asked.

Schlegel said he wanted to speak to Rehse about an appointment. He gave his name. A long silence followed and Schlegel thought the other man had just walked off, but eventually he came back and told him to come now, if that was convenient. Schlegel was about to say it was, but the other man had hung up.

He decided to check the hotel to see if Morgen was back after all. Morgen had talked of Rehse as a possible connection, according to Gestapo Müller. On the other hand, Schlegel had not told Morgen about the so-called Anton Schlegel confession mentioned by Rösti. He supposed if anyone knew anything about that Rehse might, with his archive probably a hiding place for all kinds of old secrets. For that reason Schlegel rather fancied a private conversation with the man.

It started to rain, a heavy shower that took him by surprise.

A dark saloon car with its wipers on was now parked outside the hotel. Schlegel made out two men waiting inside, one outsize silhouette behind the wheel and in the back a thin one: the fat man and the cadaver. Schlegel turned on his heel, hoping he hadn't been spotted, and quickly crossed the street, praying that his hurry would be put down to the rain.

He ran without thinking until he found himself halfway down the narrowest one-way street, too late to realise it was perfect for an ambush. He hurried on. The end of the street was in sight when he heard a car coming up behind him. As it drew level, the driver's door swung open to block Schlegel's path. The rear door swung open too: it was the sort that opened backwards, leaving Schlegel boxed in. But the cadaver was having to lean out awkwardly and without thinking Schlegel pulled him out onto the ground, kicked him out of the way, swiped the door shut and ran. At the end of the street he paused to look back and was greeted by the unintentionally comic sight of the fat man obediently reversing back down the tiny one-way street and not making a very good job of it.

The shower had stopped by the time Morgen arrived back at the hotel twenty minutes later to be greeted by the uncanniest sight: Anna Huber pacing up and down, her suitcase on the pavement. Morgen stood thinking how only a short time before he had been looking at an old photograph of her, revealing unsuspected links. Now there she was almost as though the photograph had undergone further stages of chemical development and animated her.

Whatever the reason for her delay she'd still had time to get her hair cut short, giving her the look of an Amazon warrior.

'There you are,' she said.

'And here you are,' Morgen said, trying not to sound disconcerted. 'How did you know where to find us?'

She shrugged to say it was obvious. 'The tourist office is bound to keep a record of all the bookings they make. Lucky me, it turned out to be close because I don't have money for a taxi.'

She blew out her cheeks and asked, 'Do you have a cigarette?'

Morgen gave her one, lit it and watched her greedily suck in smoke.

'It tastes foul. I love it.' She had quit a couple of years ago, she said. Her eyes glittered. Morgen wondered if she was high on something. He couldn't make her out. He asked why she hadn't come with them on the train, wondering why she was there now.

Her excuse was a delay in getting to the station because of transport problems and a feeling she was being followed.

'I probably would have missed the train anyway with all the hold-ups and I didn't want to jeopardise anything.'

She smiled sweetly.

Morgen didn't remember any particular transport difficulties that evening.

'Where are you staying?'

She didn't say and asked instead, 'Can we get a drink?'

Morgen suggested the station. She pulled a face and said she couldn't remember if there was anywhere better around.

Morgen saw he was expected to offer to carry her case. Huber travelled light; it wasn't heavy. He pictured a silk blouse, silk underwear.

Anna Huber drank a small beer, Morgen a large one. She turned the glass in slow circles. The place was full, the mood morose, nothing but departures and goodbyes. Morgen was in no hurry. Whatever misgivings he had about Anna Huber, it was a luxury to sit with a good-looking woman.

He made small talk, about how he didn't know Munich, while she continued to scrounge his cigarettes. She blew out smoke and gave him a look of complicity.

'Luring me back into bad habits.'

'I just had lunch with Hermann Fegelein,' he said.

She didn't seem thrown by the mention.

'He showed me old pictures of you at the riding academy.'

'I have known Hermann for years. I think it's safe to say that he is a shit.'

She seemed rueful as she stubbed out her butt with a scribbling action. Fegelein had implied they still socialised. Did that mean they slept together?

'Are you meeting him?'

She answered equivocally, saying, 'He'll be down for the racing. By the way, have you come across Toni Tieck while you were here?'

'No. Why? Who is he?'

'I just wondered.' Her attention seemed to drift and her earlier glitter gave way to lethargy as she seemed to be trying to rouse herself to tell him something.

'Take me to your hotel,' she said. 'I could do with putting my feet up.'

Morgen couldn't tell if she was being suggestive.

They walked slowly saying nothing. The kid behind the hotel desk watched them come in and Morgen glared, daring her to say anything, as he picked up the key.

He took Anna Huber upstairs and apologised for the poky room.

She shook off her shoes and lay on his bed, with her hands behind her head. Unlike most women she shaved her legs. Morgen sat primly on the solitary chair watching her appear to drift off.

'I don't know whether I should be telling you this,' she murmured with her eyes closed. 'It is being said that this man Toni Tieck is in possession of a document that once belonged to Schlegel's father, in which Hitler confesses to killing his niece.'

Interesting, thought Morgen, the first time it had been mentioned since Müller. It left him even more suspicious about where she fitted in. He asked how she knew.

'My brother told me.'

'And how did he come by this?'

'He overheard Tieck. He drives him into town a couple of days a week to where he sometimes works at the archive.'

So there was a Rehse connection. Morgen couldn't work her out. She was saying this fellow Tieck had what Gestapo Müller wanted, but why was she telling him?

'What is the point of this?' he asked.

'Can you help me get it?' she said, with pleading eyes.

'Why should you want it?'

'For Fredi Huber.'

'Your father?'

She said it would vindicate him, confirming what he had spent years trying to prove. 'He drove himself half mad. They persecuted him and all the other reporters who had written a word against them.'

'Is he still alive?'

'I can't say.'

Morgen thought that probably meant he was.

'He wrote a pamphlet while on the run,' she went on. 'It made use of a state attorney's unofficial inquiry, showing that the niece was killed by, or on the order of, her uncle. This document has never surfaced. My father gave it to a friend for safekeeping and that was the last he heard of both. I don't even need to see the original confession, just a copy to show my father. That would at least exonerate the pointlessness of his existence for the last ten years.'

'So, he is alive?'

'Oh, yes, and rather hiding in plain sight.'

Anna Huber closed her eyes and said, 'I must rest now, if you don't mind. Should I give your friend a consolation fuck because he seems so down about his girlfriend?' Morgen wasn't as blunt as she was and didn't say give it to him instead. 'Or do I even care about men?' she added, with languid amusement, leaving Morgen even more undecided if her being there with him was an invitation. Anna Huber drifted off while Morgen studied the eye movement beneath her closed lids and experienced a strangely intimate half hour watching a woman he barely knew sleeping. It was difficult to credit people asleep with lying.

39

The sky was black and it started to rain even harder as Schlegel made the twenty-minute walk to the archive. He used the trees for cover to check he wasn't being followed. The streets were full of umbrellas. He paused, sheltering under a tree, mesmerised by the rain, thinking about Geli Raubal's death and whether the thugs had materialised because they had been asking too many questions about her. The deluge left him wondering at the point of any of it – the war, the streets, the trees, the traffic, the very existence of the scuttling passers-by. For a moment it was like a heavy weight being lifted, to realise there was only the endurance of a pointless existence. He saw how he had rarely amounted to more than being a guest in his own life, controlled perhaps all along by the long shadow of his missing father.

Schlegel ran on through the rain, reckoning if none of it mattered he could leave whenever he wanted. The thought rather cheered him up.

The archive was housed in one wing of the Residenz, an enormous old palace. Bits were missing from bomb damage and camouflage canopies hung over sections to disguise what from the air would be a glaring target. Schlegel checked that there was no sign of the dark saloon car before ducking into the hushed sanctuary of the archive.

The central reception area overlooked a court garden in a state of neglect. A display of posters from the early days of the

Party hung on the walls. Most of the floor space was taken up with packing crates being organised by men in brown overalls who went about their business in a hushed manner.

Schlegel asked at the desk for Rehse and waited, staring at the puddle forming at his feet, until he was greeted by a tiny man with a disproportionately loud manner. Rehse was older than Schlegel was expecting, maybe even in his sixties. His mouth twisted up on one side, like half of an unsettling smile. He had what Schlegel thought of as a professor's beard. His hair was like cut corn.

He came with a pretty secretary, presumably the same one that had been missing from her desk. She smiled at Schlegel and he decided perhaps life was not so bad after all, thinking how shallow he was.

In terms of proportion and scale, Rehse rather reminded Schlegel of Dr Goebbels in his equally palatial surroundings. Also like Goebbels, Rehse started conversations in the middle, offering a running commentary on the state of the archive. A lot was being moved out to safe storage, he said, raising his eyes towards the heavens. 'Untold treasures. *Fifty* rooms!' he exclaimed, with a sweep of his arm to show the size of the operation. 'Not so many years ago it all had to be kept in my apartment.'

He made sure Schlegel admired the neo-classical surroundings before going on. 'We're a huge success. Exhibitions. Publications. Image copyright, that's where Hoffmann was smart. Every time a photograph of his gets printed he takes a cut. I understand you are interested in purchase.'

'What were you told?'

'Somebody would come from Berlin,' said Rehse vaguely. 'The white-haired one,' he added with a hiccough of a giggle. 'So not you.'

Rehse smirked, shooed the secretary away and took

Schlegel's arm in a show of friendliness, an awkward gesture given their difference in height and Schlegel's wet sleeve. Rehse had tiny feet in patent leather shoes.

'Come to my office.'

Impressive corridor one, followed by even more impressive corridor two, then a room the size of a small ballroom, with French windows and a terrace on which a wet peacock prowled, making its ghastly noise.

Rehse had a built-up chair behind a desk while the ones for guests were low. He sat and said, 'I would rather you didn't sit given the state of your clothes.'

Schlegel remained standing, sodden and uncomfortable. He said, 'I am enquiring on behalf of a third party. So far, everything has been too unspecific.'

'In what way?'

'My client has a very narrow field of interest.' He added, not quite knowing why, 'Pertaining to Herr Wolf.'

'Yes, I know,' said Rehse. Schlegel presumed Gestapo Müller had warned the man to expect them.

'This is an interesting piece,' Rehse said, producing a post-card wrapped in cellophane which he placed on the desk for Schlegel to inspect. 'Don't touch. I don't want it getting wet.'

The card showed an old picture of Munich.

'And on the other side?' asked Schlegel. Rehse turned it over for him. It wasn't stamped, dated or addressed, though the message section had been filled in; appalling handwriting, a scribbled urgency, that Schlegel read with difficulty:

Although I have braved gunfire in the trenches and
charmed rich ladies in drawing rooms and roused
huge crowds to frenzied cheering, I am sexually and
emotionally bereft.

Obviously Herr Wolf had written it, though Rehse was not saying. It was presumably there without the author's knowledge, or perhaps not. The man had made such a display of his life in terms of biography intersecting with political destiny; maybe in the early days he was less censored.

'There is supposed to be a confession too,' said Schlegel.

'Don't believe everything you hear,' said Rehse. 'Who told you about that?'

'A man in Berlin.'

'Rösti, no doubt.' Rehse snorted. 'He trades in such rumours to enable him to sell what little tat he has.'

'I am thinking about Anton Schlegel as the missing piece in all of this.'

'You are a relative, I suppose?' Rehse asked sharply.

'A long-lost one. I am told Anton Schlegel made a confession too.'

'Again Rösti, I presume. Let me show you something.'

Rehse reached into a drawer and produced two sets of books in slipcases identical to Anton Schlegel's copy of *Mein Kampf*.

Rehse said, 'These have recently been passed on to us, which makes me curious about why you are here. This copy is from the limited signed first edition of *Mein Kampf* dedicated to one Anton Schlegel.'

Schlegel, baffled by this turn of events, wondered if he were looking at a fake or whether Rösti was in the process of cheating him.

'That's my copy if you got it from Rösti,' he protested.

Rehse said nothing.

Schlegel asked, 'Does that mean you are interested in purchasing it for the archive?'

'It is of no particular value to us at the moment. Anton

Schlegel is a forgotten figure and while the edition is rare the dedicatee is of no significance. Sorry to disappoint.'

Schlegel presumed that was Rehse's way of driving his price down.

'But if Anton Schlegel did make a confession wouldn't that give the book a certain cachet?'

'I think you will find you have been misled. We acquired Anton's papers after his death. Disappointing on the whole, although there was an unsent letter to his son that amounted to a sort of confession. I expect you will find that is what Rösti was referring to.'

'To his son?' asked Schlegel, thinking his father must be dead after all if Rehse had his papers. 'Can this letter be seen?' he asked, wondering to himself: Confessing what?

'An application must be made in writing.' Rehse smirked. 'It takes time.'

Schlegel remembered Rösti saying he thought whatever was going on was part of a controlled exercise. He asked sarcastically, 'What of the letter written by Herr Wolf to his niece, surely that is of academic interest as another unsent letter to a relative? Perhaps it would also be possible to see that too, if one were to apply in writing.'

Rehse gave a withering look and said, 'Not for viewing.'

'But it exists.'

Rehse steepled his hands, a rather absurd gesture for one so tiny, unable to resist showing off. 'Let us say we were able to intervene when the letter came up for sale fifteen years ago. For performing that favour, we were rewarded with the first archive grant.' Rehse looked around at his grand surroundings and said, 'Every cloud has a silver lining. Our discretion was rewarded.'

Outside, the rain grew louder, with the first flashes of lightning and a rumble of thunder.

Rehse turned to the window and said they got quite a lot of storms at that time of year. 'Big electrical ones, to do with the mountains. The gods getting angry. Have you done anything to offend?'

It was meant as both a joke and not a joke. Schlegel turned the question around by asking, 'What did Anton Schlegel do to offend?'

'He was a man who kept his head down, but perhaps not enough,' Rehse said enigmatically.

'Concerning what?'

Rehse shrugged. 'It was said he had an unhealthy relationship with Herr Wolf's late niece.'

'And the point of any confession made by him, were it to exist, would be in connection with that?'

'Fish all you like,' Rehse said with a wave of his hand. 'As you say, *if* it exists. Speaking hypothetically, perhaps it was given to protect the dead girl's reputation. It would have been unacceptable if a Jew had subsequently confessed to having had a carnal relationship her. Whatever else Anton was, he was not Jewish.' Rehse gave a whinny and asked, 'Confessional enough for you?'

More flashes and a crash of thunder, closer, and the drumming of heavier rain. The peacock shrieked like a lost soul.

Yet Dreck the waiter had said that his father sat at the pansies' table in the Bratwurst Glöckl.

'Did you know him personally?' Schlegel asked.

'Never met the man.'

It was bucketing down now, the gap between flashes and the reports closer as the storm moved overhead.

'And Fredi Huber?'

Rehse looked up in surprise. 'Of no interest to us. He had a following in his day but what he wrote was of no lasting value.'

'Didn't his newspaper once show a mock-up of the Führer marrying a Negroid woman?'

'Exactly. Stupid, juvenile stuff.' Rehse looked out at the storm and said, 'You can't leave now until it passes. Perhaps I can get someone to show you around.'

'Your secretary, perhaps,' Schlegel said, feeling superficial.

'Married,' said Rehse, not amused.

A simultaneous flash and crash. Schlegel, tiring of this annoying little man, decided to assert himself. 'It has come to the attention of a senior party in Berlin' – lightning flash – 'that a document might surface, which if exposed' – thunder – 'could cause huge collateral damage, some of it no doubt affecting the archive. It is our task to deliver said document to the relevant party so it is removed from circulation. Just as the letter you referred to' – simultaneous flash and thunder crack – 'played a part in your institution's founding – and it is a magnificent institution – so the deliverance of this document should be seen perhaps as playing a similar role in your continuing existence.'

Rehse grunted. He didn't look that bothered. 'Excuse me a moment,' he said.

Schlegel watched him leave the room. The man walked putting one foot so directly in front of the other that any trail would look like that of a monoped. The sky was purple. The cries of the drenched peacock were drowned by the storm. Schlegel could just hear Rehse talking on the telephone outside and wondered why he couldn't have made the call in the room. He stood, still soaked through, and contemplated walking out of his life, going through the French windows into the rain, letting the grime of years wash away, trudging on until he reached the sea.

Rehse returned, looking thoughtful and waited for another round of thunder to pass.

'Come with me, while you are waiting for the storm to end. I want to show you something.'

'To do with?'

'Of personal interest to you.'

Schlegel obediently followed, curious. They went down a level to a basement. The sound of the storm grew muffled. Schlegel was reminded more of a prison or a bank with its security grilles and barred gates, controlled by combination locks.

'The inner sanctum,' said Rehse in a confidential tone, holding open another gate. Schlegel had quite lost any sense of direction. They had only made a couple of turns and walked down two or three long corridors but he doubted if he could find the way back.

'Ah, here we are,' said Rehse, opening another tall barred gateway, not giving on to a corridor as before, but a room. Rehse stepped aside for Schlegel who entered, realising too late that Rehse was locking the gate behind him.

He protested. The situation was absurd, being virtually kidnapped by this tiny man. He grabbed Rehse through the bars and lifted him off the ground. The man weighed next to nothing. Schlegel demanded to be released. The storm outside now seemed to be mocking him.

Rehse shook his head, saying, 'You have to stay here for your own good.'

'Locked up?'

'Please put me down.'

Schlegel did so and for a moment he thought Rehse might break into a malevolent jig, but he composed himself. Schlegel decided perhaps Rehse was an unlikely guardian angel, unwittingly protecting him from the return of the fat man and the cadaver; unless of course Rehse was holding him on their behalf.

Schlegel listened to Rehse's departing footsteps. The room's metal bars were like a jail in a Western film. The furnishings included a simple couch, suggesting it was sometimes used by night staff. The walls were lined with archive boxes, full of old receipts for accounts, of no interest. As he had no idea how long he would be there he stripped off his clothes, wrung them out as best he could, put on his damp underwear and arranged the rest to dry. He lay down shivering and a little feverish.

In isolation, Schlegel found he was able to visualise the niece clearly for the first time. He sensed it all had gone wrong very quickly. Wherever the final blame lay, he knew for sure that the relationship was responsible for her death.

He had a vivid image of standing next to her in the apartment, and realised he must be dreaming now, but very close to the surface, making everything appear almost tangible. She was teasing him about his white hair rather than the wretched dye. She said, 'We're not so different.' A stone-deaf old woman wandered through the night-time rooms brandishing a knife and carrying a loaf of bread. The canary was out of its cage, flying around in a panic, and instead of being yellow or green, or whatever colour canaries were supposed to be, someone had dyed it black. Even in his dream, Schlegel laughed at such ridiculous symbolism. Muted voices came from the library and Schlegel knew her uncle was talking with Anton Schlegel; the girl was behind him, saying, 'Don't go in. We must be very quiet because there is great sickness in the house.' She announced that she secretly loathed chrysanthemums; they were her uncle's choice. The last thing he remembered her saying was, 'We're the little people. They kick us around like they kick everyone around.' Then he was a small child again, standing at the bottom of a flight of stairs he didn't recognise and looking up.

He woke deciding she had shot herself after all. If the dream had shown him anything it was suicide as a state of mind, which once entered became like a refuge beyond everything. He understood it gave her the choice of reclaiming herself in the moment of obliteration: See, this what I have done.

So that was that, Schlegel thought, until a complication suggested itself. He dismissed it but it refused to go away: that she was murdered while in a suicidal state , and was thus deprived of the right to determine her own fate.

Gradually in that entombed space a presence manifested itself. Schlegel heard the scrape of chair legs, then slow footsteps, pacing endlessly back and forth. He could not tell whether they were coming from above him or were on the same level. The pacing had a drag to it. Uneven and a tapping. Someone with a limp, using a stick.

He lay listening for what seemed like an age to their rhythmic monotony. He must have dozed off without realising because the footsteps were approaching. Schlegel hurriedly dressed. He had no idea what to expect; certainly not the sight that greeted him: a grotesque, shaven-headed man, wearing a powder blue suit, who unlocked the door and quietly said, 'I am ready for you now.'

Schlegel found himself staring at one of the oddest men he had ever seen.

40

Martin Bormann, June 1934

In that last hectic week of June 1934, almost three years after Geli Raubal's death, Bormann spent his days getting rid of the loose ends still surrounding the affair: the scribblers, the badmouths, the intriguers and the ones that just wouldn't shut up.

There was mordant humour to some of Bormann's clear out. Zehnter and his head wine waiter at the Bratwurst Glöckl ostensibly went because they were fairies, though that wasn't a capital offence. The real reasons were not keeping their mouths zipped about a drunken Führer and his niece in their restaurant the night before she died, and one too many references to Adolf's 'shit-eating grin'.

Distinguished local music critic Willi Schmid was carted off and killed in a case of 'mistaken identity'. Grovelling apologies were made to his family; the 'mistake' because no one could come up with a good enough official reason for killing such a distinguished figure. It wasn't as though there was a difference of musical opinion or that his reviews were so awful.

It went back to Geli. She had been reported plotting with Schmid behind the Führer's back, planning to run away to Vienna to continue her so-called music career, even though she could barely hold a tune. Schmid, besotted, had promised introductions.

Anton Schlegel was always adamant there was no sub-stance to the rumour, but it wasn't enough to save Willi. In fact, the Schmid story was one of multiples of false infor-mation put out by Anton following the niece's death: a feint here, a dummy there, a blizzard to obscure the facts.

Then there was Fredi Huber. Down on everybody's list to go. Gutter press and what the man had written about the Führer vile enough to see him done in twice over. Yet Anton Schlegel made a point of coming to Bormann to plead Huber's case.

'What's to plead?' Bormann asked. These days he pre-tended he was busier than he was to Anton, whose falling star was typical of the Führer. Anyone to whom he felt over-indebted got the shove in the end. Ernst Röhm had made the double mistake of thinking he could stand up to the Führer and that old loyalties would save him.

Heady, pin-sharp glee became the mood of those days of tight plotting. The rest were too excited to notice Bormann's stealth. However much Heini Himmler and Göring pored over the lists at Tempelhof Airport on the Sunday at the start of the great purge, the names were a foregone conclusion because Bormann, for 'reasons of co-ordination', had made sure that they all crossed his desk.

Bormann didn't know whether to be impressed or annoyed by Anton Schlegel's revelations about Fredi Huber.

Three years before, he and Anton had worked their arses off to control the chaos surrounding the girl's death. It had been Anton's idea to say she had shot herself in the heart: 'More romantic than a bullet in the head.' The pliant Doctor Müller recorded accordingly, with his drunkard's shaking hand. Two deadbeat cops had been bribed to take witness statements and leave it at that, without viewing the body.

Bormann, still feeling his way, deferred to Anton, who

insisted, 'Push it right to the edge. Give them what they want, all the dirty hidden linen washed in public – the point being, none of it can be proven. All they will be able to conclude is the girl's confused world was about to come crashing down, so she killed herself as the only way out.'

Anton Schlegel summarised for Bormann: 'Cause chaos and control it, so that the Führer survives, and if the homos are seen as part of the problem so be it.'

Bormann asked if Anton wasn't part of that same homo clique.

Anton shrugged. 'If I have to I will acquire a wife. I have done so before. I am not unfond of women.'

Part of Bormann's suspicion during the lead-up to the 1934 bloodbath concerned how much Anton had been running on the side and he hadn't known. He had never got to the bottom of the man's relationship with the Führer and his niece, and now Anton was trying to tell him that Fredi Huber, one of the Party's most vociferous opponents, had secretly been working for them all along. Fredi fucking Huber! The Führer wanted the man's guts for garters.

Bormann asked on what grounds had Fredi been amenable. Anton knew Fredi socially, he said, making it sound casual. Fredi had told him that Party lawyers were threatening to sue over what he had already written about the suspicious nature of the niece's death and feared his employers would cave under the pressure. Anton had suggested other targets to Fredi, as a way of taking the heat off.

What Anton didn't tell Bormann was that blackmail had played its part. Family man Fredi trawled for boys in his spare time, so had no choice but cooperate.

Unlike others, Anton was looking beyond the immediate crisis to work out how what was universally being regarded as a complete disaster for the Führer's public image could in fact be exploited for political advantage.

It was already plain to Anton that the Party's internal schism with Ernst Röhm would have to be addressed in the end by violence, but he saw ground could be gained in the meantime through stealth. He steered Fredi Huber to go after Röhm and his brownshirts. Fredi obliged by turning to the wider picture.

One Fredi Huber exposé was accompanied by a cartoon of an overweight stormtrooper with a distinct resemblance to Röhm, wielding a whip and standing over a prone woman, her hands protecting her head. Wrong sex; it was boys Ernst liked knocking into shape but the point stood. Fredi reminded readers of Röhm's homosexuality, exposed by The Munich Post the previous summer. Fredi gave dire warning of high-ranking 'bachelors and homosexuals' in the Party. Fredi thundered: What did the Party's espoused sanctity of the family count for when it was led by corrupters of young boys or a man who drove women to suicide?

It was political war in the guise of grand scandal, but what no one saw, apart from Anton, was that Fredi's broadening of the attack meant the real target was already becoming diffused.

Even if Fredi Huber's material was controlled by a hidden agenda, no one would dream of mistaking the reporter for anything but a tough crusader. Anton was the only one to see that Fredi had a way of laughing up his sleeve, however much he lived in fear of exposure. Something else Bormann wasn't told – and only later came to suspect – was Anton's decision to play both ends against the middle by recommending that Fredi keep his suspicions about the Führer's involvement in his niece's death to himself, while implying he shouldn't drop them altogether, just in case, as a possible insurance.

Bormann's reaction to Anton's plea for clemency was the reasonable one of saying if no one else knew about Fredi's double role, what did it matter if he went down the pan?

Anton Schlegel's approach to Bormann turned out to be a big mistake as it backfired on him because Bormann decided if Fredi stayed then Anton had to go. He'd had his fill of pansies. They were not sentimental days. Bormann told himself he would miss Anton even so, but it was time for the sorcerer's apprentice to take over. As for Fredi, even if he was off the hook, he would still have to make a run for it as a marked man in everyone else's eyes.

41

The man standing before Schlegel in his dandy's pale suit had a pampered air and appeared so gross it looked as though someone had taken an air-pressure pump and inflated him until he was in danger of splitting, leaving Schlegel to wonder at the prospect of watching him deflate like a punctured tyre.

Flash and vulgar were the only words that came to mind. A big ring on the pinky. Another, extraordinarily, on the man's thumb, something Schlegel had never seen before. A fancy clip for the loud tie. The big shaven skull.

The man said, 'I find it easier working at night. I would have come earlier but something came up. My apologies. Follow me.'

The voice Schlegel decided was the same as the one that had answered the secretary's telephone when he had called the archive earlier.

He followed the man's awkward, scything gait, the result of a damaged foot. Stairs he could manage only one at a time. They ended up in another windowless space, much larger than the one downstairs. The man locked the door behind them: more shelves crammed with box files, this one with a desk and two reading chairs and an air of monastic contemplation. Schlegel found himself staring stupidly at the man's mismatched footwear. The left shoe was brown suede. The special built-up boot was made from extra-shiny black leather.

Seeing Schlegel looking, he said, 'It's special waterproof material. As you can see, it doesn't match.'

Schlegel felt both drawn and repulsed by such ugliness. The man's eyes appeared indifferent to the point of detachment. Schlegel couldn't say what colour they were. Pupils didn't come in black but that's what he would have said.

The man asked, 'What on earth happened to your hair?'

Schlegel couldn't be bothered to explain. The joke was wearing thin.

The man rubbed his hands vigorously over his bald scalp, brushed his shoulders and said, 'I didn't know until I lost my hair that you could still get dandruff. What colour is your hair normally?'

'White.' Schlegel felt emboldened to ask, 'Why am I here?'

The man showed his teeth, as if to say such abductions were entirely normal in his world. Schlegel suspected he could afford to be casual because he dealt in a particularly tight form of control. He remembered Rösti's suggestion of some kind of mastermind and wondered if he was looking at him.

'I am told you are after something. The seeker shall be shown,' the man announced enigmatically.

Schlegel, still shivering from his drenching, experienced a flash of trepidation: he felt as though he was sitting on top of a slide with everything about to move very fast, and he needed to have his wits about him.

'The Hitler confession?' he ventured.

The man moved towards a safe that stood under a table and worked the combination lock. 'My little black museum.'

He gave Schlegel a sly look as he produced a large box file and put it on the table. Schlegel watched as the lid was slowly opened and the contents arranged lovingly on the table. They consisted of a document pressed in Plexiglas;

what looked like a child's exercise book; and a dark green leather folder with a clasp lock.

'All fascinating in their way,' the man said, pushing the Plexiglas in Schlegel's direction. It showed a handwritten sheet, with the same scratchy writing that was on the postcard Rehse had shown him. Cheap paper and brown ink. Schlegel read:

My darling child

At first it was just the sound of laughter filling the room and gay singing as you go about your business, and he realises how little real laughter there has been in his life. Then it becomes *your* laughter, *your* singing. It took time to realise it was all about you, the adorable child. He missed you when he wasn't there and counted the days until his return, and his heart lifts on seeing you again. No harm must come to you. Absolutely not! You must be kept safe and not bruised or sullied by the filthy lusts of men. He is assailed by dread visions of what others will do, with their marbled bodies and unleashed cocks. He sees you tied down, straining against your bonds, begging and screaming for mercy, exposing your raised buttocks in offering, despite yourself, because the power of the man cannot be denied, forcing his way into that dark, forbidden hole. Out! Out! Other terrible sights besiege him. Men on their knees, begging you to defile them, to reveal their worthlessness by shitting on them, how can such things be? These men are craven, bandy-legged Jews, he knows, inviting punishment, asking to be kicked and beaten as their only path to satisfaction. And worse! In one ghastly apparition the beautiful child, no longer submissive but a wilful seductress – your magnificent naked bosom caressed lasciviously by you – stands legs spread over the prostrate Jew, who rants incoherently, twitching and frantically fingering himself as you shrug down your drawers and squat to spray a long, thin and thrilling stream of liquid gold into the man's babbling, eternally grateful mouth.

Schlegel found what he'd just read almost laughable in its crass use of surrogates; as with the account of the Jewish intruder who was supposed to have attacked the niece.

'And the point of showing me?' Schlegel asked, wondering if Herr Wolf, with his claims to be above temptations of the flesh, could have had such a dirty mind to produce such stuff. It read more like the work of a cheap pornographer.

'Context,' said the man.

'And the other items?'

The man picked up the leather folder. 'Said to be Fredi Huber's secret text. The key to the lock is missing.'

'And no one has opened it?' asked Schlegel in surprise. The lock wouldn't prove much of an obstacle.

'Some things are better for being preserved, like a fine wine not for immediate opening.'

'But it may turn out to be nothing.'

The man nodded. Schlegel suspected he was familiar with its contents and deliberate mystery was part of his game.

'And the exercise book?' Schlegel asked.

'The niece's private diary.' He pushed it in Schlegel's direction. 'What do you think?'

Schlegel looked at what seemed to consist of accounts of shopping and boyfriends and love affairs, written in a sloppy romantic style. He noted Jewish names. A single entry underscored three times: 'I can't get enough of him!' A note of her shooting target practice scores. A late entry declaring: 'I am beside myself with worry. I don't know what to do.'

'Your conclusion?' asked the man.

'It's not exactly tell-all,' said Schlegel.

'It's a poor fake, probably by Russian intelligence produced after the girl's death.'

'The reason being?'

'To discredit her to the detriment of her uncle, showing her as a promiscuous Jew lover.'

'And the man's confession that everyone is so interested in, do you have that?'

'Shall we say it is in play.'

'In play?'

'Active.'

'And the other "confession", the one by Anton Schlegel?'

Also in play.'

'What are the stakes?'

'High. In the meantime my purpose is to demonstrate that your world just got a little smaller.'

'And your role in this?'

'Discretionary. Let us say we are aware of those familiar to you. Let us say they operate within our orbit. Your old friend the art dealer Christoph, the homosexual, hanging on by the grace of others. Your stepfather, current whereabouts unknown, and your colleague Morgen's old adversary, Fegelein. We are aware of Anna Huber.'

'How do you know about her?' Schlegel asked, shocked.

The man spread his hands and said, 'She told us.'

Schlegel experienced a stab of anger, thinking Huber must have set him up all along.

The man looked apologetic. 'None of this is so extraordinary in a world of informers and secret files. The point is you will be given safe passage.'

'To where?' Schlegel asked, still shocked.

'You have been selected.'

Schlegel didn't bother to ask, selected for what?

The man went on, 'You are the only one in a position to deliver certain documentation in person to Party Secretary Bormann in Berlin.'

'I have no access to the man.'

'I heard you met him.'

'Did Fegelein tell you that?'

The other man shrugged. 'Bormann will see you when he learns your name.'

Schlegel saw his chance and said, 'Then give me the document, put me on the night train to Berlin and I will gladly see the back of this place.'

'The station is being watched.'

The two thugs, Schlegel supposed.

'The airport too?'

'We can't take that risk. We have another route out via the big race meeting tomorrow afternoon. You will be taken there and put on one of the charabancs taking racegoers back to Nuremberg. From there you can take a train to Berlin.'

'And the documentation?'

'Tomorrow.'

'And in the meantime?'

'You are safe here until then.'

As in Budapest, Schlegel had the feeling of life going on around him which he knew nothing about. With the talk now of race meetings, he wondered if his being there was not to do with his father at all but his stepfather, given his stepfather's racing connections. It led him to ask, 'Does any of this have to do with Anton Schlegel?'

The man shook his head. 'Long gone.'

'And you are?'

'Bormann's is the only name you need to know and he yours. Safer if you don't know mine.'

'And when Bormann asks on whose behalf I am acting?'

'He won't. He will know.'

The other man was sweating. Schlegel wondered if physical grotesqueness was a condition of this netherworld these strange creatures inhabited. He decided the man standing before him was actually nervous for all his air of command. Perhaps the stakes were that high. As he had been chosen to execute the delivery, Schlegel wondered if he perhaps had more of an upper hand than he'd thought.

He said, 'I want a favour in return.'

The man looked surprised by the demand.

Schlegel went on. 'Rehse said the archive has Anton Schlegel's papers.' He pointed to the objects on the table and said, 'If you are willing to share these then surely you can show me those belonging to someone described by Rehse as being of no consequence.'

'Did he say that?' the man asked sharply. He grew impatient and demanded, 'How much do you really want to know?'

'I know next to nothing. I only care that I was lied to. I am bound to wonder if these papers contain some sort of pathetic excuse.'

'The truth isn't always polite,' the man announced ponderously.

Schlegel sighed. 'Enough games. I have come a long way.'

'Like a good pilgrim,' the man said with sudden sarcasm.

Schlegel was thrown by the change of tone. The man had been almost friendly until then.

'Do you really want to know what your father was?' he insisted.

What, not who, Schlegel thought; was there a difference?

The man paused. 'Anton Schlegel was not a nice man at all.'

'Did you know him?'

'Before my time, only by reputation.'

'I came to Munich being told he was alive.'

'I can assure you he is dead. Sorry to disappoint.'

The news was almost a relief, thought Schlegel. Now he could get on with the rest of his life.

The man replaced the objects on the table back in their box and returned them to the safe, shut the door and was about to lock it when he asked, 'Are you sure you want to know?'

Schlegel didn't say no and the man opened the safe again, removed an item from another folder, and laid it on the desk.

After the man was gone, locking the door behind him, Schlegel went to the desk and looked at what had been left. It was Anton Schlegel's unsent letter, addressed to him.

42

To my son:

I write in the expectation of you never reading this, my dear August, as we shall probably never meet and it shan't be sent, and, besides, I am using it as an excuse to address myself, at a remove.

It is 1931, a rainy evening in late October and a momentous time of late.

I am mostly homosexual by nature though not exclusively as I married and produced you. I did not serve in the 1914 war, being in Shanghai where I acquired an English bride who was boyish and flat-chested, well-connected and a crashing snob, which I didn't mind as I still take a detached interest in society's foibles. Colonial life was more European than Europe, the meticulous recreation of a half-remembered dream, delineated by the tyranny of distance. Our house looked like it could have been in any European stockbroker belt, but especially English, with the addition of craven but untrustworthy Chinese servants.

I had gone to Shanghai to avoid the 1914 war because I possessed enough foresight to anticipate the bloodbath. I was not a patriot. I was familiar with my homosexuality, having practiced it and been fiddled with from an early age, including a mutual liaison with a school teacher, a man with gentle hands. The disadvantage of Shanghai was lack of opportunity for significant extracurricular activity. Chinese boys didn't appeal. Some British public schoolboys kept their hand in but tended to be pink and flabby, with parts to match. So I packed up my family and returned to Germany, to throw myself into Berlin's emerging single-sex nightlife, with its hard-up young men willing to sell themselves in lively, easygoing ways. My dear wife was otherwise engaged learning her excellent German and cultivating her own affairs. We came to a broad understanding and although sexual relations were maintained – but no little sister produced – we both knew our private interests lay elsewhere.

As for my subsequent disappearance, a scandal would make most sense – being caught with my pants down, buggering in the boardroom – but the reasons are boredom, dear boy, and insider trading, plus extensive borrowing at a time of hyperinflation, creating a fortune, hedged via accounts in Switzerland and Luxembourg. I soon created a platform that allowed me to do as I wished . . . The child bored me. I have to remind myself by that I mean you – it is too late not to be honest. You must be twelve now. I am afraid I had no aptitude for, or interest in, being a father. An insecure and clingy brat, not that our schedules coincided to any extent. Your mother showed as little concern and sometimes I wondered why we bothered with such a cumbersome asset.

I was curious about Argentina and told my wife I was thinking of scouting it out in terms of a move.

Your beloved mother was not convinced. Having worked hard to master her German, she wasn't sure she wanted or needed to add Spanish. My reason was pursuit of a young diplomat from the Argentinian embassy who was being posted home, with whom I was smitten, or so I told myself. I was quite steadfast about making the trip until I fell in with a young visitor from Munich – a military lad and brownshirt, of easy passage and exquisite orgasms.

I decided to follow him to Munich, for what I thought would be a short stopover before departing for Buenos Aires. I had already decided Munich was sufficiently diverting to dally when I received news from my Argentinian paramour that he had decided to marry, making any continued liaison difficult while not out of the question. I in turn decided I wasn't willing to play second fiddle.

I rented a house out in Feldafing where I entertained a succession of young men, for a week or two at most until I tired of them.

In many ways, I am an unassuming man of good grace and manners, possessing excellent taste, in clothes, in shoes, in the furniture I choose, the paintings I buy, and with my afternoons free I soon found myself entertained in the salons of Munich's *haut-bourgeois* matrons. I could talk persuasively on most subjects and only very occasionally was found out. It was an idle, pleasant and indulgent life. I enjoyed its shallowness. Depth doesn't interest me. I indulged in fashionable drugs and drank moderately, so was in no danger of going off the rails, but I knew I was already thinking of the next adventure.

As it happened, I had already been acquainted with that new adventure for several weeks without realising; what my afternoon matrons called 'that delightful,

funny little man'. One of my boys had dragged me
along to what he called a political evening – a gathering
of the great unwashed in a fifth-rate beer hall, getting
drunk and disorderly until a small man with a greasy
forelock walked in surrounded by brownshirt thugs,
who winked suggestively at my lad. Scuffles broke out.
Clubs were wielded, heads cracked. It seemed almost to
be a reflex action of the herd.

I at once understood the attraction of terror. Fear
costs nothing. Brutality is always respected. The
realisation marked the start of a personal recklessness.
My boy let me take him in a toilet cubicle to the
accompaniment of shouts and screams and the sharp
reports of bone on bone.

By the time we returned, order is restored.

The strange man smooths his hair into a parted
fringe and before speaking spends a long time
searching the audience, which grows suspenseful and
expectant. He starts slowly, almost too quiet to be
heard, in great rolling sentences – despondency, anger,
betrayal, hope. Word for word it doesn't add up to
much but the effect is transformative, in a guttural way.
The voice cranks up a register, cracks with emotion.
Sharp chopping gestures to emphasise a point. If he
speaks with notes he seems not to refer to them. It
is as though the man is the vessel of the voice, which
twitches him this way and that, like a storm-tossed
cork, as the response grows more tumultuous. It is the
bark of the underdog, the unheard, the voice of riot;
that much is blindingly obvious to everyone in the
room, which roars back its approval. Huge crescendo,
the man flaying his vocal chords chasing a rapturous,
barnstorming climax, showers of spittle as the rage

grows uncontainable and the promise of delivery is screamed out to foot-stomping applause. It was as though a heavy artillery bombardment – which many of those in the room would have been familiar with – had found its way into words. The audience reeled shellshocked.

Afterwards he looked like someone had switched him off. His clothes were soaked and he repeated the hair smoothing gesture.

The eyes were quite gone.

There was no getting near him with his bodyguard wrapped around him like a cloak. He appeared so spent and insignificant I doubted I would recognise him if he walked past in the street.

I became friendly with Ernst Röhm, who called himself the head queer in town. We were bound to meet, given my liking for his hard boys. Ernst sniffed out my Feldafing home and approved. Well-appointed, not too comfortable. He said it looked like I was capable of walking out at a moment's notice.

That initial meeting with Ernst was in November 1923. Herr Wolf, as he liked to call himself, I didn't encounter until later, because of the failed Party uprising and his trial and imprisonment. After his release at the end of 1924 Herr Wolf was, in effect, voiceless, being banned from public speaking. A strange first meeting in the January of the following year, organised by Ernst bringing him to Feldafing, revealed a tongue-tied man of few social graces, gormless in repose, but with a feral whiff and a marked air – the fancied runner with the longest odds.

To what extent Herr Wolf defined me or the other

way round is impossible to say. He will no doubt fulfil his political destiny regardless, but there was perhaps a brief period when my influence held sway – as an arbiter of etiquette and taste. I said, 'I can teach you all the boring things you will need to get on with the boring people. However much you despise them they will be your backbone.' I saw neediness and greed in his eyes.

Your affectionate father, A. S.

In the early stages of their friendship, Herr Wolf told Anton Schlegel that he found him like clear water over which he could skim his pebbles and watch in admiration as they skipped away.

People generally found Anton receptive, even when he wasn't that interested in them. They seemed to want to tell him their stories and he seemed to satisfy some primitive urge whereby those confessing went away with a better understanding, even though he, Anton, like a fashionable shrink, contributed nothing and, unlike a shrink, didn't charge. He decided his talent lay in the art of saying nothing or not very much.

Herr Wolf complained that he had no one else who would just listen. Everyone looked to him instead. The relationship with Röhm was breaking up.

Not long after they met, Anton became mildly obsessed on Herr Wolf's behalf with the case of Therese Neumann, a local farm girl who took to her bed paralysed and went into an ecstatic trance. Visions included Jesus on the Cross. Neumann's hands and feet wept Jesus's blood, as did her side and even her eyes: the tears of Christ indeed. She received visitations from the Blessed Virgin, purveyor of dire warnings about the state of things. Neumann declared her only nourishment was Eucharistic wafers. Fed by the body of Christ!

Neumann became a celebrated event, even among men who should have known better – including Fredi Huber. With Fredi it was sometimes difficult to tell how much he bought into the story rather than merely reporting it, but he was superstitious, and susceptible, being Bavarian and Roman Catholic and living too close to the dark forests of wild imagination.

The ostensible reason for his interest was a political dimension to Neumann's utterances: warnings that could have been written by a press office for the Roman Catholic Church trembling before godless Communism and the devil's disciples. Deep sceptics came to Neumann's bed and departed converted. Grown men left bathed in their own tears of forgiveness.

Herr Wolf was interested in Neumann as a crowd puller and asked Anton if he should visit. He considered her his antithesis and wanted to know, 'How does she do it, the business with the blood?' 'Vials probably.' 'Real blood or fake blood?' 'They live on a farm. The parents are probably in on it too.' 'We are both spoken through. My blood is the symbolic blood of racial purity, not some cheap trick. We are not fooling anyone into believing.'

Herr Wolf asked Anton to attend on his behalf and report back. Anton duly made the journey and found an austere, cell-like room with wooden shutters and whitewashed walls, full of the pervasive and honest stench of country cattle dung.

The visits were supervised by the parents. A crowd of fifteen or so was waiting that day. The mother made a show of humility, fingering her rosary beads. Her rough husband, hat clutched in both hands, announced that their daughter was 'resting' and no one should communicate with or disturb her. Three at a time, they were told, and no more than two minutes; all donations gratefully received afterwards. Anton Schlegel suspected the husband and wife operated a canny double act, which of an evening saw them sitting around with their feet up, counting their coins and joking about it. When Anton Schlegel's turn came he shuffled in with a bent-double crone in black and a fidgety girl of maybe seventeen.

Surrounded by religious accoutrements – holy water, crucifix, rosaries and tallow candles – a pale young woman lay abed, spectral in the wax white of her complexion, sculpted lids over closed eyes and only the slightest rise and fall of bedcovers to say she was alive.

The crone and the young woman fell to their knees, babbling silently.

Anton loitered after the wife came to say time was up. He listened to coins being dropped into a brass bowl by the departing visitors.

Perhaps thinking she was alone Neumann woke and blinked in surprise to find Anton staring back. They viewed each other for an eternal second with naked eyes. The woman closed hers, and sighed in contentment, relieved perhaps to have been seen through by such another perfect dissembler.

Anton left without tipping, and reported to Herr Wolf that the parents might as well open a restaurant as part of the business. The fleece of the Lamb of God against fleecing the lambs. What was the difference?

Anton was reminded of the Neumann visitation some months after Geli Raubal's death, on the last occasion that he and Herr Wolf met socially. It was early in 1932, the location a beer garden, on the first day of the year that it was warm enough to sit out. While waiting for his habitually late companion Anton passed the time reading newspapers, including a book review about Genghis Khan, which casually wrote off the millions of deaths for which the warlord was responsible as meaningless within the larger context of historical progress. Herr Wolf, when shown the review, devoured it rapaciously and laid the newspaper aside with a dreamy look while Anton thought to himself: On such moments history turns.

The niece was never mentioned between them.

Hoffmann was always telling an extravagant story of a secret nocturnal drive to visit her grave immediately after the funeral, and how on returning to the car the Führer's voice was restored, as if he had received a message sent by her from beyond, instructing him to proceed with his mission, for he immediately said, 'So now let the struggle begin, which must and shall be crowned with success.'

What tosh Hoffmann talked, thought Anton. Hoffmann's pretty secretary was, by the by, now ensconced as Herr Wolf's latest little secret. No danger of anything getting out of hand there.

With the whole sad business of Geli Raubal, Anton looked back at his own role as arbiter of what at first had been a diverting and unlikely experiment in romantic Gothic – the monster ambushed by love – until the night of Herr Wolf's drunken call when for the first time Anton saw him for what he might become: the beast unleashed.

Anton Schlegel had been the unannounced presence in Herr Wolf's reception room during the early hours of Friday, 18 September, noted by Hoffmann. Anton was the first to be summoned by a hysterical Herr Wolf shouting down the telephone that his niece had been attacked by an intruder. He arrived to be met by the astonishing sight of the virtually teetotal Herr Wolf staggering around blind drunk, hissing, 'A Jew has killed her!'

Anton checked. Not dead. A pulse. Unconscious and badly beaten.

Herr Wolf seemed scarcely to comprehend, repeating only that the girl must have forgotten to lock the front door. She was the one with the keys as he didn't bother himself with such minor inconveniences. Anton called in Bormann, who had the Party connections.

Anton did not share with Bormann what his immediate thoughts had been upon being confronted by such a wildly deranged Herr Wolf. He told himself: First, the decadent scene, with which the Party and you are too closely associated, must be jettisoned and transcended. The vociferous opposition of the press must be tamed, after being drawn. A scandal must be provoked followed by what public relations companies call an image makeover.

He addressed the pathetic, collapsed man: 'Herr Wolf, the risks are huge but they can be overcome and you will become unstoppable. The opposition will be exposed and can be disposed of when the time comes. It will be like lancing a boil.'

Herr Wolf looked up at him with crazed eyes. Nevertheless, Anton Schlegel suspected that in one of the darker recesses of the man's mind he understood perfectly what was being said.

Time for the Party to clean up its act.

Standing there in the chaos of that night, it was blindingly clear to Anton Schlegel that a sacrifice was needed and what that sacrifice had to be.

Betrayal is such an exquisite thing.

In the storm-tossed days that followed, everyone agreed it was a tragedy with the girl gone so young. Anton saw how they were all compelled to share in her death, claiming it for themselves as though she were the sacrificial victim. The tight clique surrounding Herr Wolf reflected the wider feeding frenzy, partaking in private ceremonies that Anton came to regard as acts of symbolic cannibalism. But of greatest significance was the calculated effect of Herr Wolf's grief. For all the man's devastation and suicidal state, Anton watched him coming to realise that the tragedy gave him the one element previously missing.

Depth.

Anton understood what the rest were too busy scurrying to realise: how their glorious leader needed to love, be loved and rendered loveless. The mysteries surrounding the death were irrelevant beyond the fact of her being gone: the casting asunder of Geli was the last piece in the making of Herr Wolf. Love lost forged the alchemical solution and little more than a year later he was in power.

Without her, it would not have been the same.

THE BERGHOF

43

The first race was already underway. Breezy weather, fluffy white clouds and a huge cheering crowd pressed against the rails as horses with improbable names flashed past, thundering hooves, churning turf, the going soft after the rain, the blur of jockeys in their bright silks jostling for an edge, using their whips to thrash their mounts on, the tinny report of the race's progress coming over loudspeakers with the commentator tripping over his words to keep up, two horses breaking for the lead, snorting breath, riders high in the saddle, taking hold and positioning themselves lower over the horse until their heads were level with those of their mounts as they rounded the final turn, ground shaking from the deafening hooves until they merged with the roar of the crowd. The two leading horses crossed the line neck and neck – photo finish! – and the jockeys loosened their reins and stood relaxed in the saddle to slow their mounts, and look back exhilarated at the rest of the straggling pack of already forgotten also-rans.

Schlegel watched in a daze. He had been taken there by a man who introduced himself as Thomas Huber, Anna's brother, fetching him from the archive as though that were perfectly normal and driving them out to the racetrack at Reim in the eastern suburbs. Huber, unlike his sister, was an ordinary sort, who offered a damp handshake; once fit but muscle turning to fat, the chin starting to double. He wore a cheap suit with what looked like an expensive hat. Schlegel supposed him about thirty.

He stared out of the window, wondering what to expect.

The letter. Being told the unadorned truth for once, which was what he had always thought he wanted, he now wished had not happened. He was annulled, like a dead man walking through lank space.

Schlegel was taken by Thomas Huber to the winners' enclosure where the strangest party awaited. Morgen and Anna Huber, with her aggressive new haircut. Hermann Fegelein surrounded by a crowd of sycophants. He was the owner of the winning horse. 'By a whisker!' he crowed. The Braun woman was there dressed to the nines. A man with a pencil moustache nodded at Thomas Huber and Schlegel found himself looking at an older version of the young man in Hoffmann's photograph, his father's apparent assassin, Emil Maurice. For all that, it was like any day out: bright convivial chatter, an aimlessness. Stand around and no one pays you much attention. Schlegel made for Morgen, who asked where on earth he had been.

He said, 'Unavoidably detained,' and left it at that.

Anna Huber was staring. Schlegel said, 'I see you made it.' He thought Morgen looked captivated by the woman.

'We need to talk,' he said to Morgen.

'We're here to enjoy ourselves,' Huber announced, like it was one of those deadly polite parties where everything was kept horribly light and everyone was on their way to getting smashed.

He looked around for some sign of the man in the powder

blue suit. Perhaps he didn't make public appearances. The rigmarole of the previous night suggested someone in hiding and perhaps forced to use go-betweens.

Morgen and Huber were drinking a sparkling wine. Schlegel asked if Morgen was anyone's guest in particular. Morgen said, 'It was her idea.'

'How did you find each other?' Schlegel asked but before they could answer Thomas Huber arrived carrying two bottles of beer, one of which he gave to Schlegel. Anna Huber pointed out Fegelein's wife, a darker, plainer, less showy version of her sister, Fräulein Braun, and equally well turned out. Huber dismissed Fräulein Braun as a fake blonde, and seemed sour about the sister. Schlegel watched Fegelein flirt with Fräulein Eva. Both were in a gay mood showing off by coming together for a quick mock waltz with their drinks still in their hands, in celebration of Fegelein's win. Schlegel suspected Anna Huber had her claws into Morgen. He steeled himself to approach Fegelein, thinking how since Anton Schlegel's letter everything had become *less* readable.

Fegelein looked about to give him the cold shoulder then introduced his wife, who immediately turned to someone else.

Schlegel said, 'I am looking for a strange-looking man who last time I saw him was wearing a bright blue suit. He didn't tell me his name.'

Fegelein looked at him in surprise. 'You must mean Toni Tieck.'

'If that's his name.'

'Then you have met already?' Fegelein asked sharply.

'Not intentionally,' said Schlegel.

Fegelein, with a look of supercilious concern, asked, 'Knowing that the man is your father?'

Schlegel rocked back, thinking Fegelein had to be lying. He could see nothing of himself in Tieck.

Fegelein gave him a look of mock concern as it dawned on him that Schlegel hadn't known. 'Sorry if I spoke out of turn.' He sounded anything but apologetic.

Fegelein was the last man Schlegel wanted to be told by, and he could see Fegelein knew that.

'Didn't mean to spoil your day,' Fegelein said casually. 'Anton and I go back years, or Toni as he calls himself now.'

Toni Tieck. Anton Schlegel. Ha-ha, Schlegel thought, seeing the joke, Tieck and Schlegel being joint translators of Shakespeare. The man was hiding in plain sight.

'What are you and he cooking up?' Fegelein asked in a conspiratorial tone. 'Was it he who sent you here?'

'I am supposed to be contacted,' Schlegel offered, to see if Fegelein reacted.

'What are you doing later?' Fegelein asked instead.

'Going to Nuremberg apparently.'

'You don't want to do that.'

Was it a veiled threat? Schlegel couldn't tell.

'Come back with us to the Berghof. We can sort everything out there.'

Fegelein stood looking pleased with himself, as though all was now in order. 'You really didn't know about Tieck?'

Schlegel still wasn't sure if it was a joke against him. For the life of him, he could not square his vision of the poised, rather cruel letter writer with the vulgar Michelin Man he had met.

Fegelein gave Schlegel an insincere pat on the shoulder. 'I can see I have left you with a lot on your plate. Must dash. More anon at the Berghof.'

Schlegel was sure that the apparently casual revelation had been deliberate malice and felt like socking the man.

There was more cheering as the horses passed the post.

Fegelein looked at his watch. 'Must dash. I have another horse in the next race.'

Schlegel scanned the crowd in vain search of Tieck, with no idea of what he would say to him. There was a viewing stand, bars in tents, food stalls, blared announcements on loudspeakers, paddocks, enclosures, and a separate glazed viewing area for important guests. He saw Emil Maurice up in the VIP area, standing by the window with a group and making expansive gestures. The air was heavy with the smell of cooking oil and bad food frying, interspersed with the whiff of horse dung. Schlegel passed the shiny black boots of jockeys nonchalantly riding to the winners' enclosure, their horses lathered in sweat, and he wondered if a horse actually knew if it had won a race.

The crowd was drunk to the point of fights breaking out. Litter lay everywhere. Pickpockets were at work. A woman cried out that she had just lost her purse. The sun beat down, as indifferent as the grass, which would have the place back to itself tomorrow.

Thomas Huber was talking to his sister, apparently handing her something, but too far away for Schlegel to see what. Thinking they might have something to do with Tieck's business, he went over but they offered only bright, anodyne conversation, looking rather furtive about it while agreeing that they were getting pleasantly drunk. Anna had a race card and said she had already picked a winner at 33–1.

Schlegel asked if either of them had seen Tieck. Anna Huber gave what he took for a warning look, which stopped him from asking if she knew that Tieck was really Anton Schlegel. He still couldn't believe it. It was Anna Huber and her brother who had first raised the possibility of Anton

Schlegel still being alive. He left them to it after deciding neither was to be trusted.

He wandered around and considered making himself scarce until the meeting ended and sneaking onto a coach going to Nuremberg and lying low for a while. Curiosity got the better of him when he spotted Morgen standing alone. He went over and gave him gave a hurried explanation about Tieck, not mentioning Anton Schlegel.

'I think Tieck is behind the Hitler confession,' he said, 'which I am now supposed to give to Bormann.'

'Then you have it?' Morgen was apparently not surprised by this news, leaving Schlegel to wonder as usual exactly who could be trusted.

'No, but Fegelein seems to be under the impression I do.'

'Fegelein told me he is interested in it too.'

'Who isn't?' Schlegel asked sarcastically. 'Does your authority extend to access to the Berghof?'

'I don't see why not.'

'Fegelein insists I go there with him. Tieck, on the other hand wants me to go to Nuremberg with a document I don't have and take a train from there.'

'Go to the Berghof,' said Morgen, 'and I will come with you.'

Schlegel looked up towards the glazed stand. Maurice and his gang appeared wildly drunk. Then he spotted Tieck, alone in the opposite corner, not immediately recognisable, being dressed in top hat and tails, leaning on his stick, which was what gave him away, and surveying all below in a godlike manner.

Schlegel told Morgen to wait and went up into the stand, shoving his way through the raucous crowd. Two SS guards on the door announced that entry was by permission only and tried to stop him until Schlegel shoved his badge in their faces. He saw the guests inside all wore special rosettes that gained them admission to the stand. Most were whooping drunk.

Tieck was standing with his back to Schlegel, the top hat in his hand now. The man's footwear matched, he saw. Tieck turned as if expecting him. He showed no surprise but looked strained and exhausted, like a man in the middle of a marathon session at the gaming tables.

'Hermann Fegelein wants to talk to me,' Schlegel said while asking himself if this man really could be his father.

'No surprise there,' Tieck said flatly. 'I expect Hermann is being greedy.'

'He has invited me to the Berghof.'

'When?'

'Now.'

Tieck's mood seemed to improve at that. He clenched his fist, as though ground had been gained. 'Then you must go. But first come.'

He motioned Schlegel closer to the window overlooking the winners' enclosure. Sounds of loud drunkenness continued all around. Taking Schlegel's arm, he held it tight, not in a friendly way, and pointed with the top of his stick.

'Who down there do you know?'

Schlegel thought how absurd to be standing next to this man, who didn't know he knew, yet the awful social situation prevented any mention of the fact.

Schlegel recited what he saw. Fegelein. Fegelein's wife and the Braun sister. Anna Huber and her brother. He pointed out Morgen.

'So that's Morgen,' said Tieck. 'Not how I imagined.'

'What do you know of Morgen?'

'Fegelein speaks of him as a thorn in his side. Do you trust him?'

'Fegelein, no!'

Tieck, impatient, said, 'Nobody trusts Hermann. I mean Morgen.'

No more than I trust you, Schlegel wanted to say. 'To a point,' he said as he watched Emil Maurice leave the stand and walk over to Fegelein. The man was reeling.

'Emil Maurice,' Schlegel said.

'You don't need to tell me,' said Tieck sourly.

'Wasn't he supposed to have shot you?' Touché, Schlegel thought. It was the first indication he had given that he knew the man was his father.

He watched for any flicker of reaction and got nothing.

Tieck remained silent for a long time before saying, 'There is a book in the Berghof, in the Führer's study, on the top shelf on the far left. Of sentimental value, a personal copy loaned by me to the Führer which he never returned. I expect it is still there. I doubt he even opened it. Perhaps you could bring it to me, should you have the chance.'

Schlegel looked at Tieck and wondered if the Berghof hadn't been the man's real objective all along.

'Any reason you can't fetch it yourself?' he asked, a little cruelly.

'I don't qualify for admission. As you have probably gathered, I am not supposed to exist.'

'So it's not about delivering anything now. It's about retrieving an item you don't have access to.'

'For the moment, and as you are going.' It was said with the offhand manner of a man hardly asking a favour, until Tieck's eyes unexpectedly appeared to well up as he said, 'It is the only extant momento of my childhood.'

'And the title of the book?' asked Schlegel, incredulous at this mawkish turn.

'An early edition of *The Adventures of Pinocchio.*'

Schlegel couldn't help but laugh.

'Quite so,' said Tieck, aware of the joke. 'The puppet master and the paradox of the lie. You must go now. They're getting ready to leave. Make sure you take Anna Huber. Send Morgen to me. It's important. I will wait here.' He let go of Schlegel's arm.

In terms of lies, Schlegel saw that Tieck had never intended to reveal himself as his father. But he was perfectly willing to betray his former self, Anton Schlegel, through the revelation of the letter. Strange, Schlegel thought, that the son was now entrusted with the errand of retrieving the monster's one sentimental possession. He suspected that wasn't half the story.

Back in the enclosure Fegelein's group was packing up. The best races were over and no one was hanging around.

Schlegel went over to Morgen and pointed to Tieck looking agitated in the glazed stand. 'He needs to speak to you, he says.'

Morgen shrugged and said, 'He can't be any worse than this lot.'

'Don't bet on it,' said Schlegel as Fegelein came up and clapped him on the shoulder, enough to make him stagger.

'There you are!'

Fegelein's eyes were unfocused. The man was as drunk as the rest of them. He looked at Morgen and sniggered. 'Your friend's turn to be invited. Sorry. No more room in the car.'

Schlegel gestured helplessly at Morgen as he was led away.

Fegelein gathered the women, the Braun sisters and Anna Huber. 'Ready girls?'

Anna Huber said she had other plans and wouldn't be going.

Schlegel drew Fegelein aside to ask if he could persuade Huber to change her mind. 'I quite fancy her,' he said.

Fegelein made an obscene gesture, sticking a finger into the hole made from the joined thumb and forefinger of his other hand.

Schlegel watched him talk to Anna Huber, who frowned before being persuaded. She stared at Schlegel as Fegelein escorted her to where the sisters, brightly pissed, were waiting and looking none too pleased about the extra company.

Fegelein returned to Schlegel and said, 'Mission accomplished. Here's Emil, as drunk as a lord. He's coming. Big week for the Chamber of Commerce. Have you met?'

Maurice had the inane grin of a man well away. Schlegel avoided giving his name.

The two sisters chattered on the way to the car park. Huber looked downcast. Schlegel decided there was nothing he wanted to say to her in front of the others.

Fegelein ordered, 'Girls with me. Emil, back to chauffeuring! Drive our friend here. Important guest!' He shouted to Maurice, 'Race you to the Berghof!'

Whatever Emil Maurice might once have been, it came down to being beyond drunk in charge of a motor vehicle as they headed off in pursuit of Fegelein, who swung from side to side to stop them overtaking, giving long derisive blasts on his horn, and then the houses were gone and they were crossing a silver plain, through the start of the long shadows of the sun's descent.

Maurice, cursing like the devil, chased in vain after Fegelein's more powerful motor while Schlegel sat with a rictus grin smashed across his face, thinking there were worse ways to go.

Horn blaring, they shot past a peasant on a bicycle; Schlegel didn't know how Maurice missed him. He turned and saw the man wobble into a ditch.

"Don't worry!' Maurice shouted. 'I got the Führer out of hundreds of scrapes. Vehicles in pursuit. Roadblocks. Ambushes. We stopped once for a tramp on a mountain road because Ade wanted to give him his coat and the cunt turned out to be hiding a bayonet! You have to keep your eyes about you.'

Ade! thought Schlegel. Did Führer Ade call Maurice Em?

Maurice continued yelling above the roar of the engine. 'Führer security after my time was a joke. They let someone steal Ade's Merc while he was in a café! Picture his face coming out to find that! Two of the security commanders were totally shit-faced. I know, I can see you thinking, "Speak for yourself!"'

Maurice roared with laughter as they slewed round a corner and were hit by blinding sunlight that turned everything white.

Dazzled by the play of light on the windscreen, Schlegel had the brief impression that the road and fading landscape were moving around them as they sat stationary in a time bubble, surrounded by lurking secrets so deep they acquired an air of fabulous worthlessness, the accumulation of all the lies surrounding the Führer amounting to no more than bankrupt stock.

Maurice insisted on a short cut and they climbed into the dark Alpine fastness. A deep ravine lay on Schlegel's side. Maurice drove with reckless abandon until Schlegel could see only the edge and the drop beyond. He stared in terror-stricken fascination at snow deep below, left from the previous winter, and expected at any second to find himself flying through the air towards it. How they reached the top in one piece he would never know. For a moment they were above the tree line, with a view of a valley bathed in the last of the soft light. Schlegel wanted to ask if Maurice had shot his father then realised the man had passed from beyond the stage of drunkenness where anything was possible into a state of dumb, white-knuckled desperation.

In terms of odd couples, Morgen thought he and Tieck made a pretty good pair but not half as strange as the idea of the man being Schlegel's father.

Morgen had done as Schlegel asked and approached Tieck who said, 'Take me to the Berghof.'

He was the strangest creature, Morgen thought, and like a lot of men with an almost clownish aspect probably not to be underestimated. Tieck didn't strike Morgen as a humorist, but he did make him think of a joke being played in deadly earnest.

Tieck cast around, looking uncertain, leaning on his stick, top hat awry. He wasn't drunk but from his stumbling manner he could have been as far gone as all the others staggering around. He eventually said, 'My son. I hadn't realised the effect he would have.'

Morgen stared at the man's bulging, toad-like throat, asking himself if it really could be Anton Schlegel he was looking at or someone pretending to be. The thought almost made him laugh – the notion of an impersonator in the way that the Führer had doubles. He found the idea quite in keeping with the strange, haunted world in which they had found themselves since coming to Munich.

Tieck said, 'I need Schlegel for an errand, which will guarantee my reinstatement.'

'To what?'

Tieck gave a bitter laugh. 'The land of the living.'

They left the town and headed south with the setting sun to their right.

Tieck asked who had sent Morgen and he saw no reason not to say, as Tieck probably knew more than most.

'What exactly is Müller looking for?' Tieck asked.

'He believes there is a tell-all diary written by the niece.'

'Fake.'

'The so-called Hitler confession, does that exist?'

'Oh, yes. What are your conclusions about the niece?'

Morgen said he thought her uncle did it in the early hours of the Friday morning after the night out at the Bratwurst Glöckl.

Tieck eventually said, 'Not bad.'

'End of story?' asked Morgen.

Tieck gave a high-pitched giggle. 'Good heavens, no!'

The man would not be further drawn and with that fell into a disconcerting trance, in which he appeared to sleep with his eyes open. It was not that the pupils were colourless, more that they were beyond the known spectrum, and as Morgen stared ahead at the nearly dark road he decided they were not the colour of night exactly but matched the day's dying light.

44

Schlegel could describe what he was looking at only as a beggars' banquet. They were in what Fräulein Braun insisted on calling 'below stairs', the Berghof's huge staff kitchen, which from what he could tell was on the same level as the main reception.

Maurice had driven the last of the journey in a trance, as cautiously as a man who had just passed his driving test and could recite the Highway Code backwards. They were waved through the Berghof's elaborate security system on Fegelein's telephoned say-so. By then it was too dark to make anything out and blackout prevailed. Their escorted entrance into the building was round the back, through a cloakroom full of walking sticks and umbrellas and rubber boots lying around in a state of disorder, then down a corridor past a boiler room and locked gun racks, into the big kitchen where they were greeted with sarcastic applause from Fegelein. The rest of the room didn't bear thinking about. Worst of all – the last people Schlegel expected or wanted to see – were the two thugs from Berlin: the fat man and the cadaver, lounging at the table with bottles of beer and chomping wurst. Schlegel stared, wondering if they had known he was coming. His presence scarcely seemed to register, as though they had already written him off, until the fat man laughed at Schlegel's hair and lifted his bottle in mock salute while the cadaver studiously ignored him.

The atmosphere was fetid as if the room hadn't been aired in years. The Braun sisters were squabbling over what record to play. The gramophone looked like it had been dragged in from next door. Eva won and settled for what she announced as 'hot jazz'. Everyone was smoking. Eva Braun clicked her fingers in time to the syncopated beat, gyrating lasciviously as she started doing a dance of the seven veils that didn't involve taking off any of her clothes. Fegelein was making eyes at Anna Huber, standing apart. She acknowledged Schlegel with insouciance. Fegelein's wife looked drunkenly tearful. But most extraordinary was the man sitting at the head of the table with his uniform jacket undone and hair awry, with a cigarette and a drink on the go. A Führer, if not *the* Führer; Schlegel didn't know what to call him. He thought of Hoffmann's endless, boring gallery of photographs, none of which could be labelled: The Führer relaxes with a fag and a drink.

The drunken Führer looked amiable, his mood probably about as far from his master's as it was possible to get. Some running joke seemed to be going on because everyone called him Bobby, and used the familiar address. The man's name was obviously not Bobby but whenever it came up it was greeted with hilarity.

Fräulein Braun lost her balance doing her pseudo-strip tease, crashed into a chair and grabbed Fegelein and said she needed someone to hold on to. She stood with her arm draped around her brother-in-law and ordered her sister to find a slow dance record.

Schlegel wondered about the two thugs. He supposed their job was getting rid of human garbage for the likes Bormann and now perhaps Fegelein. They appeared not bothered about him, but Schlegel sensed they were biding their time.

Emil Maurice looked dazed, like he had just been

dropped from a huge height. Fegelein had his hand positioned proprietorially on Eva Braun's arse, noticed by the sister who marched over and removed it. The room was electric. Bobby was muttering to himself in a Führer-like way and staring at Fräulein Braun, leaving Schlegel contemplating whether she took her pick of the understudies when her master was away. As for Fegelein, it would be her choice, Schlegel supposed, doubting that even Fegelein would jeopardise his position with such sexual recklessness; she, on the other hand, was probably too aware of her limitations as unofficial mistress, her current staggering notwithstanding, which was probably about being seen to let her hair down. It was obvious that the man himself was never coming back and Bobby confirmed as much, saying over, 'The Führer is gone.'

Fegelein stopped dancing with Eva Braun when her sister cut in. Fräulein Braun sat sprawled, her legs stuck out, pigeon-toed, as she kept trying to blow a stray hair back into place, laughing at the facial contortions she was having to make.

Fegelein asked Bobby, 'Are we doing the Führer walk tomorrow?'

Bobby suddenly didn't look at all happy.

'Explain the Führer routine for our guests.'

Bobby mumbled and had to be told to speak up. Then because he seemed incapable, Fegelein explained for their benefit.

'The Führer's daily exercise consists of a solitary walk from the main building down to the teahouse where he takes breakfast. Invariably he is fetched and driven back. But, and here is the thing, for around ten minutes, during which he walks alone – as, in the end, we all walk alone – a concealed gunman could shoot the Führer, without even a telescopic sight if he were a good marksman. We know the Führer is bulletproof but this needs to be tested.'

Fegelein produced white powder, which he told them when inhaled 'concentrates the senses wonderfully'. They took turns snorting it, the giggling sisters perhaps making themselves out to be less practised than they were. Bobby was talked into doing a Cossack kicking dance, to quite the wrong music, which he sportingly performed, to roars of applause, none more than from the two thugs, until he keeled over and lay panting and breathless, and Fegelein clapped his hands over his head and shouted, 'The Führer conquers Russia!'

Schlegel felt scratchy from the white powder and wanted to talk urgent rubbish to whomever would listen. The women took it in turns to dance with different men after Fegelein announced 'ladies' choice'. Even the two thugs were dragooned. Bobby declined, citing Führer protocol. Maurice danced well, sashaying the women around. The Braun sisters avoided Schlegel.

In the end, Huber offered, not looking particularly bothered. She steered Schlegel, keeping her distance.

'Why did you not come on the train?' he asked.

'Hermann invited me to fly down on the Führer's plane.' She laughed and said, 'I missed that too.'

'Why are you here now?'

Huber shrugged and said, 'I expect Hermann and I are after the same thing.'

'Which is what?'

'You,' she said enigmatically. 'Aren't you the one with what we want?'

Schlegel suspected he had been used as bait all along, but to what end?

'Isn't it you that might have something for me?' he

countered, thinking of whatever her brother had passed her at the race track and whether it had really been meant for him.

Huber said she didn't know what he was talking about but he could see she did. She broke off dancing and walked off without a word, leaving Schlegel standing there, sure that he was right.

The drug had left him feeling uselessly alert and fool-hardy enough to ask Fräulein Braun to dance. He thought she was going to snub him but she held up her hands in acceptance. She danced like a marionette. Schlegel could sense from the tension in her body how much effort went into the empty-headed brightness. She chattered on, giving him a potted history of the place and the huge improvements made, before telling him, 'We can't use the Great Hall while the Chief's away but maybe we can sneak in tomorrow and I can show you.' He sensed she was flirting and couldn't think of anything witty. He caught her eye and was reminded of salmon in aspic. Behind the fixed smile he saw the shadow of a much easier, more attractive one and he decided she must have been fun once. He thought of smashing down social barriers and telling her about his father and asking what she had really thought of Fräulein Raubal, and what sort despair had driven her in turn to attempt suicide and what she and Ade got up to in bed, if anything; and of course he didn't say anything.

But she did, venting her frustration, leaning in to whisper, 'Can't she see he fucks anything that moves, including that bitch over there. Can't she, really?'

Schlegel shuffled to keep in step as he worked out she was talking about Fegelein and Anna Huber. Fräulein Braun tilted her chin up with the look of a supplicant, their lips almost touching, as she went on urgently. 'Gretl only got married to spite me, so she could be be the adoring little wife when I never can, and now she thinks she is respect-able just because she is hitched to a drunken philanderer. Can't she see he married her for his career and nothing to do with her? He was fucking one of the bridesmaids on the morning of the wedding, that's how much she means. Are you married?'

'No.'

'I can never be married. Tell me I haven't been mad. I never doubted, until now. He won't come back.'

'Can't you go to him?'

Fräulein Braun gave a laugh of suppressed hysteria. 'You're so sweet. Nobody knows who I am. I am the little secret. I am not supposed to have a thought in my head. I am there to entertain and chatter on without a care in the world. Sometimes I think men understand nothing of women.' She gave him a startled look, as though she had said too much, and asked what he would do when it was all over.

'When everything's back to normal,' she prompted.

Schlegel could not recollect ever being asked about the future and had no answer so he asked the question back, curious.

'Have an exhibition of my photographs,' she said. 'I know I could earn a living from them but Hoffmann has always blocked me. Not any more. The man is out of favour and good riddance.'

Schlegel was wondering how much influence Fräulein Braun really had when Fegelein cut in and said to him, 'Emil and I want to show you around. A moonlight drive. Emil is rather enjoying reliving his chauffeuring days. Tells me you had tremendous fun on the way over.'

Schlegel left Fräulein Braun looking like she had sud-denly been switched off.

Maurice, playing a noisy game of Snap with the two thugs

and Bobby, saluted them with his glass, looking like he had broken the sound barrier in terms of drunkenness.

Fegelein snapped his fingers. 'Time to drive the Führer car!'

Maurice eyes grew excited at the prospect. The seven-seater Mercedes!

Fegelein, who had taken his gun belt off, strapped it back on. 'Schnapps for the road,' he said, taking a bottle.

The underground garage contained a whole pool of vehicles, the most conspicuous being the armour-plated convertible Mercedes. Maurice stared in awe, looking almost halfway sober at the prospect.

Fegelein insisted on putting the roof down and complained when he was made to help, saying the Berlin one had a button that controlled it automatically.

Fegelein told Schlegel to sit in the front and got in the back. Maurice fired the engine and reversed the purring machine out of its space, handling the vehicle as reverently as if he were conducting a sung Benediction: driving as a religious experience.

The clear skies of the afternoon had been replaced by rolling mist and a chilly night.

'All right to drive, Em?' Fegelein asked cheerfully from the back. 'Can't see a thing. Pity. Magnificent views by day.'

Like a tour guide, he described the superhuman feat of building seven kilometres of perilous mountain road taking them to the peak-top recreation house that had entertained heads of state. It been built by Bormann, he said, as a special gift for the Führer, who rarely visited because of his vertigo. Fegelein went on to tell them how he had taken advantage of the place to continue his own wedding celebrations the month before, and these had gone on for several days with them all as pissed as lords, which they couldn't have been down in the Berghof with a disapproving Führer in attendance.

They drove out of a tunnel into a grey blanket of mist that was like having one's face pressed by a wet rag.

The silence became too much for Fegelein, who announced, 'We've all become so psychotic and steeled, don't you think?'

The car's headlights seemed to reflect back on them, giving their faces a sickly glow as Maurice coaxed the Mercedes up the steep, winding road until they reached level ground. Through a break in the fog Schlegel could just make out the brooding silhouette of the mountain-top retreat.

The road ended in another tunnel, like entering a fallopian tube, which delivered them spectacularly into a domed waiting hall where they got out and waited for an elevator whose doors opened to reveal a uniformed operator, who snapped a salute.

Schlegel found it all very Jules Verne, this strange marble and concrete hideaway. The crazy tunnelling and dynamite needed to construct the road alone seemed like an act of willed hubris: nature will be conquered! Then there was the gadgetry of the lift with its telephone and clock and a flashing indicator showing the height of ascent: more than a hundred metres, leaving Schlegel wondering at the cost of it all.

They exited the lift and Fegelein led the way, turning on lights, saying there was no need for blackout in the fog. He took them up a short flight, revealing a room that came as a surprise after all the engineering. Schlegel's impression was of overwhelming Alpine kitsch, a salon with pine panelling, dominated by a huge, quite ghastly tapestry of an al fresco medieval courtly scene. Anything that wasn't brown was green, apart from an oriental carpet. The effect was expensively sickly.

'Shame the Führer hardly ever comes,' said Fegelein. 'My sister-in-law makes up for that.'

Schlegel supposed the view by day compensated for the indifferent taste. Quite out of keeping with the style of the rest of the room was a set of bronze doors. These led out on to a small terrace.

'Come and admire the non-existent view,' said Fegelein, gesturing for Maurice to remain behind.

They stepped out into the cold night. The door shut behind them. Enshrouded in mist, all Schlegel could see was the glowing tip of Fegelein's cigarette. He inched his way forward until he felt a low balustrade that didn't even reach his waist. They could be on the edge of a precipice for all he knew.

Fegelein's free hand came to rest on Schlegel's neck. 'Fabulous views during the day and this terrace is a suntrap. My wife and sister-in-law like to sunbathe *au naturel*. Now, you must have something I am interested in.'

Schlegel said, 'I don't, as a matter of fact, so I don't quite know what to say.'

The grip on his neck tightened.

'Let's not try and be clever.'

'I was supposed to be given something this afternoon but that didn't happen.'

Fegelein swore and ordered Schlegel to explain himself.

'Tieck asked me to make a delivery to Party Secretary Bormann, he didn't say what and I wasn't given it.'

He didn't say he suspected Anna Huber of having it.

'Is Tieck running you because you're his son?'

The sneer reminded Schlegel how much he had wanted to hit Fegelein earlier, for the way he had announced that Tieck was his father.

'I can't think why he chose you,' Fegelein went on, petulant now. 'He could have asked me. I work with Bormann, so why not?'

Schlegel decided to speak his mind for once. 'Because he doesn't trust you.'

He sensed Fegelein didn't know how to react to that. Do it now, he thought, balling his fist to smash Fegelein in the face, doubting he had the guts. Fegelein gave a nasty squirt of a laugh as he prodded Schlegel in the chest and took a step forward to say, 'I've had people shot for less.' With no room to swing a punch, Schlegel head-butted him instead. His forehead met cheekbone with a satisfying crack and he was surprised by how easily Fegelein went down, until he heard him squealing, begging not to be hit again, and realised the man was a complete coward. Schlegel turned away in disgust, just as the bronze doors opened to reveal Maurice squinting in a pool of yellow light, trying to make out what was going on.

Fegelein sprang to his feet, saying, 'Suddenly indisposed. Feeling better now.'

Schlegel had to admire the man's speed of recovery, acting as though nothing had happened.

'What have you got there, Em?' Fegelein asked, in a show of friendliness.

Maurice had found a guitar. 'In the music room,' he explained and played a complicated arpeggio, badly.

Fegelein stuck his hands in his pockets, dangerously relaxed already, and said, 'My wife's favourite position is kneeling against the balustrade there, being taken from behind, telling me, "Fuck the view, Hermann."'

They all laughed, even Schlegel, possessed by the spell-bound mood and dreamlike switches.

Fegelein rested his hand on Schlegel's shoulder and murmured, 'Shan't forget that.'

After that everything grew more bizarre, as though the reason to be sitting on top of a mountain in the middle of the night was to listen to a recital of Emil Maurice's clumsy music skills.

'Who has the confession, do you think?' Fegelein asked in an easy way. Schlegel didn't say, wondering why he was protecting Anna Huber. Fegelein's cheek was smarting; soon he would have quite a shiner.

They watched Maurice perform some complex finger work then, carrying on, Maurice asked, 'What confession?'

'Shall we tell?' Fegelein turned to Schlegel. 'Go on, let's hear your version.'

Schlegel looked at Maurice and said, 'There is supposed to be a document in which Hitler confesses to killing his niece.'

'Whether he did or didn't,' offered Fegelein.

Maurice carried on playing, 'He didn't.'

'We know he probably didn't,' Fegelein said, getting exasperated. 'That's not the point.'

Maurice repeated, 'He didn't. What is the point?'

'The point is the document,' said Fegelein testily.

As Fegelein seemed amenable to explaining in the grand manner of villains willing to share with lesser mortals, Schlegel asked why.

'Tactical reasons.' What these were, he wouldn't say. He dabbed his cheek with a silk handkerchief. Schlegel noted the malevolent look as Fegelein asked, 'Who would you rather be, Schlegel, you or me?'

'I would rather be a rat than you, Hermann,' Maurice answered for Schlegel.

'Ha-ha! You already are, Emil.' Fegelein turned back to Schlegel. 'Oh, go on, then, if you really must know. Reichsführer-SS Himmler—'

'Your boss,' Maurice interrupted sourly.

'Poor Em here has hard feelings,' Fegelein explained to Schlegel. 'He thinks he should have been head of the SS, but Em got shafted. Anyway, "my boss" has taken an interest in the case of the niece for years.'

Maurice was still plugging away, a polka now, sounding less rusty.

Fegelein said, 'The Reichsführer-SS has always been keen to know who spread the rumour of his involvement in her death. According to that particular story, he was supposed to have bamboozled the kid into becoming the suicide equivalent of a kamikaze pilot.' Fegelein sniggered. 'With so much scheming, in any given plot everyone's name is bound to come up.'

'What would having the confession add?' Schlegel asked.

Fegelein looked at Schlegel as though the answer were self-evident. 'Heini's a completist in terms of information.'

Schlegel supposed it was more a matter of not wanting anyone else to have it. It wouldn't be long before those closest to their master turned on him. Just as they spied on each other as a matter of course, they would all have files stacked up on the Führer.

'Back in the day . . .' Maurice began.

'Oh, let's hear no more of your "back in the day" and "old fighters" nonsense,' Fegelein interjected. He explained to Schlegel, 'Emil rode shotgun for the Führer, and he was even engaged to the niece.' He asked Maurice, 'Good fuck was she? Never had the honour myself but heard she rode like a steeplechaser.'

Maurice put down the guitar, looking like he wanted to

square up to Fegelein, who taunted, 'Poor Emil, the heartless thug with a broken heart.'

Maurice looked crushed. With Fegelein's mask firmly back in place, Schlegel found it impossible to recall him collapsed in a funk on the balcony.

'Well, Emil,' said Fegelein, standing. 'All very interesting. How your service has been rewarded, with the chair of the Munich Chamber of fucking Commerce. Bravo, old sport!'

'Don't be a cunt, Hermann,' said Maurice with cheerful unconcern and Schlegel was shocked to realise they were more or less friends after all, whatever dirt they had on each other.

Schlegel asked, 'Did you shoot Anton Schlegel?'

Maurice didn't even have to think to answer. 'In the end, no.'

Fegelein goggled. 'I didn't know that. Come on, Em, you do get around. But if the man was down to be done why disobey orders?'

'A religious visitation.'

'Oh, come now!' said Fegelein. 'Pull the other one.'

Fegelein rolled his eyes as Maurice related an improbable vision of Raubal appearing to him in the woods, telling him to spare Anton because, after his betrayal of her, he should be saved for a fate far worse, perhaps many years hence.

'What betrayal?' asked Schlegel, but Maurice only shrugged and Fegelein said, 'Time to go.'

Life's only constant, thought Schlegel: betrayal.

45

Fog rolled down off the mountains until there was neither night nor road. Tieck lowered his window, saying he could see enough of the kerb to guide them. Quicker to walk, protested Morgen, who had neither the skill nor stomach for blind driving.

They crawled on upwards into the soft white wall, until a distant clattering came from up ahead that Morgen couldn't identify, then became thundering hooves coming down the road and a scream of pure terror that seemed to last forever. Morgen stamped on the brake as the huge shape flew out of the fog: a horse, or perhaps even the devil himself, Morgen thought as the windscreen shattered, followed by a second scream so terrifying he knew it would haunt him for the rest of his life. An enormous spasm gave way to a deathly still, broken by the sound of dripping blood. Morgen felt antlers penetrating the space on either side of his seat when they could easily have impaled him. He had matches but had no wish to see the stag's dead eyes staring at him. He shoved. Nothing budged. He told Tieck to take the antler nearest him and it took an age of gruesome wrestling before the dead beast slid away off the bonnet. Morgen's hands shook as he lit up. His front was blood-spattered, his lap full of broken crystals of glass. Tieck's reaction was not shock but rage at having his journey interrupted. Morgen listened to him swear until he decided enough and got out, the scatter of glass falling from him.

The stag had taken out one headlight. The other just about illuminated the shape lying in the road. It took all Morgen's strength to pull it to one side. The beast convulsed hugely as he held its legs, sending him reeling like a man hit by an electric shock. He picked himself up and put a bullet in the animal's head, more out of fright than mercy.

46

'Does anyone know if dogs can die from eating peanuts?' the Braun sister was asking as Schlegel, Fegelein and Maurice returned to the Berghof where the atmosphere remained rancid.

The party had moved on to a more formal salon, what Fräulein Braun described as the original living room, dating from before the expansion. A huge glazed stove stood in the corner. Long banquettes ran along two walls, with a dining table, sofas and armchairs designed more for statement than comfort. Führer Bobby lay passed out on one, with drink down his jacket. The Braun sisters were curled up on sofas. The two thugs prowled like caged animals. Anna Huber seemed nervous and Schlegel wondered if more was at stake than she was letting on. They had been joined by Negus and Stasi, Eva Braun's Scotch terriers, who were being fed titbits. Emil Maurice, who had driven them back in what Schlegel could describe only as a state of suicidal concentration, looked gone. Fegelein was highly strung and continued to knock it back.

One by one they nodded off, the sprawled bodies looking like a bloodless massacre in a departure lounge. The two thugs took turns by the door. Schlegel thought it was like being stuck in hell or waiting for the end with no prospect of leaving.

Emil Maurice started to play a game of patience, a

complicated double-pack affair which he was too drunk to follow. Schlegel drifted over and said, 'Red queen on black king.' Maurice dithered until Schlegel moved the cards for him.

Looking at the fiendish complexity of the emerging ladders and their refusal to play out, Schlegel was rather reminded of the Raubal case. The cards made it easier to ask, 'That business of the vision in the woods.'

Maurice snorted. 'Stranger things have happened.' Red seven and black six across to black eight. 'Bloody hot week-end, too many jobs on,' he continued.

The lists, Schlegel supposed. 'Why were some carted off and others not?'

'You mean shot.' Maurice seemed almost relieved to talk. 'Special treatment. The way it worked. Those that were disappeared and those that were made an example of.'

'Why Anton Schlegel?'

'Orders. We weren't told why. Harlaching, Saturday, 1 July 1934. We were all sweating from the heat.'

'Did you know Anton Schlegel?'

'Are you really his son?'

Yes and no, thought Schlegel. He asked, 'Why didn't you kill him?'

He moved the two of diamonds out of the game onto the ace. Jack of hearts ladder down to black six across to black queen.

Maurice said, 'See her.' He meant Anna Huber. 'Your father had a bargaining tool.'

'Fredi Huber's scoop,' ventured Schlegel.

Maurice nodded. 'Anton said Fredi owed him his life, in exchange for the secret dossier Fredi had been compiling since the niece's death.'

'Which Anton then bartered in exchange for you sparing him.'

Maurice nodded. Schlegel asked what that had been about.

Maurice's drunken, rambling explanation boiled down to the rivalry between Maurice and Himmler. This had culminated with Himmler expelling Maurice from the SS after proof emerged of his Jewish background. The Huber scoop was offered by Anton as immunity against Himmler making any further moves against Maurice.

'A talisman, he called it.' Maurice shrugged. 'Well, he was right about that. I told Heini to fuck off and if anything happened to me there would be consequences.'

Maurice slumped back, dazed by the effort of the explanation.

'Who did Huber hold responsible for Raubal's death?' Schlegel asked, curious.

Maurice snorted. 'He didn't really. He only wanted to demonstrate that the Führer was in the apartment when the girl died.' Maurice shrugged again. 'It didn't actually prove anything. Looking back, I'm not sure if it was even a fair exchange.'

'Where is it now?' Schlegel asked, thinking of the dark green folder he had been shown in the archive basement.

'The thing is, it disappeared.' Maurice seemed to find the idea amusing.

'Did that bother you?'

'Not especially. The Führer, after leaving me to sweat, eventually made up his mind that I had his protection regardless. Old loyalties still count among those who matter.'

Schlegel was reminded of schoolboy crazes where an intense interest, like a collective fever, seizes everyone before burning itself out, leaving everyone mystified about the original attraction.

'And what did you report back about Anton Schlegel's death?' he asked.

'That the job was done. It was all say-so anyway. It was treated like a weekend shooting party ...'

At one point in the night, Schlegel, Fräulein Braun and the fat thug were the only ones awake. She came over and asked him to show her the rules of the patience game. 'I have a lot of time on my hands,' she said simply. He explained how it worked and in spite of appearing dazed she was a quick learner, though easily bored.

'I have a favour to ask,' he said. 'Would it be possible for you to show me the Führer's library?'

'I don't think so. It's private.'

'Of course,' said Schlegel. 'It's only that a relative of mine was involved in furnishing it.' As a guess, it seemed a reasonable one.

'Who was that?' she asked out of routine politeness.

He told her and could see the name meant nothing. She looked tired, he thought, in that way of someone who has just travelled a long distance.

'It would be a privilege and an honour to see it,' he went on. 'Something to tell my grandchildren.'

It seemed the only way, playing by the general rules of her household, with its pretence of manners, sentimental decorum and doing the right thing. He continued to butter her up, seeing it as his one chance of getting past the fat thug on the door. Eventually she stood and said, 'Please,' gesturing that he should follow.

The thug was forced to defer to her, saving a hostile look for Schlegel as they passed.

She led the way upstairs to a room more like a studio apartment than a study, with an expansive sitting area with a sofa and armchairs, a huge carved desk, another enormous tiled stove and expensive pale wooden panelling with inset shelves of books. Fräulein Braun explained how the building had started out as a modest holiday chalet until expansion became necessary. From what Schlegel could gather, the original building was still contained within all this gargantuan madness. Fräulein Braun, surveying the huge expanse as though it were no more than a cosy nook, declared that she thought it came closest to reflecting the Führer's modest personal taste. 'He is, in the end, a man of contemplation,' she said.

By day, the Alpine views through the tall windows would be spectacular.

'May I . . .?' asked Schlegel, pointing to the books at the end of the room.

Fräulein Braun appeared momentarily distracted, as though struck by the pointlessness of her position as mistress of an abandoned household. 'Please do,' she said, reverting to being the courteous hostess. Schlegel hadn't expected to feel sorry for the woman.

He made a show of studying the books, moving slowly towards the shelf indicated by Tieck, and there it was, *The Adventures of Pinocchio*, exactly where it was supposed to be, on the top shelf on the far left, clearly having lain undisturbed for years. Did he risk filching it? He turned to see if Fräulein Braun was watching. She was. He said, 'There's a book here, am I allowed to touch it?'

It was the wrong thing to have asked. She came over and stood next to him.

'Probably not,' she said. 'It's a private collection.'

He pointed to the book in question. She perked up when she read the title on its spine and said, 'Oh, yes, we screened the film of it here several times. We all enjoyed that.'

'You see, the book belonged to my father,' Schlegel said. 'He lent it to the Führer.'

'This very copy?' Fräulein Braun laughed and exclaimed, 'And he didn't return it!'

'How did you know?' asked Schlegel, going along with her mood.

She appeared pleased to be able to indulge the memory. 'He often used used to joke about how he was always being fined by lending libraries for overdue books in the days before he had two coins to rub together.'

She laughed again in desperate merriment and reached up but the shelf was too high for her. 'You're tall,' she said flirtatiously.

Schlegel got the book down and held it in his hands: a well-worn copy of a slim volume, which like a lot of children's books had seen its share of wear and tear. He knew nothing of his father's childhood, which his mother had never mentioned. He opened the cover and there, written on the inside fly leaf in a child's unformed hand: 'This book belongs to Anton Schlegel.'

He showed her, still wondering how to pocket it or whether he would have to try and come back later. Fräulein Braun took the book, not appearing that interested. The strangely intimate moment between them had passed. She opened the book at random. It was an illustrated edition and Schlegel found himself looking at an engraving that appeared straightforward but became increasingly disturbing.

A sticklike Pinocchio was being arrested and manhandled by two soldiers wearing old-fashioned uniforms. The image, unsettling in itself, was lent an enhanced cruelty by the arresting soldiers being given dog faces and paws instead of boots. One had a long tail protruding from under his tunic and the other's eerily human hand was clamped over Pinocchio's mouth, emphasising the exaggeratedly elongated nose.

It struck Schlegel as an example of everything that was frightening about childhood, which was perhaps why the page had been scribbled over in crayon, presumably by a very young Anton Schlegel. Fräulein Braun appeared upset and snapped the book shut. With a shiver she passed it back and exclaimed, 'What a horrible, beastly drawing!'

Schlegel made to return the book to the shelf but she quickly recited in a formal, automatic way, 'It doesn't really belong here. It's a scruffy copy anyway. Take it, please, as a souvenir of your visit and perhaps you can give it back to your father. We should go downstairs now.'

The book fitted comfortably in Schlegel's pocket and he made a private decision not to return it to his father.

Downstairs, everyone was still asleep, apart from the cadaverous thug who had replaced his colleague on the door. The collective spell cast over the room retained its hold, with everyone still laid out and mysteriously incapable of going to bed. Schlegel found himself succumbing to the room's heavy torpor. He resolved to destroy or get rid of the book, thinking it would give him a mean pleasure to spoil Tieck's plans, whatever they were. With that, he fell into a deep and exhausted sleep, afraid of what he might find in his dreams.

He woke at first light, fretful. Fegelein was already up and prowling, guarding the room and looking hungover. Outside was invisible for a dense fog that hung over everything. Schlegel watched Anna Huber wake and look around the room with a calculating air, as if planning her getaway. The Braun sisters lay abandoned on their sofas, the dogs asleep with them. A telephone rang somewhere in the house. Fegelein shook the two thugs awake, told them to come with him and they left. Führer Bobby snored on. Maurice jerked awake, stood up and announced to no one in particular that he was going to the garage to work on the Führer's car which wasn't running quite right. Schlegel suspected that tinkering with cars was about Maurice's natural level – that and violence – and everything since was a sinecure. He watched Maurice stumble off then he got up and motioned for Anna Huber to follow him onto what he presumed was a terrace. He held open the door and stepped after her ghostly silhouette into the milky opaqueness.

She asked where he had gone with Fegelein and Emil Maurice. Schlegel said Fegelein had got it wrong thinking he had the confession.

The fog was like embalming fluid.

'Why are you here?' Schlegel asked.

'I am in the process of being dumped by Hermann. He likes to show off his assets, me to his wife and her to me. But the sister-in-law has read the riot act.'

'Why?'

'Fräulein Braun found letters I wrote that Hermann left lying around. She is a terrific snooper and Hermann is careless. Anyway, she is jealous because her sister is married and she is not, and for all her elevation she is as trapped as the niece she despised.'

'Despised?'

'Because she was everything she is not. Spontaneous. Impetuous. Probably good in bed.'

Schlegel supposed Huber was better in bed than he was. Distracted by her unsettling presence, he struggled to the point, saying, 'I believe you have something that is supposed to be for me.'

She shook her head as if to say she didn't know what he was on about.

'I saw your brother give it to you. Now give it to me.'

She stood there undecided, until he said, 'Or I tell

Fegelein, who will probably not be so polite. I expect he can be nasty to women.'

Anna Huber rattily said, 'Oh, have it your way then.'

She took an envelope from her jacket and thrust it angrily into his hands just as Fegelein called for her from inside. After telling him where she was, he came out and upon seeing them asked suspiciously, 'What are you two whispering about?'

'Talking about our love lives,' Anna Huber said tartly.

Schlegel stood with his hands behind his back, holding the envelope, which from the feel of it had a wax seal to stop it from being unofficially opened.

'Breakfast. Eggs Benedict,' Fegelein announced.

Schlegel stabbed his egg yolk and thought he might heave. Breakfast was courtesy of the two thugs, another surprise, who stood basking in Fräulein Braun's praise.

'These really are very good,' she said and asked where they had learned to cook. The cadaver had been a chef at Hecker's Deele in Berlin before the war.

Fräulein Braun approved. 'Good hearty fare. Sauerkraut. Knuckle of pork.' She looked at the fat one. 'And you?'

'Catering corps.'

'Bravo. Come and work for us. We're lucky to have you. I gave the kitchen staff time off, not expecting this impromptu gathering.'

Schlegel saw she was doing her best, like a good little hausfrau, to reassert domestic order after the previous night's debacle. Best manners, properly laid table, which she had done herself. She played the good hostess to indifferent guests. Fegelein's eyes looked yellow. The bruise was coming along nicely. He had put it about that he had walked into a door after one too many and announced himself pleased as it made him look piratical. For Schlegel it was a nasty reminder of whatever Fegelein might be cooking up in revenge.

His wife complained of a crashing hangover. An unpleasant scene followed when Fegelein mixed two raw eggs and whisky, one for him, the other which he forced her to drink when she didn't want to. Fräulein Braun tried to intervene, saying she needn't. Fegelein said sweetly, 'I know what's best for Frau Fegelein.' It was a battle for property: sister or wife. Fegelein won, his face set as he watched his wife swallow the mixture before running gagging from the room.

Fräulein Braun said, 'Hermann, that wasn't necessary.'

Fegelein swatted the remark aside. 'She shouldn't drink so much. Not becoming in a woman.'

Anna Huber concentrated on her plate of food as if her whole world were reduced to that, eating birdlike portions. She avoided Schlegel's eye.

Feglein asked, 'Where's Bobby? We'll need him.'

Nobody knew.

'Gone walkabout?' asked Fegelein, who seemed amused by the idea. 'Ah, look who's here,' he said getting up.

Morgen and Tieck were shown in by the fat thug. Everyone politely ignored that Morgen's clothes were covered in blood. Fegelein greeted them like long-lost friends. Fräulein Braun laid two extra places and showed them to their seats. For a few minutes the scene was like a normal breakfast. The coffee was praised. Fegelein asked what had kept them.

Tieck recounted the adventure of their journey.

'I didn't know a stag could scream. Like nothing you have heard in your life. A miracle we weren't speared by its antlers. How was your evening?'

'Grand,' said Fegelein. 'Well, so-so actually.' He looked at

Morgen. 'That explains why he looks like he has just come from an abattoir.'

Tieck regarded the room with hooded eyes while Fegelein bided his time and Fräulein Braun prattled on. Her sister slipped back into the room, deathly pale. Anna Huber appeared disconcerted by the arrival of Tieck. Schlegel was uncomfortably aware of sharing a table with a stranger who was his father; of the envelope and the book in his pocket; and his unwillingness to do the man any favours.

With breakfast done, Fräulein Braun organised the washing-up rota, using her authority to designate Fegelein and Tieck to do the dishes and Anna Huber and Schlegel to dry. Fegelein joined in the spirit of things, stripping down to shirt and braces, and rolling up his sleeves, cheerfully taking control, telling Tieck to pass the dishes for him to wash while the others dried. He put too much soap in the water and the suds rose in a soft white mound above the level of the sink. He changed his mind about Anna Huber drying and told her to rinse the plates after he had washed them. 'New to me but my wife insists. Do you rinse?'

'Generally, yes,' said Huber.

Fegelein turned to Schlegel and said, 'It must be a woman's thing.'

Schlegel sensed Huber's nerves as Fegelein carried on casually. 'Now, there's something we all want, but the question is who has it? Young Schlegel here was meant to but he isn't a good enough liar to pretend he hasn't.'

Huber made a fair show of incomprehension. 'What are you on about, Hermann?'

Fegelein, seeming in even more of a good mood, turned to Tieck. 'You're keeping very quiet. Perhaps you've hung on to it all along. But then again if you knew where it was you wouldn't be here.'

Anna Huber held her line. 'Somebody please tell me what you're all talking about.'

Fegelein said, 'Get your handbag, there's a doll, that way I might know what I am talking about.'

'She doesn't have it,' said Schlegel, trying to decide whether he was being chivalrous. 'I do.'

Fegelein stared in feigned admiration. 'Perhaps you are a better liar than I gave you credit.' He held out his hand for the envelope.

'Fuck the washing up,' he said.

Morgen, excused kitchen duties, found himself the captive audience of the Braun sisters, who insisted on getting out their photograph albums to show endless snapshots of Berghof parties and distinguished guests in happier days. The fog hadn't lifted. Fräulein Braun said it sometimes came down for days on end.

'It's a pity you can't see anything. The view really is paradise. Look,' she said, pointing at the album. 'There's Minister Speer. So tall and handsome.'

'The wife's an old bag,' chipped in the sister.

Fräulein Braun came back with, 'Most of them are with the exception of you and Magda Goebbels.'

The sister turned to Morgen. 'Magda had a huge crush on the Führer.'

'Gerda Bormann can be quite pretty,' conceded Fräulein Braun.

'But a bit of a mooncalf and she pops out another sprog every nine months. How many now?'

'Lord knows. Eight, nine?' Fräulein Braun addressed Morgen. 'What is going on here? Everyone is behaving very strangely and who's that revolting man with the stick?'

'Horse trading, I would say. They're all interested in the same thing.'

Fräulein Braun looked up and said, 'Oh, Bobby, there you are. Too late for breakfast.'

Morgen did a double take at the extraordinary sight of this strange Führer presence who appeared to have slept in his clothes and was being addressed as though he were a toy.

Fräulein Braun said to Morgen, 'I want everyone to leave by lunchtime, before not after. I think our hospitality has been sufficiently extended. I am putting you in charge of making that clear to everyone.'

She was the only one who looked like she had made an effort, wearing a twinset and pearls, the face discreetly and immaculately painted on. The sister looked awful. Fräulein Braun produced liver salts, which she mixed with mineral water in a crystal glass taken from a sideboard.

'We have only Fachinger in the house,' she said to Morgen, offering him a glass, which Morgen accepted.

Fräulein Braun went on, 'Fachinger is the premium brand for wellbeing, health, wellness, beauty and mental performance.'

Her sister interrupted. 'You're just saying that because it's not owned by the SS.'

'No, I honestly believe it.'

Morgen, stunned by the surreal banality of the women, found himself inexplicably chipping in with, 'I think it's not widely known that the SS owns quite a lot of mineral water companies. But Fachinger?'

Fräulein Braun shook her head. 'Certainly not. Or we wouldn't be drinking it.' She explained for his benefit. 'We're no great fans of Heini. Nobody is, from what we can see.'

The sisters laughed at that. Fräulein Braun asked, 'Anyway, what's that all about, going round buying up all the bottled water?'

Morgen said he thought it was because the Reichsführer wanted to reduce alcoholic consumption by acquiring enough of the soft-drinks market to achieve price leverage.

Fräulein Braun said, 'Spare us the economics. We leave that to the boys.'

They were joined by Fegelein.

Morgen said, 'Fräulein Braun wishes us to leave.'

Fegelein put on an expression of fake surprise. 'The party's only just started!'

The others came in. Morgen thought Schlegel looked like he had woken to find himself on a rocket to the moon; Tieck was like a man holding cards up his sleeve; and Anna Huber stared at the sisters with no love lost.

He thought of his own strange interlude with her, back in the hotel room. Huber had asked him to massage her feet which he had, inexpertly. The experience wasn't as pleasant as it might have been as she hadn't washed them recently. Nothing happened. They slept chastely on the separate beds. Morgen had wondered what Schlegel would make of it when he came back. Where was the bloody boy? he remembered thinking before drifting off, and when he woke Anna Huber was gone. Morgen felt the indentation of her body on the bedcovers to check he hadn't been dreaming, then saw the message on the table, telling him to join her at the races that afternoon.

Morgen was told off by the officious little hotel concierge for 'having a woman in his room' and informed if it happened again he would be reported.

*

Fegelein looked at his watch and up at his sister-in-law. 'Just need a short chinwag with this lot then we'll be out of your hair, or shall you be coming back with us?'

'I haven't made up my mind,' Fräulein Braun said coolly.

'Let us know when you do,' Fegelein replied equably.

He wanted to use the Great Hall for the meeting. 'Showing off,' he said, grinning. He was overruled by Fräulein Braun saying it was not to be used in the Führer's absence.

'Bobby will do,' suggested Fegelein hopefully but Fräulein Braun held firm. Fegelein shrugged. 'Let's do it in the kitchen then.' He said he needed Tieck, Anna Huber and Schlegel, then pointed at Morgen. 'You too. May as well. And Bobby. All of you, come.'

Fegelein took the head of the table and told them to sit where they liked. Everyone took seats well away from him. Morgen caught Anna Huber's eye. She stared back, composed, her poker face on.

Fegelein put the envelope on the table and said to Tieck, 'Shall I be the one to break the seal?'

Without waiting for an answer, Fegelein did so and flipped the opened envelope down towards Bobby, saying, 'You read it.'

Bobby took his time, being monumentally hungover, fumbling to remove its contents, a single page at which he stared as though he were looking at Sanskrit.

Fegelein prompted, 'Führer spectacles.'

Bobby did as he was told, hooking the sides behind one ear first then the other. Morgen, watching the man, thought it was obviously not the Führer, though anyone looking through the window might think he was. The fake was like a bad painting, until he opened his mouth and the illusion fell away as he read, '"This is the confession of Anton Schlegel to Adolf Hitler, given on 20 September, 1931."'

Fegelein interrupted to say, 'Hang on. What are you talking about, man?'

Bobby stopped and said, 'I'm just reading what it says.'

Fegelein looked to Tieck and asked, 'What is this? "Confession of Anton Schlegel"?' Tieck stared back inscrutable until Fegelein told Bobby, 'Oh, just read the bloody thing!'

Bobby began and Fegelein interrupted again. 'It doesn't have to be the Führer voice. We're beyond ventriloquism.'

Bobby read flatly while everyone looked surprised by the nasal whine of his normal delivery: '"On the afternoon of Friday, 18 September, I received an urgent call from Fräulein Raubal who was alone and asked me to come to her because of what she called a terrible accident. I found the girl gushing blood, begging to be put out of her misery. She said she was pregnant – and devastated by the prospect of banishment, should anyone learn of her condition, she had in a fit of despair tried to abort herself with a coat hanger and made a mess of it. She announced she was at death's door and feared going to hell. She begged I hear her Last Confession. As I am not a priest, I told her to recite a Perfect Act of Contrition and trust in the Lord. She beseeched me to help her end it and told me to fetch her uncle's gun, requesting I do it with that. She said if she lived she would be unable to bear the shame of his disapproval. She was fading before my eyes so, to foreshorten her agony, I shot her as she asked and she died instantly.

'"I subsequently confessed this to Herr Wolf (as he chooses to be addressed by me) because he blamed himself for the girl's death. I related these facts as they happened, to spare him further guilt. Herr Wolf is a sentimental man and wept copiously, seeking confirmation that she died at once, which I assured him she had.

"'The matter of the child's paternity was never discussed between myself and Fräulein Raubal and I have no idea who the father was.'

"'Signed, Anton Schlegel.'"

Fegelein glared at Tieck to ask, 'Is that the best you're giving us? "The Hitler Confession"? Don't play me for an idiot. Where is the real one?'

Tieck raised his hands and said, 'That's it. I can only assume people mistook it to mean a confession by the man rather than one given to him.'

Tieck appeared amused by the distinction, as if he was taunting Fegelein, who obliged by losing his temper.

'You could have bloody well said instead of wasting everyone's time! What's the point of this Anton Schlegel nonsense? Is it true?'

'True in that it happened. In terms of content, no,' said Tieck.

'Then what's the bloody point?'

'The Führer could not accept that the girl had shot herself.'

'Why not?'

'Because she could only have done it to spite him.'

'To get back at him, you mean,' insisted Fegelein.

Tieck said, 'If you want to state the obvious. The man was beside himself. The only way to persuade him otherwise was to show it wasn't his fault.'

Fegelein grunted. 'So it was a psychological trick to save the man from himself. Quite good, I suppose.'

Schlegel saw how clever the ploy had been in retrieving the Führer from his suicidal state: the introduction of an unwelcome third party (the embryo); the nightmare of the botched abortion; a squeamish Führer bound to distance himself from the whole bloody mess; and the idea of a mercy killing, which precluded motives of blame or revenge on the part of the niece. Quite brilliant, in fact.

From what Schlegel could see, no one had got what they wanted, except perhaps Tieck. Fegelein and Anna Huber had been after something else.

At the same time, Schlegel realised Tieck and Fegelein – whatever their present differences – were in fact as thick as thieves, with proof of that possibly contained in Fegelein's file, reporting stolen goods found at the family riding academy where the receiver was listed as ... T.T.

Toni Tieck?

Schlegel stuck his hands in his trouser pockets, hitching his jacket back, hoping the book didn't show.

'Do you have something for me?' asked Tieck, taking Schlegel aside.

Schlegel thought to himself: Not that you're getting.

'Well?' insisted Tieck.

Schlegel disliked the man's manner as much as he did Fegelein's. Both involved the blunt expectation of those used to getting their way.

Thinking he perhaps didn't need lessons in how to lie, Schlegel held Tieck's eye as he said, 'The book wasn't there. You must have misremembered.'

Tieck's eruption expressed itself first as a rising purple flush, travelling up from his neck until he was shaking. He hissed, 'It must be there!'

'Well, it isn't,' Schlegel said flatly, meaning that it wasn't there now.

Having managed without a proper father for so long, he wondered if he could somehow undo Tieck. What really stuck in his throat was how the man expected him to do his unquestioned bidding.

They were joined by Fegelein who told Schlegel to join him on the terrace. Schlegel left Tieck looking thunderous.

Outside the fog was lifting, from the sky down, leaving below a field of white. Schlegel was struck by the incongruous sight of what was obviously the Führer's cap on the balustrade.

'I need a hand.' Fegelein sounded dangerously friendly. 'Our two friends from breakfast need to test whether it would be technically possible – only technically, you understand—'

'To shoot the Führer on his morning walk,' Schlegel finished for him.

'Did I say that already? It's essential for security.'

Schlegel looked around, trying to sound reasonable. 'The place is more or less closed down. The Führer isn't coming back, so on whose orders?'

Fegelein fingered his bruise thoughtfully.

'The Führer asked me to check in the event of his return. Nowhere in the world he loves more than here. Come to that, and God forbid, he would rather make his last stand here than in Berlin. So we are bound to check. Bobby is the obvious stand-in but Bobby unfortunately is in a state of post-performance collapse, having drunk the best part of a bottle of brandy, so legless Bobby is not up to the job.'

'Don't you have other Führers at your disposal?' Schlegel asked, in a poor attempt at sarcasm.

'Ha-ha! Very funny. None available. So put on the cap and do as you're told. The mist's lifting. It will be gone by the time we get down. See how beautiful it is.'

Up to a point, thought Schlegel; to him one mountain looked much like another.

47

Morgen found himself cornered by Frau Fegelein, who insisted on giving him and Anna Huber a guided tour. They started with the formal entrance hall, which contained an exotic collection of cacti; a strange display, thought Morgen, given the relentless Teutonic nature of the rest.

Frau Fegelein called the Führer the Chief and told them that all the interiors had been done by his favourite designer, a woman with the ability to combine statesmanship with the personal touch. Showing them around was her way of being proprietorial, Morgen thought. She struck him as a pleasant but silly woman and as insecure as her sister. He suspected rivalry.

In the Great Hall, everything was covered in dust sheets, giving the impression of a ghosted space. It was the culmination of huge rooms with oversized windows and big statements. The only item not covered was a massive globe, suggesting world domination at least. The vast window was a size of a tennis court. Fine if you wanted a mountain sitting in your lap, thought Morgen. The view was still more milky than picture postcard, though the mist was rising.

The Braun dogs appeared and took turns to hump Anna Huber's leg. Frau Fegelein took that badly and looked like she couldn't decide between slapping Huber or breaking down in tears.

Morgen heard the tapping of a stick, announcing Tieck's

arrival. Watching him approach from a distance, Morgen thought he looked like a badly assembled Frankenstein experiment.

Tieck joined them, asking unctuously, 'May I?'

He stood sweating, leaning with both hands on his stick. The two women appeared disconcerted by his presence. Morgen suspected whatever Tieck's business, it wasn't done.

Next they were shown the projection booth, which enabled the Great Hall to be turned into a cinema. The booth was as big as any commercial one, Frau Fegelein told them, with two projectors allowing for continuous screening without breaks for reel changes. She recited tales of happy nights watching Laurel and Hardy.

Then it was the gymnasium, with what looked like medieval torture machines.

Frau Fegelein stared at Anna Huber and said, 'Hermann's getting a bit of a paunch.'

Anna Huber replied meaningfully, 'He still seems in pretty good shape to me.'

They went upstairs in silence. Tieck could manage only one step at a time and they had to wait for him at the top. The bedrooms were private, Frau Fegelein said, but she could show them the Führer's study.

Tieck said, 'That would be an honour.'

They were shown into what Morgen thought looked more like a vast hotel lobby, with lots of chintz and cut flowers. With the windows dominated by such a commanding landscape he found it hard to imagine any actual work being done. They dutifully admired the mountains emerging through the fog.

Morgen noticed Tieck standing apart, making a show of studying the paintings hanging on the wooden panelling while the rest of them made polite noises about the spectacular view. Morgen decided he was rather enjoying the preposterous tour. Both Frau Fegelein and Anna Huber were in tremendous sulks. He watched Tieck move round to inspect the library with what appeared to be more than idle curiosity.

Morgen joined him. 'A good collection?' he asked.

'Average,' muttered Tieck, continuing to pass along the shelves until they got to the end and were standing by the window overlooking the terrace. Tieck gave a sharp intake of breath. Morgen noticed but was distracted by the sight of Fegelein conversing below with Schlegel, and what looked like the Führer's cap on the balustrade between them. They were joined by the two thugs carrying rifles.

Tieck grabbed Morgen's sleeve and asked urgently, 'Did Schlegel say anything to you about a book?'

Morgen saw Fegelein and the others were leaving.

Tieck insisted, 'Did he? My plan is wrecked if he refuses to cooperate.'

'Too late for that now,' Morgen said, pointing to the path below.

48

Feglein led on horseback. Schlegel walked between the two thugs, casual but sinister with their rifles. Fegelein stopped and turned to rehearse them. Schlegel was made to put on the Führer cap and take it off. Fegelein had a whistle, on which he gave a short blast. The two thugs had whistles too, giving fussy peeps in return.

Schlegel was in no doubt Fegelein had it in mind to shoot him once he had extracted maximum humiliation.

The mountains were bathed in light. Schlegel recalled the brutally hot summer's day three years before – a result of plans probably dreamt up in this very valley – when far away in the endless plains of the East he had stood in a ditch, knee-deep in bodies, administering the *coup de grâce* to those the executioners had failed to kill. He was told afterwards it wasn't necessary. The pit would be filled in anyway.

Morgen marched past Frau Fegelein and Anna Huber, asking if there was a gun cupboard. There was but the sister didn't know who had the key.

'Would Fräulein Braun know?' Morgen called back.

'She doesn't bother with that side of things. There are men for that.'

Morgen's sidearm had been removed on arrival. All he could do was go down and try and talk sense into them.

*

Fegelein's sabre rested over his shoulder, with the Führer cap stuck jauntily on the end, as they ambled slowly down the path, no one in any hurry, like they were on a stroll. Fegelein rolled comfortably with the horse's walk. 'Clip, clop,' he said echoing the sound of its hooves, leaning forward to give it an affectionate pat. He extended his arm towards the sparkling mountains and said what a beautiful day.

'Fancy your chances?' he asked Schlegel and turned to the two thugs. 'Okay, boys, take up your position. Blast of the whistle when you're ready.'

Schlegel watched them peel off into the trees.

Morgen ran down past a couple of lounging guards who paid him no attention. They both carried rifles. Morgen considered ordering them to come with him but they were blank-faced robots and clearly non-negotiable.

He ran, coughing, out of shape, through bright sun and shining dew. Fegelein and the rest were out of sight. Morgen stopped, breath heaving. He ran on. The excruciating physical effort made his glasses steam up.

A distant whistle came from up ahead.

'Put it on,' said Fegelein. Schlegel was holding the Führer cap, refusing to wear it.

'I am not the Führer,' he said.

'You are now,' snarled Fegelein.

Schlegel gripped the cap, unmoving. Fegelein shrugged, as if to say, have it your way, then whacked him across the head with the flat of his sabre, leaving Schlegel sprawled. Fegelein told him to get up. And if I lie here? Schlegel thought. Fegelein gave a blast on his whistle. Two more whistles came in reply, followed by a shot, close enough to kick dirt in Schlegel's face. He scrambled to his feet without meaning to.

'Stand to attention, soldier, and stop behaving like a snivelling coward,' Fegelein barked. The man's glazed eyes said he was back in the killing fields.

'Are you the one that complained about being splattered with blood and pieces of brain and asked to be excused duties?' Fegelein demanded. 'Or the one that begged not to be assigned to the firing squad, so we made him hold my horse for the duration of the executions? Nearly two and a half thousand that morning. That's a lot of horse holding, soldier.'

Schlegel still refused to put the cap on. The point of Fegelein's sabre jabbed into his neck.

'We had them dancing in the street. Hippity hop. Go on or I cut your tendon. Excruciating agony, I believe.'

The tip of the sabre remained resting against his throat until Schlegel felt it pierce the flesh. He put on the cap.

Morgen left the road and ran through woods trying to make up ground. He could see Fegelein on an open stretch, the horse strutting arrogantly as though Fegelein were conducting an exercise in dressage. Schlegel stood in the middle of the path, an abject sight, with the cap on. Morgen couldn't see the two thugs. Fegelein stopped and looked up at the far hillside as if calculating angles. He moved Schlegel twenty metres back, prodding him with his sabre. Schlegel stood in his new position. Fegelein fussed over the details then rode a short distance off, turned and Morgen saw him raise his hand to his mouth. Another blast, answered by two more, then another rifle shot. Schlegel stood unflinching. Morgen saw the bullet fall short. Either they were finding their range or playing with him. Fegelein's horse reared and he brought it back under control with insolent ease and gave its flank a slap.

Morgen decided the two thugs must be about level with him on the far side of the road, how high up he couldn't tell. The hill dropped into a fold and rose again even more steeply. It was all trees, with the occasional rocky outcrop and Morgen supposed they had taken up a position on one, giving them a field of fire.

Fegelein had decided to pause. He leaned forward in his saddle looking for all the world as if he were passing the time of day with Schlegel. Morgen could see the smoke from his cigarette hanging in the still air.

Fegelein said, 'Our two friends up on the hill developed a real taste for it. The fat one trampled down people at execution sites until his trousers were filled with blood. The other one made a Jew wait until last after he had asked to be shot first. Burning churches with people inside was one of their specialities, after complaints that the armoury budget was being exceeded. It was all pretty much make and match, didn't you find?'

Fegelein looked at Schlegel expectantly. 'I read your file. Einsatzgruppen B.'

Schlegel's then-boss, Arthur Nebe, had taken a squad of mainly police reservists east for what they were told would be general policing duties behind the front line. The first corpses they saw were three German airmen who had been barbecued alive. Filmed evidence showed a civilian enemy that was cunning, relentless and given to cutting out and eating the liver of any enemy.

Schlegel was there technically as a liaison officer. Under the guise of anti-partisan duties, villages were rounded up, marched off, made to dig their graves, lined up and shot. Schlegel had gone into the field to see the job was being done in the correct military manner. The shooters complained about what a tough job they had. A shrink brought in for general wellbeing told Schlegel that the trick was to normalise the process. For the perpetrators, the shrink had meant. There was nothing normal for those on the receiving end. Schlegel had walked on corpses, among geysers of blood, reloading with shaking hands. His hair hadn't been white then.

Well, his turn now. Emil Maurice had told him they had given Anton Schlegel a sporting chance, letting him run for it. He tried to imagine running and stumbling, whipped by branches, wondering if the mind froze or whether there was coherence to the terror. Running from and running to death, he thought. What if he ran now, would they shoot him down or would Fegelein display his fancy horsemanship to corral him?

'Didn't exactly distinguish yourself,' said Fegelein. 'Mental fatigue, was it? Sent home, diddums.'

Schlegel had had no stomach for witnessing such killing. A burning shame judged him not tough enough when others were. The memory, suppressed for so long, blossomed like blood in water.

Morgen decided to break cover and go down and negotiate when he heard a whistling – not one of the previous blasts, but the common or garden whistling of someone wandering down a path above him, which joined the road just past where he was standing. It looked like a patrol guard coming off duty. Slung rifle. He stopped and lit up. Morgen walked back, trying to look casual. The guard was little more than a kid. Morgen held up a cigarette for a light. 'No matches.'

The man's uniform gave him the air of a forest ranger, apart from the usual insignia. He wore short boots with cleats. He seemed grateful for the interruption.

'What's going on?' He spoke with a thick country accent.
'Target practice.'

The boy patted his pockets and a light was produced. They looked each other in the eye as the flame took hold. Morgen muttered thanks and said, 'I need to borrow your rifle.'

The boy appeared confused by that, enough for Morgen to grab his neck and knee him hard in the groin. As he jack-knifed, Morgen drove his knee into his face. The boy sat down heavily and Morgen kicked his head, thinking how he had never been any good at close combat training. At least the poor devil was out cold. His nose looked broken.

Morgen used the boy's belt to strap his arms behind his back, removed his boots and threw them away. Then he took off the socks and stuffed them in the boy's mouth, relieved him of his rifle and ammunition pouch, thought about the pistol and took that too.

Schlegel saw Morgen hare across the road just as Fegelein started to turn, leaving him no choice but to lunge to prevent Fegelein from seeing Morgen. Fegelein's holster flap was undone and Schlegel grabbed for it an act of defiance and stupidity in equal measure. Fegelein easily manoeuvred himself out of trouble as Schlegel realised he should have grabbed the man's stirrup and up-ended him.

Fegelein appeared pleased by Schlegel's initiative. 'Always better when they put on a bit of a fight or it's like shooting fish in a barrel.'

Fegelein remained elegant and in command, the snivelling of the previous night unimaginable. He said, 'Let's play a game while we're waiting. It's called "Do they run or not?". Here's a clue: they all run in the end.'

Schlegel watched Fegelein's departing back rise and fall as he trotted away. He stood his ground, knowing if he made a run for it the thugs would shoot him down before he reached the trees. He supposed Morgen's arrival offered a slither of hope but Morgen was outgunned and did he even have a weapon?

Fegelein turned and spurred his horse into a canter then a full gallop. Schlegel stood thinking about other deaths to distract from his own. Geli Raubal's, still a mystery. The agent Busl picked up by the two thugs now on the hillside. Did they swing him – one, two, three – for greater momentum? Then the split-second illusion of flight before gravity did its job. The same with Frau Busl and Gerda, flying through the air. With Gerda they had probably swept in, didn't even stop to ask, picked her up and chucked her out. Schlegel thought of the single shoe of the dead nurse, lying in the cellar. Again the two thugs, he was certain. It was what they did. And then there was the man falling from the roof of the burning clinic, which Schlegel now took as a sign of his own death foretold.

Given the choice, he would jump, for that moment's illusion of freedom, falling through time and space.

The ground shook from the charging horse. Fegelein was low in the saddle, sabre extended. Schlegel stood transfixed by the speed and momentum of the horse until it was nearly upon him and he snapped. Fegelein was right: they all run in the end.

Schlegel fled in blind panic. All he could hear was the din of hooves and Fegelein's whoops, then the sear of pain across his back as Fegelein whacked him with the sabre. As he fell he caught a glimpse of Fegelein's face suffused with pleasure at the memory of killing orgies.

Fegelein reared the horse so it danced on its hind legs and the front hooves kicked at Schlegel's face.

*

Morgen ran heedless, praying the trees provided enough cover for him not to be seen. There was no time for stealth. His fieldcraft was almost as poor as his range shooting. From the edge of the trees he had a view of Fegelein and Schlegel. He watched Fegelein repeat his charge. Schlegel held his ground until the last second and as he turned to run he appeared to be trampled underfoot.

Shooting an SS General was out of the question, though Morgen had to think twice about that as he pushed up the steeper incline, starting to panic because he could find no break in the trees. He was sweating hard. Shafts of sunlight started to penetrate the canopy as the wood started to thin and the ground, until then a bed of pine needles, became rockier. A brighter patch to Morgen's left suggested a clearing. He moved towards it and found a knoll looking back across the valley with a view of the road. Morgen crawled on his stomach to an outcrop of rock and scanned the trees opposite but saw nothing in the way of any obvious clearing.

Down below, Fegelein reverted to his previous routine, setting Schlegel up as a target. A repeat of the single blast, answered twice, followed by the shot. Morgen saw the bullet kick up in front of Schlegel, getting closer.

Schlegel stared dumbly at the spot where the bullet had just hit, thinking from Fegelein's dreamy look that he was moving in for the kill. Miraculously, he had avoided getting kicked by the horse when he went down. At least he had lost the stupid Führer cap, which lay crushed after being trampled on.

He suspected the two thugs had been told not to finish him off, allowing Fegelein the pleasure of toying. No flinch, next time, Schlegel told himself. He eyed Fegelein's stirrup, thinking if the man moved any closer he would be near enough to grab. The stirrup came almost within reach. Fegelein and his horse were between him and the guns on the hill, not allowing them a shot. Now or never, Schlegel thought. As he was about to grab the stirrup Fegelein shook his boot free and shoved it hard into Schlegel's chest, controlled his horse with a skittering sideways movement, knocking Schlegel off balance, and he went down again and lay staring up at the huge breathing belly of the horse, which stood perfectly still over him, under the control of its master.

Schlegel rolled out from under the horse and started to walk away. Let them shoot him in the back. He thought of his father and cursed him, wishing neither of them had been born.

Morgen saw what he had missed before. A sentry or hunting platform among the trees, further down than he had been looking, distance about 100 metres. The platform was open. The fat one was sitting with legs dangling over the edge, his rifle across his knees. The other one was lounging behind him. They were passing a bottle.

Fegelein was using the horse to herd Schlegel back into position. Fegelein now appeared to act with deadly intent and Morgen knew time was running out. Schlegel's spirit looked to have been been broken but then he appeared to rally and could be seen arguing with Fegelein. Fegelein had briefly dismounted to retrieve the battered Führer cap and Schlegel was refusing to wear it. The squabble concluded with Schlegel throwing the cap aside. Morgen was sure such a show of disrespect meant Schlegel was done for.

Fegelein turned away. What Morgen saw next made no sense: Schlegel standing there with what, of all things, looked like a book, rapidly flicking through it until something fell out, which he bent down to retrieve.

Of course, thought Schlegel, stuffing book and paper back in his pocket as Fegelein stopped and turned. More hiding in plain sight: the elusive confession, hidden in the book, secreted in the very lair of the beast. He knew it could be his lifeline, offered to Fegelein in a repeat of Anton's Schlegel's barter with Emil Maurice – in a desperate attempt to avoid the inevitable.

He weighed the odds and resolved to make no deal with Fegelein. With luck, the secret would die with him, thwarting everyone's intentions – a hollow triumph but a small victory nevertheless.

Morgen rapidly familiarised himself with the rifle. Standard issue, same as in Russia. Reliable if unspectacular. Bolt action. He checked the magazine: full. Every sound seemed magnified. He took up a shooting position on his front, legs spread, left arm wrapped through the rifle sling to steady the aim, and looked down the barrel. The two men suddenly seemed further away, exact distance hard to judge. Seventy-five? A hundred? A hundred and twenty? He set the sight at a hundred, remembering the trigger had a lot of give. Out of the corner of his eye, he saw Fegelein raise his arm and the fat one took up position, using the roof post of the platform to support his aim.

Fegelein blew three blasts and Morgen, thinking of the previous single blasts, took it as a signal to aim to kill. Squeeze, don't snatch, he reminded himself as the fat one whistled back his three peeps, and settled over his rifle, while his companion signalled their readiness with his three blasts. What an absurd rigmarole, thought Morgen, as he applied pressure to the trigger, deciding it was probably what they had done when rounding up villages: cheap whistles, with the sound able to carry over long distances; the two thugs were bound to have been part of Fegelein's band of killers. The current show was no doubt a version of the lethal games played over there.

The rifle kicked hard against Morgen's shoulder. The report rang in his ears and acrid cordite filled his nostrils. He released the bolt to eject the shell, rammed it shut and sighted again. The two men looked frozen in surprise. Morgen fired again, aiming lower, and saw the red starburst as the fat man flopped back. The thin one, exposed on the open platform, had nowhere to hide. He was at the top of the ladder scrambling down when Morgen got him in his sights. He aimed allowing for the man's descent, fired and saw his target swing back, one handed, his free arm raised like he was acknowledging applause, still grabbing on until he regained his grip and continued to fumble his way down. Sitting duck, thought Morgen: hope you're enjoying this. The next shot blasted the man backwards; it was like watching a swallow dive in reverse. The fat one was struggling to sit up, his squeals resembling those of a stuck pig, carrying across the valley. Morgen looked across to Fegelein and Schlegel. Schlegel was still standing and Fegelein was staring at a shoeless man hobbling down the road – the young soldier from whom he had stolen the rifle and pistol. Morgen wondered whether to take another shot at the fat man, or indeed Fegelein.

Schlegel looked like a ghost of himself, but seemed to be holding steady, Morgen thought as he joined them, his rifle over his shoulder. Contrary to all expectation, Fegelein seemed in tremendous good spirits as he dismounted and produced a carrot for his horse, offering it in the flat of his palm. The horse chomped gratefully and whinnied.

Fegelein cocked his ear at the fat man's bellows and said to Morgen, 'Well, you have proved the point of the exercise, not quite how I had in mind. Any idea why this man is bootless?'

Morgen ignored the befuddled soldier and said, 'I found this,' handing the rifle to Fegelein. 'And this,' passing over the pistol.

Fegelein chucked them to the soldier, who dropped the rifle and caught the pistol.

'Find your boots, boy,' Fegelein ordered. 'Dereliction of duty is the least of your worries. Are you drunk?'

The boy shook his head.

'Most of them are,' Fegelein announced. 'Fuck-all else to do, sitting around in guard rooms waiting for nobody to come.'

Fegelein was all bonhomie and concern, asking Schlegel, 'Are you all right?' placing a hand on his shoulder. 'Necessary exercise. Good job.'

No one mentioned Fegelein's flashback to his days clearing marshes and sabre charges.

Fegelein accompanied them back leading his horse. Morgen watched him recalculating the odds.

'Back to Berlin?' Fegelein eventually asked.

'With your permission,' Morgen replied not quite sarcastically.

'I can arrange for us to take the Führer's private train. A treat.'

'Us!' thought Morgen.

'Who exactly did you shoot, do you know?' asked Fegelein.

Morgen thought whoever they were, in the end they were probably as disposable as those they disposed of.

'To ex-cooks, as it happens,' Fegelein went on with a laugh. 'Now here's the thing. Assaulting a soldier, stealing army property. Shooting two servants of government, where does that leave you?'

'You tell me,' thought Morgen, suspecting what was coming.

'Those two in the woods knew too much anyway for their own good. I can probably write them off. Soldier boy is neither here nor there. Do you see what I am saying?'

'Tell me anyway.'

'Slate clean. You owe me. How do you spell "indebted"?'

Got the better of again, thought Morgen bitterly. He looked back at Schlegel, stumbling like he had just walked all the way back from Russia.

The Berghof came into sight.

Fegelein looked up and said, 'There's Tieck waiting.'

END

ENDGAME

49

The Führer express sped its way through the night, unhindered by the delays to regular transport, but it was very much a budget version; Fegelein had had to hide his disappointment at only three coaches – a flak wagon, radio and baggage cars. On-board staff consisted of a radio operator, a couple of soldiers to mount the ack-ack guns and a train manager.

The train had departed from the local station where it was kept in its own special section, allowing for private entry. Fräulein Braun had announced she would remain at the Berghof with her sister. If she was curious about the morning's gunfire or the whereabouts of the two thugs she made no reference to either, or to the state of the returning party, making it plain that such goings on were beneath her and typical of her duplicitous brother-in-law, whom she now treated with scarcely veiled contempt. Emil Maurice had briefly reappeared to get out as quickly as he could, driving back to Munich, leaving the rest to assemble on the empty station platform with none of them saying a word to each other. Morgen kept his own council. Schlegel remained in his shell. Tieck held himself apart. Anna Huber gravitated towards Fegelein, perhaps not done with him yet, while Fegelein, who was the only one who had managed a change of clothes, did his best to keep a cheerful face but had the shifty look of one who had overplayed his hand. He made a point of being seen to take charge, discussing sleeping arrangements with the train manager, who in turn seemed to make a point of being unusually polite to Anna Huber.

Morgen was given a sergeant's compartment in the flak wagon and Schlegel, who insisted on being left alone, put in the other ranks' room. On his return to the Berghof, he had turned his back on Tieck. Morgen had had to order Tieck, who was behaving crassly, to back down and give Schlegel time as he was in shock.

Tieck's quarters were one of three narrow sleeping berths for railway personnel in the baggage car, with a bunk, a small basin and a WC in the corridor. Fegelein and Anna Huber had separate compartments – Tieck wondered for how long – in the radio car, luxury by comparison.

He suspected that Fegelein had wangled the Führer train partly to impress Anna Huber, in hope of wheedling his way back into favour. Tieck knew Fegelein for what he was: cad, opportunist and bounder, a conventional and feckless villain.

Tieck inspected himself in the vanity mirror over the basin. Part of him wanted to rip off his face and cast aside Toni Tieck to reveal his old self underneath. He told the mirror from now on he would go back to being Anton Schlegel.

Anton cursed his son, who had locked himself in his compartment and refused to answer.

He had managed to speak to him briefly before leaving for the station to be told that Schlegel had on returning to the Berghof burned the book in the kitchen stove as an act of filial revenge for being shown Anton's letter. Anton had raised his stick in anger, realising how naive he had been in thinking he understood anything of the running sores of

family resentment. The intention always had been to lead
the boy blind, so he never learned the real identity of Toni
Tieck, until bloody Hermann Fegelein spoke out of turn.

Morgen knew he could make life difficult for Toni Tieck,
aka Anton Schlegel, as the receiver of stolen goods for
Hermann Fegelein, and anyway Tieck stood to be exposed
as others learned his real identity.

He found the man in his compartment looking crushed
and willing to talk. They started with Hermann Fegelein.
Anton Schlegel admitted that he had been living as Toni
Tieck on Fegelein's isolated stud farm outside Munich, in
exchange for 'continuing financial services'.

'Hermann had two great loves, horses and dirty money,
with women coming a poor third. When I was still Anton
Schlegel, Hermann sucked up to me because I knew how
money worked, which he didn't, being a spendthrift. After I
became Tieck, Hermann couldn't care that I was supposed
to be dead. I asked him to teach me about bloodstock and
came to appreciate animal grace in contrast to my recent
lameness. In return I educated Hermann in alternative
tactics of appropriation as it was evident that loot and its
fencing would become the main game following conquest.'

So, thought Morgen, Fegelein was just the puppet.

The other man went on. 'When Hermann went to
Warsaw in 1942, I spent long hours on the telephone teaching him how to asset strip a company as daintily as disrobing
a seduction. But Hermann was a show pony, and I came to
prefer his sidekick—'

'Kurt Becher,' Morgen interrupted.

'Quite so. Buccaneering Kurt had more élan and a talent
for pirate business and it was he who cooked up a grand plan
that had nothing to do with Fegelein.'

'Appropriation of art?'

'No, that was my son's old friend Christoph. I believe you were after Becher in Budapest.'

Even Morgen, who regarded himself as something of a connoisseur of hidden connections, was surprised by how everything joined up.

'I never got close,' he admitted.

'What was he really doing there, do you know?'

'Jews. Appropriation, wheeling and dealing, allowing some to buy their way out.'

'The *real* reason.'

Morgen admitted he had no idea.

'It was the gee-gees. Horses.' The man laughed wearily at Morgen's bafflement. 'Among his other enterprises, Becher bought horses for the SS cavalry. It was he who came up with a grand vision to use that as an opportunity to breed the finest racehorses, which would win a clean sweep of international trophies after the war. Kurt was always far sighted.'

'So he plundered the cream of Europe's bloodstock for Hermann's stud.'

'In a nutshell, and I consulted with the finest veterinary scientists on how to perfect the stock.' The man sniggered. 'So you could say it was all about animal genetics.'

Knowing that Schlegel's stepfather kept racehorses too made Morgen's next question obvious. The answer was that in such a narrow field the two men inevitably ran into each other at meetings around the country, and even as far away as Longchamp in Paris.

'Of course, he had no idea who I really was. At Longchamp I once saw him with my wife whom I was unaware at the time he had married. A sad moment. She looked ravishing. I was much changed by then, having decided physical ugliness was the best chance of survival because people avoid

454

looking, as did my wife, who anyway wouldn't have glanced twice at the vulgarian I had become. So, there you have it, a pure moment of beauty and the beast.'

'And your son's friend Christoph?' Morgen asked, still thrown by that connection.

'Ah, Christoph was what you might call the unseen thread. Here's a story. A young man arrives in Munich in the spring of 1934, still a boy really, in search of himself, a process accelerated by his abrupt seduction by an older man. A pleasurable month is spent as that man's *poulet*. First names only, until Christoph is tempted to go through his lover's desk and realises he has been seduced by his best friend's father, whom everyone believes is in South America.'

'And now?' asked Morgen.

'Christoph remains pliable and biddable, and deeply discreet through fear of exposure. Four years later he returned to Munich, on the bottom rung of the art ladder, and in one of those cellar dives that still functioned in the deeper underground he fell in with a man whom he gradually came to think, but could not quite believe, might be his former lover, but the name had changed and the appearance so transformed that the man might indeed be a different person. The matter of previous identity was never brought up. As Tieck, I cultivated two worlds – bloodstock and the archive – and Christoph became my eyes and ears in dealing with that latter.'

As for the original list with 'Schlegel. A' that started it all, it had been acquired by the archive as part of a job-lot purchase, obviously a death list that should have been destroyed. On that occasion, Christoph was asked to make the delivery.

Anton looked at Morgen and said, 'I would rather you did not tell my son about this conversation. He doesn't need to know. I have already hurt him enough.'

Morgen wondered about that. The man did not strike him as someone of sentiment or sympathy. He asked if there was anything else.

The other man cast around, giggled and finally said, 'As we're here. The train manager.'

Morgen said he had hardly noticed the man and was told that was the point.

'Perhaps in a normal world it would seem far-fetched for Anna Huber's father to turn out to be the train manager of the Führer express. Yet he is and has been for years.'

He explained how Fredi Huber, apparently a notorious opponent of the Party, was spared death because of secret services rendered but was forced nevertheless to go underground.

'The thing about Fredi was that although he was a name, he was not a face. No one really knew what he looked like and I recommended to Hermann that it might be to his advantage to have someone on the inside of such an enclosed, highly charged world.' He looked around the carriage. 'Not so much now – the train is hardly used any more – but in its day it was a hive of secrets. Telecommunications left lying around, gossip, dining-car conversations. So Fredi Huber became a vital source to Fegelein as his master Himmler was more and more excluded by Bormann.'

So that was that, thought Morgen, there wasn't a loose end he could think of. He stood to go and was left with a footnote to take away: it was Fredi Huber who had been indirectly responsible for Anna Huber's post at the Ministry of Propaganda, arranged on Fegelein's say-so after a word to the tiny doctor.

The other man looked at him and said, 'Whether the predatory Dr Goebbels added her to his conquests is neither here nor there, though Hermann thinks he probably did – as female availability is understood to be part of the contract.'

Morgen left quietly, certain that he had been told this last story in an act of almost casual, reflex cruelty because Anton Schlegel had guessed that he carried a torch for Anna Huber.

Fredi Huber, in his role of train manager, knocked on Tieck's door and asked if he wanted a whisky nightcap. Tieck, with no wink or aside, said yes he would. No ice, Fredi Huber apologised.

'As it comes is fine, with a splash of water.'

'Fachinger?'

'Of course.'

Fredi Huber regretted the lack of a dining car or kitchen. All he could offer was some biscuits, which were declined.

When Fredi Huber returned with the whisky, he said, 'I trust you are keeping well, sir?'

It was still the train manager and Tieck talking.

'As well as can be expected in difficult times,' Tieck said, still keeping to his part.

Fredi Huber turned to bid him good night.

'We're both lucky to be alive,' Tieck said, speaking for himself and Anton Schlegel.

'Indeed we all are, sir. I bid you both good night,' said Fredi Huber with a wink.

Clever devil. He wondered what Fredi did now about chasing boys. Anton Schlegel would have made quick work of the ack-ack lads.

Sleep would not come to Toni Tieck or Anton Schlegel. He got up, raised the narrow blind and sat watching the benighted land rush by. Not a single light to be seen: a gone world.

*

The train moved through the suburbs of Berlin, revealing themselves in the morning light, showing how badly the city had aged.

Thanks to the train's teleprinter, Anton was able to inform Bormann of their arrival and asked to meet, signing himself off as Schlegel. Bormann wired back to say he would come to the station. Anton was joined in the radio room by Fegelein, looking both tired and refreshed after a no doubt invigorating bout with Anna Huber, who he said was breakfasting on biscuits with her father.

Anton explained about Bormann and said he needed a place where they could talk. If Fegelein was surprised at this he gave no sign. He suggested the kitchen in the baggage car. 'More of a storeroom really, but it has folding tables and chairs. I presume you want to speak in private.' He was back to being the impeccable liaison officer.

'A last favour,' said Anton. 'Perhaps you could fetch my son.'

He had decided after all there might be an advantage to be gained from producing the boy for Bormann, but he couldn't face going himself.

Fegelein went and returned to say, 'He chooses not to come,' and Anton realised he had been stupid and undiplomatic to have sent Fegelein, thinking perhaps there was such a thing as shame after all.

The train had its own private platform away from the station. The blinds were up as the train glided to a halt, opposite a high security wall. No reason to lower them, Anton thought: Let's have a little light on the matter.

Bormann bustled in moments later. The same but different: fatter, coarser, less hair, and infinitely more power, worn lightly. If one person could see through Tieck it would be Bormann, Anton Schlegel thought. Bormann sat leaning forward on the table with his hands clasped, and

Anton realised Bormann had no idea who he was and he, Anton, had nothing to say in return because Bormann had blanked him.

'Well?' asked Bormann still curious but impatient.

Anton stood clumsily and asked to be excused for a moment. He hobbled down to Schlegel's compartment where he was sitting on the bed, staring into space.

Anton said, 'I need you to come.'

He had to say please, and add that it was his son's help he wanted. He watched him calculate, then to his surprise Schlegel agreed and followed him back down the compartment to where Bormann was waiting, looking like his time was being wasted.

Apart from a double take at the dyed hair, Bormann gave little sign of recognising Schlegel, who said he was there to represent Anton Schlegel.

Bormann threw him a quizzical look and said, 'Anton Schlegel is dead.'

Schlegel said, 'I thought so, too.'

'Why are we here then?' asked Bormann, sounding less certain.

Schlegel slowly reached into his pocket and laid the copy of *The Adventures of Pinocchio* on the table between them.

Bormann looked at it and said, 'Do we have a need for children's stories?'

Anton turned to Schlegel. 'You said—' he began and stopped, silenced by his son's contempt.

Anton Schlegel picked up the book and riffled urgently through the pages. He threw it down and said to Bormann, 'There is supposed to be more.'

Schlegel remained silent, letting Anton see how much he was enjoying the other's discomfort.

Bormann picked up the book and flipped through it,

finding nothing either. He paused to note Anton's name on the fly leaf, then looked more closely at the strange man sitting opposite him.

Anton said, 'I had intended my namesake here to act as my messenger, but I see no point in pretending now. We both know it is too late for that, given the dire state of things. I am Anton Schlegel.'

Bormann's first reaction was to laugh in disbelief; his second to say, 'Well, you have made a God Almighty mess of yourself since I last saw you! And your messenger here, what was he supposed to bring?'

'The Hitler confession.'

'We both know he didn't do it.'

Schlegel spoke up to ask, 'Which one of you brought in Emil Maurice to shoot the niece?'

They stared at him, united in their hostile silence and Schlegel knew from Anton's reaction that he was the one that hadn't known. Bormann finally said, 'A dangerous question to ask, boy.'

Schlegel was beyond caring. 'Having survived your two thugs and Fegelein, it doesn't matter a fig to me what I say.'

Since the previous morning he had acquired the indifference of the dead.

Bormann sat back. Perhaps it was a relief to be asked. 'Clear the air then.'

Schlegel spoke fluently and without hesitation. 'The girl had become a liability to Herr Wolf and the Party, putting the whole project in jeopardy. There was the domestic beating, hushed up but noted by Fredi Huber.' He looked at Anton Schlegel. 'Though who told him I suppose we will never know.' He turned back to Bormann. 'Hoffmann accused you of beating the girl.'

Bormann started to protest and Schlegel cut him short.

'The point is, whoever did, the incident threatened to undo everything.' He turned to Anton Schlegel and said, 'Hoffmann also reported someone else being there that night who did not reveal himself and that was you, I am sure of it.'

Anton conceded with a turn of the wrist as Schlegel went on.

'The logical outcome was the girl had to go to save the leadership. Herr Wolf was then got out of the way so she could be disposed of behind his back, decided jointly between the two of you.'

He looked at Bormann, who didn't appear in the least threatened by what he was being told. Schlegel continued. 'You brought in Emil Maurice. It was an a gangster-style rub-out and Maurice was the hit man.'

'Why Maurice?' asked Bormann, curious to know how Schlegel had arrived at that.

'A dumb soul, definitely stupid and an unquestioningly loyal executioner of orders, without guilt or guile. The little man with the gun. It's so obvious it's almost an anticlimax, in keeping with such a dirty, fast and squalid ending. So Maurice turned up, the familiar friendly face, old chums with the girl, and did she for a second think about the man's body count, going back years? Maurice was the perfect example of the discrepancy between the Party's grandiose image of itself and the reality of a cheap killing.' He addressed Anton. 'Of course the real value of the Huber scoop to Maurice was that it didn't name him.'

On that last afternoon of her life, Geli Raubal wandered through the different rooms of her uncle's apartment, inspecting her memories: the laughter and tears, giggling discoveries, shocking admissions, reconciliations, rows and tearful forgiveness. 'You have unleashed a storm of unbridled passion in me.' Had he really said that? Hard to imagine now. His bedroom. Single bed! Their bathroom. Her room. Single bed! Poor Hansi. He had told her how canaries were kept in mines for their ability to detect any advance warning of danger beyond human perception. She had wept at the thought of those poor birds in the dark. Taking her hands, he had said, 'We are caged creatures but I will show it is possible to be free.'

Reception room and library, books given by her as gifts: at first, 'Your ever loving niece'; then, over time: 'G xxx'. Outside, the square turning to autumn, still bright before the start of winter cold. Nothing cosy about the place. Try as she might, she could never make a nest of her room in the way she had in the mountains. The staff quarters mysteriously empty, even the deaf crone, Frau Drachs, who usually couldn't be prised away, gone, as though everyone had said goodbye without doing so. Had the crone been her protector after all, and not the sinister presence she believed her to be? Any sense of 'his' imminent coming shifted with the slow movement of light around the apartment into a growing acceptance of her abandonment. Perhaps he had never intended what he promised. Perhaps he had buckled under the pressure, temporarily, and would come nevertheless. She forgave him for beating her, putting it down to a volcanic tempestuousness, the inevitable result of the risk being run as they braced themselves for the operatic scandal about to erupt and the triumph of their love. The press would soon be on board, Anton had promised, to write up their story in all sorts of favourable ways. Bormann had been her penultimate visitor, calling unexpectedly after all the others were gone, seemingly to check on her wellbeing, saying as he left, 'I must go now. No rest for the wicked. I am sending someone over to take care of you.' She watched him depart, knowing then. In an effort to banish all negative thoughts, she sat down and wrote to a girlfriend, saying how much she was looking forward to visiting: 'When I come to Vienna – I hope very soon – we'll drive to Semmering—' She broke off in the middle of writing as the doorbell rang.

After Schlegel was finished, Bormann, the great dissembler, said he above all respected honesty. Speaking eloquently for a change, he said, 'It was a psychologically critical time. The Raubal death is now seen as an aberration, as intended. Perhaps only we know that it was a moment of great spiritual crisis.' Bormann ruminated, again unlike him. 'You're right. She would have ruined him. He was losing his mojo as it was. She wouldn't be bought off, because I tried, so she paid the price. Regrettable, but there it is.'

Schlegel saw clearly how Bormann, as the interpreter of his master's secret wishes, had decided Herr Wolf wanted her gone but was too indecisive to break off the relationship or give the order. He suspected Bormann had been uncharacteristically hesitant: it was a big decision killing family, after all.

Schlegel's only miscalculation was in the effect. He had spoken out for Geli's sake because she deserved to be accounted for and those responsible confronted. But instead of anger or threats, he was being greeted with unmistakable admiration on the part of both men, as though he had established his credentials by exposing their secret. Having shown himself capable of resolving the mystery, when none had, he appeared to be on the brink of being invited over to the other side.

Did he sigh as he reached into his pocket? He wasn't sure. He said, 'There's more.'

He produced a scrappy typed sheet of paper from his

pocket and was rewarded with a look of grateful astonishment as Anton Schlegel realised what it was.

Bormann picked it up with a look of ironic amusement and read aloud: '"Sunday, 20 September 1931. Herr Wolf admits the following."' He looked up, eyebrows raised. 'The first I've heard. To whom did he admit?'

'To Anton Schlegel, I presume,' said Schlegel.

'Ah,' said Bormann. 'Where?'

Anton answered. 'At the Berghof. He stayed briefly, after learning of her death.'

'Ah,' said Bormann, inscrutable. 'I suppose that makes sense. While the balance of his mind was disturbed.'

'The same was said of the niece,' replied Anton.

'You're right. Perhaps none of us was in his right mind,' Boorman offered in return.

Schlegel sensed an undercurrent between the two men, almost as though the blackest joke was being shared. He could make no sense of it.

Bormann resumed reading aloud:

'"It is hard to say whether Herr Wolf assumes blame for his niece's death, holding himself indirectly responsible, or whether he believes he did in fact kill her. I write this for the record. It is up to others to decide. It was a volatile relationship. Both were mercurial in temperament. Herr Wolf and his niece dined out on the evening of 17 September, returning home late. Unusually for him he drank alcohol. She said it would loosen him up. At first the effect was novel. She spent the evening being provocative. Not until they got home did Herr Wolf realise how overwrought he had become. His niece's contrary state persisted. Herr Wolf referred to her monthly moods, which badly affected her. With Herr Wolf extremely reserved about physical matters, it was some time before I grasped that he was trying to say his niece was telling him her period was late. She was infatuated with the idea of having a child. He dismissed her claims as a crude attempt at emotional blackmail. There was music on the gramophone: 'Tristan and Isolde'. The relationship had reached a crisis point. However intent he was on honouring his promise to go away with her, he wanted to delay as he needed time to arrange the future of the Party and decide on a successor."'

Bormann, who had sounded sceptical about what he was reading, looked up in surprise at that. 'Oh, come now. "Go away with her?" You made this stuff up.'

'It's what he said. Go on,' said Anton Schlegel.

Bormann continued, sounding less certain. "'I add the following observations. Guns lay around the house, whips too, contributing to an air of latent violence. Then there was the move from a tiny bedsit to this histrionic, operatic space demanding grand gestures. Herr Wolf then made a terrible miscalculation, by his own admission. Unable to comprehend what she was telling him, he proposed they go back to when she had first come to him aged nineteen and helped around the house. He pointed out she was nearly as good a cook as her mother. Herr Wolf said: 'I was only trying to suggest we return to the start and make our own secret world.' Herr Wolf believed his offer would be gratefully received. Instead he had to contend with her throwing it back in his face, saying she wasn't putting up with any demotion to below stairs. Herr Wolf pleaded poor recollection because of shock and the drink. They were both playing a part, he thought, and would come to their senses. To defuse the situation he took the canary from its cage, to offer as a token of his love. Only when he handed it to her and she screamed did he see that he had squeezed the life out of it. After that he recalled nothing, saying he had blacked out because whatever he had done was too awful to bear. She would never do anything to hurt him, therefore: 'Only I can be responsible for what happened, after taking leave of my senses.'

'"Signed, Wolf."'

Schlegel thought the confession read not like any unburdening but an attempt to own the girl's death for the sake of Herr Wolf's sentimental tragedy.

Bormann looked to Anton Schlegel, who said, 'Herr Wolf saw himself as utterly defeated. With so many accusations flying around he frequently said in the hours after, "I may as well have pulled the trigger."' He insisted I write everything down for him to sign. Later that evening, I offered my own spoken "confession", which I wrote up later, to demonstrate to him that he could not have done it.'

They sat in silence, each contemplating his position, until Schlegel spoke to Anton. 'One thing I don't understand is how you knew where the book was. Fräulein Braun told me Herr Bormann had the Berghof extensively remodelled in the years after that.'

'The archive,' said Anton as though the answer was obvious. 'I suggested Rehse have the library photographed for purposes of inventory and insurance, and for the cultural record.'

'Why not ask him to return the book? It was yours after all.'

'It was not a matter I wished to share with Rehse.'

'Why did you hide the confession there in the first place?'

'Everyone going in and out agreed to be searched for the sake of Herr Wolf's safety.'

'Yet you didn't retrieve it.'

'I was never invited back.'

'Even so, how could you know it would still be in the same place?'

'Because the books were for show. It was not a working library. Contrary to his reputation for being a voracious reader, Herr Wolf, even when I knew him, barely picked up a book.' He asked Bormann, 'Isn't that so?'

Bormann acknowledged as much. Looking at the book on the table between them, he pushed it towards Anton like a croupier advancing chips. Nodding towards Schlegel, he said with grim appreciation, 'The sorcerer's apprentice.'

He lit a cigarette, leaned back, looked at them and asked, 'Are you really telling me they were really planning to run away together, or was that the girl's fantasy?'

Anton Schlegel said nothing. August Schlegel laughed out loud, thinking the situation was a mirror of Herr Wolf's totalitarian state, with the guilty being invited to unburden whether culpable or not.

Schlegel watched them, detached: two men of such easy malevolence that their company was almost enjoyable, with none of Fegelein's neurosis. Shallow men. Anton Schlegel had admitted as much in his letter. Depth didn't interest him.

As for the pathetic Herr Wolf, Schlegel failed to comprehend the image of the man willing to give up everything for love. Perhaps his head really had been turned, a more frightening prospect almost than him killing Geli. He could see Bormann was too canny to say he hadn't known, however obviously he was internally processing this new information at a rapid rate. Schlegel wondered if there was another twist left.

Anton Schlegel was the only one who knew about their secret plan, almost impossible to imagine now. Unthinkable. Geli was Herr Wolf's Achilles heel. Career to be abandoned for private bliss. Maybe it had been a fantasy but it was one that was seriously entertained.

Geli had confessed to Anton, one night in the Chinese tower in the English Garden: 'The things he makes me do.' This would have been in late July or early August of 1931. Later, Anton would think of everything taking much longer, but it was only a few weeks, more interrupted than not by Herr Wolf's hectic schedule. Anton, intrigued by her reticence, because he thought her a forward girl and up for anything, decided to give her a crash course in sexual accommodation and depravity. He showed her his world, mad nights of giddy partying, with her awestruck, asking, 'Is it possible even to think such things?' He taught her that doing as the man asked gave her control.

'Whatever?' she asked.

'Compared to what they do here, it's nothing.' He had watched the girl grow entranced at the theatrical display of desire, power and control. He could see she was impressionable, willing and generous with her body, eager to share her delight in it. Anton showed her that her uncle's demands weren't so unusual and revealed to her much worse in smoky backrooms, in terms of beatings and aggressive penetration. He watched her calculate the odds in terms of outrage and dare and revenge against all the stuffed shirts surrounding her uncle.

She was a fast learner and duly reported back that her wolf man was willing to give it all up for her and sexual enthralment. Anton supposed it was the first time in Herr Wolf's life since his mother that a woman had treated him with generosity.

Geli's easy spirit extended to giving her body to Anton Schlegel, one balmy night on the banks of the Isar, telling him, 'I owe you and am going to give you the ride of your life,' which she duly did, leaving Anton thinking she was wasted on the emotionally clammy Herr Wolf.

In all subsequent versions of their story, the one fact agreed on was her disgust and horror at Herr Wolf's requests. Only Anton knew otherwise, summoned to the apartment to be told about their secret plan. 'And why shouldn't you?' wondered Anton, seeing nothing of the old, blazing Herr Wolf, just a content little man who had discovered the sweet jar for the first time. Herr Wolf was of course extra-susceptible to 'falling in love' as a man who never had, and being so scarred by loneliness. She whispered to Anton that they had become a magic couple.

Herr Wolf was secretly transformed.

'I can't tell you,' he said to Anton, not telling, a man with visions of angels.

He took Anton aside and instructed him. 'No one must know. In fact, they must believe the opposite. I am making you responsible for them all thinking we are not getting on.'

And so everyone came to subscribe to the fairy tale gone sour, in which the evil uncle became a controlling Bluebeard. Where others parroted the gossip put about by Anton, he suspected the lovebirds had entered a sexual playground of dare and childish delight, like two kids pretending to be doctors and nurses. Any shitting and pissing business was 'play'. As there is a pleasure to plain pissing, it wasn't hard to see the practice remaining almost innocent, even in a sexual context. Compared to the realm of pain Anton was witness to, it was, truth to tell, pretty pathetic, light rather than heavy. She told Anton she had been flattered to have her cunt drawn, giggling at how hard he had tried to get it right and how frustrated he got.

Herr Wolf clearly regarded sex as 'adult', therefore difficult. Only much later, when reminded of how childlike Geli remained, did Anton Schlegel see the actual equation: that the 'child' is seen, and sees herself, as a way of returning sex to an innocent, wondrous state. It never could have lasted because the situation was corrupting, involving secrecy as it did, and no one knew that better than Anton, on the one hand tasked with protecting what she called 'the flame of their secret love' while poisoning the well, just as no one knew better than he that the story ever since had been about a succession of dirty secrets.

He supposed in the end Herr Wolf found himself riding two horses, deluding himself into thinking he was prepared to sacrifice his career and run off with her, until on that last night they were together he snapped and hit her.

Bormann looked at Anton Schlegel, thinking: and then fucking Emil Maurice botched the job. Afterwards, Bormann alone had gone into the room to find the girl lying there to all intents dead, until she blinked. He put it down to a last involuntary reaction, until she blinked again. By then the press office had released its statement that she was dead and there she lay instead suspended in a twilight limbo, apparently brain dead but the heart still fluttering.

Bormann now saw the span of the last thirteen years as the tale of two botched jobs: the fake Führer who didn't die when he should have been blown up and the niece who blinked when she should have been dead.

Fucking Emil Maurice.

The rummy doctor was an easy buy, having been bought off before, in exchange for settlement of gambling debts. The false certificate was provided. Bormann, with vehicles at his disposal as head of the Party's automobile association, fetched one and he and Anton Schlegel covered the girl's head and carried her down the back stairs, and drove her to an abortion clinic that did Party business. Registered as 'unknown female', she was shoved in an out-of-the-way room.

Bormann, having failed to have her killed, suffered a rare loss of nerve, and hoped she would die on them. But she didn't, being of strong peasant stock. The 'body' meanwhile was smuggled overnight to Vienna, to keep the press hounds at bay. The girl was both dead and not dead. Only Bormann and Anton Schlegel knew that. Bormann admitted to himself later that he had lost his head when the girl blinked, which was why he called Anton Schlegel.

The Führer was duly informed she had shot herself, in accordance with the official version.

Anton returned from the Berghof on the evening of Sunday, 20 September, when Hoffmann turned up to take Herr Wolf to a safe house, following rumours that the press knew of his whereabouts. In the dead of night, he had had the girl taken by private ambulance to Nussbaumstrasse: Room 202, checked in under his name. Anton undid the head bandage and cut her hair off and shaved her skull then bandaged her up again. Why he did this he had no idea; a ritual perhaps, a way of claiming her. She remained clinging on to life. Anton was reminded of the Neumann woman lying in her bed and all the religious nonsense around her.

Then the revelation: looking at Geli and thinking of Neumann, Anton Schlegel realised that Herr Wolf could be initiated. She was the perfect necrophile trophy.

Herr Wolf's face shone with cracked ecstasy when he was told.

'Can it be possible she has been returned?'

He agreed there was no question of announcing her comeback from the dead because she would be turned into a ghouls' shrine.

'A miracle indeed.'

The fact that the woman was a vegetable seemed not to bother him.

'Who knows?' Herr Wolf asked.

'Me, Bormann. Now you.'

'Keep it that way. Tell Bubi to pay, whatever it costs. Absolute discretion.'

'She is registered under my name.'

Herr Wolf grasped Anton Schlegel's arm with both hands and said, 'Take me to her.'

So on the night when Hoffmann claimed the Führer paid a secret visit to his niece's graveside in Vienna, which became equated with the legend of his political rebirth, Herr Wolf was in fact dressed more like a tramp, recalling his down-and-out Vienna days, for an incognito visit to his 'sleeping princess'. Anton Schlegel, waiting discreetly outside, listened to the man's frenzied weeping. Upon seeing her he had thrown himself on his knees, howling, and clasped her hand.

The sobbing stopped and for a long time the room was silent while Anton stood in the corridor, wondered inappropriately whether the sexual nature of their relationship would continue, a thought that shocked even him. Herr Wolf emerged with a look of quiet triumph, as if to say: Now she is mine and mine alone.

Later, she was moved to the clinic in Berlin, which was why Herr Wolf insisted on going there in the summer of 1944. The intended face surgery – to allow him to vanish into the hoped for life of tranquil, anonymous obscurity – never happened, thwarted by the failure of the bomb to do its job, necessitating his return.

The clinic was also where Anton Schlegel had undergone his transformation, ten years earlier, with the surgeon describing the case as a first, in that such surgery was invariably done to make appearances more attractive, not less so. The operation left Anton horrified by the results but at least unrecognisable, a process that was continued by a fatty diet resulting in the previously slim Anton almost doubling his weight and completing his metamorphosis.

Anton visited the niece a few times as it was near where he had once lived all those years ago. He went past the house from time to time to remind himself of what he had walked away from.

Once, while passing by, he had left his old Munich guidebook in the garage when the doors were open and the cars were out, as a relic of who he once was and what he had become; he wondered if anyone would find it. He returned later with the *Mein Kampf*, with the intention of it being a possible summons for his son. By then Anton was starting to consider Bormann and building bridges, which was when he first contemplated using the boy, perhaps he saw now for vain and sentimental reasons, to see if the son was a chip off the old block.

In the clinic, hidden behind her steel door, the girl lay in her bed, looking angelic, connected to all the latest gadgetry whose tangle of wires reminded Anton of the mythical spaghetti lunch she was supposed to have shared with her uncle on that last afternoon of her life.

There was nothing to age her in whatever cocoon she now inhabited.

The only difference was her hair had grown back quite white.

His white angel.

*

Bormann folded the confession, as if to say the matter was done. A coveted document even if it was rubbish. 'Power, Bubi,' the Führer had once said, 'is about knowing or guessing others' secrets.'

He laughed and said, 'I will have a legal expert check whether it's a capital offence to kill a canary, which in the end is the only thing admitted to.'

He looked at Anton expectantly.

'Plan B,' said Anton.

'Always plan B,' acknowledged Bormann. 'Do you have one in mind?'

'Time is of the essence. We must begin straight away, unless you have already started. Within months the country will be in ruins. It's time to get the money out.'

Bormann lit a cigarette and shrugged, to say: You know me.

Outside the window, first Fegelein, then Anna Huber and last Morgen drifted past, like ghosts from another story.

Bormann looked at Schlegel then back at Anton and asked, 'And him?'

Schlegel answered for Anton, saying, 'I am with you now,' while thinking to himself: I will have you both yet.

50

One last bit of unfinished business.

Schlegel watched Bormann and his father as thick as thieves, talking, whispering, gesturing on the platform. Part of him was still standing on the Berghof road, waiting for the end that hadn't come. And now the unwanted father, at an age when most men were starting to forget theirs; he wasn't sure where that left him.

Bormann had a car. Schlegel had no idea where they were going, except north.

A clinic. Oranienburg. Schlegel had dim memories of the one that burned down having another branch there. Whatever, it made no sense. Neither Bormann nor his father was saying.

A private room behind a security gate with a combination lock that Bormann knew. Schlegel thought of the steel door he had been told about in the other clinic. A woman lay in the dark; asleep, he thought, then more than asleep he realised, on seeing the complicated machinery she was attached to. He still failed to understand the significance of their being there. Bormann and his father stood almost reverentially, their heads bowed. Schlegel could not comprehend. White hair but a young woman still; she looked little more than twenty or so, and childlike at that. As he moved closer, it dawned on him: Room 202, Schlegel A. Checked in under his father's name as cover for who she really was. Whoever would have suspected when the newspapers were full of nothing but her reported death and rafts of speculation?

In all the permutations offered, none had even begun to hint she might still be alive. The absoluteness of her death was never questioned, only the coagulation surrounding it.

Schelgel still didn't quite believe what he was looking at. Despite hair as white as his, without its ridiculous dye, the face was that of the young woman photographed by Hoffman.

He had to turn to the two men for confirmation.

Bormann inclined his head.

His father said, 'Time to let her go.'

Schlegel wondered if it was the first move in whatever diabolical plan they were hatching next, the start of the end of Herr Wolf, who no doubt would be told his niece had passed.

For a split second Schlegel saw the woman in her living death as the sister he had never had; and, before he could be asked, he reached for the switch, praying she would blink for him, and in that moment of reaching he saw his whole life start to go backwards, in reverse like he was dying, or being reborn, the image reducing as the years sped away, until it was no more than a dot, then not even that, then nothing.

THE BUTCHERS OF BERLIN

Berlin 1943.

August Schlegel lives in a world full of questions with no easy
answers. Why is he being called out on a homicide case when
he works in financial crimes? Why did the old Jewish soldier
with an Iron Cross shoot the block warden in the eye then
put a bullet through his own head? Why does Schlegel persist
with the case when no one cares because the Jews are all being
shipped out anyway? And why should Morgen, wearing the
dreaded black uniform of the SS, turn up and say
he has been assigned to work with him?

'Powerful evocation of a city living in terror'
Sunday Times Crime Club

'Ambitious, darkly atmospheric'
The Times

SIMON &
SCHUSTER

I

It was still dark as the old man dressed. The light would not come for another hour. Socks and suspenders. Trousers and braces. The underpants of which he was so ashamed, dish-wash grey and stained, for lack of soap, so threadbare they were in holes. His shoes, once good, barely held together and leaked at the slightest provocation. They smelled of the detergent used to wash the slaughterhouse floor. The medal deserved a collar, he thought. He had no cufflinks either and made do with rolled sleeves. The suit still had its waistcoat, which he wore for the little extra warmth it afforded, usually under his one sweater, which he discarded that morning, wanting to look his best. He took his overcoat, hat and scarf, which hung on the back of the door. As an afterthought, he folded his pyjamas and placed them under the pillow. He wanted the gesture to provoke some regret or nostalgia but felt nothing.

The pistol was an old Mauser C96. He appreciated the aesthetics of its distinctive box magazine in front of the trigger, the long elegant barrel and comfort of the wooden handle. His last companion of choice. His hands were cold but he would not wear gloves. He passed through the apartment, careful not to disturb the others because he wished to leave unobserved. He closed the door softly behind him, stood at the top of the stairs and stared into the descending gloom.

*

The block warden was slow to arrive. He was a short man with a childish face and the insolent, spoiled look of minor authority. He didn't see the pistol in the old man's hand until he raised his arm. He gave a small yelp of surprise, followed by his characteristically unpleasant laugh, which he never had time to finish. He was in the middle of putting on his coat, with his mouth open, when the bullet entered his head, through the eye, at which the old man had been aiming. His head snapped back from the force. Blood and bone hit the wall, followed by the bullet. He slumped back and slid down, his blood a dark smear on dirty paintwork. The remaining eye fluttered, almost coquettishly, as he hit the floor sitting, paused and rolled over.

In the booming echo of the shot the old man thought he heard footsteps stop on the stairs. Female. He knew whose and regretted he could do nothing about that; perhaps she was his angel of death after all. At least he was her avenger.

The old man turned the gun on himself, grasped the barrel in his left hand to hold it steady and pulled the trigger. The bullet travelled upwards through the unresisting flesh of his chin and tongue, missing his false teeth, into the soft palate of his mouth, passing the nasal passage, to penetrate the brain where it lodged, causing none of the messy damage of the first shot. Such a neat, clean death; the old man was gone before he hit the ground, doing more tidily for himself than his victim, who jerked and twitched like a dog in a dream.

The young woman was still standing petrified when the second shot fired. A voice in her head told her not even to think and get out. She ran with her hand over her mouth until she reached outside and spewed in the courtyard as the door banged behind her, barely stopping before she carried on running.

August Schlegel woke up in a prison cell with no recollection of how he had got there. Everything swam unpleasantly. He wondered if he were still drunk. Like a man contemplating white space on a map, he thought, 'My name is August Schlegel and the street where I live is the same as my first name, in the former Jewish quarter.' He opened one eye. Had they thrown him in the drunk tank? There were many things he disliked about himself, starting with his name. He was only twenty-five but his hair had gone quite white, which he also disliked, as he did the way it sat on top of his open, ordinary face.

The air stank of stale drink. He had a memory of throwing up during the party. The party. There had been speeches. A big room full of boozed-up men. A group of the oldest and toughest had decided to make him the butt of their lurid and preposterous tales. Stoffel claimed to have dressed as a woman for the S-Bahn murders, to act as bait. The idea was beyond imagination. Stoffel was bull-necked with a boxer's nose and a tobacco-stained moustache, which he claimed to have shaved off for his drag act. Tears of mirth ran down everyone's cheeks.

They were all reeling drunk by the end. He remembered wondering if he would end up spending the night in the cells again; it seemed to be happening more often. He recalled standing swaying, trying to read his watch, and someone saying, 'Ach! After eleven. Too late to go home. Everyone downstairs!'

Sleeping it off in the cells was standard police practice.

He must have dozed off. The next thing he knew, he was being poked awake. The reek of brutal aftershave told Schlegel it wasn't just a bad dream. He ran his furred and distended tongue around his teeth and tasted a horrible residue. He could feel his swollen liver.

'You'll do,' said Stoffel, continuing to poke him.

'What for?'

'A homicide.'

Schlegel couldn't find his hat and one glove was lost. His jacket and coat were wadded up under the bunk. At least the big leather waistcoat was still there. He kept repeating under his breath: I am not homicide. On the rare occasions Schlegel found himself drinking with the likes of Stoffel – at leaving parties, and there were plenty of those – he had a warning list in his head of subjects never to mention, however drunk. He hoped the image he had of himself regaling them hadn't happened. Stoffel's crowd were always laughing at things not in the slightest funny until someone said something really funny, when they made a point of not laughing at all.

He arrived in the garage hatless, his ungloved hand stuffed in his pocket. Stoffel was sitting in an Opel with the engine running. The garage was bitterly cold and it was no warmer in the car, whose heater didn't work.

'I am not homicide, you know,' he said to Stoffel.

'The rest are busy.'

Busy sleeping it off, he thought sourly. Where was his hat? It was a good one.

There was a hole in the floor of the car and a chilly draught blew up his legs. He suspected Stoffel wore newspaper under his vest from the way he rustled. There was much discussion about what gave the best insulation. Stoffel smoked a foul cheroot. He was a wet smoker. Schlegel was aware of not having cleaned his teeth, not that it mattered. Nearly everyone's breath reeked these days. He tasted last night's alcohol. No shortage there. Outside it began to spit. To stop from feeling sick, he concentrated on the grinding of the useless wipers and the smeared vision through the greasy windscreen.

A lot of official traffic was on the roads. Trams were crammed with commuters. Those banned from public transport trudged past with their heads down. Another grubby dawn, another working Saturday and another of those filthy colourless days found only in Berlin in winter, in the year of our Lord nineteen hundred and forty-three.

A roadblock was set up where the street had been sealed off. They were in a run-down working-class part of Wilmersdorf. Schlegel saw soldiers on standby, their scuttle helmets silhouetted in the drizzle. There were a lot of ordinary policemen too and plainclothes, as well as special Jewish marshals with armbands.

The man they were referred to wore the usual unofficial uniform of snap-brim fedora and leather trench coat. He gave them a peremptory look and said, 'Gersten.'

Gersten's hair was worn unusually long over the collar. Schlegel remained preoccupied with his hangover as they were led through an arch into a deep courtyard surrounded by dilapidated barracks-like blocks with crumbling brickwork, dark with soot.

'Two Jews,' said Gersten. He pointed to a block entrance.

'You drag me out of bed for a couple of Jews!' protested Stoffel.

'Today the Jews are all busy getting arrested. We go in at full daylight, so you have five minutes to sort them out.'

Stoffel, still grumbling, said to Schlegel, 'You tell me what happened. Consider it part of your education.'

Stoffel was already nipping from a hip flask.

They were in a ground-floor corridor that ran from front to back, outside the block warden's quarters. The staircase took up most of the space. The hall stank of cordite. One man had been shot while putting on his coat and had fallen awkwardly. The eye was a gaping hole. The other by comparison appeared formally arranged, so neat he could have been laid out by an undertaker.

Schlegel passed Stoffel the pistol using his gloved hand. Stoffel looked at the weapon in appreciation.

Schlegel said, 'The old man shot himself after shooting the other man. There may have been a witness who ran away.'

'We're not looking to complicate this.'

'I stepped over a puddle of vomit by the door.'

Stoffel inspected the soles of his shoes, yawned ostentatiously and went outside. Schlegel followed. The yard was now surrounded by troops with submachine guns and attack dogs straining their leashes. He had heard nothing of their arrival.

Gersten beckoned them over. Stoffel insisted that Jews were not the business of the criminal police. Gersten ignored him and said Stoffel still needed certification of death.

'Get the bodies out here in the meantime. They're in the way.'

Gersten nodded to an SS corporal with a bull whip, who blew a long blast on his whistle. A squadron of Jewish marshals ran in and fanned out towards the block entrances. The corporal cracked his whip and the dogs pulled on their leads, followed by the noise of doors being hammered on and kicked in, then banging and screaming and people being yelled at.

Schlegel was quite unprepared for such controlled fury. It pitched him back to that other time, which he had trained his mind to blank, during the waking hours at least.

A man upstairs yelled, 'No packing. Get dressed and out!' Stoffel was in no hurry to move the bodies by himself. He ordered a couple of marshals who were in the process of chasing out the first residents.

The men hesitated until Stoffel shouted, 'Unless you want to join the rest in the yard.'

A middle-aged woman tried to press money into Schlegel's hand, saying a terrible mistake had been made, her name should not be on the list. Schlegel looked at the pathetic amount and turned away. The woman moved on to Stoffel, who took the money and told her to wait outside. He asked her name and said he would have a word. The woman babbled her thanks.

'Go along, before I change my mind,' said Stoffel not unkindly, pocketing the money.

The sound of blows came from upstairs, followed by a sharp crack and glass being smashed.

'Dead body!' a voice shouted.

Schlegel thought perhaps the old man had been forewarned. As to where he had got the gun or why he'd shot the other man, he doubted anyone would care. Stoffel was smoking another of his foul-smelling cheroots. The tip, even wetter than the last, reminded Schlegel of a dog's dick. A steady crowd pressed downstairs. Some whimpered. Others complained about pushing. It was like watching a river surge.

Someone fell on the stairs. People started to get trampled. Schlegel tried to restore order, aware of Stoffel's sceptical gaze. The crowd seemed incapable of stopping. Schlegel was close to losing control of himself as he saw back to that flat horizon, marshland, huge summer mosquitoes, villages little more than a collection of hovels.

He pulled people up and shouted at others. A scream from under a pile of bodies seemed to act as a sign for the pushing to stop. Schlegel walked away, leaving them to sort themselves out. The air outside was absolutely still. It had stopped raining, not that it had done more than drizzle. His hands trembled in his coat pockets.

The corporal snapped his whip and ordered everyone to stop milling around. He separated the mostly elderly men. One who tried to point out his wife was screamed at. The crowd recoiled whenever the dogs showed their fangs.

The two bodies were now lying dumped in a corner by the bins, behind the rank of soldiers. The old man wasn't looking so neat now. Schlegel knelt down and put his hand inside the man's coat, like a pickpocket. The wallet he extracted was fake leather. The papers were stamped with a 'J'. Schlegel noted the name, Metzler, and the number of his apartment upstairs. The other man had no papers.

The corporal kept cracking his whip like he was Buffalo Bill. Anyone showing indecision was kicked into line by the Jewish marshals. An ugly pudding of a woman with orange hair let out a wail and ran across the yard, arms jerking like a wind-up doll. At the bins she threw herself on the body of the other man. The courtyard was momentarily stilled except for the woman's keening. The corporal stopped to look, then screamed at one of the civilians, 'You! Cockroach! Eyes front!'

Gersten had a stick of lip salve, used surreptitiously to moisten his mouth. He came over and said to Schlegel, 'The other man was the block warden, not Jewish, so it is technically a homicide.'

The woman paused her wailing to shout, 'We are German. I won't have my man touched by a Jew doctor. We were here years before this riffraff!'

Even for Stoffel this was too much. He snapped, 'What difference does it make? One dead man is the same as another.' Gersten looked worried. 'In fact, one Jew didn't shoot another. She's right. You're going to have to get a proper doctor now.'

PALE HORSE RIDING